COVEN OF WOLVES

BOOK II:
BLOOD TIES

A NOVEL BY
PETER SAENZ

doorQ Publishing l Playa del Rey, California

Published in the USA by
doorQ Publishing
8675 Falmouth Ave #306
Playa del Rey, CA 90293
www.doorq.com

ISBN-10: 069236210X
ISBN-13: 978-0692362105

Edited by David Berger
Front cover art by Jon Macy

Printed in the United States of America

FOR JOSEPH

CHAPTERS

Chapter One
WAR

SEVERAL BULLETS ZOOM PAST MY FACE, STRIKING THE BUILDING behind me. I instinctively duck behind a large metal trash Dumpster for protection. Across from me I see Nicholas similarly hiding behind a good-sized air conditioning unit. His dark hair and eyes match his dark clothing. He reaches into his jacket and pulls out a gun. It shines slightly in moon glow.

Cocking it, he yells to me, "I knew this was going to be a set-up. We should've stayed at the mansion until we got confirmation of when Jason's team was spotted."

Nicholas quickly peeks around the air conditioning unit and fires several times in our attacker's direction. Once several shots are returned, Nicholas resumes his safe position again.

Frustrated, I answer back, "We've already been through this. By then it might've been too late. If Jason really is planning an assault, we need as many provisions as we can get our hands on."

The bag filled with exotic herbs, talismans, and various other magical treasures lies at my side. I feel for the sword strapped to my back, but know it'll be of little use in a gunfight.

Adding further agitation to the situation, Nicholas says, "The cops will be here any time now if we don't end this soon. Can you hocus your pocus so that we can get the hell out of here already?"

Knowing that his mocking will strike a nerve with me, I grimace in his direction. I can see a slight grin appear on Nicholas' masculine face in response.

I take out a piece of white chalk and form a circle around myself on the ground. I scribble in a few protective symbols and sit. The look on Nicholas' face tells me I should hurry. Closing my eyes, I breathe deeply inward and focus on my spiritual center. I can feel my internal magic begin to sift and swirl within me. Soon my body is surging with energy. Using it, I will my soul self to leave my body.

Looking down, I see my physical shell sitting safely in the lotus position. The circle should protect my body from any psychic attacks while I'm away from it, while Nicholas protects it physically only a few feet away. I'm 24 years old, but looking at myself from this perspective I seem a few years older. I'm surprised at how much I've gained in muscle mass over the past few weeks, probably from all the training Nicholas has been putting me through, when I'm not double booked in conference meetings with the other members of my pack that is. My thick brown hair is also getting to be a bit too long. I'm due for a trim. Later.

I move my spirit self invisibly toward the shooters in order to get a better look at what we're up against. There are four of them. From Nicholas, I sense a resistance to my magics, a natural effect to his werewolf nature, but I try to break through as best I can. Once I do, I allow him to see what I see. When the full surveillance is given to him, I wait a few more seconds for him to process it all before I return to my body, whole again.

Opening my eyes, I look over at Nicholas. Not being a witch himself, and also still not yet used to my magics, the expression on Nicholas' face is both one of confusion and glee.

"Devin, that was awesome."

I answer back, "Focus, Nicholas."

"Right, right." he says back. "Those aren't Jason's men. According to the photos your mother showed me last week, they belong to Bobby Longo's group. This isn't a clan hit. It's a mob hit."

Ever since we legally took over my mother's family property in Boston, my family and I (both literal and otherwise) have become moving targets. Nicholas and I are part of a newly created pack of werewolves. Until recently, we were protected from our enemies by powerful magic. Once we established roots, though, all that went out the window.

On one side of the spectrum, we have the majority of the American and European werewolf clans looking to destroy us for breaking their millennia's old traditions; and, on the other, we have human mob families wanting to get rid of us for moving into their territories. The mob families have no idea that we're werewolves. Or even that a select few of us are witches either. All they know is that the daughter of a former mob Don has moved back into the old neighborhood with a hell of a lot of people in tow, and they don't like it.

That said mob daughter would be my mother, Victoria Marshall, formerly Victoria Sazia. She and my father changed their last names and went into hiding just before my mother's father was killed. I was born a year later, raised completely unaware of my true lineage. My father's name is Adam Marshall, formerly Adam Toxotis. I'm the product of one human born mafia princess and one werewolf born elite assassin. It's all new to me as a whole, but I don't have time to get bogged down with that side of my family's politics. I have my own agendas that need to be carried out. Because of this, ending the werewolf and mafia feuds takes high priority.

Nicholas, the brooding assassin across from me, is my father's younger cousin. He's several years older than I am and is the deadliest member of my pack. He and my father were high-level members of the Synoro Clan of werewolves, who currently dominate the North American continent. My father's father, Jason Toxotis, is one of the head leaders or Archons that govern that pack of wolves. That arrangement changed recently on account of me. Now, my grandfather wants me, and those with me, dead.

Forming a plan, I motion to Nicholas to stay put. A field experienced fighter, he doesn't take well to the request but he does as he's told. Taking hold of my magics again, I create a glamour spell. It's a simple enough spell that creates an illusion of my choice: in this case, the illusion of Nicholas and myself trying to make a run for it.

Sure enough, the four mob assassins take the bait and chase after the magically created figures. As the sound of stomping feet comes closer to our location, I look over and see Nicholas put his gun away and slowly reach for his swords affixed to his back. I make a hand gesture for him to put them away. I then make a fist with one hand and point to it with the other. Now, obviously surly, Nicholas narrows his eyes and prepares a fighting stance while still hidden safely behind the air conditioning unit.

When the footsteps are directly upon us, we both swing our arms outward and clip the two front running gunmen at the neck. They go down, clawing at their throats and gasping for air. We quickly disarm the remaining two assassins, knocking their guns several feet away. The now unarmed men immediately begin swinging punches at us. From their movements, I can tell that they're natural brawlers. Unlike Nicholas and I, though, they are not professionally trained in hand-to-hand combat. Nicholas firmly grabs one man's fist with his own, pulling him closer to him. He then uses the elbow of his opposite arm and brings it down forcefully onto his opponent's arm. I can hear a loud crack as the mob goon's arm bone breaks in two.

At the same time, I slam my elbow into my own opponent's face. While he is momentarily dazed, I spin around and kick him across the face as well. The werewolf blood flowing through my veins gives me a higher than normal strength level. It enhances each attack I make. My attacker falls down unconscious.

I look over and see Nicholas pivot his victim, causing him to flip in place and fall to the ground. Nicholas straddles him and is about to finish him off. Something tells me that the force he's about to use will be a killing blow. I shout to Nicholas not to kill him. Nicholas stops mid-punch. Instead of using lethal force, Nicholas follows through with a swing that merely knocks out his opponent.

Turning to face me, Nicholas says, "We won't get anywhere if we let our enemies live. You're one of my clan's Archons so I'll follow whatever orders you give me, but you're making a bad call right now."

"Nicholas, we have enough trouble on our plate with the other clans sending assassins to kill us. Spilling mob blood will only guarantee that the next hit they send will be bigger and deadlier. We need to send a message to the Longo family that we're not looking for a fight."

At that moment, a fifth gunman appears and takes aim at me. Just when he's about to fire, my familiar Fenrus magically appears and jumps at the attacker, savagely snarling and baring his teeth. The various colors of Fenrus' wolf coat of red, black, white and brown gleam beautifully as his yellow eyes shine brightly with fury. The sudden appearance of my familiar's canine form surprises the mob assassin. Once Fenrus has his victim on the ground, the new assassin's gun goes off, the bullet harmlessly hitting a nearby building instead of my face. Fenrus, now on the man's chest, carries a magic all its own. Fenrus breathes inward and barks loudly into the man's face. A concentrated force of magic mixes in with his bark, amplifying the sound to a high pitch. The effect acts like a massive physical punch, leaving the attacker out of the fight. The entire sequence takes only a few seconds, but still manages to leave both Nicholas and me shocked and shaken.

"Thanks Fenrus," I say to my friend. Fenrus woofs back softly to me in response.

Turning to the two remaining men still gasping for air on the ground, I will for my internal magics to surge forth again.

I say to Nicholas, "But we also need the Longo family to understand that we're not pushovers, either."

I magically move all five assassins together. Once their bodies meet, I feel Fenrus arrive at my side. His presence amplifies my magics, allowing me to complete my plan easily.

I use my magic to allow the two conscious men to resume their normal pitch of breathing, easing the agitation Nicholas and I caused to their tracheas. Wide-eyed, they stare at us perplexed. I emit a cold field of fear into their minds as I glamour the area to take on a red hue. I then glamour my eyes to turn pitch black. The two men begin shaking in terror.

I distort my voice magically and say to them, "You will go back to your Don and tell him that he is to leave Victoria Sazia and her people alone. She doesn't want to have anything to do with Bobby Longo's business or the business of any other Don in the city. We only want to be left alone to live in peace. As you can see, we could've killed every one of you. We did not. Tell your Don that if he sends anyone else to harm Victoria's family, the next group won't be so lucky. Do you understand?"

The two men simply stare at me. Wanting to make sure I drive the point home, I use last year's demon experience as inspiration and extend my glamour spell to transform myself into the image of a large horned monster. Reading my thoughts and wanting to get in on the act, Fenrus also glamours himself into a large demon dog several times his normal size. His now drooling mouth utters a savage growl, showing the two men a set of teeth that resembles those belonging to a shark.

"Do you understand!?!" My voice echoes around them. The faux claws on my demon hands grow a foot.

The two men scream, "Yes! Yes!" at the top of their lungs. One of the unconscious men begins to come to. Waking up to see the hellish scene I've created, he tries to yell, but no sound escapes his throat. The sudden growing wetness from the crotch of his pants speaks for him instead.

I laugh manically, both from seeing the humor found from my side of the situation, and also from wanting to further extend my fantasy performance from hell. I then rush toward the men. They scream louder. When I'm a foot from them, I use my magics to freeze them. Their movements and voices cease instantly. I then will for my glamour spell to end. Slowly, the surroundings resume their normal color. Fenrus and my creative disguises fade away, revealing our normal appearance. Off in the distance, I hear the sound of police sirens heading in our direction.

Nicholas says, "You're totally twisted! BOTH of you! What in the hell did you do to them?"

Snickering, I grab Nicholas by the arm and quickly lead him away from the scene. Fenrus follows in tow.

"They'll be fine. I just froze their minds for a moment. The last thing they'll remember is a huge demon coming at them. They'll wake up from the spell in a few moments but we gotta get out of here quickly. The police'll be here any moment."

I pick up the bag of trinkets still by the Dumpster with my free hand and hand them to Nicholas. I then will for the protection circle I created on the ground to vanish. Taking my cell phone out of my jacket pocket, I press the necessary set of buttons for the mansion's main line.

"This is Devin. Nicholas and I have the items. Bobby Longo's gang ambushed us just outside of the pick-up location, but we made it out okay. Tell my father that we'll be in Beacon Hill within the hour."

Ending the phone call, we reach our car, and the three of us get in. Normally, I let Nicholas drive but I have way too much of a rush from what just happened to not take the wheel myself. The tires screech in place as we drive away to safety.

Looking beside me, I notice Nicholas is staring at me with a strange expression.

"What?" I mentally shrug off his judgmental look.

"What in the hell was that back there? I thought witches can't reveal themselves to normal humans the same way werewolves aren't allowed to."

Flippantly I say, "That? That was nothing."

Nicholas says, "Are you kidding me? Devin, that wasn't *nothing*. Do you have any idea what you did back there? Do you know what your little stunt could potentially mean for the pack?"

Letting the rush of the moment pass, Nicholas' words hit me like a slap to the face. I know he's right. Werewolves and witches have lived hidden for thousands of years beside humans. Keeping our lives secret for so long has been the only reason why we still exist today. The few times humans discovered even rumors of our existence being something more than fairytales, myths, or old wives' tales has lead to the witch hunts of old and public burnings. Stories like the French Beast of Gévaudan and the appearance of plagues caused fear in normal humans hundreds of years ago. Fear can be a dangerous weapon. It was fear that ignited people's mania back then, bringing about the unjustified deaths of countless people and animals, many of whom were innocent of the crimes made against them. The fact that I may have just put my family in added danger suddenly dawns on me.

"You're right. I shouldn't have done that. I guess I thought that if I scared the living Bejesus out of them that they'd back off."

Nicholas says, "Well, you guessed wrong. What were you thinking? You could've put all of us in danger. The First Law among werewolves is that we kill anyone who exposes our existence. That goes for humans *and* werewolves. It's the only way to get rid of any weak members so that they can't make the same mistake twice."

"So you're gonna kill me?"

"Don't be stupid, Devin. Of course I'm not going to kill you."

"You definitely tried your hardest the first couple times we met." I hate where this line of dialogue is going. The words feel as if they're going to choke me on the way out of my throat.

Nicholas gives me a stern stare. "I was watching you as your father had asked. You saw me in my wolf form. I had to follow the code. It was either you or me. This isn't a game Devin. I need for you to know how severe we take things like this. You're a new wolf so you're gonna make mistakes. You just can't afford to make any mistakes that put the entire clan at risk."

"I'm sorry," I say.

"Sorry won't bring back the lives of the people you're supposed to be watching over. You gotta think ahead. I've been in this game my whole life. The other wolves won't be as forgiving. If you jeopardize our hidden status, and they find out you're the one responsible, any sympathizers to our cause will immediately turn against us. We can't afford that."

"I said I'm sorry. Why are you riding me so hard?"

Solemnly, Nicholas answers, "Because I care. What you did at your brother's trials a few months ago? What we're doing now? It completely throws everything we wolves have ever known or believed in out the window. Our entire history will be changed by what we decide to do next. Our new clan…the potential new members we're hoping to join us…all of us, we're not pawns in some game. We're living beings. You've met so many wolves already. You know we're not all just assassins for hire. A lot of us are people with simple families and simple lives. It's why I'm so passionate about what I do. There's a greater purpose here. That's why I was such a faithful counsel to your grandfather. And that's why I plan to be a faithful counsel to you now, too."

The next few minutes go by in silence. Nicholas' words feel like ice: cold, but still completely solid. I can't afford to make such a sloppy mistake again.

"So what should we do next?" The words stumble out, leaving a bad taste in my mouth.

As if picking up on my feelings, Nicholas says, "I defer to your rule. Hopefully, what you did back there will do just what you intended. With any luck Bobby Longo's people will be scared enough to only consider our words, and not linger too much on what they saw. I say we let this play out and hope for the best. Share what happened with the other Archons, but not with the rest of the Council. No sense stirring the pot any worse than it already is."

In my head, I hear Fenrus. "Sound advice." I agree with him.

I look at Nicholas as best I can while driving. "Why did you turn down my offer to be an Archon? You obviously have a knack for leadership. Our clan could use someone like you making the big decisions."

Nicholas looks out his side window, away from me. "I told you. I'm just a grunt. Our goddess chose you and Damon to lead our people, not me. I'll help when I can, but it's up to you to see us through this. Now let's drop the subject. Please."

The car eventually arrives at the large mansion our pack now calls home. The mansion is actually a grouping of large row houses taking up one full city block on the border of the Beacon Hill and the Back Bay neighborhoods in Boston.

The entire block and several businesses were once owned by my mother's family. Due to some legal loopholes and attorney push-throughs, we were able to get the majority of the properties and assets written back over to my mom. My mom then had everything written over to my half-brother Damon and me so that we could better direct the pack's living situation and income. The families who lived on the property prior to our arrival were the remaining Sazia family members, which included my mother's still living stepmother Julia. To say they weren't happy about the take-over is an understatement. The entire Sazia clan is currently in the process of trying to block the court ruling. Fortunately one of our pack members, Ian Dikigoros, is one of the nation's top lawyers with a lot of pull in Washington. Thanks to him, we have a roof over our heads.

Ian was once part of the Synoro Clan of wolves, just like Nicholas and my father. While there, he was put in control of a lot of key local and national committees. His placement in those groups was meant to help the American wolves get a good legal footing in the grand scheme of things. Now as a member of the Enopo Clan, his legal help has been invaluable. Though the Boston properties are in the appeals process, Ian was able to put through a legal stay of new ownership, causing the remaining Sazia family members to have to vacate the main house entirely.

Not wanting to put my distant human relatives completely out on the street, I offered to house all those displaced at a smaller property in the less exclusive neighborhood of Mission Hill. Pampered their entire lives, the well-to-do Sazias balked at the idea of having to downgrade their upper crust status. While only half of them finally agreed to the move, leaving the remaining other half to hold onto their pride and choose their own new dwellings, every one of them was vocal in their anger at the situation. Part of me did feel badly for them. The takeover was especially hard for my mother as several persons who were forced to move from their homes were close to her growing up. Not only did they feel betrayed at having to lose their homes, but also at discovering that the person responsible was a woman they once loved and thought dead.

Despite the guilt, nothing stopped my mother from putting through what was necessary. Taking ownership of her father's property meant our immediate livelihood. It also provides sanctuary for the many members of our new clan, a clan whose numbers are still trickling higher as new potentials show up sporadically on our doorstep.

Pulling into the private driveway, one of the Enopo guards sees me roll down my window and walks over.

"Your father is waiting for you in the main study."

"Thanks."

The guard then gives a silent 'all clear' signal to the hidden security team strategically placed around the area. A second later the large ornate car gate slowly swings open, allowing us to drive into the newly built underground parking stalls.

I can't help marveling at the handiwork as we drive into the new surroundings. Since the buildings above are several hundred years old, it would have taken over a year and a lot of man-power to secure the stability of each building initially, and then to later dig out the earth beneath them to accommodate the new 21st century concrete and mortar foundation that now exists. In addition to new parking stalls, alleviating the security issue of having to park on the street above, the new sub-levels also provide much needed additional housing and storage. The combined magical strain needed to finish such a big job in such a short amount of time is still exhausting to remember. Being the only magic users in the pack, Tobias, Mika, Fenrus and I had to tax everything we had, and then some. To say nothing of the back breaking physical labor the wolves put in as well. Looking at the outcome though, I am beyond proud of the teamwork our new pack has shown.

Parking in my designated spot, the three of us exit the car and are immediately greeted by my boyfriend, Tobias. He throws his arms around me, and I do the same in return.

"I heard you were attacked. Are you all right?"

I hear Nicholas grunt as he quickly walks past us holding the bag of magical supplies, and into the building entrance. Holding Tobias tighter, I say, "We're fine. Honest."

I then pull away from Tobias and grab his hand. "Come on. My father is waiting for us in the main study."

Wagging his tail happily beside us, Fenrus licks Tobias' free hand as we make our way to the elevator just ahead of us where Nicholas is impatiently waiting.

When the elevator car doors ding open, the group of us walks into a mad plethora of activity. Nicholas dives right in, weaving in and out of moving bodies toward the main doors ahead. The three of us follow.

The main study is sumptuous with its rich tapestries, beautiful oil paintings, and shelves of books lining the walls. The majority of the decadent furnishings owned by my mother's family came with the property. The only furnishings the Sazia family members were allowed to take with them were personal items and objects not paid for through the main family account. Because so many family members were taken care of in every way necessary by their mafia produced ill-gotten gains, this left quite a bit behind for us to sift through. To be honest, I couldn't care less about any of the material possessions we've inherited. The things I insisted upon that do matter to me are things like beds and buildings to house my people.

To the far right of the room, I see my father speaking to our pack's chief lawyer, Ian Dikigoros. Ian's new assistant Angela stands behind them, speedily writing notes into a booklet. Once they see us, their serious posture becomes more relaxed. My father opens his arms wide, which I dive into gratefully.

13

"My boy returns unscratched."

Ian laughs. "That's no boy. That's the wolf responsible for giving all of us hope for the future."

I release the hug with my father and shake Ian's hand.

"You're too kind," I tell Ian, feeling my face turn red. "How are things progressing with the Senate Judicial Committee? Were you able to introduce our representatives as hoped?"

Ian's face becomes slightly weather-beaten at the question.

"For the most part. I do have a lot of sway in that area, but your grandfather has put up a few new roadblocks that will take some time to get around. We're getting there, but the process is going a bit slower than expected. On a good note, the circuit judge overseeing the property rights to the Sazia family estate has just announced his verdict. I was just telling your father here that it looks like we have all titles and properties free and clear."

Nicholas chimes, "That's fantastic! All the work we put into this place won't be for nothing. And now we can move on to developing new housing and businesses in the undeveloped lands as planned."

Angela speaks up. "I'm sorry to interrupt, sir, but your meeting across town will be starting in 40 minutes. If we leave now, we should still be able to get there on time."

"Thanks, Angela." Ian turns to us again. "I'm sorry to cut my visit so short, but there's a lot to do. How about we have dinner together when I fly back from Washington next week?"

"That sounds great," I answer back. After several handshakes, Ian leaves the study, followed by Angela and two large bodyguards.

My father turns to the group of us. "Come. The others want a full report on what's happened."

My father then pushes on a hidden panel covered by a tapestry. Immediately after, one of the bookshelves slides open, revealing a series of rooms on the other side. Walking in, we pass a stock room filled with non-perishable food and water. The room on the opposite side contains several military weapons. Seeing the amount of ammunition stationed there gives me a slight chill. The lot of us finally walk into the third and final room. The room is dressed up as an elaborate meeting room, equipped with digital projection screens, security video monitors, and a main computer workstation off to the side. There are several people already present. Among them, I see my half-brother Damon standing to one side of the large round central table. He's talking to my close friend, and Tobias' figurative sister, Mika. I smile to myself as I can see the obvious chemistry between the two of them. Ah, to be 18 again.

On the other side of the table, I see my brother's mother, Gabriella Basilikos, attempting another civil discussion with my mother. My brother Damon inherited his mother's fiery red hair. All of his other physical characteristics, though, are a close match to mine and my father's, aside from our six year age difference. Due to his upbringing, though, Damon's maturity level, education, and demeanor are much more advanced than my own, which thankfully makes him an ideal Archon leader despite his young age.

I give a lot of credit to Gabriella. After my grandfather forced my father to abandon us when I was still just a kid, he immediately threw my father into a scenario that involved Gabriella having my father's pure wolf blood child. The reason for their union no longer matters. All that does matter to me now is that I have a brother that I really care about. Gabriella and my father's non-marriage arrangement wasn't romantic at all. They viewed their creating Damon as something obligated by them from tradition. They raised my brother as parents, but as far as the relationship between my father and Gabriella was concerned, there was only ever mutual respect and, over time, a solid friendship. My mother understands what happened, but the feeling of betrayal runs deep within her. I can honestly sympathize with both women and my father. I only hope that my mother can resolve her issues with my father and Gabriella for her own sanity's sake.

Once my mother looks up and locks eyes with me, her facial expression goes from one of controlled annoyance to happiness. I go over to her and embrace her. When I do, I feel wetness hit my cheek.

I pull away from my mother and look into her tear-filled eyes. "What's wrong?"

She wipes away the moisture from her face with the side of her hand. "I heard you were attacked by some of Bobby Longo's men. I'm just glad to see you're okay."

I hold my mother again. "I'm fine, really. You don't have to worry about me."

My mother shoots right back, "That's a mother's prerogative kiddo. Get used to it."

My father then puts his hands on both of our shoulders. "I don't mean to interrupt, but we need to call the meeting to order."

My mother kisses me on the cheek one last time and moves back to the table. I give Tobias a quick wink and take my place on one side of the table beside all the other Archons. Fenrus follows me and lies at my feet. Beside me sits Damon, my father Adam, Gabriella, and our newest Archon, former Basque Council Member Vincent Ichnilatis. I've only met him recently, but he has been a staunch ally to my father, Gabriella, and Damon for years when they were still attempting peace talks between the Synoro and Basque clans to end a past potential war.

On the opposite end of the table sit our clan's Council Members: my mother Victoria, Tobias, Mika, Nicholas, and a former Exallos Clan wolf named Quentin Synetos. He's proven to be an excellent morale booster for the new clan from the beginning. His knack for quick problem solving has also benefited the clan on many occasions. He and the other Council Members have voiced a great deal of points to the Archons, which helped sway a lot of our final decisions.

In general, I'm pleased with the group's choice of leaders. The only bit of disappointment I've had is not being able to make my mother and Tobias official Archon members. It was agreed upon by the others that the old rules of not allowing spouses to sit as Archons together should stay in place. Thankfully, I was able to convince the others that they, Mika and Nicholas be Council Members instead. Thus, the four of them will still have some say in the overall organization of the clan. Ultimately, though, it is the Archons whose word becomes clan law.

I look over to the side and see that another new wolf, Anne Dendronto, has stationed herself at the computer terminal. A former housewife from the Neuri Clan, Anne's sweet nature and commitment to our cause helped solidify a more permanent place for her in the new pack. Her office skills, organization ethic, and attention to detail made her the perfect choice as the official clan secretary. She sits in place, ready to record the meeting minutes.

My brother Damon speaks first.

"Thank you all for making this last minute meeting. There have been some new developments. First of all, I'd like to repeat what I just learned from my father and Ian. The Sazia properties are now turned over to us entirely. Everything's been finalized and all titles of ownership are now in our name legally."

Happy murmurs are heard throughout the room.

"Ian and his team will be facilitating the initial meetings with several land developers to see what our options are in using some of the unused land we now own, as well as comparing initial bids to make sure we stay on budget. This is fantastic news, as you all know. With more clan members showing up at the compound each week, we're starting to get tight again with our already established housing. If everything works out as planned, we should be able to break ground in a month."

Quentin says, "If it comes down to it, I don't think any of the wolves would mind sharing their homes with a few new members for the time being. At this point, we all know how it feels to be homeless and in need. We'll make do."

Smiling, Gabriella says in her French accent, "Glad to hear it. We'll keep all of you updated once we get word back from Ian. That said, I believe we have important news from Archon Devin."

All eyes are on me. I take a deep breath. "As you may know, Nicholas and I left the compound to pick-up some magical essentials I had shipped from San Francisco. They were sent to an outside P.O. Box for security reasons. The items should help the witch members of our clan further fortify the compound from outside harm, as well as strengthen our psychic perceptions a bit more. After our meeting has adjourned, if the magical casting members of the group could take the items to the designated locations and activate their mystical properties, I would greatly appreciate it."

Tobias and Mika nod their heads.

"Unfortunately, our mission wasn't entirely without issue. As you've no doubt heard, on our way back, we were ambushed by some of Bobby Longo's men. Nicholas, Fenrus, and I were able to make it out okay, but we made sure to leave our attackers alive for safety reasons. Like I told Nicholas, with the attacks we're getting from our own people, the last thing we need right now are more enemies. The mob now knows that we aren't killers but they also now know that we can defend ourselves if need be. If Bobby Longo attacks us again, then I think we should retaliate, but not before. Until that happens, we should just continue to keep our distance and play it by ear. Now that's what I think about the matter, but I want to know what each of your thoughts are."

Everyone in the room looks into each other's faces and several murmurs can be heard. With his trademark French accent, Vincent speaks first.

"First of all, we're glad to see you're all right. Were you able to get any of Bobby's people to specifically say why they were sent to attack you?"

Nicholas answers, saying, "No, but our intel has been that both of the city's remaining mob families have been twitchy since we first arrived. My guess is that Longo got antsy. According to Victoria, Bobby was the main Don her father had problems with in the past."

Speaking up, Victoria says, "It's true. A couple years before Adam and I left Boston, Bobby took over his father's mob holdings. Bobby wasn't like his father, though. Signore Longo was old school and respectful of the other Don's boundaries. His son Bobby, on the other hand, is anything but. He started pushing his business dealings into my father's territories. My father put a stop to it of course but there's been bad blood between our two families ever since. Bobby obviously wasn't successful in taking over the Sazia territories when my father died. I'm thinking he's probably looking at our arrival as his next best chance for a takeover."

Mika says, "If that's true then we'll have to be on our guard more than ever. I've just ordered the outer guards to fluctuate their patrol schedules. Say the word, and I'll have the guards doubled if necessary."

Adam replies, "That's great, but my only concern is that we're seriously taxing our combat trained wolves as it is. Short of training more wolves into military readiness, which will take some time, we'll have few soldiers available for intelligence gathering or field assignments."

Damon says, "Our clan was created with peace in mind, not war. I understand the need for fighters, but I'm loath to make killers out of cooks, librarians, and office clerks. I can go, father. I'm more than happy to get whatever intelligence we need."

Gabriella says, "That's considerate of you, *mon ami*, but you are way too recognizable. The other packs will spot you immediately. Just look at what happened with Devin tonight. I was just as against his leaving to get the supplies. The pack can't afford to lose one Archon, much less two."

Vincent interjects, saying, "I agree. No Archon or Council Member should be given dangerous assignments unless absolutely necessary. We can make an announcement to the other wolves that, if they are interested, the option of military training is available to them. Those wolves who volunteer will be trained without further obligating the remaining pack members. Would that be an acceptable alternative?"

Damon ponders the idea a moment. "Yes."

Vincent continues, saying, "Good. Quentin, Nicholas, and I will speak to the others tomorrow morning to see who's interested. Now, as for Bobby Longo, it's a tricky situation. Perhaps we can try the delicate approach. Victoria, how do you think Bobby would take an invitation to a sit-down meeting to help clear the air?"

Victoria appears deep in thought for a moment, and then says, "I don't know. Bobby is an arrogant bastard, but he's not stupid. My guess is that he'll accept the invitation, but I really don't know how it'll go from there."

Tobias replies, "I or one of the other witches can shadow the meeting to make sure everything runs smoothly. Bobby Longo is human after all, so he and his team are susceptible to our magics. But what about the city's other mob boss, Don Franco Phillipi? Will he be invited too?"

Adam says, "He'd have to be. We need to have all cards out on the table for everyone."

Victoria says, "Don Phillipi won't be a problem. He's a sweet old man who likes to keep the peace. As long as we make it clear that we have no interest in any of his territories or businesses, he'll be happy to turn the other cheek."

Vincent replies, "Well, that's good, one less thing to worry about. We're going to have to choose a neutral location for the meeting. Preferably someplace anyone won't object to." To Victoria, he asks, "When your father met with the other Dons, where did they usually meet?"

"At a little coffee shop in the center of the city on Hanover and

Wesley Place, near St. Leonard's Church. It's technically within Don Phillipi's territory but my father and the other Dons always considered it neutral ground for things they had to discuss."

"Perfect," I reply. "We'll send the invite to have both Dons meet us there the day after next. One point I want to make is that I don't want us to get bogged down with any of their internal politics. If they want to kill each other, fine. That's between them. The main point I want to get across to both families is that we are not involved or interested in any of their agendas. We only want to be left alone."

Adam then says, "We still have to discuss who will be representing us at the meeting. Any more than three of us will definitely spook the Dons. She's not an Archon, but I feel Victoria needs to be there. Both families know her, and she's probably expected. I volunteer to help escort her."

Hesitantly, I say, "I don't think that's a good idea dad. You won't be a stranger to Longo or Phillipi. They still might recognize you from when you worked for mom's father. You being there will only add more fuel to the fire."

Vincent adds, "I agree. No offense meant to you Adam, but it's probably for the best. I'm not so intimately tied to the Sazia's history, so I'll go in your place. Is there any objection?"

Adam, though obviously upset, shakes his head in compliance. I feel crushed I had to speak against my father from going, but I can't take any chances with his safety.

Vincent continues, "Good. Now, considering what Archons are left, I feel Devin would be the best choice for the third member. He is blood tied to Victoria so the Dons can't deny his attendance, and if the need arises, his magical skills will come in handy."

Damon agrees, saying, "It sounds logical to me. Devin, is that okay with you?"

Well, of course it's okay with me. We're sending my mother into the lion's den. There's nothing that will stop me from being there to protect her. I look over to my father and see that his eyes are locked on mine already. Keeping my eyes on him, I say, "I wouldn't have it any other way."

My father smiles at me, understanding that I mean to keep my mother as safe as possible. We both then look toward my mother, who is now also smiling radiantly.

Gabriella breaks the silence saying, "It's settled then. Vincent, Victoria, and Devin will represent us at the meeting. I'll have a few of the wolf guards hand deliver the messages tomorrow morning." Her French accent gives a more civilized tone to an otherwise emotionally tense meeting. "That said, is there anything anyone else would care to weigh on the matter?" Silence. "Good, then, it will be done. Further topics for discussion?"

Damon asks, "What's the present status on the other wolf clans?"

Nicholas replies, "Nothing new as of yet. The Synoro Archons Ryan, Shaun, and Brice have been trying to keep their clan in order, but their dissenting Archons Jason and Clayton are determined to create a faction against us. Word is that the two of them and their loyal wolves are setting up camp at the New Hampshire Synoro compound. Our three Synoro Archon allies can only glean bits of information from the few spies they were able to infiltrate into the compound before Jason and Clayton closed it off. We know they'll be attacking soon, but we just don't know when or how."

Adam includes, "The close proximity of the New Hampshire compound makes things more uncomfortable. They're practically at our back door. Devin, have you been able to find out anything else from your night visits there?"

My father is referencing my witch ability to leave my body when I sleep. I used to be frivolous with my power when I was younger and would peak in on the lives of the rich and famous. Imagine the juiciest reality TV show, only a lot more real. Now it's become a tool my clan desperately needs. Lately, I've been using this power to infiltrate my grandfather's Synoro compound to see if I can discover their plans for us. That changed a few days ago. Something has been blocking my access to that area. I can get up to a few feet away from the main building, but that's it. It's almost as if an invisible wall is blocking me from getting any closer. Annoyance and frustration don't even come close to describing what I feel about the matter.

"I still can't come close enough to anyone inside the main house to find out anything. Whatever Jason has found to block my access to the compound is working. I'll make another try of it tonight. With any luck, I'll be able to break through to find out what we need."

Damon asks, "Is there anything else?" Silence. "Then, the open portion of this meeting is adjourned. The Archons will now meet in private."

The Council Members and meeting secretary rise from their chairs. Tobias and Mika begin collecting the various magical artifacts, lifting them toward me as a silent confirmation that they will now take them as asked. My mother is the last member to leave.

I say to her, "Mom, I'll meet you in the garden after?"

She turns, smiles, and then exits.

Looking down at Fenrus, still at my feet, I mentally tell him, "Now the part I've been dreading."

His voice appears in my head. "It has to be done. I'm here if you need me."

Petting the top of his head with one hand and playfully grabbing at the fur on his cheek with the other, I emanate as much feelings of love as I can toward him. Fenrus licks my face in response.

My brother Damon speaks first.

"The mafia meeting will not be pretty. If Longo is anything like what Victoria says, he's not going to back down. I think we need to lay out some scenarios of what routes we can take if the meeting goes south."

"I agree," I reply.

Adam says, "I'll have a few wolves scout the area tonight. We can meet tomorrow morning to go over what they find."

Gabriella nods. "That still leaves what to do about Jason. Devin, those trinkets you brought back tonight. What exactly will they do?"

"Some are protection amulets and others are natural magic amplifiers. Depending on where they're placed, the protection amulets will slow down anyone with ill intent from entering the compound. It might have little effect on wolves, but the amulet's magic, once triggered, will psychically alert the witches in the clan. It should provide us with a small early warning window we might need."

Vincent asks, "Devin, I was wondering if you might be able to visit Bobby Longo tonight with that sleep thing you do. He doesn't know about the meeting yet, but you might get some insight on where his head is at."

Adam confirms, "That sounds like a good idea. Would you mind, son?"

"Of course not," I reply. I fidget..

Noticing, my father asks, "What is it?"

I look down to Fenrus. His eyes become a piercing blue color. In my head I hear, "I'm here for you."

In the calmest voice I can muster, I say, "Earlier tonight, when we were ambushed by Longo's men... I broke the First Law."

An almost physical silence covers the room.

After a few moments Gabrielle asks, "You changed in front of them?"

Looking at her I reply, "No, I used magic in front of them."

The look of confused horror and disappointment that falls across my father's face breaks my spirit in two. Closing my eyes, I try to shut out the image of him in my head and ignore the deep pit forming in my stomach.

"When Nicholas and I dispatched them I wanted to send a message. I wanted them to be so afraid of us that they would think twice about attacking us again. I magically put fear into them and warped their vision of us."

My father sternly asks, "Did they see you as wolves?"

Looking back at him I answer, "No. Demons."

Vincent rises up and reaches for the handle of his sword. Fenrus immediately jumps in front of me, growling in Vincent's direction, acting as my shield. Once Vincent's sword is fully released, another sword quickly finds it's way to Vincent's throat. Attached to it is my father.

His eyes bright yellow, Adam brings the side of his face to Vincent's ear and says, "If you lay one finger on my son, I'll kill you where you stand."

My father's reputation as an assassin is well known throughout the clans. His experience and skill rivaled that of even Nicholas in his time, back before he put killing aside to become his clan's Peace Ambassador.

Seeing how close he is to death, Vincent steadily states his case. "The First Law is in place for a reason. We can't put our people at risk of exposure, not even for family. Every clan worldwide knows this. It's been our way for thousands of years. Archons hold no exception."

Just as steadily, my father says, "Our way has changed."

Damon stands up and places his hand on Adam's sword arm, gently pushing it downward. Adam lowers his sword, but does not put it away. Damon then stands in front of Vincent and says, "Killing Devin will do more harm than good. Surely you must know this. Besides being publicly chosen by the Goddess, he is also a magic user. Possibly the strongest magic user our clan has. What will his death mean to the other wolves, to say nothing of the other members of his inner coven? And so close to a potential war with the Synoro *and* Longo family? Do you really want to be the person responsible for the anarchy and added loss his death will cause?"

25

Holding his ground, Vincent asks, "So we do nothing? Our people could be compromised."

Stepping forward, I answer, "I understand, and I'm sorry. I wasn't thinking when it happened. After last years' experience, it was just the first thing that came to mind. I apologize. I'll do whatever's necessary to make up for my mistake."

Gabrielle joins the now huddled group of us. She looks deeply into my eyes.

"Do you truly understand what you've done?"

Her voice has no malice or judgment. I answer her sincere question honestly.

"I do."

She holds her gaze for a few more moments before turning to Adam.

"The First Law is still valid and important for many reasons. That said, our clan is separating from the old ways more and more every day. I can see no fear in Devin's eyes, only remorse. He's made a huge mistake, and he knows it. We have to set precedent. What needs to happen here?"

Knowing what I must do, I answer, "I will step down as Archon. I'm not a true leader anyway. I've never led anyone in my life. The four of you have been doing this far longer and know what must be done. I'm still too green."

For the first time, I see anger in my brother's eyes as he turns my way. "You will not! Both Goddesses chose you for a reason. You have a responsibility to fulfill their task."

"But Damon, how can I stay an Archon when I've broken the clan's most sacred rule?"

Damon says, "We will table this discussion until after we meet with Longo. We have too much on our plate right now as it is. We can't afford to lose even one Archon. Not now."

Vincent says, "And what if tomorrow human military troops break down our door demanding the truth? What then?"

Adam intervenes, saying, "Then we'll need *more* wolves to help protect us, not less."

Turning to Vincent, I say, "I've let you down. I've possibly put our wolves in danger. I swear to you, I will make this right. I promise."

Vincent throws down his sword and storms out of the room. The feeling of loss and shame are overwhelming. I just want to crawl into myself and never return.

I turn and see my father now flanked by his new family. Anger and disappointment spread across his face. He opens his mouth to say something, and then stops. He takes a deep breath and leaves the room after Vincent.

Gabrielle walks over to me. She gently lifts my chin, smiles warmly, then leaves the room as well.

I sit at the table again.

"I've ruined everything, Damon."

"No, Devin, this is only the beginning."

Chapter Two
VOICES FROM THE PAST

ENTERING THE CENTRAL COURTYARD, AN EVENING BREEZE CARESSES my face. Sitting near the koi pond, I see my mother. As I walk up to her, I notice a cup in her hand. Sensing my approach, she rests it on the bench and stands to greet me. Her smile eases my otherwise sour disposition. She reaches out her hand to me, which I take and engulf her with a huge bear hug.

Before I let go she says, "In case you're wondering, it's just hot tea."

My mother had a problem with alcohol in her past. When my father was forced to leave us, she didn't take it well. Alcohol became her escape from the grief. Since our reunion, however, I have yet to see her with anything stronger than a Diet Coke.

Smiling, I say, "I never thought otherwise."

Looking around, she asks, "Where's your dog? He's almost always at your side."

"I sent him to check in with Tobias and Mika."

Once we sit back on the bench, she takes her cup and asks, "So are you going to tell me what's wrong or do you want to chat for a bit first?" I simply look at her. She continues. "I'm your mother. I can see it in your face."

Looking away, I say, "I just tried to give up my title as Archon and was shot down."

"What?" She grabs my face and points it back at hers. "Why would you do that?"

"I messed up mom. Earlier tonight, when Nicholas and I fought the Longos, I used magic in front of them. Keeping us secret is our main rule, and I totally screwed it up. I'm no leader. I can barely keep my own life in order." I take her hand from my face and hold it to my chest. "I'm constantly second guessing myself, and it could get these people killed. They need someone with experience, someone with skill."

Taking her hand away, and with tired eyes she says, "You have those skills Devin. Everyone here can see that but you. Why do you think these people left everything behind to join you?"

"Great, now you're mad at me, too."

With frustration in her voice, she says, "I'm not mad at you. This…", she says waving her arms toward the buildings surrounding us, "is not what I wanted for you. I wanted you to have a chance at living a normal life, away from the death and danger I grew up with. When I came back here, I didn't feel warm nostalgia. I feel trapped in a prison that killed my parents. So believe me when I tell you I could *never* be mad at you for wanting to step away from this."

Then it hits me. I never once gave any real thought to how my mother would react to being back here or how it would make her feel. It must be agony for her.

Continuing, she says, "You never knew your grandfather. He was a force to be reckoned with, kind of like Adam's father. Men like that create enemies. We were always under guard. I was homeschooled growing up. I insisted on going to public school, and it took some time, but my father finally relented. He made sure I had a bodyguard with me at all times though. It's a terrible feeling to have every part of your life controlled and dictated to you. So, I get it."

"Dad won't even talk to me, and Vincent literally wants to kill me."

Her voice lifting again, "What?"

"Don't worry about it. Dad and the others put him in check. If nothing else, it should make our meeting with the Longos more interesting."

She replies, "I'll talk to your father. We'll get things resolved."

"Mom, with all the family politics coming out, I had a question. Please, don't feel you have to answer though."

"What is it?"

I lower my voice. "How did your mother die?"

My mother closes her eyes for a moment to collect her thoughts.

"Your grandmother loved flowers. The brighter the colors and sweeter the fragrance, the more she loved them. This courtyard was made just for her so that she would always have a safe place to enjoy as many of her favorites as possible. She would go every week though down to the flower district to see new hybrids and to get fresh flowers for her bedroom. I can still smell them now."

My mother stares off into the distance for a while before continuing.

"The morning she died, she asked me if I wanted to go with her to buy new flowers. I told her no. We had fought the night before you see. I wanted to go out later than usual with some friends. She and my father said no. I refused to hug her goodbye, but she kissed me on the forehead anyway before she left. That was the last time I saw her."

"What happened?"

Wiping her eyes, she says, "She was killed. Shot down. We were told later that one of the rival families in Miami was responsible. Things were never the same between my father and me after that. I blamed him and the lifestyle he lived for my mother's death. Then, later, when he remarried, well, things got worse."

I put my hand on her shoulder. "I'm so sorry."

"I hated my father. And worse, I had no one to talk to about it. That is until your father came along. He was so handsome, but I still treated him like dirt because he was one of my father's hired help, or so I thought. He never stopped pursuing me, though. I'd come home, and there'd be a rose or some other small gift waiting for me in my bedroom. I found out later that he asked to split his time, watching over me half the time and watching over my father the other. Eventually, we became close and, after a time, we fell in love. I could never tell my father about us, but he noticed I was happier. I even let some of the walls I had put up against him start to crumble. Then, the day came when I found out your father wasn't what he said he was."

Silence.

I haven't shared with my mother that I saw first-hand what happened to her that day. When Tobias and I were still living in San Francisco, we were part of a spell that let us literally step into that day's events. It was tragic. My father was assigned to infiltrate the Sazia mafia family, gather intelligence over a few months, and then kill their leader. That leader was my mother's father, my grandfather Don Sazia. My mother walked in just before my father could carry out his contract. He gave my mother an ultimatum: she could either leave with him and go into hiding, or stay with her father and possibly be killed alongside him. She chose my father.

"I know that must've been hard for you."

My words pull her from her trancelike state.

"Yes, but ultimately I got you." She gives me a weak smile as a tear falls down her cheek.

Shame fills me as I remember all the teen angst I put her through growing up, then later running away from home to find my father. I never even bothered to contact her during that time.

"Mom, I'm so sorry for everything I put you through. I was selfish and didn't consider your feelings. I really can't apologize enough."

Reaching over to hold me, she replies, "You're with me now, kiddo. Just promise me you'll never leave again."

Holding her back tightly I tell her, "I promise." Letting her go, I continue, "It just feels nice to have family around me again. I'm surrounded daily by unfamiliar faces asking for guidance and sometimes I just feel lost. I don't have a clue of who I'm supposed to be anymore. Everything's just happening so fast. I go from being a suburban kid with a silver spoon in my mouth, to a hustler, then a witch, and now a werewolf Archon leader. I don't even know what my real name is anymore. Am I a Marshall? Toxotis? Sazia?"

"You're Devin. Always have been and always will be. No matter what life throws at you through, always remember that. You hear me?"

I sense a wave of magic sweep across the courtyard. I stand to look around. With my special sight, I can see a layer of magic envelop the buildings all around me. Noticing my reaction, my mother asks me what's wrong.

"Nothing. Tobias and Mika just activated the magical items I brought in earlier. There's a new mystic security field surrounding the property."

"Good," she says. "That takes a lot of weight off my chest. Devin?"

"Hmm?"

"What's it like being a witch?"

The question takes me by surprise.

"Well," I reply. "It's kind of like…"

Before I can fully answer, I hear savage snarling and swords clanging against each other. My mother hears it, too.

"Stay here." I tell her.

"Like hell I am!"

Racing over to the commotion, I see two of our clan guards with their swords drawn and swinging. They are surrounded by even more of our guards. Above the two central figures are mystic symbols representing the Synoro clan of wolves. Shit, the protection spell worked!

As I race over to the group, I can feel the ground beneath me begin to shift slightly. Just as I reach them, the two disguised Synoro wolves are quickly wrapped in tree roots surging from the ground beneath them. The wolves try to slice away as much of the roots as possible, but there are just too many. In a matter of seconds, thick roots and vines engulf them until only their heads are left exposed.

I hear my mother's voice ask, "Did you do that?"

"No."

To my side, I now see Tobias. His eyes are filled with eldritch energy that slowly begins to ebb as his magical command is now completed.

"Thanks." I squeeze Tobias' hand. He squeezes mine back.

"Of course." he says in all seriousness.

Mika, the Archons, and a squadron of clan guards all race in from various parts of the compound.

Vincent pushes his way forward. "What happened?"

Tobias answers, "Our spell worked. The mark above these two wolves show where their loyalties lie."

I hear my father lightly whisper into my ear, "Devin, if there's anything in their mouths, can you remove them quickly?"

I reach out my hand and close my eyes. I focus my magics to locate any foreign objects in their mouths and will them to appear in my hand. When I open my eyes I see a small swirling white light floating just above my palm. It disappears and in its place are two small brown caplets.

Behind me, I hear barking. Fenrus!

I race to the sound of my familiar's voice as fast as I can, along with a troop of guards behind me. I hear Fenrus wince in pain and then my shoulder feels as if it's been slashed. With as much magic as I can muster, I will myself to be at Fenrus' side. My body loses all sense of weight and I can feel myself magically shifting through space. In moments, I am in the main library beside Fenrus, who is now on the ground, hurt.

Angered, I look around to see several non-soldier wolves cowering in the corners with one lone armored wolf standing in the center of the room. Above his head, like the others outside, is the floating symbol of the Synoro clan. In his gloved hand he is holding a small metallic chain. Even from where I am I can sense it is made of pure silver. I keep my guard up, as I know everyday weapons can't harm a witch's familiar. Under normal circumstances, they would pass harmlessly through Fenrus. That can only mean the silver chain the intruder is holding must have some sort of magic tied to it to have hurt him like this.

Needing to get the chain out of play, I will for both of the gloves on his hands to disintegrate. When they do, the silver to flesh contact causes the wolf to yell out in pain. He drops the chain beside him. Silver is physically repulsive to werewolves. The slightest contact will cause an immediate burning sensation. Before he can react, I also will for the brown cyanide capsule in his mouth to teleport to my hand. It does.

Realizing his magical weapon is now unavailable, the wolf takes out both swords affixed to his back and his facial features develop lupine characteristics. I remove both of my swords as well and try not to let my anger at Fenrus being hurt cloud my judgment. I allow myself to partially change into my wolf form to gain better skill in battle. With my wolf vision, I see the remaining civilian wolves race out of the room, leaving us to battle alone.

Due to a miscast spell previously made, both Tobias and I were imprinted with Nicholas' fighting skills. Since forming the new pack, Nicholas and my father have been teaching us to hone those skills in daily fighting lessons. I'm now about to find out if those lessons pay off.

Growling under his breath, the wolf slowly walks sideways, sizing up what move I will make first. It is a standard Synoro strategy. If there's any apprehension on his part, he hides it well.

"You can't escape," I tell him. "You're exposed and in the middle of our fully staffed compound. Any minute now, a troop of guards will be pouring into this room. Surrender now, and I promise no harm will come to you." Transformed, even partially, I have to focus hard to form proper words. The voice that emanates from me is now savage and coarse.

My opponent remains silent, but a look of anger sweeps across his face. He surges forward, slashing his blades at me at a ferocious speed. I push my apprehension aside and focus on my teachings. For every swipe he makes, I counter with a sword block or pivot. To any normal human, we would seem as a blur of moment and flashing swords. My heightened wolf senses and reflexes, however, allow me to stay in pace with every attack my opponent makes.

The anger in the intruder's entire being is apparent. Perhaps I can use that to my advantage.

"My grandfather's clan is growing smaller every day. Join our cause. Be part of our pack."

Anger turns to fury as the wolf attacking me becomes more hostile in his swordplay, which in turn creates several weak points for me to exploit. Following Nicholas' training, as well as my instincts, I take several swipes at my opponent's breaks in defensive. The third successful attack brings him to his knees. I know I don't have much time though as his werewolf metabolism has no doubt already begun the healing process.

"I don't want to fight you! We don't have to be enemies!"

With rage in his eyes, the battered wolf answers, "I'd rather die than follow a disgusting freak like you."

Continuing his assault, the wolf manages to throw a smoke bomb onto the ground. It immediately shrouds the general area. Focusing my magics within me, I will for the smoke to disperse. As it does, the rogue wolf comes out of nowhere and stabs me in the abdomen. He's about to use his other sword to do the same, but before he can, a shout rings out and suddenly Nicholas joins the fight followed by a troop of wolves behind him. Nicholas kicks my attacker away from me, allowing me to pull out the wolf's sword and breathe. Looking down to see what the wolf has done to me, Nicholas' face gets the same look of fury my assailant had just moments ago. Nicholas' features change as he fully lets out a barrage of sword attacks on the intruder.

Tobias and Mika appear at my side and begin inspecting my wound. I wince in pain and allow my form to change back to human.

"Forget about me. Check on Fenrus. He's hurt." I tell them.

With apprehension, they do as asked. I look on at the battle before me to see two more of our wolves have joined the fight. Outnumbered and now cornered, the rogue wolf begins spinning his remaining sword in place at a high speed.

"Death to the new fag king," he says, just before using his spinning sword to decapitate himself. I look away in horror.

Trying to get up, I can feel that my body hasn't fully healed my wound yet. I push through the pain and force my way up anyway. I stagger over to Fenrus and see that both Tobias and Mika have their hands held over the nasty gash on Fenrus' shoulder. Strong energy emanates from them. After a few moments, my familiar's cut begins to shrink. Once it completely disappears, Fenrus weakly sits up and begins licking both of their faces. I go over to Fenrus and hold him.

I see Nicholas with a determined look on his face. He whispers into my ear, "You cannot engage in battle unless absolutely necessary. It's our job to get our hands dirty, not yours. Archon lives are much too valuable. I know I'm speaking out of turn, but you must know this."

Turning to face him, I say "Fenrus *is* my life. If he dies, I die."

The revelation takes him by surprise. He bows toward me, then returns to his team. "Clear the body. Take it to furnace room below. We can't leave a trace behind. Janessa, give the others the 'all clear'."

The others do as they're told. Two wolves grab the body while another grabs the head. A fourth soldier collects the dead wolf's swords and is just about to grab the small metal chain he dropped earlier.

"Ah, no, Milo. I'm gonna hold on to that if you don't mind."

The wolf nods toward me then turns to exit the room with the swords, leaving the chain on the floor behind him. I use my magics to take hold of the chain and drift it toward me. It stops a foot away from my face as I inspect it closer.

"What is that?" Mika asks.

"The wolf had it. He used it on Fenrus. It's enchanted somehow."

Tobias states, "But Jason and his remaining wolves can't manipulate magic. How could they have come up with this, and why did he go after Fenrus? Do you think they know about your bond?"

"I don't know, but I'm going to find out."

I then will for the chain to fall into my shirt pocket. At that moment, my parents enter the room. Spotting me, they run to my side.

My dad asks, "Are you okay, son?"

Spotting the blood in my midsection, my mother yells, "He's been hurt!"

"I'm fine, Mom, really." I take her hand. "The wound is just about fully healed already. I'm all right."

The look of worry in her eyes doesn't go away. I smile in appreciation and kiss her hand.

Turning to Fenrus, I send thoughts of concern his way. In my voice, I hear, "I'm fine, too."

My father says, "A few of the civilian wolves said they saw a fourth wolf with the Synoro mark above her head. She got away before she could be detained."

Mika asks, "How could so many of them have gotten in? We've been so thorough."

Nicholas includes, "That's something I'd like to know."

Adam says, "Vincent, Damon, and Gabrielle had the two Tobias captured placed in separate holding rooms. Now that we know you're safe, I'm going to join them now."

"I'm going, too." I say.

"Oh no you're not," Tobias tells me. "You need rest."

"I'm fine."

My mother chimes in. "Tobias is right. Your father and the others can question them and catch you up in the morning."

"But…"

"No buts, Devin." my father says. "It's late. You've been attacked twice tonight. Mika? Think you can lend us a magical hand?"

Turning to my father, Mika says, "Sure." Then, to me, she says, "Don't worry, Devin. Everything comes to the surface eventually. We'll figure this out."

Tobias and my mother stay behind to escort Fenrus and myself to our room. As we walk, many groups of civilian wolves look at us with a sense of worry. I look down to see that the large bloodstain on my shirt isn't helping matters. I will for it to evaporate from my clothing. The wound I received is fully healed but still a bit achy. I can feel a sympathetic pain as well on my left shoulder, a reminder of where Fenrus had his wound.

When we get to Tobias and my room, my mom gives me a hug

goodbye and tells me to get plenty of rest. She then kisses Tobias on the cheek and leaves toward her own corridor.

Once inside, a familiar feline friend greets us. Ms. Whiskers is a black and white cat that followed Tobias and me from Los Angeles to San Francisco. She became a member of a cat clan of her own there until Mika's grandmother went missing. When the move to Boston became official, I sent for her. Her eyes are almost as deep green as Mika's. Flicking her tail back and forth, Ms. Whiskers walks up to us excitedly at first, then with question.

Sniffing the air between us, she asks, "You hurt?"

As I have a magical familiar, I'm able to mentally hear Ms. Whisker's thoughts, and that of other intelligent animals. Tobias, however, doesn't hear a thing and passes Ms. Whiskers to get me a bottled water.

"Yeah" I tell her, "I got hurt today."

Sniffing again, she says, "Magic hurt, too. I can tell."

With that, Fenrus follows in behind me. Ms. Whiskers cautiously backs up and moves to the side. Respecting her space, Fenrus quickly walks past her to jump onto the bed to rest.

Tobias returns with the bottled water. I thank him and quickly drink as much of it as I can.

With a sour look on her face, Ms. Whiskers says, "Me like Bitey's sparkle, but me no trust Dumb Ones. Me not good enough for you?"

The 'sparkle' she's talking about seems to be a special vision cats possess to see magical beings. The more magic is involved, the more 'sparkle' she sees. It's a form of catnip to them. 'Bities' or 'Dumb Ones' are what felines call dogs. Of course, cats, when they refer to themselves, call each other 'Pretty Ones'.

I bend down and pet Ms. Whiskers. "You are all the cat I'll ever need, but I need Fenrus, too."

Ms. Whiskers purrs.

"What about me?" Tobias asks with a false sense of shock.

I walk over to Tobias and give him the deepest, sweetest kiss I can manage. When we finish, I tell him, "I need you the most."

Locking hands with mine, Tobias leads me over to the bed. After removing my two swords from my back and pulling off my shoes, I throw myself onto it, careful not to bump into Fenrus. Tobias takes my now empty water bottle and returns it to our room's kitchenette area. As he does, I look around the suite. It is filled with plants of different varieties. Both Tobias and my central Wiccan goddess is the Earth Mother, Gaea. She's an ancient and powerful deity whose domain is the earth itself. Having greenery in our abode is a respectful nod to her. It also strengthens Fenrus, as his magics are heightened in natural green areas. In their presence, I can feel the soreness from his shoulder wound slowly fade away.

Most witches will bind themselves to a deity of their choice, or to the Wiccan faith itself. Mika's chosen gods are the Olympian twins, Artemis, goddess of the hunt, and her brother Apollo, god of light and the arts. Werewolf clans have a goddess of their own. Millennia ago, the Greek god Zeus cursed an Arcadian king named Lycaon into becoming the first werewolf. The goddess Hecate took pity on him and gave him the ability to change back and forth between his wolf and human form. This curse and transformation ability was then extended to Lycaon's family members and a good portion of his kingdom's subjects. These werewolves and their descendants have held Hecate in high regard ever since.

Revealing herself to our pack's members recently after so many centuries has revived the wolves' belief in her. A portion of the mansion was converted into a religious sanctuary with a ceremonial altar dedicated to Hecate, or Marzanna, as the Neuri werewolves refer to her, at the head of the room. To the right of the room is a smaller altar to Gaea out of respect to Tobias and me, and a similar altar to the Olympian twins on the left of the room out of respect for Mika. These four gods have become the central religious stepping-stones for our new pack. With all the turmoil my wolves have been through, no matter what hour, I've not passed the sanctuary once without seeing at least 3 or 4 people there offering prayers to the Goddess.

When Tobias returns, he sits on the bed and gives me a sincere look.

"What is it?" I ask him.

"I'm worried for you. I get that we're in a really tough spot right now, and that you're now Archon to all these people, but you're constantly getting attacked. And when you're not attacked, you're off training hard for when you *do* get attacked. You're stressed and stretching yourself thin. I don't like what this is doing to you."

I can hear the concern in his voice. I sit up and sit cross-legged.

"Tobias, I really appreciate your concern, but I can't think about that right now. I've got to keep my eye on the bigger picture. If I relax my guard, even for a moment, it's not just me that will suffer but the entire clan. Especially after what happened earlier tonight."

Now with his curiosity peaked, Tobias says, "What do you mean?"

I tell Tobias the details of what happened during the Longo mob ambush in the alleyway earlier, as well as what happened in the Archon meeting once the Council Member portion had ended. The look on his face conveys anger. Instead of continuing to argue with me, though, Tobias walks over to a far wall and removes a sword displayed upon it.

The sword is a vintage relic from the days of European witch hunts. It was used to behead and maim countless witches in its time. Because it tragically came in contact with so much magical blood, the sword gained magical properties of its own over time. Aside from being an instrument of death, the sword can also be used to call upon witches who have died by foul ends. Both Fenrus and Ms. Whiskers take immediate notice.

Tobias lays the sword across my lap and resumes taking his seat on the bed beside me.

"What's this for?"

"Something or someone is helping your grandfather's clan to gain an advantage in attacking us." Tobias replies. "Whatever it is, even your gift to spy in spirit form can't break through to see what that is."

"And you think this will help?"

"It can't hurt to try," he answers back. "We're in Boston. This city is neighbor and home to where many witches were tortured, hanged, and drowned during the witch trials of old. I'm hopeful that maybe the spirit of one of them might be able to give us some insight into what we need to know. It helped us before, why not now?"

I take the sword in hand, examining the scabbard. It is cold. I release the sword a few inches from its housing and immediately feel a chill.

Ms. Whiskers surprises me by jumping up onto the bed and sits next to Fenrus. He tries not to show any reaction so as not to agitate her.

"Magic in that thing. Weird magic. Not sure if good or bad."

To Ms. Whiskers, I say, "This is a weapon humans used a long time ago to do bad things to 'magic ones'. Now, the magic it has is only good or bad depending on how it's used."

Smiling, Tobias asks, "She talking to you again? I swear, if I didn't know you I'd think you were schizophrenic."

Mentally, I hear Ms. Whiskers ask, "What schizo…whatever he say?"

I then hear Fenrus answer, "It means he hears voices."

"Oh," Ms. Whiskers says in awe.

The sword begins to take a life of its own. I can feel it pulsing in my hand, as if it were eager to work its magic for us. Ms. Whiskers' eyes widen. She doesn't even seem to notice Fenrus sit up beside her. In my head, I hear Fenrus say, "There are voices in that instrument that are reaching out to you both."

I look at Tobias.

"It knows."

Tobias sits cross-legged opposite me on the bed. Fenrus looks on to the left of me while Ms. Whiskers races to the right of me for a better view of what's about to happen. Her head darts back and forth with eyes widely open, making sure she doesn't miss a thing.

Completely removing the sword's scabbard and placing it aside, I lay the sword across Tobias' lap. We take one last look into each other's eyes before gingerly placing our hands on top of the blade. Once we do, ghost-like forms begin fading in and out of view all around us. Soon, the room is filled with pacing forms, mostly female, going about their own routines as if we were not there.

From out of the shadows emerge two forms. The first one is an older woman, somewhere near the age of 75 or 80 years old. She is dressed in what can best be described as simple European peasant clothes. On her shoulder sits a small but fierce looking hawk with brown plumage. She stops a few feet from the bed with her hands clasped before her. She and her hawk stare down at me with questioning eyes. Ms. Whiskers' eyes turn full black in excitement as she stares at the bird's 'sparkles' in awe.

Next to her appears a woman in her late 20s dressed in early American period clothing. She has a well-manicured hairstyle and near porcelain skin that is marred by the unsightly wound that runs around her neck.

Both Tobias and I nod toward the figures out of respect, and they do likewise. The older woman speaks first, but I am unable to make out what she is trying to convey. She speaks in what seems to be Italian. When she is through, the younger woman speaks.

"Blessed be. We are pleased to meet both you and your familiars. My name is Catherine Morrissey. This is Maria Theresa Sazia. Over the years, I have learned your present day way of speaking. Maria has not. As I am able to speak her language, I am here to translate what she says to you."

"Sazia?" I ask aloud.

"Si," the older woman responds. She continues speaking in Italian.

Again waiting until Maria has finished speaking, Elizabeth says, "Maria is your great-great grandmother, Devin. She is here to advise you on what is about to happen."

Remembering that the sword can only contact the spirits of former witches, I suddenly realize that the ancestor before me must be a witch. With knowing eyes, Maria nods as if to confirm what I had just thought.

Almost in unison, both witches speak in different languages. In doing, Elizabeth's voice changes from her previous British hinted tones to an altogether different one. It's as if my great-great grandmother's voice changed to an Italian accented English speaking one and took possession of Elizabeth's throat. I focus on Elizabeth's words but keep my eyes on the body of my grandmother.

"A great evil from my past is coming. I am here to help you defeat it. In my time, I was a powerful Stregheria or witch. I was responsible for caring for my village's health, livestock, and land. I kept my village of Ariccia safe for many years. I was not part of a coven as you are, but I was empowered by my familiar and by the god of the nearby forest, Virbius. Not everyone gave respect to what I did. Despite the blessings I gave them, because I was not Christian, many villagers would cross the street when I went to market and hid their children's faces from me. Some even coveted my power, just as they now covet yours. You could say I was the village's prized outcast.

"In another village several miles to the east lived a coven of Benandanti. They were dark witches who hid behind false light. Because they knew I was blessed with a familiar, they wanted to steal my Prezioso for themselves. They tried to turn the people against me every chance they could. They were four but weak in power. I was strong enough to keep them away. The tragedy of my story is that the

Benandanti were finally able to get to me, not through the villagers I protected, but through my own family."

Maria looks away for a moment to gather her thoughts. I'm reminded of the same mannerisms I had just seen in my mother just moments ago in the garden.

"My daughter, your great grandmother, was not blessed with my gifts. Because of this, she became bitter and spiteful with age. The Benandanti were able to use her jealousy to their advantage. They thought that once I was out of the way that they would be able to possess my familiar for themselves. They promised my daughter many rewards and blessings. She foolishly believed them, and she poisoned me. Once the Benandanti realized that when I died that my familiar died with me, they rescinded their promise to my daughter and banished her. She left our village and was forced to start another life in the New Country."

Pondering her words, I tell her, "I'm so sorry."

Catherine translates my words, to which Maria then gives a slow nod in my direction.

Maria continues, "I don't approve of the dogs you've aligned yourself with. They've been a … problem for our family as well. I only hope you'll be able to change their mongrel ways. The attacks you've received, you sense magic is involved, yes?"

"Yes!" I immediately respond. "Do you know who's been helping the Synoro sabotage us?"

With a look of foreboding, Maria says, "It's not just the Synoro you must face. Many dogs from the Old Country have joined your grandfather's cause. And not just them, they've enlisted the help of the Benandanti as well."

I look over to Tobias and see the same look of dread I feel in my heart.

Maria continues, "You must be cautious. The Benandanti have changed since my day… grown. Their current coven is no longer filled with the weak witches I knew. Supported by the large number of wolves at your door, you will need as much help as you can get to defeat these enemies."

"But, we don't have anyone else." I answer. "We're strapped as it is. We barely cemented ownership of our current home. Most of our finances go to help feed and shelter the people under my care, not to mention the stragglers who show up on our door almost daily. When we're not being attacked by werewolves, we're being shot at by mafia families."

"Bah!" she says. "I'm disgusted by this mafia nonsense. Your grandfather tarnished our family legacy with his need for power. My daughter gave the Sazias no favors by coddling him and driving ambition into his head. He took the selfishness she had and multiplied it a hundred fold. Murders, drug dealing, and extortion: all for lust of power. Your mother was right to want to leave it all behind. It breaks my heart that my line, you, have returned the family back to that way of life again."

There it is again: disappointment. I lower my head. Almost immediately, I feel a hand lift my chin up. With eyes filled with love, Tobias says, "That isn't your fault. Remember that."

Tobias then turns to my great-great grandmother and makes the surliest face I've ever seen on him. His next words surprise me.

"You can cut the pompous attitude right now. You're a relic, a phantom from a time that no longer exists. If you have information that can help us, then give it. Otherwise, you can go back to the lifeless shadows you came from."

Maria's hawk screeches in anger. Maria, however, simply looks back at Tobias as if carefully inspecting someone she never bothered to notice before.

"You have a fire within you. You'll need it if you plan to save my grandson. I won't apologize for who I am. I'm far too old for that. I will, however, respect your decisions. I came here to help you, and I plan to fulfill that obligation."

"Go on," I reply quietly.

"You must convert the half-hearted wolves to fully embrace your cause, and you must also reach out to more than just the dogs."

"Who?"

"There are others, magical beings and free thinking witches who might be able to help you. Reach out to them, and you might have a chance."

"What other magical beings? Which witches?"

With wizened eyes, she says, "I am not allowed to reveal them outright. They are under powerful protection spells that make even the dead not able to divulge who they are. That cord in your pocket. It is covered in Benandanti magic. It's signature is unmistakable to those who they've crossed before. You must use your spirit gift to seek out those others the Benandanti have wronged. Find one, and you'll find the others. That's all I can say."

I'm about to continue prodding for answers when Catherine speaks up in her own voice.

"Devin, we'll have to be ending our time here soon. We won't be able to maintain our forms here much longer. Is there anything else that you'd like to know from us?"

"Yes. Can you tell me how I can break through the mystic wall surrounding the Synoro compound?"

Catherine replies again in her own voice.

"There are two Benandanti witches with the werewolves now. They're the ones blocking you from visiting that location. They've placed a protection spell similar to your own from any magic approaching the building. You must be clever about how you try to enter. You may not be able to enter the building either directly or from above, but if your spirit self were to travel *under* the mystic blocks, you might be able to gather the information you need."

"Brilliant! It's so simple. How did we miss that?" Tobias exclaims.

I have to agree, that's one route I haven't yet been able to try. It just might work.

"Thank you. I really appreciate everything you've both said. I can't thank you enough."

Both witches nod and start to turn away. Before leaving, Maria turns back to me and says, "There is one more thing you must know. Have you never wondered who it was that hired the Synoro wolves to kill your human grandfather?"

What? Her question hits me unawares. In all the time I've had since first seeing that assassination all those months ago, I've never really sat down to think about who was behind it.

Continuing, Maria says, "The person responsible for the dogs murdering my grandson is the same person your new family will be meeting with soon: Bobby Longo."

"What!", I say this time aloud.

"The secret he's been hiding is that he's been sleeping with Victoria's step-mother for years. The putana Julia was seeing Bobby Longo secretly to give him information. What no one knew is that, just before your grandfather was killed, Julia became pregnant with Bobby's child. She hid the pregnancy from everyone but Bobby. Now that the bastard son has come of age, Bobby and Julia plan for him to take over all of your grandfather's previous holdings. Your mother showing up and taking that away from them ruined those plans. That is why they want you dead."

Anger fills me. Seeing my reaction, Maria humbly bows her head again and fades away. Catherine bows her head again, too, and says, "Blessed be" before fading as well.

Letting go of Tobias' spirit sword, I quickly put my shoes on. As I grab my own swords nearby and head toward the door, Tobias stands up.

"Where are you going?"

He throws on his shoes as well and chases after me down the hall, through many corridors and past several buildings. At one point, I look down and see Fenrus has joined pace with us as well.

When I near one of the holding rooms, I can sense that the people I need to speak to are inside. I will for the door to open. It does with a loud thud. Inside, I see Mika, my father, Nicholas, Vincent, and a handful of soldier guards inside questioning one of the Synoro spies. My dramatic entrance startles them. They reflexively grab for their weapons, but reholster them when they see who we are. Tobias, Fenrus and even Ms. Whiskers trail into the room behind me. She hisses once she sees Nicholas. Tobias picks her up and holds her.

My father asks, "Devin, what's wrong?"

I calmly turn to the guards and ask them to leave. They look at my father and Vincent with a look of confusion. Vincent gestures them to the door and they exit. I will for the door to close behind them.

The Synoro spy looks at me in disgust and says, "If you think I'm going to say anything now that *he's* here then…"

Before he can continue, I punch him hard across the face. The force of the blow knocks him out completely.

Nicholas rushes forward and says, "Devin, what are you doing?"

Fuming with anger, I turn to him and say, "Did you know that Bobby Longo was the one who put the hit out on my grandfather?"

Nicholas flinches at my question.

"No… Devin, I didn't know."

Turning to my father, I ask, "Did you?"

I can see horror in my father's eyes.

"No, only the Archons know who the pay clients are. I promise you Devin, if Bobby Longo was the one who paid to have Victoria's father killed, I didn't know about it."

I can feel tears of anger forming in my eyes. I wipe them away and walk over to a corner to gather my thoughts. A few seconds later

Mika walks over to me and asks, "Devin, how do you know this? What did you see?"

Turning to face her, I reply, "We used the witch sword to find out if someone from the spirit world could give us any information. The spirits that responded told us about Bobby Longo and more."

I retell everything that was seen and discussed earlier. When I am done, everyone in the room is deep in thought. Tobias comes over to me and uses his free hand to hold mine. I squeeze it gently in gratitude. Fenrus walks over to my opposite side and sits. When I look over at my father I can see fury overcome his face. I can relate intimately with his reaction. Being told that the mafia family that is presently trying to kill us is also same family that paid to have my mother's family destroyed years ago is definitely overwhelming.

"Dad!" My father looks at me with extreme focus. "We need more information before we react to this."

His stony facial expression doesn't change. I can sense that his anger is only put on hold. I turn to Tobias and Mika and say, "I'm going to need your help for this one."

Vincent raises his eyebrow and utters, "For what?"

I answer back, "More answers."

I walk over to the unconscious Synoro assassin and mentally ask Fenrus to join me. He does. Taking his cue, Tobias places Ms. Whiskers on the ground and walks over to my right side and takes my hand. When he does, Mika walks over to my left side and takes my other hand as well.

With determination in my voice, I say, "Resistance to magic or no resistance to magic, this wolf is gonna give us what we need to know whether he wants to or not."

I close my eyes and find my magical center. Soon, I feel it swirl around and envelop me like a warm cocoon. Soon after, I feel Mika and Tobias filled with their own magic. Slowly the three magical boundaries pulsate and blend into one another until our three individual energies become one. When our internal magics solidify around the three of us, Fenrus uses his own magics to enhance our power to a high level. The result causes the entire room to be filled with our potent magic and crackle all around us.

I open my eyes and focus on the unconscious werewolf before me. I attempt to enter his mind and am met with resistance. Unlike the normal resistance I experience when I try to use my magics on a fellow werewolf, this resistance also seems to be aided by a strange magic of its own.

In my head, I feel Fenrus' vast access to magical knowledge. I soon hear a series of words in my familiar's mental tones. I repeat them aloud, focusing on their hidden meaning. Once the words are uttered, a strange black smoke appears around the wolf's head then disappears with a gasp.

I can now sense the magic protecting the wolf has been destroyed. Feeling only the usual barriers left in place, I attempt to enter his mind again. With the surging power of my coven, I force my way past the physical walls resisting me until I gradually reach my victim's swirling rivers of memory. When I stop myself to get my bearings, I look around and find that Tobias and Mika are still with me in spirit form. Their faces carry an expression of wonder and awe. I've only attempted this on a person one time before with limited results, but for my two companions, this is an entirely new experience.

Mika asks, "Devin, was this what it was like when you entered the Neuri Archon's mind?"

"Close. The Archon's mind was awake and turbulent when I entered it. The mind we're in now is unconscious so thankfully it's not as chaotic."

Tobias adds, "Then we should act quickly since we don't know when he'll wake up. What exactly are we looking for?"

"This wolf," I say, "was protected by witch magic. That just confirms my suspicions that he may know more about the Benandanti witches helping Jason. He also might possibly be able to tell us what Jason's next move will be."

I close my eyes and focus on his memories of the Benandanti. Like a beacon, I am pulled to a specific memory in his mind. When I open them, I find that Tobias and Mika are still with me. Our surroundings, however, have changed. In almost watercolor effect, we are at an airport hangar watching the wolf whose mind we are now occupying. He and several other wolves, including the now headless spy I fought with earlier, are standing beside renegade Synoro Archons Jason and Clayton. An expensive looking jet plane pulls into the hanger to join them. Once the aircraft stops, the cabin door opens and out step three women dressed in black. The tall blonde middle witch is the obvious leader.

"Good evening, Claudia." Jason takes the lead witch's hand and kisses it. She looks slyly at him.

"Good evening. You must be Jason." She turns to Clayton. "And you, Clayton." Her Italian accent is like velvet. "I must make this short. These are the two Benandanti agents I've assigned to work with you. Each witch is an expert in a specific field, but all of my witches are trained in the deadly arts if needed."

Clayton asks "Three? You've only brought three witches?"

Claudia gives Clayton a look of annoyance, but Clayton remains unfazed. "Two actually. I must return to Italy on important matters. My sisters are more than sufficient for your needs." She points to the raven-haired witch. "Divina is our coven's mistress of divination. She'll be your eyes and ears with strategizing." She then points to the short haired red head covered completely from neck to toe. "This is Lucia. Her touch is death to anyone who lays a hand to her skin. Would you care for a demonstration?"

Her cold invitation causes the Synoro wolves to shift their feet uncomfortably.

"No, that will not be necessary." Jason's cold tone and eyes narrowed toward Claudia give her a firm warning not to test him. Claudia laughs slightly.

"You know" she says, "the fact that I'm here helping you at all is something I never thought I'd see happen. Your kind hasn't exactly been on good terms with mine for several hundred years. In fact, one of the first lessons we teach our witches is to never trust a wolf. Does that surprise you?"

With eyes still locked on Claudia, Jason replies, "Not really. Our resistance to your magics has made us the perfect weapons for hunting and killing your kind when needed. To be honest, I'm not happy to be working with you either, but the situation we are in requires it. So for the time being, we're willing to look aside our past rivalries if you are."

With a smug look on her face, Claudia pauses a moment before answering. "I am here, am I not? If what your European comrades tell me is true, then we both have a stake in seeing this new coven dead. I must return home to meet with your overseas Archons so I must unfortunately cut this meeting short. My sisters are to report back to the coven twice a day. Those are the rules. If they meet with foul play, I will know about it and the person responsible will be dealt with by me directly. This I promise you."

Claudia turns to her witches and an unspoken communication takes place. Both witches then bow their heads to her before Claudia says goodbye to them in Italian. She then turns back to the Archons, tilts her head slightly to them, then returns to the jet. As it leaves the hangar, the dark haired witch Divina approaches Jason and Clayton.

"Take us to your base. We have much to do."

Our surroundings shift, and we are now in the Synoro's New Hampshire base. It is the first sanctuary my new pack lived in just after we formed. Three of the five Synoro Archons gave us temporary shelter there until we could find a base of our own. To see Jason, Clayton, and their soldiers setting up a death camp for us in a place where we first felt safe is disconcerting.

The room we are in was at one time used as my pack's supply room. Now it looks as if the renegade Synoro have taken to using it as one of their main planning rooms. In the center is a table with many red marked maps of Boston. Wolves in full military fatigues move quickly from room to room. Leaning against the far wall is the witch Lucia with crossed arms and darting eyes as she scans her surroundings suspiciously. Her comrade Divina stands near Jason and Clayton in deep conversation.

"Your enemies are resourceful witches. They've placed magical barriers around their compound. I can't use my powers to view them as clearly as I had hoped. Lucia and I will provide you with the same mystic barriers for your base, though. It'll give us a level playing field."

Clayton says, "I don't want a level playing field. We agreed to have your kind assist us because I thought you'd give us an advantage in destroying my enemies."

Lucia asks aloud, "Your kind?"

The Archon bodyguards stop what they're doing and glare at Lucia.

Ignoring them completely, Lucia continues, "Your wolf arrogance is as big as we've been told."

Divina gives her a stern look and says, "I must apologize for my sister's tone. She forgets her place."

An unspoken communication happens between the two, after which Lucia relents her anger and slumps back against the wall behind her. Jason's bodyguards ease their tension but keep a more watchful eye on Lucia.

"As I was saying," Divina continues, "for being a new coven, your enemies are quite thorough. I need to know exactly how many witches we're dealing with and how many wolves they have under them."

Jason gives Divina a look, as if her insinuation that the witches are lording over the wolves were an insult. He replies, "As far as I can tell, there were about three witches and at least thirty to forty wolves in their pack the last time I saw them. That was several months ago though. Our intel is that more and more of my clan's subjects are joining their cause every week."

Lucia smirks. "So, your own kind turns on you? That must sting."

Jason glares at Lucia. "The only traitors I'm concerned with now are the Archons of the Enopo clan. Cut off the head and the rest of the body dies. Those wolves who have left my fold will return. You should be more concerned with those damned witches. The last I saw of them, they and their magic dog were strong enough to kill four others of their kind that opposed them and an entire pack of demon possessed humans. Killing two more witches should be child's play for them."

At this Divina raises her eyebrow. "Magic dog?"

"Yeah," Clayton interjects. "They have a dog that can do magic tricks like the witches can."

Divina looks at Lucia and the two of them form evil grins on their faces.

"I see." Divina waves her hand before her and a clouded mist forms before her. Inside the mist a blurry scene appears. In it, several figures move back and forth but not one of their identities is decipherable. Then a shape of a dog comes into screen. "Things just became interesting."

The fact that the Italian witches now know about Fenrus makes my blood run cold. To say nothing of the rage I feel toward Jason and Clayton for revealing that secret to them. The rest of the memory sifting reveals that the two Archons had four of their wolves infiltrate our pack as part of a fact-finding mission. Once the wolf whose mind I'm invading starts to stir, his thoughts become like strong raging currents, so I pull Tobias, Mika, and myself out and back into our own bodies.

Once I feel myself whole again, I open my eyes and see the

shackled wolf coming to. Letting my passions overtake me, I strike the wolf again, causing him to fall into back into unconsciousness.

"Devin!" My father grabs my hand before I can use it to strike again at the assassin. Pushing my fist slowly to my chest, Adam looks upon me and sees the obvious rage I'm exuding. He looks calmly into my eyes. "Son, that's not going to do us any good. What did you see?"

The wolf bodyguards stationed outside come back in to see what the ruckus is about. Vincent motions to them that everything is fine.

Tobias then walks over to my father and me. "We'll show you." Tobias then places my palm on my father's forehead, then takes Mika and walks her over to Vincent. He then walks himself over to Nicholas and places his palm on Nicholas' forehead, signaling Mika to do the same to Vincent. In unison, we try our best to transfer as much of what we had seen to the Archons and Nicholas. Their natural resistance to our magics makes it difficult, but we push through as best we can until the memory transfer is complete.

"Mon dieu!" Vincent exclaims.

I taking my hand away from my father. He looks at me with a confused expression. "What does this mean?"

Worried, I answer, "It means we have a third group of enemies out to get us."

Chapter Three
CUT OF THE KNIFE

SINCE SEEING THE ASSASSIN'S MEMORIES, SEVERAL THINGS HAVE changed. Vincent's previous displeasure of me has all but vanished. Instead, he's taken to asking for my specific input on every subject discussed. My father, Gabriella, and Damon even start joining the other Enopo wolf soldiers during their daily ground patrols. As for Nicholas, he's become a figurative piece of gum on my shoe. No matter how hard I try to dodge him, he usually manages to follow Fenrus and me around wherever we go. After finding out the Synoro have witches assisting them in my potential assassination, I know he's only following orders for my own safety, but finding him in my sights every minute of every day becomes a bit much. Fortunately, Tobias, Mika and my mother have noticed my aggravation and have taken to pulling him away whenever an opportunity arises.

I frustratingly realize that my continued attempts at infiltrating the New Hampshire compound remain unsuccessful. Even following my great-great grandmother's suggestion, no matter how hard I try, I simply can't break through the magical barrier protecting the renegade Synoros. My attempts at visiting Bobby Longo, however, were a lot more fruitful.

When the day comes for our rendezvous with Bobby Longo, I'm almost numb. Too much has happened and too many secrets revealed that I'm afraid I'll be of no use to anyone otherwise. Especially hard was letting my mother know that Longo was the person responsible for the hit on her father. My father and I had considered keeping that bit of news from her, fearful of how she would take it. We ultimately decided against that as it just seemed wrong to not let her know. My mother made us promise her that there would be no more secrets between us. After everything we've been through, I wasn't about to break that promise to her. Now knowing who was responsible however, I've seen a steely part of her that has me worried.

On the limo ride over, I sit beside my mother as Vincent and Nicholas sit across from us, going over the meeting notes for the 100th time. An additional Emissary wolf sits silently next to them. My mind wonders as I nod my head to everything they say. A few cars ahead of us, three of our wolf soldiers drive Tobias and Fenrus in an unmarked car. Tobias is wearing the special arm band given to us by Mika's grandmother last year. It suppresses a witch's magical aura, making it virtually invisible to any magic users. Fenrus is also suppressing his own magical aura, leaving them both blind to even my own magical sense. It's only Fenrus' mental thoughts consoling me that gives me any kind of solace about their safety. To further hide who they are, Tobias has glamoured himself and Fenrus to stay under our enemy's radar. They and their assassin bodyguards will station themselves at the park across the street from our meeting place where Tobias and Fenrus will be able to view everything happening psychically and provide assistance if needed.

My mother takes my hand and looks out the window.

"What are you thinking?" I ask her.

"Hmm? Oh, I was thinking about how long it's been since I've been down this street. The neighborhood has changed a little, but most of the buildings are still the same. My friend Alicia used to live in that building there. She and my other friend Stacy were two of the biggest tramps you'd ever meet."

I laugh. "You hung around with tramps?"

My mother smiles at me. "Hey, it was better than the nuns my dad wanted to side me with. They were a riot. I wasn't a tramp myself, mind you, but at least I was never bored. We always got into clubs for free and never had to pay for drinks."

The air feels lighter, and I can feel a smile forming on my face. My mom's guaranteed way of making any situation manageable was magical. I'm glad to see she hasn't lost her touch. I love you, Mom.

The Emissary driver turns back to us. "We're here."

The car pulls up to the curb, and the driver opens the back door for us. Nicholas steps out first and looks around, taking in the area around him. After he gives the all clear, Vincent emerges from the car behind him. Vincent then reaches his hand back into the car to help assist my mother out as well. I follow behind, protecting my mother from the rear. The two Emissary guards with us stay behind, surveying our surroundings.

The Italian coffee shop before us has a quaint look about it. The feeling I perceive is that the business has stood in this location for many years. Standing at the door's entrance, three tough looking bodyguards look at the group of us with steely eyes, sizing us up for any shortcomings. I can see holstered guns bulging out of their black designer jackets. To his credit, Nicholas continues to take the lead without breaking stride. When we get to the door, the bodyguards hold out their hands.

"This is a private meeting, and only *she's* invited."

The bodyguard speaking points to my mother and then crosses his arms, making his body become a wall between the entrance and us.

Nicholas eyes both guards coldly. "Move out of our way, or I'll move you myself."

The bodyguards put their hands on their jacket bulges, signaling a warning to Nicholas to back off. They have no idea that Nicholas is packing just as much heat. With my special vision, I can see the two Emissary swords affixed to Nicholas' back. Vincent and I are carrying sets of swords as well. My magics cloak the swords from mortal eyes, allowing the three of us to go into this meeting prepared in case things go south.

My mother steps forward. "They're with me. I'm Victoria Sazia. We have a meeting with Don Longo and Don Phillipi. You *will* let us in."

The closest bodyguard says, "We have orders to only let you in. These other mooks stay here. Especially this one." He points to Nicholas.

Nicholas takes a step forward, to which Vincent stops him by placing his hand on his shoulder. Vincent then speaks up by saying, "Nicholas will stay here, but the rest of us *are* going in. I'm Vincent Ichnilatis. I'm with Victoria. And this here is Devin Toxotis. He's Victoria's son."

The bodyguard booms, "Look Frenchy, I don't care *who* you say you are. Our orders are that only Victoria goes in. No one else. So, you either step aside, or we're gonna have us a problem here."

Annoyed that diplomacy wasn't getting us anywhere, I decide to settle the situation. Remembering the voice trick I had seen Mika's grandmother use last year, I contact Fenrus mentally. The moment I do, I feel my magical energies grow. In my mind, I hear Fenrus providing me with the mental cues needed to duplicate the spell needed.

I lock minds with the bodyguards and see their bodies go slack. For all their brutish bravado, their minds are relatively simple and easy to manipulate. In an ethereal voice I say, "You will let us pass."

Slack-jawed, they repeat, "We will let you pass."

Slowly lumbering to the side, the bodyguards leave the door free for us to enter.

Not yet finished, I say, "You will not disturb our meeting."

They repeat, "We will not disturb your meeting."

Continuing, I say, "You will help our friend make sure no one else disturbs our meeting either."

At this, Nicholas turns to me and says, "What? I'm going in there with you."

Without breaking concentration on the bodyguards, I tell Nicholas, "The Dons inside could possibly cancel our meeting if we go in with a bodyguard. We'll be fine. Stay out here and keep an eye out for the Synoro and their witches. This might be the opportunity they've been looking for."

I can tell Nicholas wants to argue, but he holds his tongue. He bows his head and stands beside the Italian bodyguards as asked.

I repeat to the oversized gorillas, "You will help our friend make sure no one else disturbs our meeting."

In unison, they echo my words.

Happy with the outcome, I release my hold on them. I then take my mother's arm and gesture for Vincent to step through the doors. Once inside, I see a nervous looking man behind the counter smiling. Not sensing any malice from him, I imagine it is the coffee shop owner. Standing by a door to a back room I see another armed guard. This one, however, is familiar to me. It is one of Longo's men who attacked Nicholas and me only a few days ago. His right arm is in a cast, obviously the result of Nicholas breaking it from before. Seeing me with my mother, his face pales. He is about to reach for his gun with his still working hand when I put my finger to my lips.

"Shhhh!"

I produce thoughts of sleep and project my will toward him. Instantly the hired hand's eyes start to flutter, and he silently falls to the ground. The shop owner sees the man fall but does nothing, opting to ring his hands repeatedly instead. Vincent gives me a look, but I say in the lowest breath possible, "It's only temporary. He'll wake up in a few minutes."

Under normal circumstances, no one would be able to hear what I had just said, but with our keen wolf hearing I can see that both Vincent and my mother understood what was said completely.

We make our way through the doorway to see a separate dinner room with a table in the center. Standing beside it are Dons Franco Phillipi and Bobby Longo with one other man I've never seen before. Don Phillipi, an older man with wizened eyes, has little hair —stark white- growing on his head just above his ears. Beside him is the unknown middle aged man with similar features. Something tells me that this must be a son of his.

Longo has a look of animosity on his face that I don't bother to acknowledge. He shifts his weight, revealing another figure at the table. Previously blocked by Longo's large frame, Julia Sazia looks on at our entrance with a sour expression.

My mother asks, "What is *she* doing here?"

Julia scowls at my mother.

Longo forcefully says in a thick Boston accent, "She's here as my guest. Who are these two? I told my men that you were to come in alone."

With steely eyes, I stare straight at Longo and say, "I'm Victoria's son, Devin. But then you know that already, don't you?"

"Watch your tone, boy." From his demeanor, I can tell that Longo isn't used to having anyone challenge him. I flash him a sinister smile and see his ire rise.

Wanting to end the negatively escalating tête-à-tête, Vincent says, "My name is Vincent Ichnilatis. I help oversee the people Victoria houses at her family property. Anything discussed affects them, and therefore, me."

Now eyeing Vincent, Longo asks, "So you're the new Don she's been giving everything to?"

Standing as erect as possible, Vincent responds, "I am *no* such thing. If we're permitted to converse like civilized people, you will realize that your ideas about what's going at the Sazia manor are wildly exaggerated."

With one eye squinted, Longo asks, "Are you calling me a liar?"

At this, Don Phillipi puts his hands up. "Enough of this. This meeting hasn't even started and we're already taking several steps backward." He surprisingly doesn't have a Boston accent at all. Instead, it's a general American accent with a slight hint of Italian. Yelling to the storeowner in the next room, Don Phillipi says, "Angelo, we need two more chairs in here." Returning his attention back to the room, he then says, "This part of the city is under my control, and I will *not* be disrespected. Everyone here will speak civil or we're gonna have a problem on our hands, capish?"

Keeping an eye on Vincent, Longo adjusts his belt and sits. Immediately after, the storeowner quickly comes in and places two additional chairs at the table. Once he does, he swiftly leaves the room. Don Phillipi motions for everyone to sit, and we do. I sit to the right of my mother, and Vincent sits to her left.

Continuing, Don Phillipi says, "My name is Franco Phillipi." Motioning to the man now sitting beside him, "And this is my son Sam. He's my trusted advisor and will be sitting in on the meeting. Obviously, you already know Bobby Longo. Bobby and I are both in charge of most of Boston. Until recently, Julia here was controlling what was left of Don Sazia's businesses. Now that Victoria is back, though, that seems to have changed. This meeting is to find out exactly where she stands, and what she plans to do with her father's former holdings."

My mother takes a moment to look around the room to make sure she has everyone's attention before saying, "Let's get right to it. Everyone here knows that I took over my father's properties and accounts, and everyone here also knows that all those titles are now in my son's name, and also in the name of his half-brother Damon. The whys are no one's business but my own, suffice it to say that any mob ties my father had while he was alive are not included in the takeover. That part of my father's legacy my present family and I don't want anything to do with.

"Through my father, I know about every dirty deal that has gone on in this city. I know who does what, where it happens, and what outside companies are involved. The thing of it is, I really don't care. As far as I'm concerned, both of your families can have all of it. You can keep your drug running and racketeering, but leave my family and me out of it."

Sam Phillipi shouts, "Now, hold on!"

My mother stares down Sam and says, "Hold nothing. We've known each other since we were kids, Sam. Let's not pretend to not know what's really going on here. In fact, your hands aren't lily white either."

Longo chimes in, saying, "So we're just supposed to take your word for it that Sazia's former turf is now up for grabs? I've seen the heat you have at your compound and the number of people you've got there. Ain't nobody gonna have that kinda firepower sittin' around for no reason. What's really going on there?"

All four of the mobsters lean in, eager to hear my mother's response. I answer instead.

"We have armed guards because of the two of you. They're there for our survival. It's as simple as that. And as for the people we're housing, they're all struggling families who have nowhere else to go. We're giving them a second chance to get back on their feet. We're not stupid. We knew that once my mother returned and took over the properties willed to her, you two could possibly have an issue with it. Since we've already been attacked by Longo's men, it just proves that our suspicions were right."

Placing his knuckles on the flat of the table, Longo stretches his face as close to me as possible.

"You got no proof anyone from my family went after any of yous. Say one more lie like that and you're gonna be spittin' teeth for a week."

Reaching into my jacket pocket, I feel for the blank pieces of paper I had put there earlier. Once I feel them, I mentally recall the memory of Longo's men attacking Nicholas and me. Using my magic, I will images from that memory to imprint onto the paper. Once the spell completes, I remove the papers from my pocket and throw them on the table. Both families see the newly made photos and begin pawing at them.

Continuing, I say, "One thing I'm not is a liar. As you can see, those are your men holding guns and getting physical with a colleague and me. We made sure not to hurt your men too much, though. As you now know, my family and I can take care of ourselves pretty well. So believe me when I say, anyone else that comes after any of my family in the future won't be treated with kid gloves. Next time, they get cut to pieces."

Longo clenches the table with all his strength, trying hard not to give into his rage.

Don Phillipi says, "If what you're saying is true, and you really do stay out of the family business for good, you have my word that no one in my family will take any strikes against you." Turning to Longo, Don Phillipi asks, "What about you Bobby? Where do you stand?"

Physically sweating now from the taxing restraint of his rage, Longo grits his teeth and grumbles under his breath.

With a stern sound in his voice, Don Phillipi asks again, "What?"

Choking back his volatile emotions, Longo says, "We'll stand down, too."

Furious, the once silent Julia jumps to her feet, knocking her chair to the floor behind her. "What? You're letting them walk away scott free? What about my property? What about…"

Longo turns to Julia and says, "Not. Now."

Exasperated, Julia says, "But…"

Smirking, my mother tells her, "Careful, Julia, you wouldn't want to have a stroke from all the excitement."

Anger fumes across Julia's face. I can tell she wants to lunge at my mother, but Longo's stern facial expression seems to be holding her back.

My mother narrows her eyes at Julia and says, "And you don't *have* any property. My father left everything to me in his will. You knew that when you married him. The state court came back with its final verdict that his will stands as is. *You* have nothing."

Grabbing her purse, Julia points it at my mother saying, "You haven't heard the last of me, Victoria. Not by a long shot!"

As Julia strides toward the doorway, my mother adds, "Running off to see your son?"

Julia stops in her tracks, and Longo jerks his head in our direction. Seeing she's hit a nerve, my mother smirks and leans back in her chair a bit. "Stephen Carver, right? Seems funny to me that you put him under your maiden name. Especially since he looks so much like his father."

As if the wind were knocked from her, Julia slowly turns back to us and in a breathy voice says, "What? I don't know what you're…"

All color has drained from her face.

"Cut the crap, Julia." My mother's false sense of unknowing is now completely gone. "Did you really think you'd be able to keep him a secret forever?"

Longo's expression turns from anger to one of utter shock.

Confused, Don Phillipi asks, "What son? Don Sazia had a son?"

"No," my mother responds. "I'm my father's only child. No, Julia's son is the bastard child of another man. A man she was seeing behind my father's back for years. A man in this very room, actually."

Don Phillipi says, "That can't be true!"

"Oh, but it is." my mother replies. "Ask Don Longo. I'm sure he can tell you exactly who Little Stevie's parents are and why they want my father's properties back so badly. Of course, he isn't so little anymore. Just came of age a few years ago, if I'm not mistaken. Isn't that right, Bobby?"

Something in Longo snaps. He takes the table and tosses it aside as if it were a toy. Don Phillipi and Sam fall to the floor, trying to avoid being hit by the table in the process. As Bobby is about to jump on top of my mother with his hands in a choking position in front of him, I reach for one of the invisibly cloaked blades strapped to my back. Just before he reaches my mother, I uncloak the blade and swing it at Longo, stopping just as the razor's edge barely nicks his neck. Longo immediately stops his advancement and freezes in place.

"Lay one hand on my mother, and you'll see just how deadly serious I am about the promise I made earlier. Wanna test me?"

In shock and pulling Victoria back to safety, Vincent says, "Stop this! This isn't what we wanted!"

Don Phillipi, now being helped up by Sam, says, "Oh but it's just begun. I see what's at play here now." Turning to Longo, Don Phillipi continues, "You wanna have things set up for your son to takeover Sazia's part of the city, Longo? You wanna expand your territory? A war? Well, you've got one."

Eyes ablaze, Longo pushes the blade away from his neck and runs to the doorway yelling, "Kill them, now!"

Just as Longo grabs Julia and runs out of the room, two human figures emerge from either side of the room's doorway, blocking the path for anyone else to exit. My instincts go into overdrive as I sense they are wolves. I reach for the second cloaked blade affixed to my back and release it. I see Vincent does the same. Once released from their scabbards, the swords can be seen again by the human eye.

"Mom, get Don Phillipi and Sam and go to the far corner of the room."

As Vincent lines up beside me, the two figures come into the light. They are both female assassins with similar features. Their brown colored uniforms tell me they are Emissaries from the Neuri clan.

In a low voice Vincent says, "Rachael and Jacqueline Dendronto. They're the Neuri's deadliest agents."

Seeing Neuri Emissaries fulfilling a contract in the Americas is surprising to me. With Don Phillipi and Sam in the room, I won't be able to use any of my magics in battle. I accept that realization knowing that magic will have little use against wolves anyway. Once the two warriors remove their own swords, the fight begins.

Charging in a standard Neuri style, the two assassins are upon us at an incredible speed. Silver blades flash as both my learned and imprinted fighting techniques overtake my body's instincts. Though older in age, I look next to me and can see Vincent is holding his own.

I'm almost overwhelmed by the fighting grace our two opponents possess. They act as one, taking over the other's sword thrusts and pivot follow-throughs as if they share the same mind. Like quicksilver, their attacks change to include hand and foot attacks in addition to their masterful swordplay. The shift takes both Vincent and me by surprise as each of us are struck, knocking us back a step. I barely have any time to recover as I immediately block several more sword and body swings.

Reaching into one of her uniform pouches, Rachael Dendronto quickly pulls out a chain, swinging it in my direction as she does.

The chain wraps around my neck, preventing me from backing away. Using her strength, Rachael then jerks the chain toward her, pulling me along with it. As I am forced forward, I strike her as hard as I can in the mid-section with the hilt of both of my swords. Seeing what has happened, Jacqueline grabs the chain still attached to my neck, holding my face firmly in place as she kicks me hard across the bridge of my nose. A normal human would've been killed instantly. Fortunately for me, my wolf biology makes my body much more resistant to damage and heals at a much faster pace.

Spinning in place, I swing my leg in a circular pattern, knocking Jacqueline off balance. I move to strike down upon her once she hits the floor, but Rachael kicks me in my side before I can do any damage, forcing me to take several steps backward. Vincent leaps over Jacqueline, blocking a sword strike Rachael sends my way with his own.

Jacqueline jumps to her feet and pulls a short tube from one of her uniform pouches. As she puts the tube to her mouth, I immediately know she is about to send a poisoned dart in our direction. I mentally lock onto the dart and send a magical push. Jacqueline drops the tube and immediately grabs for her throat and mouth as the dart's direction is rebounded back to her. Rachael sees what's happened and leaps into the air, kicking both Vincent and me in the chest. Running to her sister's side, Rachael reaches into her uniform again and throws a metallic ball onto the ground. A wall of gray smoke erupts from it, clouding the two assassins from our view. When the smoke disperses, the Neuri Emissaries are nowhere to be found.

Removing the chain from my neck, I rush over to my mother and the others.

"Are all of you all right?"

My mother nods her head. Shaken, Don Phillipi says, "That bastard took a hit out on us!"

Grabbing his father's sport coat, Sam says, "We're leaving, now!"

Not budging, Don Phillipi says to me, "I will not forget what happened this day. Either by Longo *or* by you. I'm in your debt."

With that, Don Phillipi submits to his son's continued coat pulls and the two of them race out of the room.

Vincent takes my mother's arm and says, "We need to leave as well."

As we make our way out of the coffeehouse, we see both of Longo's guards lying on the ground outside of the entrance doors. I can't sense any life from them. Nicholas and our two other Emissary guards are nearby and out of breath. Their clothes are ripped in several places, probably from blade swipes. Nicholas looks the most hurt. He is leaning against the next building, holding one of his arms as if in pain.

Seeing us, he stumbles toward us. "The Exallos! Three of them appeared out of nowhere. It all happened so fast!"

I see the now dead Exallos assassins on the ground. I go over to Nicholas and help him stand.

At that, Tobias, Fenrus and their bodyguards run onto the scene. "Are you all right?" he asks.

It's then that I realize he's no longer cloaked under his glamour spell. His ripped clothing and dirt stained cheek tell me he and the others were ambushed as well.

"I'm fine. Are you?"

Although I can feel Nicholas is gaining strength to stand on his own, I can tell he's not yet on top of his game yet. Tobias notices also and supports him on Nicholas' opposite side. Nicholas, despite being annoyed at Tobias' presence, submits to being helped and places his arms around the both of us for added support.

"We're all fine," Tobias continues. "Emissaries from the Basque clan ambushed us just as I sensed you were being attacked. They held us in place for a while and just like that, they retreated."

I give Fenrus a good look over. Understanding my concern, Fenrus licks my hand as Tobias and I walk Nicholas toward our town car.

"That confirms it," Vincent says. "The Old World clans have joined with the Synoro against us."

In my head, I can hear Fenrus tell me, "Devin, something is happening at the compound. We have to get there soon."

"Dad!" I say aloud. Turning to the others, I say, "Fenrus says that something is happening at the manor. Everyone get to the limo. We're leaving now!"

Still supporting Nicholas, we help him walk to the limo parked just a few feet away. Just as we're about to reach it, one of our bodyguards stops us.

"Wait!"

He sniffs the air.

"There's a bomb on this car. It'll be triggered once the engine is started."

"How do you know?" I ask the wolf.

He tells me, "I was an Exallos Emissary before I joined your pack. I can smell the trademark oils and adhesive glue they use for their car bombs."

Off in the distance, I can hear police sirens headed in our direction. Knowing time is of the essence, I will for a nearby van's alarm to turn off and its doors to open.

"Everyone, get in the van."

Tobias and I place Nicholas gently inside. I then run to the driver's door and sit behind the steering wheel. Vincent sits in the passenger seat. Once everyone is accounted for and the rest of the vehicle's doors are closed, I magically will for the van's engine and systems to start. As I speed us away from the scene, I send a mental prayer of thanks to the goddess for seeing all of my people alive during our ordeal.

I look at the area between my seat and Vincent's to see Fenrus sitting patiently. I telepathically ask him what he senses happening at the manor. In my head, I can hear the sounds of swords clanging against one another, screams, and gunshots. I press down harder on the gas pedal.

Seeing my mind is engaged with Fenrus, Vincent asks, "What is it?"

"It's the manor. It's under attack."

"By whom? The Synoro? Is your father all right?" my mother asks.

"I don't know," I reply. "We need to get there fast. Vanessa, you are to guard my mother once we get there. Take her to a safe room with the rest of the pack innocents."

"Yes Archon," the bodyguard responds.

"Devin...," my mother says with a sound of annoyance.

Still looking forward, I say, "Mom, I have no idea how many people are attacking the compound, and I can't get a lock on where Dad is. Please, can you just do this for me?"

Relenting, she says, "Yes."

"The rest of you," Vincent interjects, "assess the battleground upon arrival and assist where needed."

Tobias' face appears to my right. I can feel his hand on my left shoulder, hugging my seat. Still looking forward I ask him, "How's Nicholas doing?"

From behind me, I hear Nicholas, "I'm right here you know. I can answer for myself. I'm healing and should be battle ready by the time we arrive."

Without missing a beat, Tobias says, "He'll unfortunately live."

"Again, I'm right here."

Ahead of me, I see a car swerve sharply into my lane. From the back window, a hand emerges and tosses a pipe onto the ground. I widen my eyes and veer into the slow lane. Once I do, the pipe explodes in the space my vehicle once was. Still beside me, Tobias waves his hand at the car of assassins in front of us. The car is then tossed aside wildly onto the pedestrian free sidewalk.

A second car then appears to my left. Inside, a brown uniformed Emissary is readying an automatic rifle.

Vincent cries out, "Devin!"

"I see it." I turn onto a right side street. The car chasing us is too late to follow and misses the turn.

Focusing on my internal magics, I concentrate on the van we're driving. I imagine its outer appearance changing. In my mind, it transforms into a VW Bug. I then push my will outward, causing the glamour spell to take effect.

My mother yells, "Turn here! To the left!"

I do, and we're back on the main road again. I see the car of gun toting assassins from earlier, only now they zoom past us.

Confused, Vincent exclaims, "They didn't shoot at us. Where are they going?"

Tobias replies, "Devin glamoured the van. They don't see us anymore."

Two more cars pass us, speeding after the car of assassins. As they pass I can see more rival clan Emissaries in each vehicle.

"Obviously, they were meant to detain us for a while. We need to get to the compound."

My words sound desperate as I punch on the accelerator again for all it's worth. A few short minutes later, we arrive into our neighborhood. As I approach, I hear Tobias. "Devin! Stop!"

I slam on the breaks just as I realize we are about to hit a mystical barrier. When we come to a complete stop, I see we are only inches from having hit it. Everyone leaves the van and gathers together near the front of the van.

"What is it?" my mother asks.

With a voice of frustration, Tobias says, "Someone put up a magical wall around the compound, different from the one we put in place. It has to be those Italian witches."

I scan the wall and sense Tobias is right. I gingerly reach out to the wall and instantly feel repelled. Given werewolves' natural resistance to magic, I'm sure we can break through with enough diligence, but time is a luxury we don't have at the moment.

From Nicholas, I hear, "Did you say your ancestor told you that you might be able to go under those witches' barriers? Wouldn't that help us now?"

Tobias says, "We can give it a shot."

Tobias looks around and sees no one but the group of us in sight. Content we aren't being watched, he then waves his hand in a circle motion around us, and I feel magic.

"To hide us from prying eyes," he explains. Turning to Fenrus he asks, "Can you help me with this?"

Fenrus looks to me as if asking for permission. I nod my head.

Tobias then spreads his fingers widely apart, and I can feel the ground below us start to sink. Within seconds we are lowered into the ground by several feet. When we stop I can barely see due to the darkness. I extend my hand and will for a light orb to appear. I can see dirt and stone all around us.

Tobias feels the rock wall and says, "The barrier is still there. We'll have to go down further."

Again, the floor beneath us sinks lower still. With our new light source, I can see the looks of nervous uncertainty on the faces of everyone around me. Finally, we stop, and Tobias says, "Eureka!"

Tobias places his hand on the rock wall again, and this time a tunnel begins to form. As we walk into it, the ground we previously stood upon begins to rise, sealing the ground up behind us. The tunnel continues to move forward and finally stops several yards ahead of us. When we reach the end, Tobias places his hand on the tunnel's ceiling. Suddenly the dirt and stone above us begin to part and the floor beneath us begins to push us upward. After a couple of minutes, we are back in daylight again, and I disperse my light orb.

I look over to my mother and see she is as white as a sheet.

"Are you okay?"

Trying to regain her composure, she says, "I'm claustrophobic. Always have been since I was a kid."

Hugging her, Tobias says, "I'm so sorry, Victoria. It was really the fastest way to get us past the barrier."

"I'll be fine." she reassures us. "I just need air."

Ahead of us, there are sounds of gunfire. The fact that we couldn't hear them before tells me that the wall previously blocking us was meant not only to keep us out, but to also mask any signs of the battle from the outside world.

I hold Tobias' hand, and we both magically scan the battleground before us.

Tobias says, "All four rival clans are at the compound. They've got a group of our pack flanked at the east end. There are a few smaller battles happening in the central courtyard."

"What about the innocents?" Vincent asks.

I check the underground bunkers with my extra sight.

"They're accounted for." I say. "They're all in the underground safety quarters, but there are several wolves attempting to breach the walls."

"What about your father?" my mother asks.

Tobias immediately says, "He's at the west end with Mika, Damon, and Gabriella. They're battling Jason's wolves and the witches. I…"

At this, he is thrown backward onto the ground.

"Tobias!"

Now holding his head, Tobias says, "I'll be okay, Devin. The witches obviously know we're here."

I help Tobias back to his feet.

Taking charge, Vincent says to three of the bodyguards, "You three, aid our wolves at the east end of the compound." To the two remaining bodyguards, he says, "The rest of you stop the wolves attacking underground. Keep those innocents safe!"

Concerned, one of the bodyguards says, "But Archon, our duty is to guard you and Devin as well."

At this Nicholas says, "Go. I'll watch over them."

They nod. One of them, the wolf I assigned to watch over my mother, stands beside my mom and says, "I'll get your mother into the underground bunker with the others. I won't let anything happen to her."

"Thank you," I tell the Emissary. I hug my mother before she is quickly escorted away. The remainder of the wolf guards then scatter in different directions.

"Right," Vincent adds. "Let's get to your father and destroy those witches."

I pet Fenrus, nervous for his safety. In my head, I hear, "Don't worry about me. I'll be on my guard."

Sending Fenrus mental thoughts of love, the group of us runs toward the west side of the compound with swords drawn.

We reach the courtyard first. Outsiders attack the Enopo wolves, but once our kinsmen arrive, the wolves' eyes show relief. In all, we can see three skirmishes.

Nicholas and Vincent race to one group and the tide turns to our pack's favor almost immediately. I can see Nicholas is at full strength again as he attacks several Basque and Neuri wolves ferociously.

Before he reaches his battle group, Tobias magically causes a nearby cement garden bench to rise in the air and immediately flies toward his group of invaders. They all land on the ground motionless. The Enopo wolves nod their heads to Tobias and join Vincent and Nicholas in battle.

Tobias then joins me in battle with the third group. Fenrus easily phases through every sword swing made at him, a luxury I don't have as common weapons cannot harm familiars. I, on the other hand, must block each attack skillfully and with a counter attack of my own.

Using his swords now, I can see that Tobias's arrival has turned the tide. Also imprinted with Nicholas' sword and hand-to-hand training, Tobias is a blur of silver sword swipes and air kicks. After a few moments, the remaining outsider wolves fall in battle.

Looking to see how Nicholas and Vincent are doing, I see they've succeeded also as brown, grey, and red Emissary assassins lie scattered in their wake. Even from across the courtyard, I can hear Vincent telling the remaining Enopo Emissaries to help their clan members on the west side of the compound. As they leave, I turn to my own set of remaining wolves next to me and tell them to do the same.

As they disappear from sight, Nicholas and Vincent arrive at our side again.

"Are you okay?" Vincent asks the three of us.

I look at Tobias and Fenrus. "We're okay. Let's go."

We continue our route toward where my father, brother, and Gabriella are located. I can sense magic being used on a second story level. Looking up at one of the windows, I can see colorful magic flashing brightly. Desperate to get my entire team up there, I look around for anything I can use.

"There!" I tell the others, pointing at a large piece of flagstone situated into the garden pathway. "Everyone stand on that stone!"

Once they do, I tell everyone to hold on as I magically will the stone into the air, toward the window above. Once we are level with the window, the situation above comes into view. Before us, I can see two groups of people. At one end of the hallway are Jason, Clayton, the two Benandanti witches Divina and Lucia, and three Synoro Emissaries. At the other end are my father, Mika, Gabriella, Damon and two Enopo Emissaries. Both groups have barricaded themselves behind large piles of hallway furniture. The wolves are shooting guns at one another while the witches send streams of magic toward the opposite end group. I knew that Mika was providing Damon with private lessons in the Craft once we discovered that he possessed some magical potential, but I am surprised to see him already able to produce magical shields on his own.

In a low voice, I hear Nicholas say, "Witches' magic has less impact on us when we're in our full wolf form."

Vincent replies, "Agreed. The witches might know we're here, but they don't yet know we're almost on top of them. Shift and attack while we still have the surprise advantage. Devin and Tobias, can you handle the wolves' weapons?"

Tobias says, "Consider it done."

I immediately summon the wild part of myself to come forth. As each of us leaps off the stone and through the now breaking glass window, I can feel my body surge with energy. My clothing rips and tears away as my new fur suit self fully emerges. I land on two canine feet, now a full foot taller than my usual 6'1" stature. As my comrades land beside me, we roar at our enemies in defiance.

Tobias and I focus our attention on the weapons the Synoro wolves are holding, willing them to fly toward us. The weapons leave our enemies' hands, but once they are in mid-flight, the Benandanti witches stop their progress, pulling them back as best they can. The magical tug-of-war ends quickly once Fenrus sends a wall of magical will at the witches, knocking them down and breaking their concentration. The guns and swords finish their travel toward us, leaving our werewolf enemies weaponless.

Seeing our arrival, my once-pinned family comes out into the open, grabbing the new weapons as they join us. In an exhausted voice I hear Mika say, "Thank goodness you came. I don't know how much longer Damon and I could hold up our shields."

A look of fury sweeps across Jason and Clayton's faces. They howl in anger, to which their bodyguards react by shifting into their full wolf forms, bounding toward us at an impressive speed. Nicholas, Gabriella, and my father meet them head on as the rest of us watch to see what the Synoro Archons and Benandanti witches will do next.

I ask Fenrus to stay beside me, nervous the rogue witches will try something. He does, and I immediately feel my strength levels rise due to being in such close proximity to him while in full werewolf form. I watch in awe as my family battles the Synoro wolves. A few moments into it, two of the Synoro wolves fall in battle. The remaining wolf continues his battle diligently against the three Enopo wolves, but eventually he, too, proves no match for my family.

Clayton and Jason are about to engage as well, but the witch Divina puts her arm across their chest, holding them in place. She then nods her head to Lucia. Smiling sinisterly, Lucia walks confidently to the three wolves, removing her black gloves along the way. She reaches Nicholas first. He swings his razor sharp claws at her several times. Lucia impossibly dodges each swipe and reaches for his neck. As soon as she does, Nicholas starts to spasm and falls to the ground, convulsing. He reverts to his human form and passes out, still lightly convulsing. Seeing what has happened, Gabriella and my father shift halfway to their human forms as well, maintaining a sleek hybrid look. They reach for the silver swords still attached to their backs.

Just as Lucia is about to reach for Gabriella, Tobias and I let loose with a wave of chaos magic. Seeing the attack in time, Lucia wills for a shield to block our magic. Divina adds her strength to Lucia's shield, causing our attack to have no effect on our intended victim. My father takes advantage of the distraction, grabbing Nicholas' arm and dragging him to safety along the wall. He then feels for a pulse on Nicholas' neck before returning his attention back to the witches.

Swinging her swords at a ferocious speed, Gabriella steps toward Lucia. Surprised by the flurry before her, Lucia takes a step backward. Before the swords reach her, Lucia magically pulls them away from Gabriella. The swords fly to opposite sides of the hallway. Before Lucia can make another move against her, Gabriella kicks Lucia hard in the chest. She then spins and place and uses her other foot to strike

Lucia across her face. Lucia falls to one knee, holding a hand to the side of her mouth where blood is newly forming.

Seeing that Gabriella is about to follow through with another attack, Lucia rolls to the side and grabs Gabriella's arm. Pulling her down, Lucia takes Gabriella's hair and throws her aside. Gabriella rolls across the ground, convulsing in place.

"Ama!" Damon shouts.

Angered, he transforms into his human/wolf hybrid form. Before he does anything rash, I revert to human and shout to him. "Damon, stop! They can't be beat with force. You, Vincent, and dad watch Jason and Clayton. Mika, Tobias and I will handle the witches."

Growling in anger, Damon holds his place, pondering my words. He then relents, siding toward Gabriella to cradle her on the ground, all the while keeping a close eye on the witches.

Tobias reverts to human and lines up beside Mika and me. In my head, I tell Fenrus to stand with my father and the others. He does. I then ask him to help amplify the three of our magics. Instantly, I feel a surge of additional strength coursing through me. Looking at Mika and Tobias, I can tell they are just as mystically empowered.

Lucia looks to Divina, her face full of concern. Calmly, Divina leaves Jason and Clayton to walk over to Lucia's side. The two experienced witches look at us sternly. I can feel them mustering their own internal magics. Gaea, help guide us through this.

Within moments a green haze begins to envelop the two Italian witches. The haze takes shape, eventually forming a large energy dragon. The dragon roars and swipes one of its claws at us. The three of us immediately put up mystic shields, but the force of the blow still sends us tumbling to the ground. As we jump back up, the dragon roars again and readies for another swipe with its other energy claw. Instead of trying to deflect the attack, we each dodge it instead, summersaulting to the left and right.

I look at Divina and Lucia, still standing together inside the base of the dragon. They are standing perfectly still, their eyes clouded over in a bright green glow. It's then that I realize that to defeat the dragon I must first defeat its creators. I send a force bolt at the witches, but the hide of the dragon easily deflects it. The dragon notices my attack and makes for another swipe at me directly. I jump out of the way just in time.

I notice Mika waving her hands in place. A white energy forms from her hands. I then look back over to Divina and Lucia. A part of their clothing rips off each of them and quickly covers their faces. The two witches' concentration is broken as they both try desperately to remove the now animated cloths from blocking their air to breathe. The lack of concentration also causes the energy dragon to disintegrate before us.

Not wanting to lose the window of opportunity, I send a powerful pain hex at the witches. Tobias does the same. The hexes hit them just as the witches pull away the clothing blocking their vision. They shriek as it hits them full force. They both fly backward screaming in pain.

Jason and Clayton look on in surprised anger. Shifting to their full werewolf forms, they charge at us. The look of determination on their faces tells me that they mean business.

Jason focuses his attacks on me while Clayton takes on Tobias. Shifting to my hybrid human/wolf form, I calm myself, allowing my imprinted and learned fighting skills to take over. I dodge several claw swipes and block several more bite attempts. My enhanced wolf form gives me increased speed and agility without having to use the added size and weight of my full were persona. My grandfather's attacks are relentless. My continued avoidance of his attempted kill strikes only makes him angrier. Its a weakness I use to my advantage, as I exploit several of his sloppy fight moves.

I use one such opportunity to pivot and magically enhance my body's strength, sending a powerful uppercut punch to Jason's head.

The blow staggers him. The look of disorientation spreads across his face. Knowing I won't get this opportunity again, I enhance the strength to my legs and strike Jason again with a roundhouse kick. This does the trick as Jason falls to the floor, unconscious.

Turning to Tobias, I can see he is evenly sparring with Clayton. As opposed to Jason, Clayton is much faster in his movements. I use my magic to lock onto what's left of Clayton's clothes, holding him in place with them as best I can. Tobias seizes the opportunity and smashes both fists onto either side of Clayton's head. He then follows through with an additional punch to Clayton's head. Clayton, too, falls to the floor.

Just as I'm about ask Tobias if he is all right, I'm hit with a strong pain hex. My wolf form nullifies most of the effect, but not all of it. I turn to see that both Divina and Lucia are back on their feet. Gone is Divina's former calm and collected demeanor. Replacing it is a look of angry and eager determination. Lucia looks just as deadly as ever.

Mika magically pushes the two unconscious Synoro Archons toward my father and the others. They start binding the Archon's hands behind their backs all while watching the continuing battle before them. I'm thankful to see Nicholas and Gabriella starting to come out of their previously debilitating states. I can tell this surprises Lucia as I doubt any of her previous victims were able to walk away from her death touch. Thank the goddess for werewolf durability.

In unison, both Benandanti witches pull out their devotional amulets from underneath their clothes, laying them on top of their chests. The gems inside the metal outlined casing glow radiantly. Divina's amulet is blue while Lucia's has a green hue to it. Both pieces begin pulsing, sending waves of energy around them.

In my head, I hear Fenrus say, "They are calling to someone. I don't like this." In a new protective mode, I ask Fenrus to stand by my side. He does. Fenrus continues, saying, "They are calling something dark. The three of you need to silence them…*now!*"

I can feel that the last bit was communicated not only to me, but also to Tobias and Mika. The three of us hold our hands out before us. Closing our eyes, we will for the calling to end. White light emanates from our outstretched hands. The light slowly edges toward the Italian witches. The pulse coming from their devotional amulets stops once it hits our white wall, which angers them immensely. They send disruption spells at our wall, but Fenrus uses his own magics to block their potency.

Just as the white wall is about to envelop them, a dark, swirling cloud appears behind them. It grows until it becomes wide enough for several people to walk through. The three of us rescind our spell as whatever was being called has arrived. Divina and Lucia smile at us devilishly.

I can make out several figures taking shape within the vortex. Three figures form, the central form tall and upright while the other two are child sized and hunched over. Finally emerging from the darkness is the Benandanti witch leader Claudia. Flanked at each of her sides are two grossly deformed beings. They have green skin, large odd sized noses, and makeshift clothing.

I hear Fenrus say, "Goblins!"

Claudia eyes the three of us, then looks at the rest of my pack now behind us. Still a bit groggy, Nicholas and Gabriella slowly get to their feet and take in what is happening. Divina speaks to Claudia in Italian. Claudia answers back, keeping her eyes firmly locked on us. She then looks down toward Fenrus and smiles sinisterly.

Joining her witch sisters, Claudia speaks a form of gibberish to the goblins. They cackle and eye Fenrus with eyes of desire. My blood turns cold as I can tell they mean to do my familiar harm. Petting him at my side, I mentally tell Fenrus that I don't like what is happening. He confirms that even compared to the three witches now before us that the goblins are even more dangerous. Not wanting him to be susceptible to them, I ask Fenrus to merge with me as he used to before I learned how to shift into my werewolf form on my own. He does and I feel my body grow stronger and larger as more of my wolf characteristics begin to manifest. The goblins shriek angrily at the disappearance of Fenrus. The Benandanti witches look just as surprised and angered.

I look beside me and see Mika and Tobias shifting to their full wolf forms. Despite their ferocious appearance though, they both stare calmly at the newly arrived adversaries. I slip my claws into theirs. The bond we have with each other strengthens and I can feel our energies meld into one another. Our union creates a wall of energy around us. Between that and our natural werewolf resistance to outside magics, goblins or no, I know we still have an even fight.

Claudia says in an Italian accent, "How did you do that? I've never known for a familiar to bond with their witch in such a way."

I remain silent, not wanting to divulge any information that she could use against me.

Seeing that I won't be forthcoming, Claudia smiles, "You know, not many witches are blessed with a familiar. They are rare, and each is unique. The sisters who originally formed our coven many years ago knew this. I'm surprised to see someone so young with one, though. You must be a very skilled witch to possess it."

Claudia calls back her goblins with a hand gesture. They submit, taking several steps backward. I can feel my family gathering behind us, ready to pounce if needed.

Seeing their positioning, Claudia adds, "We don't have to fight you know. We were told that before you became beasts that you were powerful witches in your own right. That witches have now become wolves is what drew us to you in the first place. It's never happened before. I don't know if you know of the legacy we witches have had with wolves in the past. We are the bitterest of enemies. You see, even though we both live in secret from humans, it was the wolves that betrayed us to mortals and exposed our existence hundreds of years ago. This lead to the witch-hunts, torture, and eventual murders of thousands of witches through the ages. Murdered because of the selfishness of werewolves. So believe me when I say, I and countless covens around the world have no love for these beasts."

Claudia looks down at the bound and unconscious bodies of Jason at Clayton at my father's feet. The look of disgust sweeps across her face.

"These Archons are nothing but cowards and hypocrites. They send their enemies to destroy members of their own family." Looking back at me, she continues, "You don't have to be like them. Leave this place. Come with us." Looking at Tobias and Mika, she adds, "All of you. Be part of our coven. We will offer you sanctuary. If you stay here, you will find nothing but death."

We stand our ground, looking wordlessly at the coven before us. Claudia speaks to Divina again in Italian. Divina's eyes turn solid white when she's through. I am reminded of when Mika's grandmother Anna would use her gift of foresight. Her eyes did something similar when she would use her divination skills. Knowing that Divina is a seer like Anna, I can only imagine what she is trying to envision. After a few moments, Divina's eyes return to normal. She answers something back to Claudia in Italian.

"My sister Divina is a seer." Claudia takes a step closer. "She confirms that you all will die if you stay this course."

Mika says, "Your coven just tried to kill us yourselves. Why should we trust you?" Her werewolf voice is strong and rough.

Claudia says, "We have no loyalties to these mongrels. We were simply hired to do a job. Nothing more. We had no idea that you were goddess blessed. We will call off this assignment if you join us. You have my word."

Tobias says, "So you admit your only interest then is to have Devin and his familiar as part of your coven. You want their power." Claudia says nothing. Tobias continues, saying "That doesn't make you better than the wolves. Your hands are just as dirty. You dishonor the Craft. You are nothing more than common initiators."

The expression on Claudia's face turns dark. She screams as she releases a stream of red energy at us. Still locking hands, the three of us concentrate on our protective shield, willing for it to remain strong. It blocks Claudia's attack easily. Seeing that her magic had no effect, Claudia yells to the goblins in the gibberish she spoke only moments earlier. They shriek and begin bounding toward us.

In my head, I hear Fenrus say, "Don't let them touch us. Any of us. Their touch is more deadly than the Benandanti's touch was."

Fenrus' eager and optimistic tone is tinged with something I've never heard from him before. Fear. My protective instincts are again raised as I mentally plot out our next action.

Using the protective dome, I will for it to pulse outward in order to strike our opponents. I've used this tactic before in my previous battles with my first coven. This time however the spell has no effect as the goblins easily charge through the protective dome as if it weren't there.

Just as they are about to lunge upon us, a set of bolos spin through the air, locking onto the goblins, sending them several feet backwards. They struggle at first, but in seconds the goblins are back on their feet. As they rise, the bolo ropes binding their bodies disintegrate into dust and falls into small piles of ash at their misshapen feet.

"Fenrus says that these goblins are deadly to the touch. Don't let them get their hands on you." I make sure my words are loud enough for all of my present pack to hear.

Tobias magically grabs a nearby chair and flings it at the goblins. They grab it and toss it toward Tobias instead. Our mystic shield stops it from hitting him, but the impact causes ripples to shimmer across our force field. Mika sends a swarm of her light daggers at the goblins. This proves to be a bit more effective as they are unable to dodge all of them, wincing in pain once they are struck.

Lucia sends a green bolt toward Mika. Surprisingly, it's Damon who blocks the attack with a self-made magical force shield of his own. Claudia seems slightly impressed, but casually waves her hand toward Damon. His shield disappears and he is knocked back several feet. My father grabs him in mid-push.

My father roars, "Devin, you three take care of the witches. We'll handle the monsters they brought with them."

At this, the non-magical werewolves remove their swords and charge at the goblins. I can see fear in the goblins' faces at the sight of the silver of their swords. Satisfied my kinsmen now stand a chance, I return my attention to our magical adversaries.

Divina flings her hands up, causing all of the foreign objects in our immediately vicinity to be thrown away from our dual area. Claudia smiles, saying, "This is your last chance. You might have youth on your side, but we have experience. You won't win."

Finally acknowledging her, I answer, "If you think you're the first coven to challenge us, you're sadly mistaken."

Claudia's smile disappears as her expression changes into outright disgust. Dipped in venom, Claudia says, "Have it your way."

The three witches send magical hexes at us in unison. Blue, green and red energies strike our barrier. Our bodies are nudged backwards slightly by the effort of holding the eldritch shield in place. We raise our hands forward and make a pushing motion. Their energies dissipate in response. My mind, I realize, is now linked to Tobias and Mika's on a primal level. Seeing that their previous hex had no effect, the Benandanti coven send a larger barrage of destructive magic our way. This time, we are knocked backward harder, but the shield still holds. I have a feeling, however, that the next wave of magic sent at us just might tax the limits of our shield.

In Tobias' mind, I see the image of a funnel. Just as the next blast of magic is sent our way, the three of us mentally envision our shield wrapping around their magic and redirecting it back at them. The shield does just that, causing the witches to scream as they are forced to block their own magic.

Trying to take advantage of the momentary distraction, I imagine the ground beneath the witches rising and push my will outward. The witches are then knocked off their feet, to which Mika sends another spray of her white light daggers in their direction. Divina sees them in time as she teleports a few feet away from the others, but Claudia and Lucia scream out in pain once they are hit.

Divina's eyes go stark white and suddenly the three of us are no longer at the Boston mansion. Confused, we look around and find ourselves in a large pit. The black stone walls rise up several feet above our heads. Standing on top of the wall above us is Divina. A slight clanking sound is heard at our feet. Looking down, I see that the three of us have iron shackles fit tightly around our ankles. The shackles then extend into chains, each of which is bolted to a central post. Looking up again, I see that Lucia and Claudia have now joined their witch sister.

Mika asks, "What is going on? What are we doing here?"

Just then water begins to rush in from small holes at the base of the pit. Within seconds the water completely covers the lower half of our bodies. Tobias pulls in vain at the chains tying us to the center post. Mika and I try to help him. The water continues to rise and soon is up to our shoulders. Above us the witches laugh at our situation. We each inhale a large amount of air just as the water completely submerges our heads. Panic stricken, we continue to pull at the chains, hoping they will give way.

In my head, I hear Fenrus say, "This is an illusion. If you continue to act as if it is real, you will die. Fight it! Fight it all of you!"

Looking at each other, we stop pulling at the chains and let ourselves float. I reach out and grab hold of Tobias and Mika's hands, giving them a look of sincere trust. They look back at me with apprehension. I project calm toward them and close my eyes. I then let go of my breath, imagining myself back at the Boston mansion. I feel magic all around me explode and break apart. Opening my eyes, I find myself back in the mansion hallway. Despite knowing our almost watery grave was an illusion, my clothing is dripping with water. Tobias and Mika appear beside me. The look of shock on Divina's face tells me that we may just be the first people to break her power of illusion.

The three of them extend their hands and energy blades appear in them. In response, the three of us reach back and draw our own silver blades from their scabbards. The sword battle that follows can only be described as surreal. Although they are no match for our wolf speed, the energy weapons the Italian witches use are powerful, which taxes our enhanced strength.

We each take on an individual opponent. While I face Claudia, Mika selects Lucia while Tobias battles Divina. Claudia's eyes flash red as I continue to block each of her attacks. Her fighting style is like nothing I've experienced before. It carries an old world feel to it but is by no means gentle. In fact, it is brutal and direct. I adapt as best I can, but can't seem to land a blow of my own despite my many attempts.

When Claudia brings down her sword directly on top of me, I block it with my own sword. Thinking she will follow through with another sword attack, Claudia surprises me with a magical one instead, sending a crimson bolt directly into my face. With no time to react, my senses and coordination go out the window when it hits me.

"Devin!" I hear my father cry out.

The world around me starts to spin as my body's nerve endings light afire. Landing on my back, I can feel a good portion of wind being knocked out of me. I begin to revert back to my full human form. I know I must snap my body back upright, but the ringing in my head stops me from doing that.

I feel someone grab the hair from the top of my head and pull me up into a sitting position. I then feel a cheek against mine and a blade at my throat. It nicks me in the process. My vision is still blurred, but my sense of smell returns, telling me that my captor is Claudia. I want to teleport away, but even if I had the full senses to do so, because Claudia is holding on so tightly to my being, she would be shunted away along with me. Instead I stay where I am, waiting for the spinning and head pounding to cease.

Beside me, I hear, "One more move and your precious new Archon gets his throat slit."

I feel magical presences materializing near me. The scent of Divina and Lucia manifest along with them. They speak a bit in Italian to each other, then return their attention to the rest of the room.

Claudia continues, "Our contract with the wolves is done. We are taking this one with us, though. Any attempt to follow us, and he dies."

I regain a portion of my vision and can see one of the goblins shuffling toward me with a gemmed locket in hand. It reminds me of a devotional amulet, only larger. Inside me, I can hear Fenrus whimpering as the goblin's deranged grin gets closer.

On the far wall several feet behind the goblin, I also notice a white orb materialize. It grows larger and quickly becomes a swirling white gown. Once it is fully materialized, I can see a familiar face along with it. It seems to be the youthful form of Mika's grandmother, Anna Geist. Her signature Eye of Bastet necklace and matching bracelet and ring confirm my deduction. Just as the goblin is about to extend the locket toward me, Anna releases a destructive white lightning bolt at him. The goblin flies several feet away, screaming in pain.

Waving her hands again, I feel a powerful blast emanate from Anna, causing Claudia and the other Benandanti witches to be tossed away from me, tumbling into a pile nearby.

A look of fury on Anna's face is the first clear image I see as the pounding in my head subsides. The power I feel emanating from her is something I haven't felt since the goddesses Gaea and Hecate revealed themselves to the werewolves last year when the Enopo pack was formed. Where is this level of magic coming from?

The second goblin charges at Anna, then stops mid-way, falling to the ground in pain. Waving her hand, Anna sends the now pain filled goblin through a glass window. My wolf hearing allows me to hear a thud below a second later.

In an eldritch voice that I've never heard before, Anna booms at the invading witches, "Hear me now, deceivers, anyone who lays a hand on this one faces my wrath!"

Anna points toward Mika as we all look on in awe. The voice she now uses is definitely not Anna's. Not only is the sentence structure all wrong, but it carries a trace of an accent. If I'm not mistaken, the accent is close to Egyptian.

The Benandanti witches gather themselves up and scream at Anna as they release a full blast of hexes at her. Anna flings her hand in an upward motion. The hexes change direction in response. The blast hits the roof, leaving a dark scorch mark behind. Anna then points toward the witches and a series of white electric bolts emanate from under their feet. The witches scream again, this time in pain.

Seeing that all of our enemies are now out of commission, Mika gingerly approaches Anna.

"Grandmomma?"

Anna turns her attention toward Mika. Looking at her coldly, Anna says, "Your grandmomma is no longer in control. I now command this vessel and do with it as I see fit."

Approaching Anna as well, Tobias asks, "Who are you, then?"

Lifting her chin dramatically, Anna replies, "I am here out of obligation to the vessel I must, for now, rely upon. I have no real care for this vessel's brood, but I am tied to an oath I contracted with it when we first were joined. I am one of the oldest of gods hidden away from this world for far too long. You shall know my name soon enough."

Struggling to move, I notice Claudia trying to crawl across the ground toward us. I can only assume she is not in full control of her motor skills as her attempts border on the pitiful. The rest of her coven is still out cold. Her remaining goblin helper hobbles over to his mistress and tries to help her up. Anna watches with a sneer on her face.

Desperately, Mika pleads to Anna. "Grandmomma, I know you're still in there somewhere. I love you. I miss you. Come back to me!"

Anna hovers toward Mika at a supernatural speed. She looks directly into Mika's face. The cold stare remains. "As I said, your grandmomma cannot be reached. Attempt to interfere with our arrangement and oath or no, you will be felled just as these insignificant casters have been."

Just then, from around the corner, I see Ms. Whiskers enter the foray. She hisses savagely at Anna, who surprisingly backs away and covers her face with her arm. Anna then disappears via a white orb, then into nothingness.

Near me, I can hear Claudia struggling to speak the goblin gibberish she uttered earlier. I turn back to see the goblin hand her the jeweled locket. She takes it awkwardly in hand, and then looks at me. Suddenly, a squadron of Synoro werewolves rushes into the room. Startled, Claudia disappears for a moment then reappears beside me. The locket swings open as she plunges it toward my chest. As it strikes hard into me, pain fills every pore of my body. I feel as if part of my soul is being ripped from me and into the locket. In my head, I can hear Fenrus screaming my name over and over again. Darkness overtakes me, and the world disappears around me.

Chapter Four
VIRBIUS

WHEN I OPEN MY EYES AGAIN, I FIND MYSELF BACK IN MY QUARTERS. Tobias, Mika, my parents, and Damon surround my bed. I feel cold and sickly. Nausea fills my stomach, and I can feel sweat on my brow. I grab the blankets on top of me and pull them up to my chin, shivering in the process. I'm so tired.

"What happened?"

Grabbing a cold, wet hand towel, my mother applies it to my forehead.

"You were knocked cold for several hours," she replies. "We were afraid you were never going to wake up."

Her red eyes and still wet eye lashes tells me just how serious she is. I look around the room one more time.

"Where's Fenrus?"

Everyone looks at one another with apprehension.

Tobias answers saying, "The Benandanti have him."

Panic and shock fill me, deadening all my other ailments.

Sitting up, I yell, "What?"

I feel as if I were just told that my only child has been kidnapped.

I desperately ask, "Where are the Benandanti now?"

With a lump in his throat, Tobias answers, "We don't know. Just after Claudia took Fenrus' essence into her amulet, her goblin opened a portal and teleported all of them away."

I throw the covers off me and try to get out of bed. The room spins immediately, and I fall back onto the mattress. My mother grabs me by the shoulders and gently places me back onto the pillow. Tears fill my eyes as I curl up into a ball as the last moments of our battle with Claudia flood back into my mind. I wail lightly in grief and helplessness. Fenrus…no, no…

Nicholas then runs into the room. "I thought I heard Devin. Is he awake?"

As I continue to mull over my loss, I can hear my father answer, "He just woke up. He's still weak, though. He needs more rest."

"I'm right here, you know!" I snap at my father. I don't mean to sound so vindictive toward him, but the words fly out of my mouth before I can stop them.

Heartbroken, my father says, "I'm sorry, Devin. I didn't mean…"

I stop him before he can say another word. "No, I'm sorry, Dad. It's not your fault. It's just that Fenrus is out there somewhere, and I have no idea what those Benandanti witches are going to do to him! I need to get out of here. I need to find him."

My mother places her face in front of mine. "You're not going anywhere. Not just now anyway. I know what you're going through, Devin. Believe me. When you ran away to look for your father, I had no idea what had happened to you either. I had no way of getting ahold of you to make sure you were all right. I worried every single day you were gone. We're going to find Fenrus, but you need to rest right now. Regain your strength and then we can put our heads together to figure this out. We're not giving up on him, I promise."

I psychically call out to Fenrus, desperately listening for an answer. Nothing. I call out again. Still nothing. More tears fill my eyes as the emptiness in my stomach overtakes me. Seeing my helplessness, my mother takes me into her arms to console me. I can hear my father ushering several people out of the room. When I finally have my composure again, I release my hold on her and see that only Tobias is now with us.

Easing me back onto the bed, my mother says, "If you need anything, Nicholas is posted just outside your door. Tobias will fill you in on everything else that's happened. Please, try to take it easy for the next couple days. I love you, sweetheart."

She then kisses my forehead and leaves the room. Tobias immediately takes her place on the bed beside me. He pushes the loose hairs away from my face, a custom I'm familiar with him doing. It eases my pain a bit.

"We have to get Fenrus back, Tobias."

"I know For your own safety, too. If something bad happens to your familiar, it happens to you as well."

"What are we going to do?" I ask. "We don't even know where they could've taken him. Do you think they're in Italy?"

I try to get up again, but the dizziness in my head sends me back down. Tobias puts his hand on my shoulder.

"I honestly don't know, but your parents are right, Devin, you need to rest. Just lie back and try to get more sleep."

Remembering our battle earlier, I ask him, "Wait! Anna! What did Ms. Whiskers do to her? How's Mika?"

Tobias' face now has a forlorn look to it. "Mika's doing as well as can be expected. Damon and I are giving her as much support as we can. As for Ms. Whiskers, you can ask her yourself."

At that, Tobias points to the far window. In it, I see Ms. Whiskers perched and looking directly at me.

"Ms. Whiskers!"

At that, she jumps off the window shelf and over to the bed. Once on, she walks over to my chest, gets on top, and then sits. I immediately start petting her, allowing her presence to help ease the pain of not having Fenrus with me.

I hear her say, "You not look so good. Not a lot of sparkle on you now. Feel better soon?"

"I hope so." I reply. "Earlier, when you hissed at Mika's grandmother, what happened? How were you able to scare her like that?"

"No!" she answers back in all seriousness. I stop petting her. "*Not* Anna. Anna is a good magic one. Only Anna's body. Dark goddess in her now. I sense bad magic, strong magic and came to see who it from. Then me see her and know something wrong. Us Pretty Ones teach our kittens about bad goddess. Protect our litter against her if have to. Bad goddess bring terrible evil everywhere she go."

Confused, I ask, "But who is this bad goddess? What's her name?"

Ms. Whiskers takes a step back. "Oh, me *never* call her name. Call to her could bring bad luck all by itself. Only say that bad goddess is daughter of most powerful of Pretty One's gods. Powerful mother banished bad daughter long long time ago. Now she back me guess. Must stay on guard all time now."

"Daughter of your god? Do you mean Sekhmet, the Egyptian war god?"

Ms. Whiskers' fur immediately puffs up as she arches her back, hissing at me.

"Told you not say name! Could come back and do bad things!"

Petting her, I reply, "I'm sorry, Ms. Whiskers. I don't mean any disrespect, but I needed to know her name. Knowing her name will help us find out how to stop her and get the real Anna back."

Ms. Whisker's back fur settles back down, and she allows me to continue petting her. Tobias gets a look of horror on his face.

"Did I hear you right? Did you just say that Anna is possessed by—"

I shush Tobias before he can repeat the name. "Yes, at least that's what Ms. Whiskers just told me anyway."

Tobias stands up and paces back and forth beside the bed. He then stops.

"Wait a second, Anna's FAMILIAR is named Sekhmet. The last two times we saw Anna, he wasn't with her. What do you think that means?"

I look at Ms. Whiskers and see that the mention of Anna's familiar with the same name doesn't seem to faze her. This makes sense as in magic, it's *who* you direct your words or intention to mentally that is important. Perhaps she knows that directing the name Sekhmet, though the same name as the goddess, to Anna's familiar doesn't necessarily empower the other.

"Ms. Whiskers." I think a second on how to phrase my question best so as not to upset her. "When you sensed the bad goddess earlier, was Anna's familiar, the orange cat you liked named Sekhmet, could you sense if he was there or not?"

Ms. Whiskers starts purring at the mention of her beloved.

"No. Me not sense him since we all lived at Anna's. He too smart. Never side with bad goddess."

Looking into her green eyes, I ask, "How is it you were able to scare off the bad goddess?"

Matter of factly, Ms. Whiskers replies, "Me am servant of Pretty One's goddess. What me see, she see. I warn my goddess that bad daughter up to no good with roar. Me roar warning *and* to let bad goddess know I die to stop her."

A sad look then forms on her face as she steps off my chest and returns back to the window. I can tell that she misses Anna's familiar just as much as I miss Fenrus.

Turning back to Tobias, I say, "Ms. Whiskers says that she doesn't know what happened to Anna's familiar. The last time she saw him was back in San Francisco. Evidently, the goddess possessing Anna was afraid Bastet would be aware of her presence if seen through the eyes of Ms. Whiskers. That's probably why she left so quickly."

My mind goes back to Fenrus, locked inside Claudia's locket. Suddenly, our previous mafia hits and clan wars don't mean a thing to me. What matters now is that I get Fenrus back. It's not how a leader should think, I know, but it's how I feel. I can't betray my people, though. I need to plan to keep them safe and get my familiar back at the same time.

Snapping me back out of my thoughts, Tobias says, "I'll leave you to get some rest, but there's something else you need to know. Just before the Benandanti witches escaped, Ryan, Shaun, and Brice from the Synoro clan arrived with their armies. The Archons were able to take back the New Hampshire compound. They were told about the attack on our base just after. The three of them came to help and were able to capture the remaining renegade Synoro members. They've been using our base to contact the various other compounds to let them know to prepare their stockades for prisoners. Your father and the other Enopo Archons are going to meet with them later this evening. And *no*, you are not to attend. Adam said that he'll report back to you with what was discussed tomorrow."

Tobias kisses me on the cheek.

"I'm going to check in on Mika. I know she's still shaken over seeing Anna. Get some sleep, and I'll be back in a bit."

Tobias leaves and an eerie silence falls over the room. I see that Ms. Whiskers is still staring out the window as I watch her tail flick back and forth. Watching its rhythmic movement, my eyes become drowsy, and it's all I can do to keep them open. I stop fighting it and succumb to the exhaustion.

I feel as if I'm falling backward between a series of thick, silky blankets. I allow my spirit self to close its eyes as well, allowing the feeling of soft comfort to overtake me. When my descent finally slows to a gentle stop, I open my eyes and find myself standing in strange surroundings. I'm in a forest I've never visited before. The light filtering through the trees spotlight several large boulders and gorgeous trees that stretch as high as apartment buildings. The green grass and moss at my feet are cool to the touch and almost sumptuous. I can sense earth magic all around me. The surging energy is almost electric.

It's then that I notice a faint path head of me. The streaming sunlight shifts slightly to spotlight it, inviting me to follow. Not feeling any danger, I do just that. Still apprehensive at first, the sweet sounds of birds chirping ease my mind as I pick up my pace a bit. Ahead, I see what seems to be a gathering of hummingbirds flitting back and forth in the air. As I get closer, I discover that what I'm seeing aren't hummingbirds at all but small fairy type creatures. Where in the heck am I?

The fairies smile, waving me to continue forward. Now happily flying around me, the sound of their wings flapping at an incredible speed soon changes to include flute-like music. Do their wings really create music? As I continue walking, I realize that the music isn't coming from them at all, but from somewhere else ahead.

The music continues to grow louder and louder until I come upon a tree stump set several feet off the path. Sitting upon it is a manlike creature. It is bare-chested, but where his waist begins starts a thick growth of bristly brown fur. Looking down at his legs I see that they are not human, but legs belonging to a goat or mule. The curly hair on top of his head is the same color on his cloven legs, but two short curly horns jut out on top. Recognizing the creature from various picture books as a child, I realize the man in front of me a satyr, one of the Greek creatures of myth.

The satyr continues playing his flute, which looks to be several reeds twined together. He looks at me directly but stays his ground, still focused on playing his music. I understand that such an unearthly creature would frighten any normal person. I mentally tell myself that being a practiced witch and werewolf myself, I know should better. Calming my nerves, I see a large rock positioned on the opposite side of the trail. I quietly backup to sit upon it and wait for the satyr to finish his song.

The satyr's eyes are a multitude of shades of brown. It reminds me of Tobias' hazel eyes, only much more brilliant. His stare is intense but thankfully distant. When he finally finishes playing, I do what comes naturally and softly clap into my hands. The satyr places his instrument into a sack hanging off his side.

"That was beautiful," I say.

The satyr nods his head, signaling the compliment's acceptance. Slowly, the satyr stands up and begins walking toward me. The way his cloven hooves glide beneath him is almost magical. Unsure of what to do, I sit up straight and strategize several possible escape routes.

When he is close to ten feet from reaching me, he stops. Looking me over, the satyr says, "I've never seen one like you before. You're hiding your true form, but I see it clear as day. You are wolf. A wolf covered in magic. How did you come to be?"

I'm stunned. Can he really see my wolf self even though I'm in my human form? I double-check my arms to verify I haven't shifted by accident. No, I see my normal skin. His eyes. His eyes must be able to see more than what is usually visible.

"Yes. I am a wolf, but I am also a witch. The power from both creatures flows within me. You must be quite a seer to be able to view the wolf in my present form. Actually, I'm surprised you can see me at all. It usually takes a while before magical beings can see my spirit self."

The satyr stands as straight as possible, adding a foot to his usual height. He eyes me suspiciously.

"How did you come here? Are you a ghost? I can see right through you."

Smiling, I say, "No, not a ghost. My name is Devin Toxotis. One of my abilities as a witch lets me free my spirit self from my body while I sleep. I'm able to wander different parts of the world. Usually, I only travel to man-made places. I've never been anywhere like this before or met anyone quite like you. Where am I exactly?"

Continuing to eye me for a few moments, the satyr says, "You are in the sacred forest of Virbius. The exact location, I cannot tell you, Devin Toxotis. It is a secret location known only to those under Virbius' care. I am Fallon, one of the few remaining satyrs."

Virbius. The name immediately draws me back to my earlier experience speaking to the ghost of my great-great-grandmother, Maria. She mentioned that she and her familiar were under the protection of a nearby forest god named Virbius. Returning my attention back to the satyr, I bow my head slightly.

"Pleased to make your acquaintance."

Fallon crosses his arms, never breaking his direct stare. "What do you want here? We haven't had strangers enter our forest in centuries. Who sent you?"

I can tell from his questioning that winning him over won't be an easy feat.

"No one sent me." I respond. "When engaged, my dream-self ability sends me to places where I need to be. There is no rhyme or reason to it, but over the years, I've learned to trust it, no matter where I end up. I don't mean you or anyone else in this forest any harm, but whatever force guides my gift sent me here. There is something or someone here that I am supposed to see."

Standing still for a moment, I become uncomfortable in the awkward silence. Fallon just stands there looking at me with no movement. It's almost as if he is searching my soul for any form of malcontent. When I think I won't be able to take the staring anymore, Fallon drops his hands and rests them on his hips.

"There are many creatures here," he says. "All of whom are either only a handful or the last of their kind. This is our sanctuary. We live here in peace. If you are to speak to anyone, then it will be to Virbius. *He* will be able to see through to your true intentions. Come, this way."

Fallon starts walking along the path. Getting up, I follow behind him, making sure to keep a comfortable distance away out of respect. His hooves allow him to move at a faster pace than normal. I allow my internal wolf speed to surface enough to keep pace with him.

Several minutes into our walk, we pass a spring where several water creatures splash each other playfully. Upon seeing me though, they become frightened and sink beneath the waterline. Several more minutes pass before I hear clanging. When we finally reach the source of the noise, I see a small building build off the pathway. Inside, I see a creature through the large open windows that looks to be a minotaur. It's bull face and neck are attached to a sinewy chiseled frame. He is hammering a metal object upon a large anvil. Just like the water nymphs before him, the minotaur gets a surprised look upon its face when it notices me. Different from the nymphs, though, he holds his hammer tightly, ready to use it as a weapon if needed.

"Come," Fallon utters, coaxing me forward.

Eventually, the path leads to a forest clearing. In the middle is an elaborate altar made of stones, pieces of wood, and gem-like crystals. Plant life grows abundantly around the altar, and several daisy flowers have taken root on the base of the altar's pillars.

Fallon holds his hand out, signaling me to stop my descent. I sense powerful magic here. Not quite on the level I felt from my goddesses

Gaea or Hecate, but still far above the magic levels an ordinary witch exudes. I stop, waiting for Fallon to tell me what to do next.

Sensing my questioning thoughts, Fallon says, "Now, we wait for Virbius."

Knowing that an altar is typically a place meant for offerings to the gods, I look at my surroundings. Nearby, I see a trickling brook. I respectfully leave Fallon for a moment, picking up a large bowled leaf along the way to the water source. I use the leaf to scoop up a bit of cool liquid and carry it carefully back to the altar. I place it gently on top, and then slowly drop to my knees before it. I lower my head and center myself mentally for what I am about to do next.

I pray at the altar, thanking the new god for his kind consideration. I tell him my name and inform him that I am a simple witch, supplicated first to Gaea, then to her daughter Hecate. I ask his permission to speak with him that I may better understand my purpose for being in his domain. I offer the sacred water as a symbol of peace and thanks, with no ill intent meant on my part.

I sense a powerful presence manifest behind me. Not yet done with my task, I gently continue with the memorized verse for the divine, as is proper custom for any witch. When I am done, I close with the words 'Blessed Be,' head still bowed in respect. I then slowly rise to my feet and turn to face the being standing behind me.

Virbius' power emanates from him, letting me know that his defenses are raised. The forest god is tall with full coal black hair and eyes. His pale white skin causes quite a contrast between the two. He's exceedingly beautiful. He has a strong Roman nose and a chiseled physique. His bare torso is hairless but supple with muscles. Around his neck is a necklace holding a simple stone. His brown basic cloth pants are loose but the muscle definition in his legs can still be seen. He is also barefoot, which seems practical for a god whose domain is a forest setting. Around his wrists are metallic looking gauntlets that carry an ethereal sheen to them. Overall, Virbius is visually striking.

Out of respect, I bow my head to him slightly. As Virbius looks me over, Fallon, who is standing beside him, steps back several paces, never taking his eyes off me. He continues until he steps into the trees surrounding us and disappears into the foliage.

When Virbius finally speaks, his voice is strong, deep and masculine, yet still somehow melodic.

"It's been some time since I've received an offering from anyone outside of this forest, and so formally at that. Still, I do not trust members of the casting realm so you'll forgive my bluntness. Why do you come here, Devin Toxotis? I have no ties to either of your central gods."

Keeping his gaze, I reply, "I go with the whim of my Wiccan gifts mighty Virbius. The will of my magics brought me here unknowingly. I was hoping you would be able to shed some light as to why."

Virbius raises an eyebrow and ponders his thoughts a moment before saying, "This forest is a place of refuge for many beings who can no longer find safety in the outside world of man, a hidden place that is shadowed by me from mortal eyes. They are all under my care. I am their guardian and protector. Are you here with the intent to harm?"

"No!" I answer. "Nothing like that at all."

I can feel Virbius scanning my being for truth.

Continuing, he says, "Then, perhaps you are seeking sanctuary from those whom conspire against you?"

Fenrus' face comes back to mind.

"No," I say. "I'm the leader of a group of my own. I understand the responsibility on your shoulders. My people are under attack by several groups who covet who we are and what we have, but no, I'm not looking for sanctuary from my duties. I cherish them. If I'm looking for anything, it's to make peace between my people's clans and to get back something that was stolen from me."

Virbius uses a hand to rub one of the gauntlets he wears. He then looks down, deep in thought.

"A clan of classless men stole a precious token from my family once." Looking back at me again, Virbius says, "The item that was taken from you wasn't an object though, was it? In your mind, I see what you are thinking of. It is a wolf. A pet perhaps?"

I shake my head. "No, not a pet. What was taken from me was my soul."

Virbius gets a look of bewilderment.

"Your soul?"

The emotional ache and feeling of helplessness from losing Fenrus fills my heart again.

"Yeah. In my world, if a god feels especially tied to one of their witch followers, he or she can bless that witch with a gift. He or she takes a portion of the witch's soul and adds a portion of his or her own magic to it in order to create a companion for the witch to cherish. We call these companions *familiars*. The wolf you see in my mind is my familiar. His name is Fenrus."

Virbius nods.

"I know what you speak of, Devin Toxotis. Years ago, a caster, or witch as you call them, came to my attention. As she lived on the outskirts of this forest, her natural power drew my curiosity. In time, I discovered the caster had a good heart and helped many people in her time. When a group of dark casters came to ask her to join them, she refused. They were relentless, though, and threatened to kill her if she did not. Normally, dormant gods to the outside world such as I rarely step into the lives of mortals, especially if a mortal does not call them upon to begin with. I could sense her desperation and put that tenet aside. I gave the caster what you call a familiar so that she would be strong enough to defend herself against her enemies."

My reason for coming to Virbius' domain becomes clear.

"The witch you helped was my great-grandmother, Maria Sazia. And the dark casters you mentioned are the Benandanti."

Virbius says, "Could it be?"

Again, I can sense his magical stare searching my mind for truth. "It is." he confirms.

I continue. "It was the Benandanti who stole my familiar from me. He is more than a companion, though. As a piece of my soul, he's like my own child. It's as if a part of me is missing, and I'm worried of what might happen to him. Do you have any insight on how I might be able to get Fenrus back to me?"

I notice Virbius' shoulders settle downward a bit, and the strong magical defenses that were raised slowly lessen.

"I can feel the sorrow in your heart. Your words are true. The goodness I sensed in Maria I also feel in you. Were it that I could easily affect the outside world as I did millennia ago when I was still known, I would return your familiar to you now. Alas, those days are long past. Now, my godly reach is limited to this forest. I was only able to help your grandmother as she built her home on the fringes of my domain. If your Fenrus were near, I'd sense it. Unfortunately, I do not. I am sorry, Devin Toxotis."

Whatever hope I had only moments ago of getting Fenrus back instantly disappears. I can feel my wolf nature yearning to howl longingly in grief. Seeing the ghostly tears form in my eyes, Virbius looks on in sympathetic pain.

"I may not be able to return your familiar, Devin Toxotis, but what I can give you is knowledge. Perhaps that will be able to help you in your quest."

Intrigued, I ask, "Knowledge of what?"

"Knowledge on why the Benandanti want your familiar to begin with."

His words strike home.

"Please. Anything you can tell me would help."

Nodding his head, Virbius waves his arm and the two of us are suddenly in a different part of the forest. Near us is a large pile of boulders with a small waterfall emanating from somewhere on top. On one of the lower boulders, I see an indentation, which has collected water. Virbius walks over to it and motions for me to join him.

"With this, we will be able to see into the outside world. It will show you what the Benandanti truly are after."

Virbius waves his hand over the pool of water. It ripples and soon images begin to form within. I see a group of witches. Altogether there are eight, three of whom I recognize. Claudia stands at the head of an elaborate table and addresses the others. I'm surprised to see two of the witches have what look to be familiars beside them. Beside one female witch is a snake, coiled around her arm. Next to another witch is a large black cat. Even through the scrying pool, I can feel their energy.

When Claudia speaks, it is in Italian, which I don't understand. As if he understands my immediate issue, Virbius places two fingers at my temple. Within moments of him removing his hand from me, the speech Claudia is giving becomes clear.

"I've called all of you here for a very important reason. Just recently, Divina has had a vision of an event to come. This event will change everything as we know it. Not just for us witches, but for the entire world."

At this, Claudia motions for Divina to take over. Once Divina takes her place at the head of the table, Claudia takes a step back to allow her room. Divina bows slightly to Claudia, and then speaks.

"As you all know, my visions allow me to see into the past, present, and future. The future, though, is often cloudy and hard to decipher. This is because the future is not yet set and can be changed by our actions in the here and now. For the first time since realizing my gift, I was able to see a future event with no trouble what so ever. This vision was clear and precise. In my vision, I saw a large battlefield. It was unlike any war I have ever witnessed. This war was not between mortals, witches, or even any other group of earthly beings. The war I saw was being fought by gods."

The coven erupts in murmurs. I can see Claudia eyeing each witch, taking in her various reactions. Finally, the witch with the cat familiar asks, "When will this battle happen? Where? Who are these gods?"

Divina answers, saying, "I can't tell you when the gods will battle as I couldn't sense a specific point in time, but I can tell you that it seemed as if it will happen soon, somewhere here in Italy. In the vision, I recognized the flowers and fields of our homeland. Some gods I was able to recognize like Gaea, Mars, and Hecate. Others, I didn't recognize at all. There were dark gods clouded in shadow, others I've never seen before, and the rest I believe are Egyptian. Those gods are unknown to me, but I recognized their origin as they wore animal heads and dressed in that type fashion."

My blood runs cold as my mind returns to our earlier skirmish with Anna and how Ms. Whiskers revealed that the Egyptian war god Sekhmet had possessed her. Is that what the war god is up to? Is she gathering her strength for some god battle that will be happening soon? I'm now fearful for Anna and for whatever Sekhmet may be forcing her to do.

Divina continues. "During this battle, I see many humans killed. The terrain is torn and altered. Hidden societies like ours are revealed. Witches, wolves, satyrs, even goblins and demons…they are all exposed in this war. The magical world won't be secret anymore. And, what's worse, a long dormant Titan will awaken. The mere sight of his eye opening from sleep shakes even my abilities. Once this happens, I can see nothing else for our world's future. It's as if all life goes blank."

I can feel Virbius' power begin to swirl and gather around him. I turn to see the expression on his face now has a look of worry. Remembering the goddess Hecate's anger from only a few months ago, I can see a similar response from Virbius as the forest in our immediate area changes to incorporate a red tinge to its otherwise green coloring. My attention is snapped away from the forest god, though, when I hear Claudia speak from the pool of water before me.

"The familiars in our possession are the key to our survival. We must use their magic to protect our coven from the devastation the oncoming god war will bring."

Lucia speaks up from the table. "But, we don't yet have all the familiars' masters controlled yet. You know as well as any of us that only the familiar's master can properly access their full potential. Without either the familiar or its master to channel our will for us, we run the risk of killing both."

Claudia looks at Lucia with a smile.

"True, but if we cannot coax the remaining masters to join our cause, then we have no choice but to drain both beings dry of their magics to augment our own. It'll provide us with only a temporary strengthening of our pooled magics, but if Divina's vision is correct, then we will do what we must for the benefit of the coven."

Sweat forms on my brow and my heart begins pounding as my worry for Fenrus doubles. Turning back to Virbius, I see that his mind is still in turmoil over the god war revelation. Agitation forms as all of the troubles on my shoulders flash across my face. The clan war with the wolves, the mob war in Boston, the Benandanti stealing Fenrus, and now an oncoming god war that will leave the world destroyed. It's all too much.

I ask Virbius, "Can you sense if the Seer in the pool is telling the truth? Could she be at all mistaken?"

Slowly drawing his attention back to me, Virbius registers my question and moves closer to the pool. Looking into it, I can tell he is focusing potent magics toward the moving figure of Divina.

"I sense that what she is saying is true. Or at least that the female caster *believes* that her vision is true." Now looking directly at me,

Virbius continues. "Devin, there hasn't been a war among the gods in millennia. Even then, those wars were internal to one another. The various pantheons of gods have never intermingled before. This is very serious. The level of godly power that will be used could destroy every living being on the planet. This war must be stopped."

The look of focused concern on Virbius' face tells me clearly that our discovery is a complete game changer. Something then dawns on me.

"Virbius, the witches in the vision… My people just battled them a few hours ago, but from the looks of them, you'd never have known they were in a fight. Can you tell me when their coven meeting happened? Was this recent?"

Virbius places his hand over the pool of water and closes his eyes. A few moments later he says, "The vision we saw happened a few months ago. Three or four perhaps."

Pondering the time in my head, I say, "If they're gathering familiars, then that must be why they accepted our rival wolf clan's invitation to help attack our pack. If Anna was still with us, she might've been able to warn us of their coming."

Virbius stiffens.

"What is it?"

Almost apologetically, Virbius answers, "I don't normally make it a habit of invading people's minds, but in your thoughts earlier… You were remembering a friend of yours named Anna and that she is being possessed by an Egyptian god."

Nodding my head, I reply, "Yes, the Egyptian war god Sekhmet. She somehow possessed Anna and took her away from us last year. We haven't seen her until just recently when the Benandanti attacked us. Anna's central gods are Isis and Bastet, good deities from Egypt. She must be Sekhmet's prisoner, as she would never align herself with someone so dangerous. I'm worried about what may happen to her, especially now."

Virbius closes his arms around himself and begins to pace back and forth.

"I've had visions recently of your friend Anna. I've seen her here, in my wood, beckoning me to follow her outside of my domain. In my wood, I possess the might of a god. Nowhere near as strong as the gods still worshipped today, but among my subjects here, I'm strong enough to protect them if needed. Out in the world of man, I would be a ghost of a being. A relic from a time gone by. I don't know why this Anna would ask this of me, but I would never leave my people. They need me and I them."

Anna? Here? How could that be?

I reply back, "The goddess Sekhmet hasn't been worshipped in thousands of years. The only persons who even think of her now are teachers and history buffs. Her followers today are almost non-existent. With no one to worship her, she needs to gather her strength again. That must be why she's latched herself onto Anna. She's like a parasite surviving off a host. The jewelry must be the key. Everything changed once Anna was reunited with another piece of the set."

Virbius then stops his pacing and stares at me.

"There is something else, Devin Toxotis. Over the centuries, I've become more than just a simple forest god. Since I was first given my godhood, many creatures have called out to me. Beings who've been hunted and near death. Their souls call out for sanctuary, for peace."

Virbius spreads his arms wide.

"The woods you see around you, they are filled with these beings. You've seen several of them during your time here, but there are much more. I provide them with a place to live out their days outside of violence for as long as they wish to be under my care."

"For as long... You mean you give your subjects immortality?"

Nodding, Virbius answers, "Yes, if that is what they desire. Some choose to forgo immortality altogether, though, in order to die peacefully among their own kind or with friends and loved ones in old age. I grant them whatever calling they feel is right for them. In turn, they provide me with their appreciation and worship. We rely on each other symbiotically. Where once I was simply a god of the forest, I am now also a god of refuge."

Virbius moves back over to the pool and stands beside it.

"It's this refuge aspect that has allowed me to know when my service is requested in the outside world. Look into the pool, Devin Toxotis, and see what being's souls call out to me now."

Peering into the water, I see it ripple once more as several new figures take shape. In it, I see a squadron of Emissary wolf soldiers herding several families into a building. The Emissary's brown clothing tells me that they are from the Neuri clan. The children clutch to their parents' sides crying in fear. The various civilians being wrangled together look shocked and unsure of what is happening.

Once inside, the various families are met with additional Emissary soldiers and two very official looking men. One of the men I recognize. He is the Neuri Archon whose mind I entered last year during my brother Damon's trial by combat.

Several of the family members recognize him and try speaking to him, only to have the Emissary soldiers push them back with the automatic weapons they hold in their hands. The Archons seem unfazed by the cold and brutish way their people are being treated. They merely look on at the helpless families with their hands held behind their backs.

Knowing that I don't understand the language the eastern European wolves speak, Virbius again places the tips of his fingers to my temple. A slight wave of magic fills my mind after which he removes his fingers. I can then understand the low dialogues happening between the family members as they try to console themselves.

The familiar Neuri Archon then tells the group assembled, "As you know, a new clan has recently formed. They are attempting to coerce our people to join their pitiful cause. We've heard of rebels within our own clan who are sympathetic to joining them. This will not be tolerated. Traitors to our clan are traitors to everything we believe in. The dissenters will be weeded out and made an example of."

The Archon eyes the families as they cower in his presence. The other Archon then takes over speaking to the citizens.

"This intrusion is necessary for the good of our people. Prove your allegiance to the Neuri, and you will be able to go back to your everyday lives. Prove yourself to be allies to our enemies and you will be killed in front of everyone here."

One of the family members says, "Archon, we are faithful to the clan always. Please, let my family return home. In Marzanna's name, please. The children are frightened."

Coldly, the Archon replies, "No one is going anywhere until we see with our own eyes who here are true allies to the Neuri. One by one, you will all transform before us to see what fur color your wolf selves possess. If they remain brown, then you will be allowed to return to your homes. If they are the color of the Enopo, then it proves what side your heart is true to and you will be killed."

The various families whimper and cry among one another. My heart is in my throat as I watch what is happening in horror. A man is pushed from the crowd toward the Archons. He stumbles forward and almost falls at their feet.

"Change!" one of the Emissaries barks.

With shaking hands, the man loosens his dress shirt's collar and changes into his hybrid wolf/human form. His fur coloring is brown.

One of the Archons says, "You are Neuri. You may return home."

The man looks back at the group collected and says, "But my family…"

The other Archon coldly says, "Your Archon said you are to return home. Go!"

Still shaking, the man changes back to his full human form and slowly walks toward the building doors. He constantly looks back at his wife and son, still with the others, before finally exiting the building.

"You!" another Emissary shouts at the man's wife. "You're next."

The Emissary shoves the woman toward the Archons, holding back her crying seven-year-old child with the others. The woman sheepishly approaches the Archons and takes a big gulp of air. She closes her eyes and shifts to her wolf/human hybrid form. Unlike her husband, though, her fur is a combination of colors: brown, red, white, gray and black—the colors of the Enopo clan. The crowd behind her gasps. The moment her colors are fully exposed, one of the Archons releases his sword and lops off the woman's head.

My blood runs cold as the woman's body falls to the ground with her head rolling a few feet beside it. Her child screams hysterically as the woman's friends and neighbors cry loudly themselves. Several people cover the eyes of their children, not letting them look at the body now on the ground.

Several Emissaries carry the body and head away as another Emissary shouts, "The child is next."

The faces on the crowd look perplexed and horrified even more than before. One woman says, "But, he's just a child!"

The Emissary takes the waling boy and throws him in front of the Archons.

"Change!" the Emissary yells, but the boy just stays on the ground crying for his now dead mother. Tears fill my eyes as I watch in disbelief at what is happening.

"Change, I said!" The Emissary digs his claws into the child's shoulder. The boy screams even louder as the pain instinctively shifts him into wolf form. Just like his mother before him, his fur is the many shaded colors of the Enopo clan. The Emissary sees this and steps away as the Archon raises his sword into the air another time. I turn away as the sword comes down, sobbing against my shoulder. I close my eyes tightly and try to block the sounds of the many wolves crying out again, this time at the child's death.

I turn to Virbius, hardly able to contain my grief.

"How could they do this?" I ask him. "How could they do this to their own people? Innocents…"

My voice trails off, unable to complete my train of thought. I cover my face with my hands as I sob uncontrollably. I feel Virbius' arms wrap around me in comfort. I rest my face against his chest, heaving in my grief. A stream of tears gathers between my flesh and his.

Softly, Virbius says, "I've learned a long time ago that death is inevitable. In this case, though, it is unjust and cruel. The many other wolf cullings I've seen with other members of your kind were just as hard to…"

I pull away from Virbius sharply in order to get a good look at his face.

"Others? Are you telling me that the other clans are doing this too?"

With sympathetic eyes, Virbius says, "Yes. All throughout Europe, your kind have been holding such tests. Many wolves have been lost. Many others still are on the run or in hiding. I've felt their calls, though indirectly, for help for many months now."

"And you did nothing?" My head spins with emotion. I know I shouldn't speak this way to a god, but my passions are taking control.

Thankfully, Virbius isn't a vengeful god, or so it seems, as he responds in a soft voice, "I wouldn't survive in the outside world. My power isn't strong enough. And even if I were, it is forbidden for a god to interfere in the lives of modern men unless called upon specifically."

"I'm sorry." I stammer.

My mind races as I wipe the tears from my eyes. How could I've not realized this before? The majority of the European Archons are holding desperately to the old ways. To them, the Enopo are a threat that must be eliminated. They'd do anything to end any decent in their ranks. Those poor people...all killed simply for what they believe. It's more than I can bear.

"I've got to do something. I've got to help the remaining wolves in hiding before they're killed, too." I ask Virbius, "Is it possible for my people to find sanctuary here? I mean, if I can get them to call on your name, can you give them protection in your realm?"

Virbius' ebony eyes sparkle slightly. From my understanding of gods, I know that each of them gains strength by the thoughts and devotion of their followers. Virbius knows how many wolves are out there and that their call to him would give him added strength. I'm hoping that it is a temptation that will work in my favor.

"With the prospect of an oncoming god war, I'll need as many followers as I can to marshal my strength. But, Devin, there are so many of your kind scattered across the globe. How do you intend to get to all of them in time?"

Oh ,if only Fenrus were here. No, I can't think that way. I'm an Archon now and must lead with my head. What would my father do?

"Virbius, Anna had a personal item from her goddess Bastet. It was a bracelet that granted her the ability to travel anywhere in the world in the blink of an eye. As a witch, I have this ability, but at a reduced level. I'm only strong enough to travel a few feet before my magics are taxed. Could you provide me with something similar? Something that will allow me to get to the long range wolves in hiding and bring them back here?"

A look of apprehension appears on the god's face.

"The trinket your friend possesses must've been god blessed when she was still at the height of her reign. To transfer that much magic would leave me weak. Too weak to defend my people. Perhaps if I had more followers..."

"My people, Virbius, they are followers of Hecate. With the introduction of my new clan, my followers learned to incorporate the goddess Gaea and the Olympian twins into their faith system as well. If I were to have them include you in their prayers also, would that work? Would you be strong enough then?"

At the mention of the Olympian twins, I see Virbius' entire aura change. He is now at attention and ponders for a moment.

"Yes, I believe it might. How soon would you be able to do this?"

I smile at Virbius, wiping the remaining ghostly traces of tears from my face.

"As soon as I return to my body I'll erect a space for you in our mansion's temple. I'll then instruct my people to mention your name in prayer. Once they know what the European wolves are doing to their own and how you are willing to help protect them, they'll have no choice but to accept you into their hearts."

A smile goes across Virbius' face. He bows his head slightly and removes the necklace from around his neck. With the upmost care, he places it around mine.

"This token I give to you, Devin Toxotis. When I am yet strong enough, it will provide you with the power you seek. When that time comes, may you be successful in your mission. May you be watched over by your people's chosen pantheon until then."

At this, Virbius places both hands on either side of my head and kisses my forehead. A warm sensation floods through me as I feel myself leaving the forest god's domain. Within moments, I feel myself back in my body, refreshed and full of vigor. Sitting on my chest, I see Ms. Whiskers. Her eyes are huge as she inspects my face in detail. Feeling at my neck, I feel Virbius' necklace. I hold it in hand and send a silent prayer of thanks.

With excitement in her voice, Ms. Whiskers says, "You have *lots* and *lots* of sparkle on you! What happen? Where go?"

I smile at the beautiful feline and say, "I went to find help, and I think I might've found it."

Chapter Five
CONVICTION

I QUICKLY SHOWER AND GET INTO A FRESH SET OF DARK COLORED clothes. I take my Emissary swords and affix them to my back in the traditional way. I spot the special leather bracelet Anna gave to Tobias last year and fasten it to my wrist. I'm instantly covered in its magical veil, which is meant to hide any trace of magic its wearer possesses from outsiders. I then put my cell phone, wallet and passport in pocket before leaving the room. Something stops me as I look at the far wall. Hanging there is the spirit sword. I somehow know it might be needed and remove it and its scabbard from their wall holdings, carrying it in hand.

Just as I am about to reach for the doorknob to leave, Ms. Whiskers asks, "Where go now?"

"I have to meet with some of my people for a few minutes. I might need your help later, though. Can you meet me in the garage in an hour?"

"Yes!"

I pet her a couple times on top of her head and then scratch the bottom of her chin before leaving my room, careful to leave the door open enough for her to walk through when she's ready. I immediately see Nicholas standing outside. He's obviously surprised at my appearance and attire.

"What are you doing up? You're supposed to be resting."

His gruff tone is mixed with care. Walking toward my direction, I see Tobias and Mika. A look of concern goes across their faces as well. Tobias notices the leather band on my wrist and his concern turns to fear.

When they get within earshot, I say, "I'm fine. There's a lot of things that have to be done, but first I need to get to the temple room downstairs."

"The temple?" Mika's voice sounds confused.

"Yes." I say. "Let's go. I'll explain along the way."

I hand the spirit sword to Tobias, and he affixes it onto his back. He then locks his fingers with mine as I speak. The four of us walk quickly down several corridors as I recount my spirit travel experience with Virbius to the others. Just as my story ends, we arrive at the entrance to the temple. Due to the late hour, I see that it is thankfully empty. The few lit candles remaining flicker in front of the various god stations.

The four of us bow our heads in solemn respect to the sacred space and quietly go toward the stations most familiar to us. Nicholas goes toward the statue of Hecate and kneels at the red velvet cushions before it. Mika similarly goes toward the statues of the twin Olympian gods Artemis and Apollo. Tobias and I then make our way toward the statue of Gaea, kneeling at her altar. Each station has a plaque, depicting the name of each god represented.

In unison, the four of us take a blessed incense stick from the various vases near each altar and light them using the flames from the candles still lit by the many devotees before us. We hold the incense between our folded hands as we begin our traditional prayers of thanks to our gods.

When I hear the whispered prayers of the others end, I keep my head bowed and focus my thoughts on what I'm about to ask.

Aloud, I say, "Oh great gods of the Enopo Clan of Wolves. We come to you now at a very dark hour. We've learned of an oncoming god war, a war that could beget the end of all things. One of your kind has graciously agreed to help us in this desperate time. The forest god Virbius has agreed to house our wayward wolves that are now being hunted and killed by the other wolf clans. But, he needs our help. Without the added prayers of our people, he is not yet strong enough to reach the wolves in need. We ask for your blessing to include him in this sacred temple that he may better assist not only our people, but also to aid you better in the oncoming war. We ask that we have your favor to have the others in our care accept him in their hearts as well. We ask for a sign that we have your blessing to include this new god among you, as you have blessed the inclusion of the twin gods Artemis and Apollo before. Please, show us your will."

At that, the remaining unlit candles in the temple light, filling the room in a warm glow. There is then a creaking sound that continues until the marble floor beside the statue of Gaea begins to buckle and crack. Out of the central crack, we each see a plant emerge. It grows upward at an incredible rate until it becomes the size of a small tree. The incense sticks in our hands suddenly are pulled away and encircle the tree, spinning around it. Soon, the incense crumbles to dust, filling the cracks of the tree as it continues to grow. When the tree reaches ten feet, it finally stops. The tree's bark turns a dark cherry color, and fragrant flowers bloom among its many leaves.

I lower my head in gratitude. "Blessed be."

The four of us gather in front of the addition to the temple and bow our heads. Tobias and Mika then use their magics to clear away any debris around the tree as Nicholas goes into a back room to retrieve a spare devotional kneeling bar. Once he places it in front of the tree, the four of us move a table behind the kneeling apparatus and begin placing more candle votives and incense sticks upon it, similar to how the other god stations are prepared. Just as we are finishing, a squadron of Enopo soldiers enters the temple. At first concerned, upon seeing me they drop their defenses.

"Archon." One of the soldiers bows his head. "We were told you were resting. We heard a commotion and came to investigate." The soldiers then look at the tree behind us with confusion.

I give them a hold motion with my hand, and they obey as asked. I focus on my magical center, willing my magics to come forth. I then look at the tree and see the name of the forest god in my mind's eye. I will my magics toward the now living representation of our newest god. The word *VIRBIUS* then appears on the tree's bark. Instantly, I feel the necklace around my neck shudder with its own magic, although it's still not yet strong enough to transport me with the ability of Anna's bracelet. I also know that once the other wolves in our clan know his name and worship in his presence, Virbius' power will grow, as it has enhanced the other gods within the temple. This is our only chance to have my plan to succeed. I'll have to remember to have one of the temple keepers have an official plaque made for Virbius' space similar to the ones already in place in front of the others. The etched name in the tree's bark will have to do for now.

Knowing our work is done for the most part, I turn back and give the soldier a weak smile saying, "Everything's fine here. Are our Synoro Archon allies still in the mansion?"

Snapping his attention back to me, the soldier answers, "Yes, they are meeting with your father and the other Archons now."

"Good. We'll see them then."

The soldier bows again and makes room for us to pass as we leave the temple.

On our way to the Council and Archon meeting room, I see several bullet holes etched into walls, broken furniture, and smashed windows—remnants of Jason's invasion. I'm drawn back to my own battle in the opposite wing and remember Fenrus' cries for help. No, I can't let my emotions get to me. Not now. Focus, Devin. Stick to the plan. The Benandanti won't do anything to him until the god war begins. We still have time.

The Synoro and Enopo Emissaries guarding the Archon meeting room are surprised to see me, but move aside to let me through. Nicholas stands with them, but they look at one another uncomfortably when they realize that Tobias and Mika are not staying behind as well. To ease their apprehension, I tell them, "These are two of my most trusted Enopo Council Members and fellow witches. They are needed in the meeting."

They bow their heads in compliance as we continue through without interruption.

Inside, we see all of the Enopo Archons are at the meeting table along with the three Synoro Archons sympathetic to our cause. They each turn their heads at our arrival with surprise. They get to their feet out of respect. I bow slightly in return.

Before they can say anything about the two other wolves with me, I say, "Please forgive my intrusion. This is Tobias Mann and Mika Williams. They are part of the Enopo Council and are part of my inner coven as well. They are needed for what I'm about to say."

My father says, "Devin, we didn't think you'd be up for this meeting. Please…"

He motions for a space next to him, which I take. Tobias and

Mika sit at two other seats at the table as everyone else sits as well. Once the formalities are made, I tell everyone about my spirit travel to Virbius' forest domain and what was discovered there. As with Tobias, Mika and Nicholas before them, the looks on the various Archons' faces change to shock and horror.

I take a breath and say, "What I need to know from the Synoro Archons is if any of you have heard any intel of Jason or Clayton killing Enopo wolves. I need to know if they were killing their own kind like the Neuri or other European wolves have been."

The Synoro Archons look at one another. Finally Archon Brice, who has had the most contact with our clan, speaks.

"We were just discussing this with your fellow Archons. One of the reasons we've pushed to reclaim the New Hampshire compound is that we've received a report from one of our spies that Clayton grouped several families in that area and killed the members he found with Enopo fur coloring. Killing innocent wolves, no matter what clan they are from, is something abhorrent to all of us. We wanted to stop the slaughter before it got out of hand."

Gabriella clears her throat. I can see that she's been crying. "They've also just confirmed your story an hour ago from their Archon counterparts. My own father is guilty of this crime."

Gabriella's father, Gregoire Basilikos, is one of the Basque clan of Archons. He is just as against our formation as my grandfather is. Damon puts his arm around his mother to console her. He then looks up and says, "We still have Jason, Clayton, and their soldiers in custody. We haven't had time to question them. We have no idea if the Synoro killings were orchestrated by both of them or if Clayton was acting alone."

To the Synoro Archons I say, "I need to know where you all stand."

Brice asks, "What do you mean? I just said that we are against the killings."

"I understand that." I say. "What I need to know is where do you stand on the future of our kind. This infighting is destroying the wolf nation. You heard it yourselves from the goddess Hecate and Gaea. The old ways are going to end. They chose the Enopo to lead the other clans into unity, the way it used to be millennia ago. What my clan needs to know is if you wish to continue supporting the Synoro and keep things as before, or if you are willing to throw away the old way of thinking all together."

Vincent says, "Devin! The Synoro Archons present have been nothing but supportive of us."

"Yes." I answer. "They have. But, there is a god war coming. That war could mean the end of everything as we know it. We don't have time to second-guess our alliances. We need to know now who will stand with us until the end. When we met with local mob bosses to try to squash any animosity between our clan and their families, Neuri assassins on the mob bosses' orders attacked us. Then we were attacked en route back to our compound by a group of other European clans. Then, during our battle with Jason's wolves once we got here, an outside coven of witches working with Jason and Clayton attacked us. Our enemies are growing in numbers. We need to hold all of our allies as close to the vest as possible. So I ask the Synoro Archons again, will you cling to the name Synoro or will you side with your wolf brothers as a unified race?"

The three of them look at each other as they let what I am asking sink in.

Finally, Archon Shaun answers. "What you want to know is if we'll cast aside the Synoro clan entirely in order to become part of the Enopo clan. Is that it?"

Adamantly, I say, "No. That's not what I'm asking at all. I'm asking you to cast aside the Synoro, Enopo, Basque, Exallos, Neuri, Lykaion...*all* of them. I'm asking that *we* as a race don't tie ourselves down to *any* clan name. I'm asking us to embrace all wolves, both here and across the pond, under a united wolf nation. No more kill assignments. No more clan territories. No more divisions. I need to know because, when this war hits, we're going to need everyone united in support of each another if we're going to survive."

Ryan, one of the Synoro Archons asks, "And if we choose to stay Synoro? What then? Will we become your enemies, too?"

Vincent, about to lose his cool says, "I'm *sure* Archon Devin meant to discuss this line of questioning with us prior to your visit Archons, but I can assure you, your help with us will *not* be thrown out of the window or be forgotten. This coven will always remain allies with the three of you."

I rise to my feet and stare down Vincent before saying, "You will *not* speak over me Vincent, and you will *not* speak for me ever again either. Am I clear?"

The tone of the room becomes heavy. I can sense even those closest to me may be questioning my timing and choice of words. I then turn back to the Synoro Archons. They have obviously raised their defenses.

I lower my voice. "You have nothing to fear from anyone in this room. Of that, you have my solemn vow. I just need to know where your loyalties lie. If you choose to stay Synoro, I can't guarantee your safety. I can't risk safeguarding any wolf that will turn on us once the war begins. I don't take this station lightly." I then look at Vincent again, making sure he fully comprehends my meaning. "Not anymore."

Vincent gulps but keeps eye contact.

Speaking again to the Synoro Archons, I say, "I don't mean to show any disrespect or inconsideration, but we have a huge responsibility and now have little time to do it in. I need to know that your hearts are in this just as much as ours are."

I can tell my words have finally gotten through. They look at each other one final time before Bryce says, "The three of us will have to discuss this in private. You should have your answer in the morning." He then looks to his companions. "Agreed?"

They both nod their heads. "Agreed."

"Thank you." I say. "No matter what answer you give us, you have my upmost respect. Vincent is right. I won't forget everything you've done for us. I just hope we can rely on each other for what's about to happen."

The three Archons then rise from their seats. Bryce nods then says, "We have a lot to discuss, both with each other and with our contacts in Europe. We'll meet with you at the same time tomorrow evening." To me he says, "I'm sure your other Archons will catch you up on everything else we've discussed."

The rest of the room rises as well. My father says, "We look forward to it. Until then, our compound, or what's left of it, is at your service. Each of your rooms should have Skype capability should you need to conference any European Archon."

"Thank you." Shaun says.

They then leave, closing the door behind them. Vincent waits a few seconds to pass then angrily says, "How *dare* you undermine me in front of outside clan Archons! I've never been so rudely insulted..."

Glaring back at him, I say, "If you're still referring to us as a clan, then you obviously haven't been listening to a goddamned word I've said. Get on board, or get out Vincent." Turning to the rest of the room, I say, "That goes for everyone. We *need* to be on the same page, otherwise we're just as dead as those murdered wolves. I can't stress this enough."

Damon says, "Brother, it was completely wrong of you to demand this kind of change on us and not discuss it with us beforehand. How can we back you in front of the others if we don't even know what it is you're fighting for?"

The Ambassador in Damon makes sense, but I don't have time to second-guess what I need to do.

"You're right. I should've spoken to you privately beforehand, but there was no time. There's a lot we have to do as a group, and a lot that I must do on my own. We need to act now."

With concern, Tobias asks, "What? What do you mean alone?"

I see fear in Tobias' face.

Solemnly, I say, "I'll get to that in a moment. First, I need for all of you to do something very important. Tobias, Mika and I, just before the meeting, approached our gods about including Virbius as part of our pantheon. They accepted. We need for all of our wolves to know how important it is to accept Virbius as one of them. It's only with his strength that we'll be able to rescue all the wolves in hiding."

I show them the necklace around my neck.

"This is a totem for Virbius. Once enough of our people think on him, he'll be strong enough to empower it. Then I'll be able to use it to transport all the wolves to safety individually. Once that's done, we're going to need to get through to the European Archons. They need to know that if they stay on the path they're on, they'll be defenseless in the oncoming god war. They'll need us if they want to survive."

Gabriella says, "Convincing them will be quite difficult. They don't trust us as it is."

"Then we've got to rally as many allies as we can to try to save the wolves that are willing to make peace. It's the only way."

My father asks, "So that's why you cornered the Synoro Archons the way you did. I agree with your brother that it wasn't the right way to go about it, but I get it. What else do you need for us to do?"

I feel a bit disappointed in myself as I let down both my father and Damon, but I have to be a strong leader for the wolves.

I answer my father saying, "Right now, we need to focus on the wolves in hiding. If we can get Brice, Shaun, and Ryan to put the Synoro aside, we'll have a lot more safe houses in the Americas to house as many wolves as possible, both here and abroad. As of now, we don't have enough space at this compound, so there's only Virbius' domain for us to count on at the moment."

My father's expression changes as if he's thinking about what to say next. Finally, he says, "I know it's a sore subject, but what about the Benandanti? They still have Fenrus."

I bite my lip and say, "I have to believe that Fenrus is safe for the time being. The Benandanti need to keep him alive, and they need me to help control him. If my hunch is right, they'll try to contact me again to get me to join their coven. I'll cross that bridge when I come to it. For now, we've got to stay focused on the wolves."

Gruffly, Vincent adds, "We're still at war with the Longo family too. Or have you forgotten?"

I look at him and try my best not to be so spiteful. I calmly say, "No, I haven't forgotten. Fortunately for us, we're not the only family Longo's after. On a good note, it seems we may at least have a shaky alliance with Don Phillipi and his family. We're gonna need it if we plan to have Longo remedied. Try meeting with Phillipi. See if he's willing to aid us, and offer our protection to him and his family in exchange. We can't let this mob war sidetrack us from our main goal: the future for our people."

Damon asks, "And when the wolves are safe, what then? How are we going to survive the god war?"

Turning back to Tobias and Mika, I say, "That's where my coven comes in. I'm sorry to be asking so much of you two, but I don't see any other choice. Anna is the key. If we can de-possess her, we might stand a chance at ending this war before it begins." Back to the other Archons I say, "Tomorrow when you meet with the Synoro, tell them our plan. Get them to help support us. If they wish to stay divided into clans, well, we'll just have to continue our plan without them."

Concerned, my father says, "You sound as if you won't to be here for the meeting."

I meet his gaze. "I'm not. I'm leaving this end of the plan for all of you to take over. Until Virbius is strong enough to aid me, I have to get to those other wolves before it's too late for them. Virbius' forest is in Italy. I'm leaving to get a head start there as soon as possible."

Mika grabs me by the shoulder and says, "Devin, going after those wolves alone is suicide! The Benandanti are based in Italy, too. Witch or no witch, without Fenrus, you're a walking target for the Benandanti *and* the European Archons."

Tobias says, "You're not going alone, Devin. We're going with you."

Suddenly, from the corner of the room I hear someone else say, "So am I."

All eyes turn to see Nicholas standing in the doorway. He has a look of determination. I'm humbled by the devotion around me. "Thank you, all of you, but not all the European Archons are looking to kill us. I'll talk to our allies there as well, if I can. Besides, I can't guarantee anyone's safety. The wolves at this end are gonna need as much direction as possible. We can't lose a single leader. Not now."

Tobias says, "After what we went through last year, you know we're stronger together. You're gonna need as much help as possible too. We've been through this."

Gabriella says, "We'll be fine here. We'll work with our Synoro allies as much as possible. Whatever they decide, they should still be able to help us with the mob families. Perhaps a private meeting with Don Phillipi would help. We'll try our best to convince Bryce and the others to give our wolves access to their other compounds, too."

Tobias makes sure he is in my range of view, then reaffirms, "See? They have things covered on this end. We're going with you."

I can tell Tobias isn't taking no for an answer. I mouth to him and Mika, "Thank you." I then turn to Nicholas and nod my head.

My father then takes me into a tight hug and whispers into my ear, "You don't have to do this, son."

I hug him back just as tightly and say, "Yes, I do. Take care of Mom."

Vincent's voice breaks our moment.

"I can arrange for one of our jets to fly you to Italy this evening."

Releasing the hug I give my father, I look at Vincent. I can't tell if his offer to help is out of sincere concern or if he is offering for the sheer gratitude of getting rid of me.

I say, "Thanks, but with the amount of wolves and witches looking for us, I don't think it'll be safe using one of our registered transports. I'll arrange for alternate transportation."

Damon steps forward. "But, what if something happens?"

I smile at him. I know he's concerned about me, but the look he gives Mika tells me that I'm not the only one. I assuage him by saying, "We should be fine. I or one of the others will contact you periodically."

Soon all of my family joins around me for farewell hugs. I have no idea when I'll be able to see them again, so I take in as much love from them as I can. Looking up from our hold, I see Vincent standing by himself. It's then that I realize just how hard being an Archon in our group must be for him. Not only did the other clans hate us, but also all the other Archons in our group have some sort of family tie to one another.

Walking over to him, I say, "I know it's been difficult for you here. And, for that I sincerely apologize. I didn't mean to disrespect or demean you in front of the others. Not on purpose. I want you to know how much I appreciate working with you. We haven't always agreed, but I do need someone to question me from time to time. It's the only way we're going to keep these wolves safe. So, thank you. If something does happen, I'm honored to know you will be helping to lead our people."

I hold out my hand. Vincent looks at it a moment, then clasps it with his.

"I wish you safe travels." The tone in his voice tells me he means it.

"Thank you."

Looking back at Tobias, Mika, and Nicholas, I tell them, "We've got to go."

Damon then takes Mika and gives her a passionate kiss on the lips. When they finish, Mika says, "We might not've gotten as far in your magic lessons as I'd like, but at least I was able to teach you how to create shields. Use it, Damon. You keep yourself safe until I return."

Damon tells her, "I'll pray to the goddess for your safe return every day."

They hug one another one last time before Mika leaves his side to join my pack of travelers. I look at my father again. His warm smile is the last image I hold before leaving through the door. When we walk through, I see my mother on the other side. I see tears in her eyes.

Tobias notices our need for privacy and says, "The three of us need to get a change of clothes and a few other things for the trip. We'll meet you in the garage in a few minutes."

I nod at him as he, Mika, and Nicholas disappear down a corridor.

"You said that you'd never leave again." The pain in my mother's voice breaks my heart. I try to say something, anything, but every word is caught in my throat.

Finally, I'm able to mutter out, "I'm sorry."

"No." she answers. "Not this time. I'm not going through the hell of wondering where you are or if you're even alive again. I won't."

Dejectedly, I reply, "Mom, those bastards in Europe are killing wolves. They're dying because they believe in our cause of unity. If it were me out there, wouldn't you want someone to help save me?"

"But it's *not* you Devin! You can't help everyone everywhere. It's not humanly possible. Don't we have enough danger here as it is? Why are you going out to find more?"

"But I'm not finding more, mom." I say. "The danger is already out there, and like it or not I'm the cause of it all. I stepped into these people's lives and now everything's turned on its head. These people are relying on me to make things right. I have to try."

My mother straightens her arms at her side and says, "Then take me with you."

"What? No. It's too dangerous."

Leaning in, my mother says, "Devin Marshall, I'm not taking no for an answer. I'm not going to sit idly by until I hear word that you've been killed. You *will* take me with you, and that's all there is to it."

Her eyes shift to a yellow color and I know she is serious.

"Dad would never allow it." I say, desperate for reason.

"I'm my own woman, Devin. I don't answer to anyone. Not even your father. I'm going or so help me…!" The trademark staunchness I remember as a child hasn't diminished in the slightest.

Just then, a voice behind me says, "Vickie, Devin's right. You're not battle trained. It'll be too dangerous for you."

My father comes out of the meeting room and gently takes my mother by her arms. He continues saying, "I swore I'd be there to protect you, and I'm keeping my word. I'll be able to keep you safe here. Where Devin is going, there's no guarantee what will happen."

Crestfallen, my mother tells him, "So you're fine sending our son off to slaughter, alone?"

With kindness in his voice, he says, "But he won't be alone. He's going with two other witches and our clan's best fighter. He couldn't be better guarded."

Frustrated, my mother says, "I know that, Adam, but you're missing the point. We may never see our son again." Turning back to me, my mother continues saying, "I'm going with you Devin. That's my final word."

Exhausted, my father says, "Vickie…" My mother turns to him and stares at him harshly. He stares back, but with sadness in his eyes.

"You're afraid you're going to lose Devin. If you go, I'm afraid I'll lose you both. That, I don't think I can take. Not again."

My mother's hard edge softens a bit. She puts her hand softly on his cheek. My father covers her hand with his. Tears fill my mother's eyes as she rests her head in my father's chest and quietly sobs. In a low tone, I hear my mother say, "I'm losing him again."

Having my mother break down emotionally is too much for me to take. Doubt fills my mind as I reach to hold my parents in my arms. Almost immediately, I feel both their arms wrap around me tightly. Memories of being a child in Scottsdale come flooding back to me, back to a time when all I had in life was my mom, my dad, and their love. It was simpler then. I'd give anything to have things go back, before I knew anything about werewolves, witches, mafias or gods.

Somewhere in the back of my head, I hear a voice say, "You know what you must do, Devin."

The voice is soft and warm. It fills me with confidence. It reminds me that I'm not a child anymore, but an adult leader. In my heart, I know the voice belongs to the goddess Gaea. I send her humbled thoughts of thanks and devotion. I mentally tell her that I haven't forgotten my promise to her.

I release my hold on my parents and wipe away the tears from my eyes. They look back at me with love.

My father reaffirms his previous words by saying, "Devin battled a squadron of trained werewolves last year and survived. It was the most amazing thing I've ever seen. I have faith in him. With the team he's assembled, I know he'll be safe. He *will* come back to us."

My mother kisses my cheek and returns to my father's side. I know I now have her blessing, too.

"I love you both." I tell them.

"We love you too, son." My father's voice fills my heart.

I turn and leave, content in knowing I'm doing the right thing.

As I enter the garage, I see Tobias, Mika, and Nicholas putting bags into the trunk of one of the service cars. They each have a set of swords affixed to their backs. On top of the car hood, I see Ms. Whiskers happily flicking her tail.

Closing the trunk, Nicholas says, "We packed light. What's our next move from here?"

"We need a jet." I answer. "I'm planning on calling in a favor."

Mika nods and says, "Let's get to it then."

Seeing Ms. Whiskers, Tobias says, "I think she thinks she's coming with us."

"She is." I say. "Now let's go."

We all climb into the car: me in the driver's seat, Tobias in the passenger seat, and Mika and Nicholas in the back. Ms. Whiskers jumps into the front seat area also, but stops and hisses at Nicholas once she sees how close he is.

Nicholas says, "That cat hates me. Why is she coming?"

I rev the car and start the journey out of the underground parking garage.

"Ms. Whiskers is coming because this little cat scares the goddess possessing Anna, and she might come in handy with finding her too. And the reason she hates you," I say, "is because you tried to kill her last year. Maybe if you apologize to her and ask for her forgiveness, she'll be nicer."

"Are you freakin' kidding me?" You can cut the incredulity in Nicholas' voice with a knife.

"I am. I talk with her all the time. Her feelings are just as real as any of ours." I try not to sound so arrogant, but the look on Nicholas' face from the rear view mirror tells me that he's not buying it. Tobias picks up Ms. Whiskers and places her on his lap. She calms down and begins purring once he starts petting her.

When we reach the exit to the garage, I wave to the set of soldiers at guard. They open the gate for us to pass. I drive through just as the sun is starting to rise. Pulling away from the compound I say a silent prayer to our gods to keep the people inside its walls safe.

A few feet from the driveway, I remember the mystical barrier that previously stopped us from returning to our base. I scan the area magically and can't sense any lingering trace of it. I can only assume that, once the Benandanti made their escape, the magic they gave the barrier must've faded away with them.

After a few minutes, Mika breaks the silence.

"Devin, so am I right in assuming that, once the wolves in hiding are free, we're going to try to find my grandmomma again? We couldn't find her before. What makes you think we'll be able to find her this time?"

Looking at Mika in the rearview mirror, I say, "The god possessing Anna said that she was obligated to protect you, that it had an oath with Anna. I'm thinking that you're the key to finding her. I'm hoping that Ms. Whiskers here might also be a failsafe for our protection."

Confused, Mika asks, "Then how are we going to de-possess her after we find her?"

I sigh. "That part I haven't fully figured out yet. We have a few days to think on it though. We'll come up with something. I have faith."

I can see Mika's reflection smile kindly at me and return the thanks with a smile of my own. I feel a warmness on my chest, look down, and see the necklace Virbius gave me is glowing. Ms. Whiskers notices it too as her eyes become big as saucers.

"Devin," Tobias asks, "what's happening with your necklace?"

I can feel energy starting to fill the stone hanging from the cord around my neck.

"It has to be our people," I answer. "They must be up by now and discovered Virbius' tree in the devotional chamber. Their prayers are giving him strength."

When my companions notice what streets we've already reached, they panic.

"Devin, Don Phillipi's compound is just two blocks away. Turn around. We're too close to his territory." Tobias grabs me by the shoulder. "Wait. *He's* not the person you're calling in a favor from."

Continuing forward, I say, "Yeah, it is."

Nicholas leans forward. "You can't be serious. They're armed to the teeth right now. You're still our Archon Devin, but you're leading us into a death trap. These people are in the middle of a war of their own. They'll see us as a threat."

I pull the car over to the curb and park. I then turn to face everyone in the car. "Don Phillipi might be our only chance of making it to Europe without our enemies knowing. We need to see if he has a jet we can use so we can enter the country under the radar."

Tobias says, "Devin, that's crazy! They aren't going to just give us a jet. Hell, they may not even let us in the front door. Maybe your necklace is strong enough now to take us to Europe on its own."

I take the necklace in hand and close my eyes. I focus on my magical center and have my sorceries engulf the enchantments of the necklace. I feel the levels of magic within it. When I'm done, I take Tobias' hand and say, "No. It's getting stronger, but it's still not strong enough to teleport all of us yet. It's gonna need time to get there. In the meanwhile, we need to stay optimistic. We won't get through this unless we have faith."

Nicholas says, "But going in as a group is way too risky. One of us will have to go in alone. Say the word, and I'll go, Archon."

Mika responds, "Don Phillipi will only respond to Devin. I think we all know that. Devin, are you sure you want to do this?"

I look at Mika and say, "It's our only alternative."

I give Tobias a quick kiss on the mouth, then reach back and kiss Mika on the cheek. Before he can protest, I grab Nicholas and give him a tight, quick hug. He apprehensively accepts it.

I then return to my seat. "Wait here. I should be back in a few minutes. Wish me luck."

Together, Tobias and Mika say, "Blessed be."

I leave the car, tossing the keys to Tobias. I then jog in the direction of Don Phillipi's compound. Not wanting to look opposing, I glamour the swords on my back to become invisible. I make sure my pace, upon reaching the compound, is calm but direct. I see several guards posted at the front gate. I take a deep breath and walk over to them. Upon seeing me, they get a look of alarm and reach inside their coat jackets.

"I'm Devin Toxotis," I say, "Victoria Sazia's son. I'm here to speak to Don Phillipi."

The lot of them looks around suspiciously, expecting a group of armed men to jump in at any moment.

Understanding their apprehension, I say, "I promise you. I've come alone. It's important I speak to your Don now."

One of the men grabs me and throws me up against the gate, feeling my sides for any weapons. I'm thankful they miss my back completely, avoiding my swords hidden from view. They find my passport and cash, confiscating them from me. Satisfied I'm unarmed, the goon tells one of the others that I'm clean and to call it in. I wait quietly as they relay the word of my presence to those inside.

After a few minutes, a team of more armed men arrive inside the gate and it opens. One of them takes me by the arm while the others surround me. Once again, I'm frisked.

"This is all he had on him," the guard from earlier says. He hands my passport and money to the new guard, and we all walk toward the main house. Normally, the grounds would be lovely to look at with their lush green hedges and brick walkways. That beauty is overshadowed by the amounts of armed men patrolling the compound.

When we get to the front doors, they open. What seems to be a butler directs the men to a side room. The man holding my arm takes me inside while the others wait at the doorway. Inside are more men that are armed. Near a large mantle is Sam Phillipi.

The man holding my arm says, "The guys were right. He's clean. This was all he had on him."

The guard throws down my passport and money on a table.

"Thanks," Sam says. "I have my men here. We should be fine."

The guard lets go of my arm and leaves the room. I reach for my passport and money, placing them back in my pocket. Sam walks over to me.

"Why are you here?"

"Let me cut to the chase. I'm here for a favor."

From behind me, I hear a voice with a trace of an Italian accent say, "You want help to leave the country."

I turn around and see Don Phillipi standing in the doorway.

Alarmed, Sam says, "Pop, you shouldn't be here. I can take care of this."

Don Phillipi says, "I am the head of this house. One day it will be yours, but until that day, I oversee the family decisions."

"But…," Sam starts to say.

Raising two fingers toward his son, Don Phillipi turns to me and again asks, "Is that the favor you need from me, Don Sazia? I noticed you have a passport. Only a man on the run would be carrying that."

In the most respectful tone I can muster, I say, "I mentioned to you before in our meeting that I am no Don. My family is out of that lifestyle. Whatever mafia ties my grandfather had are gone. I meant that."

Don Phillipi eyes me for a few moments before gesturing toward one of the couches taking up the room. I nod to him and sit as instructed. Don Phillipi takes a seat on the couch opposite of me while Sam and the guards stay standing, ready to aid their Don if called for.

Once we are settled, Don Phillipi eyes me again before saying,

"Forgive me for being so blunt, but for someone who's no longer in the business, you and your family are armed almost as fully as my own family is. If you are no longer in the business, why do you need so much protection?"

Meeting his gaze, I reply, "Just like my mother's family, my father's side has some powerful enemies as well. They have a long reach. I need to make sure the people we are caring for are safe."

Raising an eyebrow, Don Phillip asks, "Who are these people? Why do they need protection?"

"They were once loyal to my father's family, but like my parents and me, they wanted to leave that world behind. They came to us asking for protection. They want nothing more than to live normal lives outside of dictatorial rules. I promised them that I would do whatever I could to make sure they get their wish. The best way to look at it is sort of as a witness protection program."

Smiling, the Don says, "Ah, but then you are still in the business. The rationality behind it may be different, but you are still the head giving orders just like I do."

"I beg to differ Don Phillipi, but call it what you will." I know this line of questioning will only mire me more in mafia politics, so I try to deflect it as best as I can.

"The main point I wish to make," I continue, "is that you have no need to worry about my family. We have no vendetta against you and have no interest in any of your business or territories. We only wish to be left in peace."

The Don says, "And your family's enemies? Who are they? Are they something my family should be worried about should we provide you this favor?"

Don Phillipi's question is something I've never previously thought of. Will his helping me put him in added danger? I look back at him. "No more danger than you already are."

Don Phillipi thinks on it for a few minutes. He walks over to Sam. They speak in Italian to one another. Somehow, I am able to understand what they are saying.

Son, what do you think?

It's too dangerous, Papa. We're already at war with Longo. Send him away. We have too much on our plate as it is.

And what about our debt? That boy saved both our lives.

Sam looks at me.

There's too much going on right now.

I can see that Sam is working against me. In Italian, I reply, "I'm not asking for either of you to get involved in my family problems. That's my burden to bear. The favor I ask for is a jet. I need to travel to Europe unannounced to take care of some affairs there. Help provide me with this, and you can consider your debt fulfilled."

The two of them get a look of surprise.

Don Phillipi says, "Forgive me. I didn't know you spoke Italian."

I just look at him respectfully. He then turns back to Sam, and they speak in hushed tones. My keen wolf hearing picks up every word.

If all he's asking for is a plane, then we won't have to do a thing.

But, Papa, those jets are expensive. If he loses it, it'll cost us thousands.

Bah, we have four of them. We'll never miss it. Besides, a few thousand in exchange for saving our lives is nothing.

If you say so, Papa.

The two of them turn back to me.

Sam says, "We'll grant your favor. We have a private hanger at the airport. I'll arrange to have one of the pilots take you anywhere you want to go."

My heart feels as if it has dropped from my throat back to my chest. Thank you, Gaea.

I nod to them. "You have my sincere thanks."

"You know," Don Phillipi says, "I've seen you fight at our earlier meeting. Something tells me you could kill every one of us in this room easily. Your family…can they all fight like this?"

"Some. It comes from a part of my father's family we are trying to separate from."

Looking at his father as if he understands his line of questioning, Sam says to me, "Your people who can fight like you do, would you be willing to hire any of them out? My father…there is no price I wouldn't pay for his safety."

Don Phillipi puts his hand on his son's back in gratitude. I look at the both of them and understand their need. Hesitantly, I say, "I personally can't make any promises at the moment. Do you have a pen and paper?"

One of the bodyguards goes to a far desk and comes back with both. I take it and scribble a name and telephone number on it. I then extend it back to the bodyguard, who then gives it to Sam.

Continuing, I say, "Call that number and ask for the name I've written. It belongs to my father. Tell him what we've discussed. I'm sure both our families will need each other's support if we plan to make it through this."

Sam lifts the note toward me and says, "Thank you. I won't forget this."

Just then, one of the guards from earlier comes into the room and says, "Don Phillipi, we just got word that Longo hit one of the factories downtown."

Sam turns to me and says, "I'm afraid our meeting must end. I'll make sure everything is arranged once you get to the airport. Good luck on your trip."

He then takes his father's hand and guides him out of the room. Half of the guards in the room follow them out, and the other half escort me to the front door. The guards from earlier escort me back to the gate. I walk through and immediately make for the car several blocks away.

When I get there, I can see looks of relief on my family's faces. I get in, take the keys from Tobias, and rev the engine awake.

Tobias asks, "So, what did they say? Do we have transportation to Europe?"

Peeling away from the curb, I answer, "We got a jet. I'm thinking we might have to make a pit stop before Europe, though."

Confused, Nicholas asks, "Pit stop? Where?"

Smiling, I say, "San Francisco. We need to pick up an old friend."

Chapter 6
THE OLD WORLD

"I CAN'T BELIEVE I'M GOING TO EUROPE! THIS IS SO FREAKIN' EXCITING!"

Nicholas grunts, annoyed at the heightened joy emanating from Brian.

Coming over to the empty seat beside me, Nicholas sits and bluntly says, "I still don't get why we had to pick him up. That guy is annoying as hell. Are you sure he's necessary? According to the First Law..."

I cut him off. "I know what the First Law says, but we're making an exception with him. Brian Gardener is an expert on ancient cultures and supernatural phenomenon. He owns a shop in San Francisco filled with rare magical items. He also has many connections around the globe. We might need his help with what we're about to do."

Nicholas says, "If the other clans find out that he's human, they won't be as merciful."

I look at Nicholas. "If we followed the First Law completely, my brother would be dead, as would I be. There have to be exceptions, Nicholas. You must see that."

Nicholas looks back at Brian, watching as he jumps from one jet window to look out at the night sky clouds, then to another. Nicholas turns back to me and grumpily says, "I guess. You did tell him he could get killed on this mission though, right?"

I look at the two large bags Brian brought on board with him now resting on the ground. I'm hopeful something in one of them will be something we can use for our adventure ahead.

"I told him everything." I reply. "He knows what to expect. I'm just grateful he committed to coming despite the danger to him."

Falling into one of the chairs across from me, Brian says, "So your boy Virbius, he's real? I mean, actual flesh and blood real?"

I feel the necklace around my neck. I can sense it's still not yet strong enough. I then look back at Brian and say, "Yeah, he's real."

Tobias steps out of the jet's washroom, closing the door behind him. He sits down across from Nicholas. Mika puts down the book she's reading and joins in on the conversation.

"You know," she says, "the god Virbius has strong ties to one of my own gods. He was a human prince once, the son of King Theseus of Athens and the Amazon Queen Hippolyta."

With a look of interest, Brian says, "Hey, I know that story! It started with one of the 12 Labors of Hercules in ancient Greece, right?"

Politely Mika responds, "Yes, it did. One of Hercules' labors was to steal the Amazon Queen's girdle or belt. It carried a great status, you see, so anyone possessing it was often considered unstoppable in battle. On his labor, Hercules took his friend Theseus along with him. When Theseus first saw Hippolyta, he fell deeply in love with her. When Hercules stole the girdle from Hippolyta, Theseus begged the Amazon queen for forgiveness. She did and eventually married him. She bore him a son, whom they named Hippolytus.

"When Hippolytus grew into adulthood, he was supposed to be very physically beautiful. Every woman in the kingdom wanted him, even Theseus' later wife Phaedra."

Brian guffaws and says, "I only heard of that kind of stuff happening in the Deep South."

Ignoring his remark, Mika continues, saying, "Hippolytus shunned all his women suitors, though, choosing to remain a chaste follower of the virgin goddess Artemis instead. Artemis adored Hippolytus and considered him one of her favorite devotees. Angered that Hippolytus ignored her advances, Phaedra told her husband that Hippolytus had raped her."

The look of shock on even Nicholas' face tells me that everyone listening now has Mika's full attention.

Noticing this, Mika smiles and continues. "Believing her, Theseus cursed his son. He prayed to his central god Poseidon that he kill Hippolytus immediately. Hearing the king's wishes, the sea god caused a monstrous bull to appear out of the sea foam. Hippolytus was riding a chariot on the beach at the time. When his horses saw the gigantic monster, they reared up and bolted for safety. Hippolytus, unfortunately, got caught up in the chariot's reins and was dragged to his death."

Completely appalled, Tobias says, "That's terrible!"

Agreeing, Mika says, "It was. That's why when the goddess Artemis heard about what had happened, she had the Olympian god Asclepius resurrect Hippolytus from the dead. Afraid Zeus would be angered at the resurrection; Artemis renamed him Virbius and gave him domain over one of her sacred forests in Italy. In her domain, and now with power of his own, Zeus couldn't locate Hippolytus so he killed Asclepius instead, in anger."

Disgusted, Brian says, "That Phaedra was a bitch!"

"She got hers, though." Mika relishes in saying, "After hearing of Hippolytus' death, Phaedra was consumed by guilt and killed herself."

"What about Virbius' mother, Hippolyta? What happened to her?" I ask.

"No one really knows." Mika responds. "There are some theories that she died during the Attic War, but the texts never say for certain what exactly happened to Hippolyta after Hippolytus was born."

Something makes me think back to my earlier visit with Virbius, of him rubbing the gauntlets on his arms. In my head, I can clearly recall him saying, "*A clan of classless men stole a precious token from my family once.*"

To Mika, I ask, "Do you know whatever happened to Hippolyta's belt?"

She thinks a moment, and then says, "According to the myths, Hercules supposedly gave it to King Eurystheus, who then gave it to his daughter Admete. There's no record of what happened to the belt after that."

Brian chimes in. "I deal in ancient items all the time. I've never heard a peep about the belt appearing in modern times. My guess is that it's been lost to the ages."

"Actually," I say, "I may be off, but I think Virbius may've had an added part in the belt's history after all. When I met with him, he had two distinctive gauntlets, one on each arm."

Tobias asks, "Gauntlets? Are you thinking they're forged from his mother's belt?"

"I can't say for sure," I answer, "but it would make sense."

I feel a warmness at my neck. I look down and see my necklace is slightly glowing. I use my magics to scan the necklace's source, feeling more magic within the necklace than before. I smile.

Noticing my expression and the necklace's glow, Mika asks, "Devin, is it…?"

"Not yet," I answer, "but it's getting close."

Nervously, Brian says, "Uh, last time an item like that was used, it made your friend Anna disappear. You sure this won't be more of the same?"

Mika looks sad at the mention of her grandmother. I then think on Virbius and the general feeling I had in his presence.

I tell Brian, "I have faith it won't."

From her new expression, I can tell my reassurance just helped lift Mika's spirits.

Over the speakers, we hear the pilot say, "We'll be reaching Rome in a few moments. Please take your seats and fasten your seatbelts. We should be landing soon."

The excitement in Brian's eyes intensifies. I have to force myself to not laugh aloud as I look over at Nicholas and see him rolling his eyes in response.

Once we're all fastened in, Tobias says, "So, once we land, we make our way to Virbius' forest in Ariccia? We're gonna need transport."

I hold Virbius' necklace in hand and say, "I'm hoping that won't be necessary by the time we disembark the plane."

Ms. Whiskers jumps onto my lap and curls up into a ball. I pet her, which causes her to purr loudly. I'm suddenly reminded of how much I miss Fenrus. I close my eyes and send him a prayer of love and devotion, asking the goddess to watch over him until I can reach him. When I open my eyes, I see Tobias looking back at me with eyes of love.

"First thing's first." Tobias says.

Everyone looks at Tobias as he closes his eyes and takes a deep breath. I can feel his magic stirring within. A softness envelops the room and green energy slowly emanates from him. Though each person reacts differently to his magics, we each allow his green energy to wash over us. Looking over at Mika, she too has her eyes closed and is emanating a power of her own. It mingles with Tobias', and then overcomes each of us as well. I can tell the magics they are using are a subtle cloaking spell. I close my eyes and follow suit. When the spell is complete, the six of us, including Ms. Whiskers, are hidden under our three individual cloaking spells. The spell changes our appearance, though only slightly, and masks any trace of magic we possess.

Confused, Brian asks, "What did you guys just do?"

Turning to Brian, Tobias says, "We created a multi-layer cloaking spell to mask us from the wolves and witches looking for us. I was afraid it might not work since werewolves are resistant to magic. Thankfully, the spell managed to lock onto our clothing. As long as we wear them, we should be fine."

Continuing Tobias' line of thought, Mika says, "If we change clothes, we'll have to perform the spell again, but we should be good for the time being."

The ingenuity of my fellow coven amazes me. I'm grateful to have them with me.

As the jet begins its descent, I meditate, allowing my magics to recharge. Once we touch ground, I know we'll be our own, and I'm going to need to be as well rested as possible. With my eyes closed, I think about my parents. I have no idea how they're doing. I can see my mother's face in my mind. How I miss her already.

Suddenly, the world around me drops. I feel myself being transported to another location. No longer sitting, I slam my feet onto solid ground and try to balance myself. When I open my eyes, I'm standing in the rose garden back at the Boston compound. Next to me is my mother. She's feeding the fish in the koi pond. Around us, many other wolves are clearing and repairing debris from the earlier battle on the grounds.

Sensing my presence, my mother turns and sees me. She looks slightly confused. "Devin?"

I'm then reminded of the cloaking spell my coven put me under. I nod my head toward her and say, "It's a bit of a disguise."

My mother's eyes light up immediately. "Devin!" she gasps as she throws her arms around me. "It *is* you! You're back!"

I hug her back briefly, but then gently pull away to better face her again.

"It's my necklace, Mom. Virbius strengthened it enough so that I can travel long distances." Looking around, I ask her, "Where's Dad?"

Rubbing my cheek and looking me over, she replies, "Interrogating Jason." She stops and looks around me as well. She asks, "Where's your team?"

"About to land in Rome." I reply. "I've got to get back to them before they get worried. Mom, *please* promise me something. Try to get more of the wolves to pray in the temple. It's only with their prayers in the presence of our gods that the necklace will get stronger. Do you think you can do that?"

With sincerity in her eyes, she says, "Of course." She holds me tightly again and says, "I love you, Devin."

I hug her again. "I love you, too, Mom."

When she finally loosens her hug, I close my eyes and think of my coven on the jet. I focus on the necklace and ask it to send me to them. Just as before, the world around me drops and I feel myself being transported. My feet slam back onto ground, but when I open my eyes, I see that I'm no longer in the Boston garden but back in the jet with the others. The motion of the jet causes me to lose my balance so I grasp onto a nearby chair to stop myself from falling.

Tobias, Mika, and Nicholas already have their seatbelts unfastened and are standing in the cabin, perplexed. Tobias spots me first and rushes over to me.

"Where did you go?" he asks, his voice trembling.

The others surround me, inspecting me to make sure I'm all right.

"The necklace." I say. "It transported me back to Boston. It works!"

Nicholas asks, "So it can take us to Virbius now?"

"No." I reply. "For now it's still single rider only. It doesn't have enough strength, so we're still playing the waiting game."

"Still," Mika says, "that's great news!"

The fasten seatbelts light dings again, signaling us to resume our seats. When I get back to mine I see Ms. Whiskers looking at me fully awake and annoyed.

"Sorry." I tell her. "I'll give you a fair warning next time that happens."

She then moves over to an empty seat, curls up into a ball and feigns sleep.

We land immediately after and begin taxiing over to one of the large private hangers. We each unbuckle our seatbelts and suspiciously eye the outer world viewed through the individual windows. Though dark outside, we see several service personnel doing menial work here and there.

"I don't see anything." Nicholas says.

"Nothing here, either." Mika confirms.

Brian looks suspiciously out of his window. "You sure?"

Nicholas adds, "Yeah. I don't smell wolf or magic here. Still, everyone should stay on guard."

When the jet stops, the pilot and co-pilot emerge from the cockpit soon after. The head pilot says, "We're going to have to refuel before we head back to Boston. Do you have arrangements to return on your own or do you need for us to wait until you're done with whatever it is you need in Rome?"

Tobias lifts his arm toward the two pilots and spreads his fingers. The pilots freeze in place. Mika lifts her arm as well and the two men close their eyes, falling to the floor, unconscious.

Brian asks, "What… What did you two do to them?"

Mika smiles. "They're just resting."

Tobias adds, "And they're now susceptible to suggestion." Tobias kneels down and says into their ears, "You two will wake in five minutes refreshed and content. You will not remember anything about the passengers you transported. You will arrange to fly back to Boston once the jet is refueled. You will tell your employer that everything went fine."

Tobias then stands up and rejoins us. He turns to Brian and says, "Not as flashy as the 'Jedi Mind Trick' Anna gave you last year, but it'll do."

I motion to the various bags lining one side of the jet. "Everyone, gear up. The sooner we're out of here the better."

Mika makes a few clicking sounds to Ms. Whiskers, and she jumps onto Mika's shoulder. The rest of us grab the bags.

Looking out the window again, Nicholas says, "I think I see some officials heading this way. Probably the Visa passport checkers. What should we do?"

"Well," I say, "we may not be able to teleport long distances as a group yet, but we should be able to teleport a few feet." I point to the hanger doorway visible from the window. "There. Mika, Tobias, you know what to do."

They nod in response and lay free hands on Nicholas and Brian's backs. Making sure I make physical contact with them as well, we each close our eyes and focus on our internal magics. I try to tap into the magic of the necklace as well as we imagine the lot of us teleporting to the spot I mentioned. The magic takes hold and the next moment we're all outside. I can see that Brian has a dazed expression, but he quickly shakes it off once he sees the rest of us making for another building across the way.

Whispering loudly, he says, "Hey! Wait up!"

When we get to the next aluminum framed building, we duck behind several stacked crates not yet loaded inside. With our enhanced hearing, we listen as the airport officials knock several times on the jet door.

Nicholas says, "If those two aren't gonna wake for another five minutes, then more security will be arriving. It's not safe here. We need to vacate the vicinity. I think we should…"

Nicholas stops speaking and sniffs the air. He motions us to stay quiet. He then gives the hand gesture to stay put. He fluidly slips out one of the swords on his back and steps away from us, silently blending into the building's shadow. A few moments later, a man wearing the brown Emissary garb the Neuri werewolf clan wore steps out of the hanger. The assassin sniffs the air, then turns the corner toward us and sniffs again. Once he reaches Nicholas' spot, Nicholas grabs him by the hair with one hand and slits the assassin's throat with the other. The others and I instinctively grab for our throats, horrified at what we've just seen. Nicholas gently places the now dead assassin on the ground, and then returns back to us. I'm reminded that although Tobias and I both magically possess all of Nicholas' natural fighting skills, the one thing we lack is his willingness to kill.

Nicholas says, "The European wolves must be keeping tabs on all the air and sea ports. Once that Emissary fails to report in, this place will be swarming with wolves. We need to get out of here fast."

I spot one of the loading trucks not being used and gratefully see that the keys are still in the ignition.

"There!" I say.

We quickly get to the vehicle and squeeze inside. Nicholas takes the wheel and within moments, we're traveling toward one of the service roads leading away from the airport. At the end of the road is a small storage building. It's thankfully deserted but still has several parked cars beside it. Nicholas parks the loading truck we're in, and we make our way to one of the larger vans. Nicholas takes his sword and slides it down the van driver side window. We hear a click and the car's alarm light goes dead. As we pile into the new vehicle, I see

Nicholas finagling several wires underneath the steering wheel. Once the engine starts, I thank the goddess for a successful arrival.

When we get to the city's surface streets, Mika takes out a small stick from her pocket and places it on her hand. She closes her eyes and mutters a few words under her breath. The stick lifts off slightly from her hand and slowly points south. Mika leans forward and extends her hand between the driver and passenger seats. Seeing the motion of the stick, Nicholas nods his head and veers the car southbound.

Rome is bustling with people and lights. I'm amazed at both the old world and modern metropolitan feel the city has. Starbucks coffee houses and McDonalds fast food businesses flank ancient buildings caringly preserved through the ages. Under normal circumstances, I'd be completely excited. We're close to the birthplace of my Italian family after all. My spirit yearns to explore and relish the history around me. Instead, I force myself to steady my goal in mind and carry an apprehensive feeling of the unknown future that lies ahead for my team and me. I look over at Brian and can't help but smile, though. Despite our near brush with death, like earlier, Brian's face clings to the window, eyeing the glitz and glamour of his surroundings. His boyish love of life warms my fearful heart.

We eventually drive onto Via Appia Nuova and the bustling city begins to get smaller and more rural. When we pass a sign announcing the Parco Regionale dei Castelli Romani several kilometers ahead, the necklace around my neck becomes a bit warmer. Somehow, I know that this green area is where we have to go.

"We're getting close," I say.

Mika's stick pointer confirms it. The green forests eventually come into view. I'm brought back to the lush forests from my visit with Virbius earlier. My necklace begins to pulse, the light it emits becoming noticeable. I scan the necklace magically and know it's at full strength. I close my eyes and imagine the van and everyone in it transported into Virbius' domain. The feeling of being transported overtakes me. Within moments, the highway road we are on disappears and a simple dirt path replaces it. Nicholas slams on the breaks, causing all of us to lurch forward.

"What the hell just happened?" Nicholas demands.

"Where are we?" Tobias asks.

"We're here, in Virbius' realm," I say. "The necklace brought us here. It's ready!"

Up ahead, we see ghost figures of park rangers removing a fallen tree trunk in the road. The truck they use is ghostlike as well. We all look at each other in confusion.

Keeping his eyes on the ghosts, Nicholas says, "Stay here."

Nicholas puts the van in park and gingerly steps out with the engine still running. He slowly moves over to the working park rangers. They act as if they don't even see us, instead going about their business. When he reaches them, Nicholas stretches his arm out to touch them but his hand only grasps open air. He then tries to touch their work truck, but the same response happens. He looks back at us confused.

The rest of us get out of the van and join Nicholas. Just as before, when we try to touch the oblivious workers our hands moves easily through them.

"Are they ghosts?" Mika asks.

A familiar voice says, "In a way."

We all look over to the direction the voice came from. Standing there is Fallon, the satyr I met from before. Nicholas immediately removes the two swords from his back. I put my arm across Nicholas' chest.

"You can put the swords away. This is Fallon. I met him earlier in my spirit travels. He's the one who introduced me to Virbius."

Slowly, Nicholas replaces his swords, eyeing Fallon suspiciously. Tobias and Mika bow their heads slightly toward Fallon as a sign of greeting while Brian simply looks opened mouthed at the satyr. Ms. Whiskers hisses at the creature, unsure of what to make of him.

Fallon sneers at Ms. Whiskers, as if insulted. "As I was saying," Fallon continues, "these humans are in a way ghosts. Our forest occupies the same space as the human forest these men care for. We exist on two different planes. Virbius has allowed us to be aware of what happens to the earthbound space the humans roam, but they have no inkling of our existence. It's been this way for millennia." Fallon looks at Brian and adds, "Until now that is."

Finished with their work, the human park rangers get into their truck and drive off. We all stare as the truck first drives through us, then through our van parked several yards away and into the darkness.

"Come." Fallon climbs into the van. "The sun will be up soon. Virbius will be waiting for us."

We all get back into the van, unsure of what just happened. Ms. Whiskers immediately jumps into my lap, suspicious of Fallon. I can see the hairs on the back of Nicholas' neck are at attention, but he drives us further along the dirt pathway per Fallon's direction.

After a few minutes, Brian says, "Okay, I can't hold it in anymore. I just gotta ask...you're a satyr, right?"

With an eyebrow raised, Fallon says, "Keen observation. Yes, I'm a satyr."

Brian gushes, "Wow, that is, like, so cool. Are there more of you here?"

"Yes," Fallon politely responds. "Our numbers are a shadow of what they once were when we still lived among men, but there is still a small tribe living in these woods."

Continuing his line of questioning, Brian asks, "So why aren't there any girl satyr?"

With a shocked look on his face, Fallon asks, "What?"

"In the pictures and stories," Brian continues, "I've never once seen a girl satyr. Do they exist? Do any live among you?"

159

Fallon leans back to better look at Brian. "You sure ask a lot of questions for a human."

"So do they?" Brian asks again.

Looking back toward the windshield ahead, Fallon says, "No. We're male only. Our mothers were nanny goats once blessed by the all-father Pan. You, wolf assassin, turn the chariot to the right at the next break in the path."

I can tell Nicholas is annoyed at being given orders by a complete stranger, but he complies.

"Pan!" Brian exclaims. "I forgot all about him. He was your leader thousands of years ago, right? Is he here too?"

All color fades from Fallon's face. He slowly turns to Brian and says, "The Great God Pan was murdered thousands of years ago. It was a horrific time for all satyr. We do not speak of it. I would ask that you respect that and ask no more questions where he is concerned."

Brian puts up his hands and says, "Sorry, my bad. It won't happen again."

"Fallon," I ask, "what do you know about goblins? Are any in Virbius' care here?"

Confused again, Fallon responds, "No. Goblins are dark creatures. They're much too dangerous and vicious. Virbius only extends his protection to peaceful beings. Why do you ask?"

Memories of the previous battle against the Benandanti witches come to mind.

"Evil witches, or casters as you know them, have an alliance with a group of goblins. They stole something precious to me. I can battle fellow witches, but I know almost nothing about goblins other than they fear silver. I need to know more about them before I attempt to get back what they stole from me."

Fallon ponders inwardly before saying, "Goblins are powerful magic users in their own right. They are earth born demons. As such, they can travel at will between the netherworld and the mortal world.

They crave souls. It is the only thing that can sustain them. If a group of casters is in league with them, then whatever arrangement they've made between themselves can't be good. I don't know what item they've taken from you, Devin Toxotis, but whatever it is, it would mean death to try to retrieve it."

My heart sinks upon hearing his words. I feel both Tobias and Mika rubbing my shoulders in sympathy.

Ahead of us, I can now see the clearing containing the altar to Virbius. Nicholas stops the van and turns off the engine. As we all climb out, I notice Brian rifling through one of his bags before joining us at the altar. Tobias, Mika, and I each take a piece of nature in hand. I take a leaf and retrieve more water from the nearby brook. Tobias grabs a handful of earth. Mika takes the stick she held earlier and sets it aflame. We then place each of our offerings on the altar, kneel, and begin our prayers of respect and observance.

Once our prayers are over, a breeze strokes my face, and I sense a new presence behind us. My coven and I stand and turn to face our newest arrival. As before, the god Virbius is now standing in the clearing. Somehow, he appears to be even stronger, more beautiful, and more powerful than before.

"Greetings," the forest god says. "I welcome you all to my realm."

We all bow our heads, all of us, that is, except for Brian who instead begins searching through his pockets. When he finds what he is looking for, he removes it and takes several steps toward Virbius. He then gets down on one knee and holds up the object before the deity.

"To the forest god Virbius," Brian says, "I offer you this token of my humble respect. I was told it once belonged to your mother's people. I hope you find my gift an acceptable offering."

All eyes then focus onto what's in Brian's hands. There, plain as day, I see a small dagger. The blade is a bit dull and the leather handle is tattered, but it still has a simple beauty all its own. Virbius takes the dagger from Brian and inspects it. I see a grin beginning to form on his face. A few moments later, this grin becomes one of the most dazzling smiles I've ever seen. Virbius wraps his arms around Brian's shoulders and lifts him off the ground. Though a bit taken aback by being manhandled, Brian sheepishly smiles back at Virbius, happy at the god's non-anger.

After putting Brian down, Virbius says to him, "This has to be one of the best gifts given to me in many centuries. Thank you. I can sense your apprehension as to whether it's an authentic piece. I assure you, it is. These were given to dignitaries on ambassadorial events. They're the only Amazonian weapons men, outside of myself, were allowed to possess."

Virbius holds the dagger up into the air, and it begins to shimmer. We all watch as the blade's dullness becomes sharp and polished. The tattered handle refits itself and becomes rejuvenated. A small gem then appears at the handle's base where once a small hole had been.

Ms. Whisker's face becomes enraptured as I hear her say, "So many beautiful sparkles!"

Virbius hands the dagger back to Brian and says, "I'm sure as a collector you'd like to hold onto this a while longer. With my compliments."

Brian takes the dagger back and nods. Virbius then looks down at Ms. Whiskers, almost as if he had heard her speak. He then gets down on one knee and motions for the small feline to come to him. She hesitates at first, but then complies with his request. When she reaches him, Virbius begins petting the cat with one hand and creating magical lights with the other. Ms. Whiskers' purring becomes noticeable as she begins batting at the lights happily.

Virbius looks up to me. "When I was still mortal, I had several cats of my own. It's been so long since I've seen one."

The forest god then stands, leaving the magical lights behind for Ms. Whiskers to continue to play with. He then comes over and reaches for my necklace. Holding it in hand, he smiles again and says, "We were successful. I'm glad. Come, you all must be famished. You must eat and rest a bit before you go off on your next trial."

My thoughts go out to the many European wolves scared and in hiding. I'm fearful that some may be being killed at this very moment with no one to help them. I want to leave to try to help as many as I can, but looking at my team beside me, I know they'll need as much rest and as many resources as possible. Besides, I need more insight from Virbius on the best strategy to take.

Fallon leads our group to a side path. Several yards into it, we find a cottage. Fallon opens the door, and we all file in one by one. I'm surprised by the large interior once inside. The home must be enchanted, as the interior size is three times as large as what the outside frame implies. A large hearth, lit and toasty, sits to the right with a wall of books beside it. In front is a cozy sitting area with several plush chairs draped with the most beautiful blankets. Wooden stairs lead upward to several open rooms. To the left of us is an eating area, complete with a large table, a feast of foods spread out upon it, and chairs. Plates and goblets surround the cornucopia of food as if protecting the bountiful delights from falling off the table itself.

Fallon motions for us to take a seat of our choice at the table. We comply. Virbius arrives last and takes a seat at the head of the table, next to me. Fallon then sits at the other end of the table, opposite Virbius. Looking at the food before us, I notice that it is completely vegetarian. Not one piece of meat is displayed.

Perhaps reading my mind, Virbius says to everyone, "You'll find that in my realm, we consider all life precious. We do not kill here. Instead, we live off the land. Fallon here is quite the food preparer. I dare you to find anything as scrumptious in the mortal world as the food he's prepared before you."

Fallon bows his head to Virbius.

I say to Virbius and Fallon, "On behalf of my kinsmen, I thank you for your kind hospitality."

Virbius motions to the food on the table. Everyone takes several items and places them on his or her plates. I put down a saucer and fill it with water for Ms. Whiskers. Brian walks over to her, too, takes out a sandwich from his pocket, and removes the many layers of meat from it. He then gives it to Ms. Whiskers who eats it happily. I thank him for his generosity. He smiles and takes his seat.

As we eat, I tell Virbius about the mafia attack, the later wolf invasion, and more detail about our battle with the Benandanti coven. He arches an eyebrow once he hears about their alliance with goblins. Seeing his reaction, I tell him that Fallon had mentioned that goblins were earth-born demons and not allowed in his realm. I then go on to tell him about our previous battle with my old coven and how they too had foolishly used demons as allies.

When my story is over, Virbius leans back in his chair and ponders a bit.

"The inclusion of goblins and demons," Virbius says, "this deeply troubles me. Nature typically creates a balance between the light and the dark. Casters should know this. That they would make agreements with such dark creatures, thus giving darkness added power, is dangerous. It tips the scale in their favor. This is a bad omen. I will have to confer with my fellow gods."

The look on Mika's face lightens. Virbius notices her happy demeanor and smiles.

He says to her, "You are a follower of Artemis, like myself. I can sense the kinship. It is because of you that she and her brother are part of your people's pantheon, is it not?"

Mika blushes and says, "Yes. I grew up on stories from ancient cultures like Egypt, Greece, Scandinavia, and the East. Of all the stories though, my heart always came back to the Olympian twins.

Something about them fascinated me. Compared to the other gods, they were young but still powerful. The held grace and respect. I admire that."

Virbius says, "In my time, Artemis was a great power on her own. When I was still human, I was able to travel to her shrine in Turkey. It was one of the most amazing temples you could ever have imagined. It's beauty and size rivaled that of even Zeus himself. It broke my heart to learn that mortal men destroyed it long ago. Had I the power to leave this forest, I would recreate it for her. I owe Artemis my life."

"Were you a follower of her brother Apollo, too?" Mika asks.

"I held respect for him," Virbius answers, "but no, I wasn't one of his supplicants." He then turns to Tobias and says, "And your ties are with the Earth Mother Gaea, like Devin, yes?"

"Yeah," Tobias answers. "So were my parents before me. They weren't as powerful of casters as we are, but they taught me the love and respect of Gaea at an early age."

Virbius says, "Our dominion may be similar, but my godly power is but a shadow of her great might. Gods fall in and out of favor over time, but her devotion has never diminished since time immemorial. In one way or another, man has always treasured her. Few gods can say the same."

I notice Virbius look over at Nicholas. Nicholas looks up, sensing he is being watched. The two of them lock eyes for a moment. Virbius looks as if he is searching for something whereas Nicholas' defiant pose says that he is not to be trifled with. Virbius eventually smiles.

"I'm not a witch like them," Nicholas finally says. "I'm just a soldier, nothing more."

Virbius leans toward Nicholas and says, "You sell yourself short, my friend. You are far more than just that. There's passion in you. Loyalty. Honor. Those things carry a heavy weight with me. You wolves worship the goddess Hecate, correct?"

Nicholas takes a piece of bread and uses it to sop up some sauce on his plate. "Yes," he finally says.

Seeing how uninterested Nicholas is in conversation, I begin telling Virbius the story of how the wolves were first created as a curse by Zeus, then of how the goddess Hecate stepped in to aid the wolves in their time of need. The look on Nicholas' face tells me that he is uneasy with my revealing to Virbius, Fallon, and Brian the wolves' long held secret origins, but as his Archon, I know he is not about to question me in front of an audience.

When I finish my story, Virbius says, "Hecate is right. The rivalry your people have over territory brings dishonor to the history of your kind. I understand better the difficult mission you have in front of you, Devin Toxotis."

By now, we are all satisfied with dinner. Fallon sees this and begins removing our plates, motioning us to move into the living room area. Virbius follows us in but doesn't take a seat.

The forest god addresses us. "I know we have a lot to discuss, but I must attend to something first. Rest, and I will return as soon as I am able."

With that, he disappears, leaving my team to ourselves again.

Brian says, "Boy, people come and go so quickly here."

Tobias smirks. "I caught that *Wizard of Oz* reference."

Virbius' absence confuses me as I was hoping to get his advice on a strategy for our rescue mission. I'm disappointed and at a loss for words. Just then, Brian grabs one of his bags and brings it into the middle of our area. We all look at him, now interested in what he has to show us.

Pawing through the bag, Brian says, "I didn't have a lot of time to plan out what to bring, so this is what we have to work with."

Brian takes out a small, bronze staff. As he holds it up, the metallic coating shines in the morning light now streaming through the window. He flicks the staff a couple times and spikes erupt from the top part of the mace. He flicks it again and the spikes retract.

"This," Brian says, "is a relic from the Middle Ages. The religious authority created it to torture heretics."

Nicholas takes it, flicking it in the air to master the weapon's spike release. Brian goes back into his bag and pulls out a medallion. The blue and white colors are reminiscent of the Turkish Nazar amulets said to ward off evil. I look it over. It's old, far older than I imagined.

Brian says, "One of my clients in Turkey sent this to me. He said it was a powerful charm, one that his family had had for many generations. Supposedly, it has a special talent only ones with 'the gift' can see. I really didn't know what he meant by 'gift,' but I thought one of you might be able to figure it out."

Aside from its age, I don't notice anything especially unique about the medallion. I will for my internal magics to fill my being. With my now magically amplified eyes, I look again at the medallion. Still nothing. I hold it in hand and close my eyes. I startle myself. The moment my eyes close, I feel as if they are still open. Only the room suddenly shifts somehow. Instead of seeing what was in front of me, my vision allows me to see Fallon in the kitchen behind me washing the plates we just ate from. When I open my eyes again, I no longer see Fallon but my team as before.

Everyone's faces tell me that he or she is eager and curious to know what it is I just experienced. Instead of telling them, I pass the medallion to Mika. She goes through the same motions I just did, trying to figure out what it can do. When her body jerks a bit, I know she's discovered the trick. She opens her eyes, smiles, and passes it to Tobias. Once he discovers its secret as well, he passes it to Nicholas. Nicholas, unfortunately, isn't able to access magic and thus misses the medallion's ability completely. He looks at it like it's some worthless toy and tosses it back to me.

"So, what does that doohickey do after all?" Nicholas asks.

Mika says, "It lets you see what is happening behind you. It must be a witch's totem because it seems to only work for magic users."

"Witch's totem?" Nicholas asks again.

Brian answers, "They're special items specifically attuned for magical use. Witches have been collecting and using them for hundreds of years. Or, at least, that's what my books say. I never knew that's what this was."

Tobias says, "Anna's necklace was a witch's totem, just like the rest of the jewelry of Bastet. Devin's necklace is now a totem as well."

"Which reminds me." Brian says. He reaches into the bag and pulls out a leather bracelet. He tosses it to me. It's the same band I gave him last year to help him hide from San Francisco witches trying to locate him magically.

"But…," I'm stopped by the sight of Brian holding his hand up.

"It's yours," he says. "The witches looking for me are long gone, but yours aren't. If the Benandanti are teaming up with the European wolves then you're gonna need that way more than I do."

I'm humbled by his generosity. "Thanks, Brian." I say.

Brian nods his head toward me and continues looking through his bag. Just before he pulls his next item out, my magical senses go into overload. A massive spike in power is released somewhere in the forest outside. The amount of magic makes me weary, and I stumble a bit before finding my balance. Looking up, I see Tobias and Mika feel it, too.

With deep concern, Nicholas asks, "What is it?"

"Something in the forest," Tobias says. "I've never felt that much magic before."

Fallon comes out of the kitchen. "I sense something, too. Do you think it's Virbius?"

Mika says, "Virbius doesn't have that level of magic. We need to see what it is. We need to make sure Virbius is all right."

A look of fear comes across Fallon's face. "If something happens to Virbius, then we're all exposed. We won't be able to survive in modern man's world."

"That won't happen," I say. "Come. We're following the magic spike to its source."

Nicholas locks his hand on my shoulder.

"Archon," he says, "it could be dangerous. What if the Benandanti and the European wolves found us here? We'll be slaughtered."

I gently take Nicholas' hand off my shoulder, resting it back on his chest. I softly say to him, "Without Virbius, we have no place to house the European wolves on the run. He and his people need our protection, too. Do you understand?"

Nicholas looks at me a moment. I see a connection to my words in his face. Taking a step back, Nicholas flicks Brian's mace in the air, releasing its spikes.

"I do," He says. Walking to the front door, Nicholas opens it and says, "Lead the way."

Walking in front of the house, my fellow witches and I inhale. Once we sense where the magic is coming from, the three of us say as one, "There" pointing to our destination.

Tobias, Mika, Nicholas, and I remove our shoes and put them in our packs. We then begin shifting around the items in our clothing. Noticing this, Brian asks, "What are you doing?"

Nicholas says, "We'll travel faster in our full wolf forms."

Scratching his head, Brian says, "But your clothes…"

Mika says, "We've learned since being turned that modern day werewolves have adapted to the whole 'torn clothes' thing over the years."

Grabbing the sleeve to her top, Mika pulls at it, showing how easily it stretches and snaps back to its original shape. Brian lifts his eyebrows in recognition.

When all items are adjusted, the four of us begin our change. I call to that wild part of myself and will it to come forth. My body begins growing, my limbs changing. Fur begins to grow out of every pore on my body. I can feel my face elongate outwards. My mouth fills with sharp canine teeth. My hands become large, savage claws. My new wolf vision becomes sharper than before. My clothing expands to form fit to my new exterior snugly. A sensation of invincible energy overcomes my body. When I feel myself completely transformed, I howl my pleasure into the morning air. Soon I hear more wolf howls beside me. I look around myself and see that the others have completed their change as well.

I then look over to Brian. Complete shock and fear fills his face. He seems frozen. Terror fills the air around him. I hadn't thought about how he would react to our transformation, and now feel badly for him.

I go down on all fours and nudge him with my nose. I then lick him on his cheek, saying as best as I can in my full beast form, "Snap out of it, will ya? We need you in the right frame of mind."

Brian shakily wipes away the wolf slobber from his cheek.

"I, uh, never saw anything like that before. It's…pretty freakin' scary."

Tobias gets on all fours as well and walks over to us. "You'll be fine," he says in his gravelly wolf voice. "You'll be safe with us. We'll protect you."

Tobias then lowers himself to the ground, inviting Brian to get onto his back. Brian looks unsure.

Seeing his apprehension, I say, "We need to get to the source of the magic. Get on."

Brian closes his eyes and gingerly climbs onto Tobias, making sure to lean his chest over the two swords already affixed to the wolf beast's back. Ms. Whiskers climbs up with him, nosing into Brian's stomach. He lifts his shirt, allowing Ms. Whiskers to get under it. Once she's comfortable, he tucks the front of his shirt into his pants, snuggly pinning the feline in place.

With his eyes still closed, under his breath I hear Brian say, "I thought they were gonna be big wolves like in *True Blood* or the *Twilight* movies, not the scary killer looking were-beasts from the slasher films."

I chuckle to myself as Tobias raises himself off the ground. I then see Fallon emerge from the cottage's front entrance. He is brandishing a bow and has several arrows affixed to his back. He sees us, takes a deep breath, and says, "May Virbius watch and protect us."

Nicholas asks him, "Are you fast?"

Fallon guffaws and says, "Satyrs are as fast as any wolf. Let's go."

I look at my team to see if they are ready. Everyone is now on all fours and nodding his or her heads. And, just like that we take off through the woods. I must say, werewolves move extremely fast. I keep looking back at Fallon and Brian to make sure they are still with us. Fallon runs along side of us with ease. With Brian, however, I notice that his knuckles are bone white and that he's holding on to Tobias' fur for dear life.

We pass several other forest creatures during our travel. A male and female Cyclops hold on to each other, unsure of what to make of us as we pass. A flock of pixies scatter out of a large bush as we speed past it also. Further still, we pass a small lake where a unicorn drinks water. It stops to look up to see who is running by.

I can feel the magic ahead becoming stronger. I keep my guard up for any surprise attack. I pray to my gods that Virbius and his people stay safe.

From alongside us, more satyr appear from the forest. They each hold bows and arrows as they match our speed, headed in the same direction. I sense no animosity from them, but rather that they are there to help. I'm thankful for their assist and put more energy into the run.

Up ahead, I see white light breaking through the trees. We're here. As we leap into the clearing, we growl to make our presence known. I snarl and look around, expecting to see either our enemies or Virbius in battle. We find neither. Instead of enemies, we see our most powerful allies standing together.

In the clearing, I see our entire Pantheon. Sitting upon her earth-formed throne is the earth goddess Gaea, old and wise. Her daughter Hecate rests her hand on the back of the throne, eyeing our arrival. The golden shift dress and flaming red hair that forms a gorgeous mane around her face displays a great power all her own. Virbius is next to them, strong and beautiful. Two similar looking gods stand at the other side of the throne, a male and female. The male's hair is light blond, and almost seems to shine in the sun. The female has red hair braided to one side. She is dressed in battle gear and is holding the most beautiful bow I have ever seen. These two must be the twin Olympian gods, Artemis and Apollo.

Standing in front of our gods is a wizened, old man. He is leaning heavily on a large wooden staff. He is bare-chested and bare-footed, but wears a long tattered skirt that goes down to his ankles.

The old man weakly smiles at us and says, "Welcome to The Old World, young ones."

Chapter 7
MEETING OF THE GODS

I'M SPEECHLESS AS I BOW LOW IN RESPECT BEFORE THE GODLY pantheon. The other wolves do the same. Brian takes advantage of the moment to slide off Tobias and back onto solid ground. He then untucks his shirt, allowing Ms. Whiskers to jump to the ground as well. She takes in her surroundings and eyes everyone suspiciously, staying close to my ankles.

I begin shifting back to my human form, signaling the others to do the same. When I feel myself fully human again, I bow slightly to the assembled gods and say, "Please forgive our intrusion. We thought…"

The goddess Gaea chuckles and says, "You thought one of your gods was in danger and came to assist him. My boy, your bravery rivals that of Hercules himself."

The look on Virbius' face sours at the mention of the demi-god. Gaea notices, nodding her head to him in respect before turning back to my team and me.

Virbius steps beside the old man in front, saying, "As you can see, I am quite all right. I am flattered you would put yourself in danger for my safety, though. You bring honor to all of us here."

Virbius places his hands on the shoulders of the old man. "This," Virbius says, "is the god Priapus. He's lived in this forest with us for millennia."

The old man nods in our direction, then says, "I am pleased to meet you all. I've heard quite a bit about you from my companions here. My boy, you and your clan have a huge task ahead of you. It brings me great pleasure to be able to see the faces of our champions first hand before I say goodbye."

Tobias speaks up, asking, "Goodbye?"

Priapus smiles faintly. "Yes. My time is ending. It happens for some of us. I am giving Virbius the only gift I have left in me. I'm giving him the remaining traces of my godhood."

"I don't understand," I say, confused at the entire situation.

Gaea explains. "This meeting you've come upon is a requiem for one of our own. Priapus was once the god of gardens and fertility. His domain carried through Greece, Italy, and Turkey. That, unfortunately, was a long time ago. People and things have changed since then. We know of the impending god war. We are here to marshal our strength for the battle ahead."

Continuing where she left off, Priapus says, "I wouldn't last a minute in a war against other gods for, you see, I'm a ghost of what I once was. This forest was the only thing giving me any vestige of life. For me, obliteration will come with either a swift godly attack or transcendence into the void. I choose the latter." Turning to Virbius, Priapus says in a tender voice, "May what little life I have left bless yours with the added strength you will need."

Priapus then embraces Virbius, dropping his walking staff onto the ground.

Virbius returns the hug, saying, "You will live on in my heart, brother."

At that, the physical form that comprises the god Priapus begins to discorporate into bright white lights that then begin to swirl around Virbius, finally absorbing themselves into him. Virbius gains a few inches in height, and his muscle tone becomes more robust than before. Virbius lifts slightly off the ground with his arms stretched far beside him in fists. He lifts his chin into the air as a single tear falls from his closed eyes.

"It is done," he whispers as he slowly descends back onto solid ground.

Continuing his decent, Virbius allows his knees to ease onto the dirt below, grasping the rich earth with his hands. Green energy pulses between him and the ground below. He rests a moment before standing tall again. When he is upright, he stretches his hand toward Priapus' staff, still on the ground. It moves toward Virbius, changing shape in mid-air. The now swirling staff surrounds Virbius and becomes new godly visages. Whereas Virbius before wore only cloth pants, he now wears finely tailored green clothing under brown wooden armor. The other gods nod their heads in approval.

Turing to us, Virbius says, "Let word be spread, the green god Priapus is now gone forever."

The Satyr around us sniff back their tears. The tallest of them says, "As with the Great God Pan, we will spread the word to the others. Long live Virbius, protector of us all."

All of the Satyr, including Fallon, spread out in various directions, quickly exiting the clearing. I look on at Virbius, saddened by the look on his face at the loss of his comrade.

Artemis says, "Don't be sad, young ones. Priapus gave Virbius the strength to continue his reign. It is the most selfless gift any of us gods could give."

Apollo says, "My sister speaks truth. Just as our father passed his strength into us when he grew tired of his relic status, you will find that a piece of their souls will always live on in a new form."

Hecate steps forward, eyeing Ms. Whiskers. Her intent stare on my cat changes my feeling of sadness to one of protection. I pick up Ms. Whiskers and hold her in my arms. Hecate sees my defensive pose, stops, and smiles.

"Now that Virbius' gift has been given," she says, "I believe we need to address the spy among us." Hecate points to Ms. Whiskers. "There."

Alarms go off in my head. What is she talking about? Do they plan to do something to my cat? Flashes of the Benandanti kidnapping Fenrus comes to mind, as I hold onto Ms. Whiskers even tighter.

"What spy?" I ask defensively.

I feel Nicholas get closer to my right, and Tobias closer to my left. Mika gets in front of Brian, ready to shield him from whatever might happen next. Gaea sees our agitation and gives me a look of comfort. She then looks at Ms. Whiskers and says calmly, "We know you are there. Reveal yourself."

I feel energy emanating from the cat in my arms. Still afraid for her safety, I continue to hold onto her despite my confusion. The energy then transfers from Ms. Whiskers to an area in front of the pantheon. I look down at Ms. Whiskers to see if she is all right. Her big green eyes tell me that she is just as confused as I am. The energy first takes a humanoid shape, and then begins to solidify. In moments, a cat-headed woman stands before us, clad in ancient Egyptian clothing. All my senses tell me that it is the goddess Bastet.

"Greetings from the remnant halls of my people." Bastet's voice is velvety, sensual, and traced in an Egyptian accent. It is as sleek and graceful as a feline.

"Why are you here?" Hecate asks bluntly.

"I am here to ask for your help. My daughter Sekhmet has returned from her exile. She is gathering gods to aid her in her bloody retribution against me and my fellow gods." Bastet's large cat eyes look at each god before her, scanning them for any sense of compassion. "I fear what may happen should she gather enough strength behind her."

Apollo says, "You are not of our realm. What do we care if an outer pantheon falls?"

Turning to him, Bastet says, "They will not stop at just my pantheon. Once they are done with us, they will continue their slaughter across all faiths until they alone reign supreme. These gods...they are desperate. They are forgotten gods from patchwork pantheons from all across the globe. My daughter has made them many promises in return for their servitude."

Virbius says, "The cat goddess is right. Her daughter has visited me here in this grove. She enticed me to join her. She promised me a return to the old ways if I agreed to follow her. I refused."

Mika speaks up, saying to Bastet, "Your daughter is in possession of my grandmomma, Anna Geist. She is a priestess of yours."

Sympathetically, Bastet says, "Yes. Anna was one of my most faithful followers. The majority of my strength comes from my children." Bastet motions to Ms. Whiskers who bows. Bastet smiles weakly, nodding her head. "Human followers are rare, however, especially ones as powerful as Anna. It saddens me greatly to know Sekhmet has one such as her captive."

Mika pleads, "We mean to rescue her. She's not in control of what she's doing. Please, is there any way we can separate her from your daughter?"

Bastet says, "My daughter has been powerless for thousands of years. She is still weak and requires a host body until she is strong enough to sustain a form of her own. She will not give Anna up easily."

Mika asks again, "But *is* there a way?"

Turning back to the pantheon, Bastet says, "With their help, it may be a possible."

Gaea asks, "What did you do to this Sekhmet to enrage her? Why was she banished?"

Bastet replies, "Long ago, I gave birth to two godlings. They were Maahes and Sekhmet, twin children of Bastet and Ra. They were to be fierce protectors for our pantheon and of our followers. While Maahes stayed true to his path, Sekhmet did not. She relished in her station, bringing about many needless wars. Innocent blood was spilt in her name. I did the only thing I could to stop her bloodshed. As was done to the god Osiris, I dismembered her and scattered her remains across the globe. I hid them in my sacred jewelry, giving them to my faithful priestesses, making them promise that none of the pieces would ever be rejoined again."

"It's true then," Tobias says. "When Anna's necklace was rejoined with the bracelet last year, it rejuvenated the goddess Sekhmet. That must be why Anna left us in San Francisco with no warning."

Continuing his train of thought, I say, "And we've since seen her wearing the Ring of Bastet as well. All three pieces are joined together again."

Artemis asks Bastet, "Your daughter, she is a war goddess?"

"Yes," Bastet answers.

Apollo asks, "And what of your son, Maahes? Is he still part of your pantheon? Perhaps he can help tame your daughter."

Bastet gets a look of sadness. "My son is no more. His followers died thousands of years ago. His will to live died with them. All that is left of him is here." Bastet places her hand on her heart and closes her eyes.

Gaea rises from her throne and walks over to the Egyptian

goddess. She embraces her, which surprises Bastet. Feeling no animosity from Gaea, Bastet holds Gaea in return.

After a few moments, Gaea gently pulls away from Bastet and says, "Aside from earthly domain, my station is that of mother. I feel your pain. I, too, have seen my children wage needless war against each other and perish over foolish notions. It was too much for me to bear, so I retreated into myself for many years in grief. You are ancient and wise, like me. Perhaps our kinship will benefit our survival. Let us speak together to plan our strategies, away from prying eyes."

The other gods nod.

"Before we go," Virbius says, "we must first address our subjects on their task ahead of them."

The line of gods all turn to our direction. A feeling of intimidation floods into me.

Virbius smiles kindly, saying, "Saving your people is a huge undertaking. We must reserve our strength for the war ahead, but we won't let you go racing into danger unaided. Powerful casters as you are, you will still need our gifts to ensure your safety and success."

The Olympian gods gather and hold hands. An unearthly glow encases them as they stare at us intently. I turn to see that Tobias and Mika's devotional amulets are rising off their chests. They separate from the chains holding them and move toward the gods. They then stop mid-way and begin to change.

The amulets grow several times larger than their normal size. Tobias' amulet stretches outward and begins to form wings. The center of the amulet becomes fuller, forming the body of a falcon. When fully formed, it materializes feathers, talons, a beak, and the darkest eyes imaginable. It shrieks into the air, making its presence known. It then flaps its wings, circling the clearing several times. Tobias stretches out his arm, signaling the falcon to come to him. It does.

Mika's amulet similarly begins to morph. It develops fluffy shaped legs and feet, a short body and pointed ears. White fur begins to appear on the form, and soon a snowy bobcat takes shape. It leaps onto the ground and looks back at Mika with its deep orange eyes. Mika is in tears as she squats to the ground, allowing the bobcat to run into her arms. Tobias watches Mika and pets his falcon proudly.

Tobias and Mika then look up at their gods and in unison say, "Thank you."

Their now-broken chains solidify back into a full circle, gaining the same unearthly glow the gods have. The gods then look toward Nicholas and the glow develops around his neck as well. Once the godly spell is complete, I see that the three of them now have necklaces around their necks similar to mine.

Hecate says, "The witches now all have companions assigned to them to augment their casting strength. The wolves as a whole now also have the ability to travel where needed in the blink of an eye. Use these gifts well, my subjects, for we will not be able to aid you again for some time. The remainder of our strength will be needed for battle."

Bastet steps forward and asks, "What about this one?" motioning to Brian.

Virbius says, "A guest of our followers. He holds no true ties to any of us."

Confused, Bastet says, "But he aids your wolves despite his mortal status?"

Virbius nods his head. Bastet look on at Brian.

"It seems to me," Bastet says, "that his devotion to your cause should not go unaided."

Bastet's eyes glow dramatically. Still in my arms, I notice that Ms. Whisker's eyes glow just as intensely in response.

When both eyes return to their normal pitch, Bastet says to Brian, "Keep my subject close to you at all times. She will protect you if needed."

Completely dumbfounded at everything occurring, Brian nods his head, letting out a weak, "Uh-huh."

Gaea then says to us, "Safety be yours on your mission. We will meet again."

The gods then all disappear in the blink of an eye. The bright white energy they held before begins to fade as the forest resumes its normal luster.

Feeling Ms. Whiskers wrangling in my arms, I put her down and walk over to Tobias and Mika. I look at their new familiars, and then back into my family's eyes. I smile largely as I can feel tears forming in my own eyes. Still holding his falcon, Tobias opens his free arm widely. I close in and embrace him, kissing him on the neck in the process. I then go to Mika and hug her as well.

"What are their names?" I ask them while wiping away a tear with the side of my hand.

Tobias and Mika each look at their familiars, and I know an unspoken conversation is happening between them.

Tobias finally says, "My familiar's name is Hadrian."

I nod my head to the bird, to which he nods his head back.

Mika says, "Her name is Fydan."

Ms. Whiskers cautiously approaches Fydan, finally touching noses with her. They then begin chasing each other around the wooded clearing. At one point, I can faintly hear Ms. Whiskers say, "So many sparkles!"

Tobias and Mika suddenly look at each other in recognition.

"Did you hear that?" Mika asks.

Tobias smiles. "Yeah, I did!"

Scratching his head, Nicholas asks, "Hear what?"

I turn to Nicholas and say, "I think Mika and Tobias can finally hear cat speech."

"Wait," Brian says. "So they're like your telepathic dog? You guys can mentally communicate with these animals?"

The mention of Fenrus brings a shroud of sadness to me. Happy as I am at the generous gifts Tobias and Mika were given, seeing their familiars now also reminds me of my own familiar and how confused and alone he must be.

Tobias flings his arm upwards, letting Hadrian once again glide in the air above us. He comes over to me and says, "We'll get Fenrus back. I promise."

Looking at him, I ask, "How did you…"

Smiling sweetly, Tobias says, "I just know." Embracing me, my heart softens again at the amount of love I know he has for me.

I lean into his hug and say, "Thank you." Still holding Tobias, I look over at Mika and say, "And we'll help get Anna back too. I promise."

Mika smiles at me warmly. "I know." she says. "I've always had faith that you'd try."

Looking over at Nicholas, I can see he is confused at the necklace now around his neck. He grabs at it as if he's unsure if he likes it or not. Releasing my hold with Tobias, I begin to walk over to Nicholas when suddenly he disappears. I hear a gasp behind me, so I turn around. I then see Nicholas standing at the opposite edge of the clearing with a perplexed look.

"Did you see," Nicholas begins to say, and then disappears again, only to rematerialize a couple feet in front of me. His eyes become large as he tries to gain his balance. I reach out and grab him before he can fall backwards.

"The necklaces…," Mika says. "They work!"

Mika touches her own necklace with one hand and closes her eyes. She too disappears and reappears at the opposite end of the clearing. I look over at Tobias. He tests his necklace as well and disappears from the clearing altogether. A few moments later, he reappears with snow on the top of his head and shoulders.

"Where did you go?" I ask him.

Smiling, he says, "To the Swiss Alps."

"Blessed be." I say, sending our gods a brief silent prayer of thanks.

Brian runs over and says, "Whoa! That's like the coolest thing ever! Too bad your bosses didn't give me one."

I say to him, "They're not our bosses. They're our gods. And according to Bastet, you have a personal protector of your own, right over there."

I point to Ms. Whiskers, who is now rolling around with Fydan in a playful wrestling match. Brian looks at Ms. Whiskers, then at me. His expression tells me that he isn't impressed.

"So, what now?" Nicholas asks.

I look at him and say loudly so that everyone can hear me, "Now we do what we came here to do. Now we go save our people."

"But we still don't have a plan," Tobias says.

Fydan stops playing with Ms. Whiskers and looks at the lot of us. She sits regally, puffing her chest out with pride. I hear her voice in my head say, "The gods gave us their plan. You are to spread out and transport as many of your kind as possible to this forest. They will be protected from the outside world here."

By the looks of wonder on Nicholas and Brian's faces, I can tell they, too, received Fydan's mental communication.

Mika crouches down, addressing Fydan. "But, how will we know where they are? How will we even recognize them?"

Hadrian lands on a tree branch. I then hear his voice say, "The necklaces will guide you to them. Focus on your people. See them in your mind. The necklaces will do the rest. They are in hiding, so they won't know whom to trust. Convince them of who you are."

Fydan quickly adds, "You must also be aware that your enemies may be near, so be ever on guard. Vigilance is key."

Nicholas says, "We've never done this before. Most of us have necklaces to travel individually, but I think we should rescue the first few groups as a team before we split up."

Mika looks concerned at Brian and asks, "Do we need to have Brian on the rescue missions? No offence meant, but I think we could probably move a lot faster without him. I don't think he's trained for anything like this."

"No offense taken," Brian says. "I'm willing to help, but I think you're right. I probably won't be of much help in a fight. I'm a pacifist."

Thinking on it a moment, I say, "Brian will stay here then to help Fallon and the others prepare for our return with the other wolves. Brian, if you could keep an eye on Ms. Whiskers while we're gone, I'd really appreciate it."

Completely taken aback, Ms. Whiskers says, "Me go, too! Me stay with new sparkle friend!"

Tobias gets down on one knee and pets Ms. Whiskers, saying, "It's way too dangerous for you, alley cat. You could get hurt. Stay here and take care of the others until we get back. Okay? For us?"

Ms. Whiskers moves just out of hand reach from Tobias, turns her back to us, and says, "Fine, but me no like."

Tobias happily reaches over, picks her up and plants several kisses on her. He then says, "Come on, let's regroup at Fallon's cottage."

Just after Hadrian lands back on Tobias' arm, he, his familiar, and Ms. Whiskers then disappear. I walk over to Brian and place one hand on his shoulder. I then wait to make sure Mika, Nicholas, and Fydan teleport as well before I jaunt Brian and myself back to the cottage. When we arrive, we find Fallon waiting for us in the living room. I can see his eyes are bloodshot red.

After getting his new bearings, Brian says, "I don't think I'll ever get used to that."

"I'm sorry about Priapus. Are you all right?" I ask Fallon.

"I'll be fine," he answers. "Priapus was very...special to me. We've known each other for many centuries. He will be missed."

I give his shoulder a warm squeeze then pull back, wanting to give him his space.

Pointing to the new familiars, Fallon says, "I've never seen them in our woods before. More friends of yours?"

Nicholas motions to Tobias and Mika saying, "They're their souls."

Nicholas' words surprise me. He's normally always quiet and never talks about our magics. By the smiles on Tobias and Mika's faces, I can tell that they too picked up on Nicholas' newly budding openness.

Fallon shrugs his shoulders in response and says, "If you say so." He then notices our necklaces and asks, "Those your souls, too?"

Brian excitedly says, "Nope. Those gods from before give them as gifts. They help our team teleport anywhere we want."

I smile at the word '*team*'. I've never thought about us in that way before, or at least not consciously, anyway. It brings about more respect and love I have for the people around me.

"Now," I say. "We know what we have to do. I don't want to drag out any of our jaunts longer than necessary. We go in, we get our people, and we get right back out as soon as possible. Our main objective is their safety. Fallon, where do you want for us to have the wolves arrive?"

Fallon answers, "By Virbius' altar. It's the most central location and is wide enough to accommodate groups of people. I'll have other forest residents on hand to assist the different families to their temporary lodgings."

Mika asks, "Lodgings?"

"Yes," Fallon says. "Virbius made accommodations for your wolves. It's gonna be a little tight with the number of wolves we're expecting, but we should be able to manage."

Tobias says to Fallon, "Thank you, to you and the others for opening your homes and helping us when we barely know each other."

Fallon looks kindly at Tobias and says, "This forest is a refuge for all of us who can't make it out there in man's world for one reason or another. Having your people here strengthens our security and Virbius' power. If this god war is really gonna happen, we're gonna need as many of your wolves as we can get for all of our sakes."

"Brian is gonna stay behind," I say, "to lend a hand to you and the others."

Brian compliments my statement by saying, "Yeah, whatever you need. I'm here to help."

Fallon nods his head. "Good. We'll need it."

I look at my fellow wolves and take in their measure. "You all ready, then?"

The three of them say, "Yes."

Tobias places Hadrian on the back of one of the wooden dining chairs, petting him several times after. Hadrian then turns into beads of golden light that go into Tobias' chest. Mika then squats down and gently scratches Fydan under her chin several times. Fydan too becomes white lights and goes into Mika's body. My thoughts go back to Fenrus, remembering how he was able to do the same unification with me. Sadness overtakes my heart. Looking down, I see Ms. Whiskers staring up at me with big, round eyes.

"You come back, right?"

"I wouldn't leave you, you know that." I tell her. "Just stay by Brian and protect him, okay?"

"Me will," she says back. "No get hurt, okay? Me be sad if you get hurt."

My heart stings a little at her words. I pick her up and give her a kiss on the cheek.

"I'll try my best." I tell her. I look at Ms. Whiskers and then back to my team. Goddess, please, watch over them. They are my heart and my soul.

Suddenly, I sense Nicholas who was previously beside me disappear. I put Ms. Whiskers down and look around the room. A moment later, he rematerializes with his arms filled with cans of cat food. I stare at him perplexed.

"What?" Nicholas says. "Virbius said that they're vegetarians here. Cats are carnivores. She's gonna need these."

I look on speechless as stoic, no nonsense, killer Nicholas puts the small individual cans of cat food on the dining room table. Will wonders never cease?

Once we regroup, I say, "Okay, everyone follow my lead. I'm going to think about the wolves in hiding, the ones that are most in danger. Concentrate on my travel. It should put us all in the same place. Everyone got that?"

All three wolves nod their heads in agreement.

"All right," I say. "Then let's go, and remember, be ready for anything."

I close my eyes and think about the Enopo wolves on the run. I try to lock onto the emotions of them and ask to be pulled to the ones most in need. I feel my body shift locations. The feeling is still slightly disorienting, but I focus my mind and balance my body as best I can. When I feel solid ground beneath me, I open my eyes.

In front of me, I see a family huddled in a corner of a building. Their faces are dirt stained and the look in their eyes is pure terror. I can sense they are wolves. In front of them is a squadron of Neuri Emissaries. They are pointing automatic machine guns directly at the family, ready to pull their triggers.

"No!" I hear Mika scream beside me. Instantly, I see a wave of her white magic daggers fly from her hands, directly at the werewolf assassins. As they painfully strike, I turn to Tobias.

"Get the family and take them to sanctuary," I tell him.

Tobias nods and disappears. He rematerializes beside the wolf family, squatting somewhat to meet their gaze. They look on at him just as terrified as before.

Nicholas, Mika, and I then remove our swords and attack the Emissaries with everything we have. It is six against three, but our magics level our odds a bit. The Neuri wolves shift into their half wolf forms, giving their normal strength an added boost. The three of us do the same. From the corner of my vision, I see the wolf family look at our fur coloring and their terror softens a bit.

I take on the nearest Emissary to me, using my sword to slice at his hand still holding a gun. A moment later, the hand and gun fall to the floor without the rest of the wolf. The assassin howls in pain. I spin kick him across his face, knocking him down to the ground. I then use my two swords to slice into his chest, sensing I've struck his heart with one sword and his lung with the other. I then use my swords for leverage as I flip over the now dead wolf, kicking my next opponent squarely in the chest on the way toward my landing. He goes down, too.

Looking again at the family, I see that Tobias has shifted into his half wolf form, allowing the family to see his fur coloring. He extends his hand to them.

Just then, I feel a set of claws rake across my right cheek. I growl and look at my attacker. Grabbing the next claw swipe before it can make contact, I forcefully twist the assassin's wrist, listening for the expected snap of bone. Once I hear it, I turn slightly, placing the wolf's arm onto my shoulder and pivot forward. The wolf tumbles over me and onto the ground. I shift further into my wolf form and bite into my enemy's throat. Feeling his jugular fully in my teeth, I bite down hard then jerk myself up. The taste of the assassin's blood fills my mouth. I look down and see he's now dead.

I look at the family again and see the father slowly reaching out to take Tobias' hand. The moment he does, they disappear. Turning around, I see Nicholas pulling his swords out of his final opponent and Mika using her swords to behead the last of hers.

"Are you two all right?" I ask as I magically will for my victim's blood on my mouth and neck to disappear.

Nicholas looks at Mika then says back to me, "We're fine."

"Good," I respond. "Tobias transported the family. Let's get out of here before more Emissaries arrive."

The three of us then teleport back to Virbius' altar. Tobias smiles at our arrival, while the Enopo family looks on at us scared and confused.

"You're safe," I tell them. My words don't register with them. It's then that I realize that I spoke to them in English. Trying to correct my mistake, I focus on the blessing Virbius gave me during my first visit to his realm. I then say in the Neuri language, "You are safe here. I am Devin Toxotis, Archon to the Enopo Clan. The other clans cannot find you here."

Relief spreads across the family's faces. The wife and two children begin to cry. The father comes over to me and says, "I thought we were dead like the others before us. Thank you. Thank you for saving my family."

He then embraces me tightly. I'm taken aback by his response. I pat his back several times in understanding.

"It's my duty," I tell him. He lets go, allowing me to face him again. "Are there any other families like yours in hiding that you know of? We are going to try to save as many of them as we can."

Sadness consumes the stranger's face. "No. Not anymore. There were two other families in my village that sympathized with the Enopo. When our fur color changed, our Archons had one family killed. When we learned we were next, the rest of us ran. I think the Emissaries managed to catch several members of the other family, but if there were any survivors, I don't know where they would be. It was all I could do to keep my own family in hiding."

The man's wife says, "My husband's name is Sergei, and I am Potashka. We are in your debt, Archon."

Just then, Fallon, Brian, Ms. Whiskers and a large centaur enter the altar area. The family shrinks back in fear.

"Don't be afraid," I say. "These are friends. They will take you to a temporary place to stay while we go to look to rescue more of our clan."

The little girl then jumps up and says excitedly, "Halflings!"

Her brother takes his face out of his mother's arm to look. His eyes widen, and he says, "They *are* Halflings!"

I look on at the family in confusion. The father says under his breath, "The old stories are true. I didn't think there were any left."

Fallon takes charge, saying, "Come. Your leader and his team must be off again soon. We'll take you to a place where you can rest and get something to eat."

The parents look at me with uncertainty. I tell them, "It's okay. They will help you until we return."

The two children break their grip from their mother, running toward Fallon with happy cheers.

"We get to play with Halflings! We get to play with Halflings!"

Their parents get a look of alarm on their faces until Brian steps forward. He speaks to them in what sounds to be Russian. The words sound foreign at first but in moments, the words begin to make sense.

"…to worry about. These people are here to help. Come. We need to make room for more rescues in this area."

Sergei goes to Potashka and holds her by the waist. "Come to me." he then barks at his children. They gingerly return to their parents, but keep their eyes wide in awe at Fallon and the Centaur.

Fallon gestures toward a path leading off from the altar area. "This way."

As they slowly follow Fallon, I grab Brian's arm and ask, "Was that Russian?"

He smirks at me and says, "Yeah, but don't act so surprised. I have a double Masters degree from UC San Francisco and speak eight languages. Give me some credit. I'm not *just* looks and charm, ya know."

I smile at Brian, impressed. "Thanks. I'm sure that'll come in handy. How did you know they also spoke Russian?"

Brian answers, "Deductive reasoning. I couldn't understand that mish-mash language you were speaking, but I did manage to get the names Sergei and Potashka in the conversation. With names like that, I figured they probably spoke Russian as well."

"Good work," Tobias says. "On a good note, I think these necklaces provide more than just teleportation. I was able to make out what most of you two were saying to the rescues."

"Me, too." Nicholas confirms. "Okay, the first wolves are in, but there's a lot more to go." The sound in his voice is a mixture of satisfaction and determination. "I suggest we head out for the next batch while there's still light out."

"Agreed. Who knows what the rest are going through?" Mika says.

"All right." I say. "Same as before. Everyone ready?"

More nods of yes abound. I close my eyes and focus again on the wolves in most need of our help. I can feel the world shift around me. When I feel firm ground beneath me, I open my eyes.

I'm in a dark room. The only light is coming from a long, thin, horizontal window that runs along the ceiling of the wall to my right. In front of me, I see about ten or twelve figures of people. They look on my team and me frozen in fear. Outside of the window, I hear booming voices speaking a foreign language. After a few moments, the voices become clear.

"…spy said they are in the room below. Quickly, before they can escape!"

The sound of many stomping feet erupts, becoming louder as they head toward the building.

Nicholas changes into his hybrid form, showing his fur coloring. "Enopo," he says forcefully. "Come!"

The others don't know what to do, so he reaches out and grabs a couple by the hand. They scream out and disappear with Nicholas. The others look confused. I focus on the language used by the Emissary soldiers outside and say, "Come with us or die here at their hands. There is no time left. Decide!"

I'm unsure of my words, as I've never spoken that language before. I hope I got my general meaning across. A couple of the hidden wolves step forward and offer their hands. Mika takes them quickly and disappears. Nicholas then reappears and takes several more away. Tobias takes three and disappears as well. Just as I place my hands on the two remaining wolves, I hear doors breaking behind me. I teleport us to safety moments before the Emissary assassins are upon us.

Once back in the altar, area I see the other rescued wolves, scared and confused just as Sergei and Potashka before them. In better light I now see that the majority of the wolves are only teenagers. Many are crying and huddled together in clenched hugs.

"You are safe," I hear Tobias say in the new language. "We are far away from the Emissaries. There are other Enopo wolves here that were rescued too."

One of the wolves slows her crying and lets go of the boy she is holding on to. She looks in my direction and says, "You're Devin. You're the Enopo Archon."

"Yes," I reply. "I am."

Fury quickly comes across her face as she charges at me, pounding the flat of her fists into my chest. "This is all your fault! It's your fault they killed my sister! It's your fault my parents are dead!"

Her words hit me like an emotional sledgehammer. Mika goes to pull the girl off me, but before she can, the girl's grief becomes too much as she collapses on the ground choking on her tears. She rolls around on the ground completely inconsolable to anything but her grief.

Mika picks her up gently and looks into her face. "Devin didn't kill your family. That was your former clan's doing. It was the doing of an outdated regime who would rather keep its people under its rule of thumb than let them live the lives they want for themselves. I am sorry about your family, I really am, but this was not Devin's doing. It was your former Archon's and no one else's."

The girl falls into Mika's shoulder, crying hysterically. Mika pets her hair, softly shushing her cries until the girl's sobs become a subtle whimper.

Brian and two of the new Satyr from earlier then walk into the altar area. Mika takes the girl's head again and says, "We are going to stop them from killing more innocents. I promise you. But, you have to keep strong. The Archon is right. You are safe here." Mika then addresses the other wolves. "You are *all* safe here. Please, go with our friends. They will take you someplace to eat and rest." Mika then looks back at the girl in her hands. "Do you think you can do that?"

The girl nods her head then gives Mika one last tearful hug. Mika hugs her back before letting her go so that she can join her friends now following Brian and the others.

When they are out of view, Tobias turns to me. "Devin, she didn't mean it. You've got to know that."

"Actually, she did," I tell him. "But I can't let that faze me. More wolves out there need our help. I've got to focus on them right now."

Tobias looks deeply into my eyes then says, "You're right. Are you up for the next jaunt?"

I nod my head several times. "I'll be fine. Let's go."

A dozen more similar rescue missions happen, taxing our stamina, but we trudge on. Although a small percentage of the wolves we reach still scorn their losses, all are grateful for our rescue. Exhaustion on the many faces holds a big impact on all of us, even Nicholas. He finally relents in allowing us to split up into smaller teams. I understand the obligation he probably has to want to protect his cousin's son and Archon, but I now get that he also understands that more rescues will occur with our branching out.

Still thinking it's not safe to travel individually, I decide to put us in two pairs. Initially I plan to pair myself with Tobias, but Nicholas insists that he travel with me instead. Seeing there is no changing his mind, Tobias and Mika submit and agree to partner together. I give Tobias a kiss and Mika a hug, making them promise that if they get into any trouble that they teleport themselves back to sanctuary at any cost. They make me promise the same. Watching them disappear together without me was heart breaking, but I keep in mind that it's for the good of our people.

I turn back to Nicholas and thank him. He shrugs and says, "It's like you said. It's our duty."

I surprise Nicholas with a tight hug. I feel nothing back for a few moments, but finally he hugs me, though awkwardly. Pulling away, I say nothing else to him since I know that where Nicholas is concerned, words generally aren't needed.

The next couple of hours flash by as we continue our efforts. The rescues remain as scared and confused as ever, but thankfully the presence of hunting Emissaries around them begins to dwindle to fewer and fewer instances. This relaxes the tension a bit, but I remain on guard nonetheless.

On one particular travel, I notice something. Just as I convince the rescue of who we are, I sense a unique presence nearby. I don't sense any hostility from the entity, but am leery that it might be a Benandanti trick. Sensing my apprehension, Nicholas asks, "What's wrong?"

"I don't know," I answer. "I can't place it, but there's someone nearby. Someone magical."

"Other witches?" Nicholas asks.

"I can't...tell really, but there's magic involved somehow." I look at the rescue and realize I'm just confusing him further. "Let's get this one back. We'll figure out what it is later."

When we rematerialize in the forest's altar area, we see Tobias and Mika sitting on the ground beside their familiars with looks of exhaustion. After I see the last rescue escorted off to his temporary digs, I walk over to Tobias and Mika and collapse next to them on the ground. Not only is my body physically tired, but I'm mentally drained as well.

I close my eyes and say, "I can't make another jump, not for a while anyway."

Tobias lays his head on my stomach and says, "We know how you feel."

Mika then rests her head on Tobias' stomach and says, "At least the ones in most danger are safe. We can focus on the rest tomorrow."

I weakly raise my hand into the air. Tobias and Mika slap my palm sluggishly before letting them fall to their sides like dead weight. I then turn my head and look for Nicholas. I see him standing at the edge of the altar area, looking off at the nearby brook. He picks up a small rock and throws it in. Solitary like always.

I close my eyes again and hear myself breathing deeply. I'm too tired to do anything else. I hear myself say, "I'm just going to keep my eyes closed for a few more minutes. Just for a few more..."

My voice trails off as exhaustion overtakes me. Pillows of unconsciousness wrap themselves around my head as I surrender to their embrace. The stress in my body and mind leave me as I fall softly into vast emptiness. The feeling has never felt so welcome.

After a few minutes of blissful nothingness, the darkness around me slowly begins to lighten. I realize I'm now in some sort of ancient underground tomb or mosque. The smell of incense and patchouli fill the air. Flickering torches hang off gorgeous mosaicked pillars. The ground is well-worn dirt. To the far left wall, pitchers of drinks sit, and on the other wall sits a beautifully ornate statue of gold.

I inspect it closer. It's a rudimentary figure of a woman standing upright with her hands clasped firmly to her sides. Beside her ankle is a figure of a dog sitting upright and at attention. A faint memory of my father comes to mind. During one of our spells, my coven and I were able to visit the past. In it, we witnessed my father telling my brother the origins of the wolf nations. In the story, he explained that the goddess Hecate was always depicted with a wolf at her side, a signal to her ties to our people.

I go over to the mosaic pictograms. They show a man-wolf at the door of a large shrine, cowering in fear. The next picture shows a large woman with her hand now on the wolf's head. The next one shows the wolf transformed fully into a man, and bowing to the large woman. The last picture I see shows many wolves standing before the large woman, bowing in submission as well.

My senses go wild as I feel the arrival of another magical presence in the room. I can sense it's the same presence from earlier during my last rescue mission. I quickly turn to see a man leaning against a far table, staring directly at me. His hair is stark white and his eyes are yellow. The youthfulness in his face tells me that he is my age, somewhere in his mid-twenties. He is wearing a white tunic top and black loose cloth pants. At his side is a tall wooden staff.

"Those mosaics are over three thousand years old. They were made by the first of your wolf ancestors." His voice is rich and dripping with a sensuous Greek accent.

"Who are you?"

He smiles. "My name is Idaios. You are at the home of the Lykaion clan, under Mount Lykaion in Arcadia, Greece."

My eyes widen. Being in the stronghold of an outside clan raises my defenses. I can tell Idaios sees my apprehension.

"You have nothing to fear from anyone here," he tells me. "Unlike our other brethren, we don't hold feuds against our own kind. As long as you respect our status of neutrality, you are free to come and go as you wish."

"You're a witch," I say. "You're both a werewolf and a witch, like me."

Idaios looks off to the side. "Yes. We are."

I ask, "We?"

Idaios walks over to another wall of mosaics, gently touching a few of the pictograms with his fingertips.

"The Lykaion clan has always been a strong follower of Hecate. Dare I say, stronger followers than any of the other clans since we were first created. For thousands of years, we've stayed true to her worship." Turning back to me, Idaios says, "You—you are trained in the academics of gods. Tell me what you know of the goddess Hecate."

Thinking a moment, I reply, "Hecate was a Titan, daughter to my central god Gaea. She was one of the few Titans to have been given amnesty by the Titan's children, the Olympians, once they dethroned their parents and cast them into Tartarus. Zeus was especially respectful to the goddess for some reason. Once the Olympians took power, Hecate formed a strong bond with her niece Demeter and her great-niece Artemis. Together the three of them formed a triple goddess union that the various phases of the moon symbolize: the crescent moon, or maiden, represents Artemis; the half moon, or mother, represents Demeter; and the full moon, or crone, represents Hecate."

Lifting an eyebrow, Idaios asks, "And what dominion does Hecate hold?"

"She holds sway over several things," I reply. "She oversees wild places, the moon, crossroads, and..." Then, it dawns on me. "Magic."

"Yes, magic." Idaios repeats. He then motions to the mosaic. "It's all here."

I walk over to the new mosaic, carefully inspecting it. Several images show the white furred wolf followers bowing to the large female figure from earlier. The woman places her hands on the heads of several followers. In other pictures, they show the white wolves using magic to help grow plants and heal the sick.

"Wolves, you see," Idaios continues, "are inherently magical beings. Magic is a byproduct of the curse that created us."

Idaios lifts his palm in front of me. A green image of a wolf running in place manifests above it.

"As a reward for our continued worship," he says, "our goddess enhanced our internal magics, allowing the Lykaion clan to create outer magics of our own."

Closing his palm, the green wolf disappears back into nothingness.

"So you see," he says, "in this we are much alike. Magic binds us. It is the reason your original fur coloring was partly white. It's for this reason I called you here. We've been watching you for some time."

"What do you mean you called me here?" I ask. "You've been watching me?"

"Yes. We've been following you since your magics first manifested."

I look into Idaios' eyes, trying to gauge his intent. His cool stare holds no malice, only calm fact.

"Why?" I ask.

Idaios smiles. "Because whether you know it or not, you are destined to bring about a great change to the world. Our seers have foretold this many years ago. For millennia, we've kept our existence from humans and the secrets of our clan hidden from even the other wolves. Now, all things will change. Our goddess has seen a new age approaching. She's seen you at the center of that change. Our goddess has tasked us to help see you through to the end of your mission. Your fight is now ours."

From the room's various doorways step in many other figures. The various men and women I notice all have stark white hair and yellow eyes. Like Idaios, they wear white tunics and black cloth pants. They surround the room until there is no room left.

I hear Idaios say from somewhere in the crowd, "Today, we will make our presence known."

I feel a jolt and open my eyes. Looking around, I see that I'm back in Virbius' wooded altar clearing. Startled, Tobias takes my shoulder and asks, "What is it, Devin?"

I hear a growl, and Nicholas runs over to us.

"We're under attack!" he says, holding both of his blades at the ready. "Prepare yourselves!"

Hadrian flaps his wings dramatically and screeches into the air. Fydan gets in front of Mika with her back arched, hissing in defiance. I look around and see many yellow-lit eyes staring at us from the dark spaces between the trees surrounding the clearing. The scent I pick up from them is the same scent of incense and patchouli I noticed in the Lykaion temple earlier. I stand up and put my hand on Nicholas' shoulder. He looks back at me, confused. Slowly the various Lykaion wolves step out of the shadows and into the altar area. I notice Idaios, who bows slightly to me.

To Nicholas and the others I say, "They're not here to attack us. These are the Lykaion wolves. By Hecate's decree, they're here to help us win our fight."

Chapter 8
ALLIANCE

W E CAN HEAR A SUDDEN RUSH OF FEET FROM VARIOUS POINTS OF the forest around us. I look at the standing Lykaions and know that they're not creating the disturbance. Just as the stomping feet are upon us, the Lykaions raise their hands into the air. A moment later, a clear shield envelopes the clearing, stopping any other being from entering. It's then that I see Fallon and the others banging on the mystic shield with swords and bows drawn. They look on at us, unsure of our safety or how to get through.

"Witches!" Tobias says in surprise.

I walk over to Fallon on the other side of the shield and notice Brian next to him, ax in hand. Hissing at his feet is Ms. Whiskers.

"These aren't enemies." I say to them. "They are part of a secret clan of werewolves called the Lykaion. The goddess Hecate sent them to help us."

Slowly, the forest inhabitants lower their weapons, still cautiously eyeing the Lykaion wolves. I look over to Idaios. He nods. The white haired wolves then raise their hands into the air again, causing the clear magical shield to fade back into open air.

I motion to Idaios. "This is Idaios. I believe he is the Archon to the Lykaion."

Idaios shakes his head.

"No," he says. "We don't use those terms or see ourselves in that type of structure. Our leader is Hecate. We follow her will and hers alone. We are all equals in our clan. If I hold any distinction between the others here, it is that I am a high-ranking priest. Nothing more."

"My mistake." I say.

Mika turns to one of the female Lykaion wolves next to her and asks, "You're all witches? Like us?"

"Yes," the wolf says directly. "Hecate blessed us with the gift of magic thousands of years ago."

"Thousands?" I ask. I then turn to Idaios and ask him, "You're immortal?"

Idaios nods. "Another gift from the goddess."

It occurs to me just how special the Lykaions are to their goddess. Her angry chastising speech to the other clans last year now begins to make more sense.

Fallon says, "We're already at capacity as it is with the wolves you brought in earlier. I don't know if we can house these new wolves comfortably."

Idaios says, "No need to trouble yourselves. See to the others. We are only here to discuss with you our intentions."

Nicholas sheaths his swords. He then crosses his arms, saying, "What *are* your intentions?"

Idaios takes in Nicholas' measure, seeing he is not about to roll out the welcome mat like the others and I have.

Idaios continues, saying, "My clan will continue your mission to rescue the remaining Enopo wolves from danger. You and your team have more dire needs at the moment."

"Dire?" Tobias asks.

"Yes," the female Lykaion wolf says. "I am Danae, a fellow priestess from my clan. The goddess gave us omens in dreams, explaining what must be done. If our visions are correct, your mission now is to confront your enemies and resolve our people's internal struggles."

Idaios says, "Your enemies are more complex than you know. They are tied to one another in ways that will soon become clear. Do not underestimate them."

With defeat in her voice, Mika says, "We have so many enemies at the moment. Which one of them do we go after first?"

Danae says, "Like Idaios mentioned, things are not as they seem. Your enemies are central to one another. Go after one, and you go after them all."

Remembering our previous conversation, I say to Idaios, "Earlier you said we were destined to bring about a great change. That we were no longer going to be hidden. What did you mean by that?"

Idaios exchanges a look with Danae.

Danae says, "The world you see around you will soon be no more. The battle our gods will engage in…it will reveal the Hidden Ones to man. If our gods triumph, our kind has a chance at survival despite the reveal. If our gods were to lose, a Dark Age will replace the modern world as we know it and our future is uncertain. Either way, our people need to put aside our differences to face whatever future awaits us as a united pack. If we remain splintered as we are, our kind may become all but extinct. You, Devin, must take the charge of unifying our people before this war happens."

"Me?" I ask.

Idaios says, "Don't act so surprised, Devin. You've already created many changes within the wolf nation within a short span of time. Unification is our only key to survival. Our gods believe you can achieve this for us. We're here to help guarantee your success. It will take a village to complete this mission, but the head of that village must be you."

I feel stunned. I look at Tobias, Mika, and Nicholas. I'm at a complete loss of words.

Danae says, "This is a lot to take in, we know, but now is not the time for second guessing. You must prepare for what is coming, for all of our sakes."

Idaios looks at me inquisitively. "We will leave now to save the rest of the members of your clan. Should you require our help," Idaios motions to our necklaces, "you know how you can find us."

The Lykaion wolves' eyes glow bright yellow. In a flash, they all disappear, leaving my team alone again with Virbius' subjects. My head spins as my thoughts go into shock.

"Devin," Nicholas says somewhere far off from my mind. "*Devin!*" he snaps, bringing me back to attention. Nicholas turns to Tobias and Mika, saying, "Follow us." Then to Brian and the others he says, "We'll be back."

Nicholas then places his hand on my shoulder, and I feel the two of us being whisked away from where we were previously standing. When our surroundings settle again, I look around to see that we're now in Nicholas' private quarters back in Boston. A moment later, I see Tobias, Mika, and their familiars materialize beside us.

Nicholas looks into my eyes and says, "I need to know what's going through your head."

I still feel stunned, but try to shake it out of the fog of my mind as best as possible.

Tobias asks in a soft tone, "Devin, are you okay?"

"This is all just happening so fast," I answer. "We keep jumping from one fire to another, and now I'm told the entire freaking building is gonna be an inferno, and I'm the only one with a hose."

"That's not what they said," Mika replies. "You might be the captain, but you have an entire team here to help you. You're not alone, Devin."

In her face, I see sincere devotion and smile weakly.

"Thank you," I say. Turning to the others, I tell them, "Thank you. All of you."

Nicholas says, "Those Greek wolves were right. You can't second-guess yourself. We're your Counsel. What trepidations do you have? You need to put everything out on the table otherwise we stand to lose everything."

"I'm just… I'm afraid I'm gonna make a move that puts everyone in danger. I'm afraid more people are gonna die on my watch."

"Devin," Tobias says, "we're already in danger. We can't help that."

"I know," I say. "But I'm not a trained Archon. I've made mistakes—huge ones. I used my magics in front of humans, I've lost my familiar to a rival coven, our wolves in Boston have a mob hit out on them, our wolves in Europe have been hunted and slaughtered for months without us even knowing about it… I don't know if I'm the right person to solve all these problems *and* to take on the job of unifying our people globally. It's more than my mind can even process."

Nicholas says, "The rule of a good leader is to take what you can handle one step at a time. No one is expecting you to do it all overnight, Devin. We're on a time crunch, yeah, but I don't think our gods even believe you can do it all instantly."

Tobias places his hand on my arm and says, "Devin, you need to stop focusing on what you've done wrong in the past and instead look at all the accomplishments you've made so far. Those wolves look up to you. We all do."

Looking deep into his eyes I say, "Did you see that girl's face? Her entire family was killed. All…gone."

Angrily, Mika says, "Those Archon bastards did that Devin, not you. Not any of us. You did the right thing coming to rescue them. That girl could be dead now, too, if it wasn't for you. Everyone in the camp knows that, even she does. It's time you realized that yourself."

I know she's right, but it still doesn't make me feel any better about the losses already made.

"All right." I say. "I've got to realize that this thing is happening whether I like it or not. You're right. I can't let the bad things get to me. There are too many people relying on us."

Tobias asks, "So what's our next step?"

Mika says, "I think we should try to rescue Fenrus. We'll be stronger once he's back with us."

My heart breaks as I utter the next few words.

"No. I want Fenrus back more than you could know, but he's safe where he is. At least for the time being anyway. The Benandanti need both him and me for whatever plan they've concocted."

"But Devin…" Tobias starts to say.

"No. Since the Lykaion wolves are saving the remaining European Enopo members, we now need to shift our focus on safeguarding our Boston members from Bobby Longo's mob hit. They now take priority."

"Good move," Nicholas replies. "We need to check to see if the Synoro Archons joined our cause or if this is something we have to handle on our own. Having them on our side would make things so much easier. But, all that can wait 'til morning. I know we're all still exhausted from today's assignments. I suggest we go back to the rescue camp, check in on everyone, and tackle our new assignment in the morning."

"Yeah," I say. "I'm thinking we're gonna need as much rest for tomorrow as possible. Let's regroup with the others."

Tobias says to Mika and Nicholas, "You two go ahead. I'd like a couple more minutes with Devin if you don't mind."

They both nod and disappear from the room. Once they are gone, Tobias hugs me tightly. In my ear, he says, "I know you're going through a lot right now, Devin. I just want you to know I love you. I'll always be here for you."

I hold Tobias back just as tightly.

"I love you, too." I say in return. "If there's one thing I regret where you're concerned is that we haven't had any time to do anything as a real couple. We haven't even gone on a real date."

Tobias chuckles. "So you're saying fighting witches and brawling with werewolves isn't romantic enough for you?"

I laugh then pull away slightly to better see his face.

"You know what I mean," I reply. "This life isn't easy on a relationship. I've seen how rocky and complicated it's made my parents' marriage. I don't want that for us. If we...*when* we make it through this, I want you to know I plan to make that up to you. I promise."

Tobias smiles and pushes away the hair from my forehead.

"You don't have to make any promises to me. I see how you feel about me every day. It's one thing I never have to question. You're an Archon, and that takes a lot of your time. I understand that. You do what you need to and don't worry about me. I know where we are, and I'm here for the long haul. On that *I* promise."

I kiss Tobias deeply, moved by his words. I have no idea what I've done to deserve such a wonderful man in my life.

When I feel the kiss is over, I smile. "Come on. Let's not keep the others waiting."

The world around us shifts again, and we find ourselves back in Virbius' forest. Around us, I see several wolves gathering wood. Others I see taking buckets of water from the nearby stream. Brian notices us and jogs over with Ms. Whiskers beside him.

"You're back."

Ms. Whiskers follows with, "So many sparkle people here now. Not bright sparkle like you but still pretty."

"How are we doing on the housing?" I ask him.

Scratching his head, Brian says, "It's getting a bit tight. We could do with a few more dorms if possible."

Tobias nods, saying, "Leave that to me."

He then turns to face an open area of the forest. Pointing to it, his eyes begin to glow dramatically. The ground slightly shifts beneath us. The ground of the open forest area begins to rumble as mounds of earth pillar upward. Tobias then begins to mold open air. The action causes the earth pillars to bend and shape themselves. Everyone in the camp stops and stares at the amazing occurrence. When Tobias is through, there, standing in the now gone opening, is a crude but stable building made of earth.

Tobias' shoulders go slack once the spell is over. He weakly says to us, "It's not Buckingham Palace, but it should do."

I peck him on the cheek. "Thank you."

I walk over to the structure and inspect it, helping fortify its foundation and create window openings on various walls. Once inside, I see Tobias has created a second level to match the large first floor space with individual rooms. A stairway made of earth provides access. I'm impressed. His familiar has definitely amped up his power levels.

In a flash, I see Ms. Whiskers zoom up the stairs, eyeing everything in curiosity.

Brian and Tobias walk in as well. I say to them, "Mika and I will create another one on the opposite end of the camp. That should provide us more room for the wolves still to come."

Brian says, "That's great, but we're still gonna need more supplies like blankets and such. Do you mind if I borrow the van to get some essentials?"

"Not at all," I say. "Just take Ms. Whiskers with you for protection."

Brian snickers. "Yeah, okay." Then yelling to the upper floor he says, "Ya hear that, ya little fuzz ball? We're going on an errand. You've got ten minutes."

Ms. Whiskers looks down from her lofty height at us for a moment, and then goes back to investigating the new building. We walk out of the building as curious camp wolves go in, looking at Tobias' creation. Fallon arrives and joins us. He looks at the new earth building in awe.

"Great Pan…," he exclaims. Then turning to me he says, "You did this?"

I shake my head. "No. Tobias and his familiar."

At that, Tobias' familiar Hadrian manifests from his chest and flies to the top of the new structure. He puffs out his chest.

Brian says to Fallon, "The witches are gonna make one or two more to accommodate the wolves still coming in. I just got a hall pass to head into the city to get some more supplies."

Fallon says, "Hall pass?"

"Sorry," Brian says. "I forgot you don't know modern day lingo. Mr. Wolf here said it was okay for me to leave for a few minutes."

I know Brian is just itching to get into the city to explore. I can tell Fallon can see the twinkle in his eyes as well.

Fallon inhales deeply and says, "Stay out of the public eye as best you can. We don't know which agents out there know you're with us. Get what we need and come right back."

Still tired, I say to Brian, "I could teleport you if you want."

Tobias says, "No! That's too dangerous. Especially since we're so spent at the moment." Turning to Brian, Tobias adds, "Do you need any money? I have some American bills in my bag back at Fallon's cabin."

Brian winks his eye, taking out a wad of Euro bills from one of his many pockets.

"I got that covered." He grins slyly.

I grab Brian and give him my best bear hug.

"Thanks," I tell him. "I know you don't have to be here helping us, but you've been a real friend and ally. It means a lot to the pack and me."

Brian pats my back a couple times then pulls away, saying, "If what you say is going down really is happening, being under your watch is probably the safest place I can be. Symbiosis, my friend. Symbiosis."

He then puts his pointer finger and thumb into the sides of his mouth and whistles loudly.

"Hey, cat! Let's go!"

Ms. Whiskers comes bounding out of the cabin toward Brian's feet.

"Him annoying," Ms. Whiskers says.

Correcting her, I say, "No, him kind and generous. Now, you remember your goddess' wishes. You watch over him and keep him out of trouble. Okay?"

Sighing, she says, "Me know."

We watch as the unlikely duo walk off toward the path leading to the car. I say a silent prayer of protection as the path leads them around several trees and eventually out of sight.

Mika and Nicholas then join us.

Nicholas asks, "Where are they going?" motioning to the now empty path.

"Supplies," I answer back. "We need to make a couple more dorms for the wolves. Mika, do you think you can help me with that?"

With concern in his voice, Nicholas says, "Devin, you don't have your familiar anymore. Do you think you'll have enough strength? Maybe Mika and Tobias should handle that." Turning to them, he adds, "If that's all right with you two."

Mika says, "Nicholas is right. I can see how exhausted you are.

Tobias and I will handle this. I'm sure the wolves in the camp would appreciate you checking in on them though."

"You sure?" I ask them.

Tobias answers, "Positive. Go see to the others, and we'll see you in a bit."

I hug both of them.

"I love you guys," I say.

As they walk off with Fallon, Nicholas motions to the opposite direction. I follow him, and soon we're in the heart of the camp. Several wolves notice us and walk over. We receive more sincere thanks and gestures of gratitude for their rescue. I ask several of them if they are settled in or need anything else from us. The wolves' kindness knows no bounds as they say they are fine but wanted to know if there's anything they could do for us in return. I smile, saying that their safety is all that is needed.

At one point, I hear some shrieking, so I turn around to see the commotion. I look to see a young Centaur galloping across the camp with two squealing children sitting upon his back. They are the two Russian children from my earlier rescue. Their parents Sergei and Potashka follow the Centaur closely, fearful their children might fall off. I smile at the amusing scene before me.

Just then, I feel a light tap on my shoulder. I see it is a young boy, no more than sixteen.

"Excuse me, Archon," he says, "but if you have a moment, I was wondering if you'd like to hear us play?"

"Play?" Nicholas asks.

Now sheepishly grinning, the boy says, "Yeah. I'm Paul. My friends and I had a band before all this happened, and we thought if we played a few songs that it might get everyone's mind off what's going on. We don't have our normal instruments, but several of the Halflings here gave us some of theirs. Would you want to listen?"

"I'd be honored," I tell him.

Excited, he grabs my hand and leads me to toward one of the buildings.

"The others are gonna love this!" he says. "We've never performed for an Archon before. Oh, and, don't worry about Lia. She was upset before, but I think she's doing a lot better now."

"Who's Lia?" I ask him.

"She's the girl who was upset with you when you first brought us here. I knew her family. They were close. She's the lead singer for our band. We're called The Curse. It's a play on the curse Zeus gave our people a long time ago. I hope you like us."

As we get closer to the building, I see several teenagers standing together, some with stringed instruments. A small group of older wolves have gathered to see what they are doing. I see Lia standing in the middle of the group, and my heart sinks. I remember my pack's words from earlier and try not to let my grief show.

Lia sees the three of us approach and locks eyes with me. I do my best to keep her stare. She eventually turns to retrieve something. Nicholas steps in front of me in a protective stance. I gently put my hand on his shoulder, letting him know that I'll be all right. When Lia turns back around, she is holding something.

Slowly walking up to me, she hands me the item. I take it and see it's a picture of Lia standing with what looks to be her parents and another young girl.

"This is a photo my family took a few days before they came for us. That's my parents and my little sister." Lia's voice trails off at the end. I try to gain my composure as waves of grief wash over me.

"I'm really sorry about your family, Lia." I tell her. "I can't even begin to imagine what you've been going through. If there's anything I can do, I'll do my best to help in any way possible."

Locking eyes again, Lia says in a weak voice, "Make sure this doesn't happen to any more of us."

Her words hit home. Before I know what I'm doing, I pick her up in my arms and hold her tightly. I feel her arms wrap around me, too.

"I promise to try," I tell her, still held tight in my embrace. When I feel her tears fall against my neck, I feel the same sorrowful tears in my eyes as well.

When I feel the tightness of her hug lessen, I let go of her and hand her back her photo.

I motion to the forest around us, saying, "This forest is protected by our gods. Not just Hecate, but an entire pantheon of gods who've sworn to stand by us. The other clans can't get to any of you here. I'm going to try my best to get as many of our people to this sanctuary as possible. When everyone is accounted for, I'm going to see that the Archons who did this to you pay for what they've done."

Still with tears in her eyes, Lia asks, "Promise?"

I hold the side of her face. "I promise."

Wiping her tears away, Lia collects herself. "Good. Come with us. I want you to hear a song I wrote last year when we heard you and your brother won your combat challenge. It's written in our original language, so only wolves would understand what I'm saying. The song's about you." Seeing the look of apprehension on my face, she adds, "Don't worry. It's a good thing."

We walk over to the rest of the teenagers, and I introduce Nicholas and myself. They look at me star struck and introduce themselves as well. Nicholas and I then take a seat on the ground, facing the young musicians. They begin shaking off any nervousness they have and take their makeshift instruments. I'm captivated by what I see next. Nearly everyone in the camp walks over and joins us. Looking to the left and right of me, I see a small sea of wolves and other forest creatures all sitting together, eagerly waiting to hear The Curse play.

Lia softly clears her throat, and then closes her eyes. The musicians begin playing and Lia begins to sing.

"Night falls, and the moon rises high.

There's cold darkness, but I feel you nearby.
I'm chased by others, nowhere to hide.
Come join the fight, for tomorrow we die.
"Only together do we stand a chance.
It's not the safest place, but this is our dance.
Amulet gleams, magic takes hold.
Release your fury, and behold…
"I'm in a coven, a coven of wolves.
I should be frightened, but it feels way too good.
I'm in a coven, I'm misunderstood.
Come run, run, run, with the wolves.
"You stalk your prey, and you pull me in close.
I hunger for you, you're my drug, you're my dose.
In a trance, I'm in your dangerous game.
If I lose myself, I have no one to blame.
"Running for our lives, with no end in sight.
Push through the pain, oh how I need your light.
Save me from darkness I have within.
The moon is up, let the change begin.
"I'm in a coven, a coven of wolves.
I should be frightened, but it feels way too good.
I'm in a coven, I'm misunderstood.
Come run, run, run, with the wolves.
"They're coming now, run, don't let me fall.
We're pinned up now, with our backs against the wall.
Succumb to the wildness at a fever pitch.
Let go of it all, become were and witch.
"I'm in a coven, a coven of wolves.
I should be frightened, but it feels way too good.
I'm in a coven, I'm misunderstood.
Come run, run, run, with the wolves.
Come run, run, run, with the wolves."

When the song ends, silence goes across the forest. Lia slowly opens her eyes and as she does everyone in attendance begins to cheer. She and her band become reddened but bow gratefully to their audience.

I'm then reminded that this is what I'm really fighting for. Not for control, power, or territory like the other wolves, but for the people who are looking to me for protection. They have so much promise ahead of them. No matter what happens, I have to keep them in heart and mind.

The audience shouts for more. Gingerly, the musicians play a few more songs as the large crowd before them sways to their melodies. At the third song in, Tobias and Mika join us. I notice their exhaustion but they smile and begin swaying along with everyone around them.

I wait for a couple more songs to finish before I motion my team to join me. I get up from my seat and go over to Lia, giving her a big hug and shaking the hands of each musician. Tobias, Mika, and Nicholas do the same.

I then turn to the crowd behind me and focus on my god touched necklace, asking it to help me translate what I'm about to say in the universal Greek wolfen language.

"Please," I say, "enjoy more music from this wonderful group. If you need anything, there are many Halflings here to assist you. The Lykaion wolves will be bringing more of us here throughout the night. Please welcome the newcomers, and let them know they are safe. We have a lot planned for the next few days, but I hope to see you all again tomorrow."

At that, the entire sea of wolves stands and bows to the lot of us. I hold my composure but inside I am overwhelmed at the solidarity they have. We bow back and begin walking back to our cabin. Along the way, Fallon, Fydan, and Hadrian join us.

Nodding in our direction, Fallon says, "The new lodgings your witches created are superb, but if those white wolves bring more of your brood to the camp, we might run out of space again. I had no idea there were so many of you."

"Neither did I," I answer back solemnly. "You know, Fallon, our cabin is much too big for the handful of us. You can house more wolves there if need be. Unlike our clansmen, we have the gift of teleportation. To save the wolves some room, the lot of us will shift over to the Boston compound and sleep there." Turning to my team, I ask, "Would that be okay?"

They all nod in agreement. The exhaustion in their eyes tells me that the sooner we can get to bed the better.

Fallon says, "It's settled then, and thank you."

Tobias says, "We'll see you in the morning, Fallon. Are the rest of you ready?"

"I'll say," Mika yawns.

"All right." I answer. "Let's get going, then. Is everyone ready?"

After more nods, we each hold on to the shoulder (or in Hadrian's case, wing) of the person next to us and close our eyes. We focus on our Boston home. In moments, our surroundings shift and we find ourselves in Tobias and my private Boston room quarters. The process takes more of a toll on us, leaving us downright ready to faint. The sun shines brightly through the window, temporarily blinding us from our previous nighttime setting. After blocking its rays from our eyes, we all stare at the king sized bed before us with longing. I've never been so happy to see pillows before. In unison, we all fall onto the bed, glorying in its comfort. Within seconds, all of us are asleep.

Time suddenly has no significance as my comatose mind stays darkly blank for quite some time. Whether I'm in this state for hours or days is entirely beyond my comprehension. My body slowly recharges itself from the taxing energies needed. I'm too tired even to let my dream-self wander out on its own.

When I finally have some sense of life recognition, it's to the sensation of being shaken awake by a set of strong hands. Slowly opening my eyes, I see a vague shape of a man looming over me. As my vision focuses, I see that its one of my Enopo bodyguards from the Boston compound. He's desperately trying to snap our attention to him.

"Archon, Archon, you must wake up."

Nicholas bolts upright. "What is it, Owen?"

Now, Owen, seeing that the entire group of us is awake, says, "The other Archons, they left a few hours ago with Don Phillipi and his men to ambush Longo. I was doing my usual property surveillance…I had no idea you were back until just now."

Wiping the last of the sleep from my eyes, I ask, "What day is it?"

Confused, Owen says, "It's Tuesday, Archon."

Mika says, "We've lost two days!"

Tobias then asks Owen, "Is Devin the only Archon left in the complex?"

"Enopo Archon, yes." Owen replies. Turning to Devin, he says, "Your grandfather is still locked up and under guard though. He hasn't given us anything new we can use. Your father thought it best to deal with Longo's family before you returned."

Concerned, I ask, "What about Clayton, the other Synoro Archon?"

Owen looks uneasy. "He escaped. We still don't know how."

Any sense of lingering sleep now disappears upon hearing this horrible news.

"The other Enopo Archons, did they say where they were going specifically?" Tobias asks.

Owen nods. "Don Phillipi got word that Longo was going to be personally overseeing a boat arrival at the docks tonight. They're heading there to set up an ambush."

At this, Fydan arches her back and hisses. We all look over to her and see that her eyes have transformed completely white.

217

"What is it?" I ask Mika. She stares forward as if she is looking into another world, one where none of us exists.

Almost trance-like, Mika says, "Fydan…she's getting a vision. It looks like…oh, my God! It's a trap! Longo knows they're coming. And the boat Longo is waiting for…the Benandanti are on it! Claudia brought her entire coven!"

My heart sinks at the thought of my family and people going up against them on their own.

Turning to Tobias and Mika, I say, "Gather as many magical supplies as possible. We're going to need everything we've got."

They nod, then disappear along with their familiars. Then to Owen I say, "Try to get one of the Archons on the phone. Warn them that Longo and the Benandanti are waiting for them. Tell them to hold off on the attack and wait for my instructions."

Owen nods, racing out of the room.

Confused, Nicholas asks, "Why don't we just teleport there and warn them ourselves?"

Focusing his attention, I say, "Owen said that the boat is supposed to arrive this evening. Look out the window. There's still daylight. That gives us a little bit of time to turn this to our favor."

"Are you forgetting that the Benandanti have seers in their coven? What's to say they don't already know what's going to happen?" Nicholas asks.

Placing my hand on his shoulder, I smile. "Have faith. The Benandanti aren't the only witches with tricks up their sleeves."

******

Walking into the padded cell, I see my grandfather sitting at a table with his hands shackled behind him. Once he sees me, his face becomes sour.

Taking the chair across from him, I sit and say, "Hello, Jason."

He turns his head away from me and remains silent.

Cordially, I say, "I know I'm the last person you want to speak to, so let me just say, you don't have to. All you have to do is listen."

Since I still haven't gotten a proper response from him, I continue.

"I know that Clayton and many of the other Archons overseas sent kill squads to get rid of members of my clan globally."

Turning to me, Jason says, "My son told me that, but I refuse to believe it. I hate you and everything you've done to my people, but clan or no clan, I'd never consent to killing innocent wolves without precedent. If what you're saying is true, Clayton is a traitor to wolves everywhere and will be dealt with. *If* it's true."

"Good," I say. "Then you'll be happy to hear that I was able to save a good portion of the Enopo wolves before the Emissaries could get to them all. The survivors are in hiding and protected by our gods."

Jason looks away from me again.

"Hecate is one of those gods, you know. She has stood by us since my clan first came into being. But then you'd know that since you were there when she publicly claimed us as her own. She's recently joined forces with several other gods. She's created a new pantheon that will help guide and protect her wolves and anyone else who'll join her."

Jason squirms in his seat a bit.

"Not only are we protected by this new team of gods," I say, "but the Lykaion wolves have joined our cause too at Hecate's behest, as well as the world's remaining Halflings."

This jolts Jason, who now sits up and looks at me with surprise.

Continuing, I say, "But all that may not matter in the long run. You see, the world as you know it may not even exist soon. Everything around you...wolves, humans, cities, landscapes...all of it could be incinerated in the blink of an eye."

"What do you mean?"

"Hecate and her collected gods," I answer, "are being challenged by a team of dark gods. Many of them are angry, bitter, and scornful. They don't just mean to take power. They want to make an example of their might. They're willing to destroy half of the world and its people to prove their power. My gods and even magical seers like the Benandanti witches you yourself work with have seen this."

"You're bluffing!" Jason snaps. "Those witches never said anything about the end of the world happening. You're trying to confuse me."

"I'm not," I answer. "Use your wolf hearing and training to see if I'm lying. Whether you believe me or not, a god war is coming, and we're all fodder standing in its way."

The look on Jason's face becomes stoic. I can tell he knows I'm not lying, but I also know he'd never concede to it.

"This wolf war you've created?" I continue, "Ultimately, it will mean nothing. What's the use of fighting for rule when your subjects will all soon be dead? I concede this fight. All that matters to me now is that we get our people to safety, far enough away from the godly blowout."

Squinting his eyes to better focus on my face, Jason says, "Let me get this straight, you're conceding? You're declaring defeat and giving up your title of Archon?"

"I am," I say. "I never wanted that title to begin with. That's also why I'm going to set you free."

"You're...you're what?"

"Free," I confirm. "If what you said earlier about wanting to protect all innocent wolves is true, then I'm willing to turn over my Archon title to a leader who will guard and protect these people, no matter what clan they align themselves with. I will concede and free you on two conditions."

Suspicious, Jason says, "Go on..."

"First of all, you must know that my clan wants nothing to do with the assassin side of our culture. The clans have made more than enough money from that venture. They want to live normal lives as a unified nation, free from internal wars. Promise me you won't rule them in the old ways they are trying to run from. Promise me they won't ever be part of your old world."

Jason stares at me for a long moment. I can see he is mulling over what this means. In essence, he knows he will be ruling over two different clans, each with its own set of guidelines. After a few moments he says, "Go on."

Nodding, I then say, "Second, you must let my team and me do what we can to save our people. You must let us stop this god war from happening. Not just for the wolves, but for every living thing on the planet."

At this, Tobias, Mika, and Nicholas enter the room. They stand behind me, signaling to my grandfather that they stand by what I just said. Jason leans back in his chair, pondering my proposal. I notice him stare at Nicholas.

"You mean to tell me," he says, "you and this scraggly bunch of makeshift wolves are gonna take on a team of gods? You honestly think you will be able to make even a scratch in something like a god level war?"

I calmly reply, "We're going to try."

Jason laughs. Still eyeing Nicholas with contempt, Jason asks him, "You're still siding with him? This bastard half-breed who's just declared his defeat to me, who thinks he can stop gods?"

In a steely voice, Nicholas says, "I do, Uncle."

A sense of humbled pride wells up within me at hearing Nicholas' response. His words mean more to me than he could possibly know.

Jason then tells Nicholas in the old wolf language, "You even wear their trinkets," motioning to the necklace around Nicholas' neck. "You're becoming just like this little faggot."

I immediately focus my thoughts on my own necklace, asking it to help me translate my words into the same Greek wolf language

Jason is using. Angrily, I then say to Jason, "This faggot fought off three witch covens, a gang of demons, mob enforcers, and countless troops of your own best fighters several times over. I'd say he's siding with a winning team. Don't you?"

Jason's eyes glow yellow in anger. Grunting, Jason says in English, "Say you're a really good liar. Say you've convinced these three of what you've just told me. How am I supposed to believe this god war really is happening? How am I supposed to know you're not simply tricking me into not killing you as soon as I get the chance?"

Looking him dead in the eye, I reply, "You can try to kill me, but by now you know just how hard that is to do. If blood is all you're after, then maybe you aren't fit for the title of Archon after all. Petty revenge only tarnishes the title you hold. You and I both know that."

My words strike Jason hard. His expression tells me that I've gotten through to some hidden part of him.

Continuing, I say, "We know your faction is working with Bobby Longo, and we know they're meeting with the Benandanti at the docks tonight. You want proof that what I'm saying is true? Then ask the Benandanti yourself once they arrive. Use your skills to make sure you know what they're saying is true. Maybe then you'll see the big picture and what's really at stake here."

Jason looks hard at me, then to my team. I can see the wheels turning in his head. A couple minutes of quiet silence go by before Jason finally says, "I agree to your conditions and accept your defeat."

I know his inclusion of the word 'defeat' is meant as a dig against me, but I don't let him see my annoyance at his childish taunting. I motion to one of the guards in the room. He looks at me uneasily, then hesitantly goes behind Jason and removes his arm shackles. He then crouches lower and removes his ankle shackles as well. Jason stands and rubs his wrists.

Looking at me with one eyebrow raised, he motions to the other

Emissary soldiers in the room and says, "You've told your people about this changeover, I trust?"

"They're your people now, too" I say, "and yes, I have. Since the Longos and Benandanti are planning to attack us this evening, I hope you have a plan in mind to help stop that from happening."

With a stern voice, Jason says, "Never you mind about that. I'm Archon of this clan now, and I will do everything in my power to make sure every wolf is safe. You go and fight your gods, if they really even exist that is. I'll question those Italian witches as soon as they land. If I find out you really are lying to me, I will use everything I have to track you and your witches down and destroy you." He then turns to Nicholas and adds, "That goes for you, too."

I try to suppress the anger I feel at his verbal attacks at Nicholas, and bow my head.

"I'll be standing with my father and brother," I tell Jason, "to make sure they know about the agreement we just made. Once you confirm the truth, leave the witches to us. Clayton, his wolves, and the mob teams will be your responsibility."

Jason guffaws. "You four against Claudia's full coven? Ha! You barely survived the last fight. You're as good as dead."

I stand up and back myself closer to my team. I then say to my grandfather, "We'll see."

The lot of us then close our eyes and focus on my father. The world around us disappears, and then shifts itself to a new location. Before us, I see my father standing beside Vincent, my brother Damon, and the three Synoro Archons Brice, Shaun, and Ryan. I'm surprised to see Brice, Shaun, and Ryan's battle garb now displaying the colors of the Enopo clan. The lot of them and their personal guards startle at our sudden appearance. Once they realize who we are, their demeanor relaxes a bit.

"Devin!" my father happily exclaims. He rushes over to us and hugs me tightly. I hear my brother just as happily calling out to Mika, and she to him. My father then releases his hold and hugs Nicholas, too. I can see Nicholas hold my father a little tighter than usual. My father notices this as well and asks him if he's okay. Nicholas just shrugs it off and says, "I'll be fine."

My father looks at his cousin one more time. The look of concern lingers in his eyes a bit before he finally turns to give Tobias a hug as well.

"Where are Don Phillipi and his people?" I ask.

Damon lets go of his hold on Mika. "They're back at their mansion. We're in radio contact with them but Don Phillipi and his son won't be part of the actual fight."

My father asks, "So it's over? The overseas Enopo wolves are safe?"

"Yeah," I answer. "The few remaining Enopo wolves still in hiding are being collected by the Lykaion wolves.

Shocked, Vincent asks, "The Lykaion? You were able to convince them of our cause?"

"Not us," Tobias replies. "Hecate."

Vincent bows his head and mutters, "Praise be to the Great Lady."

Nicholas notices the Synoro Archons and asks, "Forgive my bluntness, Archons, but your clothing... It's not Synoro. Have you switched clans?"

Brice answers, "Yes, we and the wolves loyal to us are Enopo now. With everything going on, it just seemed like the right decision to make. If our goddess trusts you, then so should we."

At that, my mother and Gabriella enter the meeting room. Their eyes light up when they see us.

"Devin!" my mother cries. She rushes over to Tobias and me, hugging us both tightly. "You're all safe!"

Gabriella goes over to Mika and hugs her as well, saying, "We are so happy to see you, *mon amis*, especially now. Don Phillipi and his men are working with us. We're about to end the American end of this war once and for all."

"No!" Mika says loudly "It's a trap. Longo and Clayton know you're here. They're waiting for the Benandanti to arrive so that they can attack you together. You have to hold off your attack."

Shaun asks, "How do you know this?"

Turning to Mika, Tobias says, "Show them."

Mika closes her eyes, and I feel her internal magics rise. A moment later, her familiar Fydan springs forth from her body, landing onto the ground in front of her. Everyone in the room looks on in awe as the magical being stretches, then walks over to her mistress, sitting at her feet.

"This is Fydan," I tell the wolves in the room. "Our gods blessed Mika with a familiar of her own. She has Mika's family gift to see. Through her, Mika was able to foresee the Benandanti's arrival."

Surprised, my mother says, "Isn't it supposed to be a rare honor to be gifted with a familiar? Well done, girl!"

The pride in Mika's eyes almost sparkles.

"I'm not the only one," Mika says.

She then points to Tobias. Once she does, Tobias releases his own familiar. It darts from his chest and into the air before him. It glides in a circle around the room before landing on a nearby table.

Beaming, Tobias says, "This is my familiar, Hadrian."

At this, Hadrian spreads his wings and gives his audience a regal bow.

Happily, my father asks, "So does this mean you were able to rescue Fenrus, too?"

My high spirits fall at hearing my father's well-meaning question.

"No," I say. "We haven't had time to try. The Benandanti still have him."

Sincerely, my father says, "I'm sorry, Devin. I just thought…"

"It's okay," I tell him. "I have faith we'll get him again. You need to know one more thing, though. I was able to get another Archon to side with our people."

With my wolfen sense, I can subtly hear Tobias holding his breath.

Vincent asks, "So, you were able to meet with some of the European wolves after all?"

"No," I say again. "Not European, American. My grandfather, Jason Toxotis."

With horror, my father passionately asks, "What are you saying, Devin? My father hates everything to do with this clan. He's locked up back at the compound. He's a danger to everything we stand for."

"Not anymore," I tell him. "I made a bargain with him."

Confused, Gabriella asks, "What bargain could you give him that would make him change his view of us?"

"Rule," I tell her. "I agreed to step down from my role as Archon so that he could take my place."

Gasps and murmurs fill the room.

Angrily, my father says, "Devin, do you have any idea what you've done? The title of Archon is a sacred station. He'll use his authority to destroy this clan from within!"

My brother Damon calmly steps forward and says to my father, "No, I don't think he will." Damon then looks at me and says, "I see what you've done. You know that our grandfather would do anything to protect the wolves under his care. By making him an Archon to the Enopo, you've forced him to put that same set of protection on us. He's now honor bound to do so. That's a move I would never have thought of."

I search my brother's eyes. I can tell he sees just how hard a decision and risk that was for me. He gives me a warm smile. My eyes begin to mist at knowing his understanding is sincere.

Ryan says, "But how can we be sure of that? I've been an Archon at his side for many years. He would die for his people if need be, but he just as strongly hates our new clan."

Tobias says, "Jason will be coming here to meet with everyone. He doesn't yet fully believe that the god war is coming. We'll know what side he's really on once he speaks to the Benandanti. When they confirm what their seers know, his next actions will tell us if he can be trusted or not."

I can see I still haven't quite convinced my father, Vincent, or the three new Enopo Archons.

"Look," I tell everyone in the room.

I focus on my internal magics and picture my new surroundings in mind. I then wave my arm, willing for a visual layout to manifest in the center of the room. Before us, we see the boat dock area, several buildings, and open pier locations. I then cause several individual areas to light up in different colors.

"I know I took a huge gamble and that we're outnumbered as it is," I say, "but I have to have faith that my decision will benefit the clan. Some of you might have doubts, but believe me, this just may work in our favor. I do have a plan. Now listen carefully as I'm going to need every one of you. The timing for this has to be perfect."

Everyone in the room moves in as I relay what I have in mind, listening in earnest.

Chapter Nine
FIGHT

I watch from an afar building as Longo and his men pace one of the larger piers below. Many groups of armed guards patrol the entire area, ready to act if needed. The ammunition they carry makes them seem as if they're prepared to go into war. With my enhanced wolf vision, I can see a scowl on Longo's face as clear as day. He's no doubt agitated at the prospect of possibly being attacked at any minute.

Using my magics, I confirm the intel we received earlier, and my own suspicions. Scattered in buildings around Longo's men I also sense the presence of other clan wolves in hiding. They are all just as heavily stocked with weaponry but are even more deadly. I give a silent prayer to our gods, hoping they will watch over and protect us in what we're about to do.

Looking at a dusty clock on a far wall, I see that it is close to eight o'clock. The boat carrying the Benandanti coven should be arriving at any minute. The moon in the sky is crescent, but still provides an abundant amount of light needed.

A few of Longo's men begin to stir. They point to the harbor. Looking out, a large yacht can be seen drifting toward the docks. Seemingly out of nowhere, several ropes from the ship begin throwing themselves toward several of the mob goons standing by the docking posts. They grab the ropes and begin to tie them off, securing the large vessel.

I can sense a great deal of magic aboard the yacht. The Benandanti aren't even attempting to mask their presence. A few moments later, a walking plank is lowered from the ship, and Claudia appears at the edge of the boat, looking down at the surroundings below. She is wearing a red designer suit and high heels. The color reminds me of the crimson colored cloak Malik wore when we last battled a year ago. A shiver runs through me.

As Claudia carefully walks down the plank, many more figures follow in line behind her. They all wear heavy black and green uniforms. As opposed to our last meeting, I don't see any goblins among her coven. Mentally taking in their number as they emerge from the ship, I count twenty-seven witches total. Panic hits me as I realize that that's way more than the number I previously saw in Virbius' scrying pool. My heartbeat quickens, but I close my eyes and try willing for it to slow its pace. My mind can't have any doubt or distractions right now. My family, my gods, the Halflings, Lia, and the rest of the wolf refugees need me. We can do this. We just have to stick to the plan.

Once the entire coven gathers together on the dock, Longo walks over to them, searching through the crowd, as if looking for a familiar face. I use my keen wolf hearing to try to focus in on what they're saying.

Gruffly, Longo tells Claudia, "I hope you had a safe trip."

Claudia notices Longo's fidgeting and says, "It was pleasant, thank you."

She then raises her hand above her head and motions for someone from her coven to step forward. The crowd parts somewhat and a figure walks through. Before I can make out his face, Longo grabs the young man and places him in a bear hold embrace. This confuses me somewhat. What's that all about?

From one of the buildings, a woman screams out, "Stephen!"

I'm surprised to see my mother's step-mother Julia run out from the building and over to Longo and the young man. Like Longo, Julia embraces the dark clothed male. I send out as subtle of a magical scan as possible toward the figure, hoping none of the witches in the coven will notice. My assumption is confirmed. He's a witch. Can it be? Is Bobby Longo and Julia's son a witch and a member of Claudia's coven?

Just then, I hear the approach of a car engine. The people on the ground below eventually hear it, too. All eyes stare in the direction of the oncoming vehicle. Longo's men hold their guns to their shoulders, ready to shoot if necessary. Longo gets in front of Julia and their son, shielding them with his own body. Several of Longo's men then begin walking toward the car area, cutting it off from getting anywhere near the pier.

A few moments go by before I hear a familiar angry voice bark, "Get the hell out of my way. You know who I am! They're waiting for me!"

Storming through the squadron of bodyguards, I see my grandfather. He's alone and dressed in full Synoro battle gear. He continues walking toward Longo's area, but then a newly emerged figure stops him before he can get to them. I sharpen my vision and see that it's Clayton.

Focusing my hearing again, I hear Clayton whisper to my grandfather, "Jason, you got free! What are you doing here? We can't be seen yet. You'll ruin our plans."

Angrily, Jason says aloud, "Your plans are already ruined. They already know you're here."

"What?" Clayton asks, confused. "But..."

Before he can continue, Jason asks, "Is it true you put a death mark out on the Enopo commoners?"

Horror goes across Clayton's face, but he remains silent. Pushing past him, Jason continues his way to Longo and Claudia with Clayton closely in tow. The level of animosity on Longo's face matches my grandfather's.

"What the hell do you think you're doing old man?" Longo snaps at Jason. "You assassin types are supposed to be lying low!"

Jason looks Longo in the eye fiercely before turning his attention to Claudia. Several of her coven members move forward to her side, but she gives them a subtle hand gesture to stay where they are.

"You!" Jason barks. "You have fortune tellers in your group. Did they already tip you off to what I'm about to ask you?"

Claudia raises one eyebrow. I can tell the fortune tellers remark struck a nerve.

She holds in her anger, calmly addressing Jason by saying, "My *seers* told me many things, but regarding what is about to come out of that primitive mouth of yours, I haven't the slightest idea."

Jason focuses his gaze on her and says, "Tell me true, witch, is there or is there not going to be a possible world-ending god war?"

Claudia's eyes widen as she takes a half step backward.

"I...I have no idea what you're talking about, dog." she answers.

I don't have to use my wolf hearing to listen to her heartbeat to realize she is lying. Her obvious bodily reaction to Jason's question gives her away immediately.

In a steely voice, Jason says, "That's all I had to hear."

In the blink of an eye, Jason removes his swords and swings them in the air at lightning speed. The first blade slices through Clayton's neck, causing the Archon's head to fall off to the side. His second blade is about to do the same to Claudia when one of her witches quickly hits Jason with some sort of magic bolt. Before his blade can touch Claudia, the chaos magic sends Jason hurling several feet backwards. Jason rolls with the tumble, eventually landing on all fours. He looks up to reveal his eyes have become bright yellow.

"Synoro wolves!" he yells into the night, "Kill the humans, your Archon commands you!"

Out of the shadows, the once hidden Synoro wolves begin pouring out, attacking the humans in earnest. Longo looks on in horror as the majority of his men are slaughtered in front of him.

Turning to her coven, Claudia tells them in Italian, "Scatter. You all know what you must do."

With that, the majority of her coven teleport to different points of the pier. They place several unknown items strategically on the ground, then teleport to new locations. The remaining coven members stay behind, creating a wall of protection around their mistress. I notice that two of the witches that stayed behind are the masters of the familiars I previously saw in Virbius' scrying pool. The snake familiar is resting comfortably on its master's shoulders, and the black cat is snuggly at its master's feet as well.

Longo takes out a pistol from his inner jacket, pointing it at Jason. Jason rolls out of the way of the oncoming bullets, charging at Longo with blades still in hand. In seconds, he reaches Longo and raises his sword. Seeing his father is about to be attacked, Stephen sends a magical bolt at Jason, but the experienced wolf merely shrugs off its effects. As Jason is about to bring down his blade on Longo, another set of swords blocks the attack. That's when I see the Neuri assassins Rachael and Jacqueline Dendronto. Rachael quickly kicks Jason away from Longo, providing them more space.

Smirking, Longo says, "Bet you's forgot I paid your pals overseas a nice penny for these two's services. Way I see it, the only one getting killed around here is you."

The Dendronto sisters walk toward Jason, with blades at the ready. Several Synoro Emissaries nearby see the situation and run to their Archon's side.

Forcefully, Jason tells the assassins in the old world wolf language, "You two have an obligation to aid your own kind, not these cattle. Stand aside."

Smirking, Jacqueline replies, "You are not our Archon. We were instructed to aid our client and that's what we're going to do."

Rachael then yells aloud in the Neuri tongue, "Neuri! Protect this human."

She points to Longo as many more wolves emerge from hidden locations. As opposed to Jason's men who wear black assassin gear, these new entries wear the trademark brown Neuri clothing, denoting their allegiance. They form a wall around Longo with swords drawn. Longo smugly crosses his arms in defiance to Jason.

Angrily, Jason yells out, "You're being played for fools! This human is of no consequence to us anymore. The Italian witch hid something from us. Hecate and her allies are about to go into battle. A battle that could destroy everything we know. We need to put aside our differences and get our people to safety before it's too late!"

The Dendronto sisters begin laughing. Jacqueline then says, "The ramblings of an old fool. We were paid to do a job, and we're not leaving until our contract is complete."

The look on Jason's face begins to change. It's almost as if some sort of new understanding or realization is taking place in his mind.

He pauses a moment then says, "Exallos and Basque clans, I speak the truth. Reveal your allegiance. Will you side with me or these arrogant upstarts?"

The remaining wolves then emerge from the last of their hiding spots. Wolves dressed in either gray or green assassin gear stare first at Jason, then to the Dendronto sisters.

"Use your skills!" Jason announces. "See if I'm lying. A god war is coming, and we may not survive it. Come with me so that we might find safety. Side with them, and you're as good as dead."

Rachael says, "Betray your clan laws, and your own clans will kill you themselves! Remember who you are. We have a job to do. Help us fulfill it! This wolf just killed his own fellow Archon. You can't trust a word he says."

Frustrated by his lack of understanding, Longo points his gun at Jason again and says, "Fuck this!"

He fires several rounds at Jason. One bullet manages to hit him in the shoulder. As Jason falls to the ground, his Emissary assassins begin to charge at the Neuri wolves. Half of the Exallos and Basque wolves join them while the other half sides with the Dendronto sisters and Neuri. Soon the entire dock is filled with the sounds of clashing swords.

With the wolves now occupied, I know it's my turn to make my move. I look down at the figure of a dog shaped being at my side and ask, "Are you ready?"

The dog looks up at me and nods its head. I take off the leather band that masks my magical presence and place it in my pocket. I then pet the dog's head and close my eyes. I will myself to teleport to an area in front of Claudia. When I open my eyes, I see her standing before me. The dog from before nudges my leg, letting me know it's still at my side.

Claudia looks at me coolly. My appearance hasn't surprised her in the least. Longo and Julia on the other hand look downright gob smacked. Looking down at my legs, Claudia spots my animal companion and her eyes widen.

"What is that?" she asks.

"You don't recognize my familiar, Fenrus?" I answer.

"It can't be! Your familiar is our prisoner," she says, grasping at a chain around her neck. Being closer to her persona, I'm now able to sense a familiar magic attached to the bauble she's protecting. Bingo.

Smiling at her, I say, "Your skills must be waning Benandanti. Even a novice level witch would be able to sense that this is a magical familiar."

Claudia stares down at the creature again, then back at me. I can see the light of desire in her eyes. She wants the familiar a great deal. She then looks over to the familiars in her own coven. The expression on her face tells me that they are mentally confirming to her that I indeed am standing beside a fellow familiar.

"I can sense its godly power. You are not lying. Your companion is a familiar." Claudia submits. "How is this possible?"

"How my familiar came to be is of no concern of yours," I tell her. "Your trifling here is done. Your allies fight among themselves. You've lost. Go home. You have no more business here."

"Arrogant cur."

The words come from the witch to Claudia's left. I look at her face and see that it's Lucia. To Claudia's right, I see Divina, looking at me, perplexed. On the other side of Divina is Longo's son, Stephen Carver. He looks almost as young as my brother Damon. My mother is right—he does look strikingly like his father. His mother Julia clings to his arm, eyeing me with contempt.

Longo looks at me angrily. Then to Claudia he says, "This punk is a witch, too?"

"Yes," she answers. "And quite possibly one of my coven's newest members."

"What?" Longo yells.

Claudia's eyes narrow as she stares at Longo. Longo, seeing the look of danger in her face, holds back what he was about to say next.

"I'll never be part of your coven, Claudia!" I say defiantly.

Claudia looks back at me and her eyes resume their normal pitch. A slight smile forms on her face. Just then, one of the Synoro wolves near me notices my presence outside of the wolf battle skirmish. He begins to charge at me when Claudia makes a nearby barrel fly in his direction, knocking him to the ground unconscious. Claudia then motions to her coven. In unison, they raise their hands. A magical wall of energy then separates the area we are in from the wolf battle several feet away.

I look down at the dog at my side and tell it, "Go, Fenrus, find safety."

At that, the dog disappears. Claudia grasps at open air before her, driven with anxiety at the familiar's sudden disappearance. Catching herself, she softens her demeanor again. Divina whispers something into her ear. With my wolf hearing I make out the words, "I can't see where the creature has gone."

To myself I think, "Good."

Several of Claudia's coven members who were previously dispatched now teleport back to join her again. Nodding in their direction, Claudia places her manicured hands into the front pockets of her jacket.

She then says to me, "This charade with the wolves has gone far enough. I'm laying all my cards out on the table, as you Americans say. I only agreed to work with these mongrels so that I could get to you. I needed to test you to see if you were strong enough. Your grandfather is right. There is a god war coming, and we're going to need every bit of power we can get our hands on if we plan to survive it. Familiars are the key. Witches are powerful, but familiars have something we don't. They have divinity. With their help, we might be strong enough to ensure our survival. So, now do you see our predicament? Now do you see why we need you?"

"And the others?" I ask. "What of them? What about the wolves, humans, and every other living being on the planet? Do you have a failsafe for them, too?"

Lucia speaks up, saying, "Those dogs deserve death. Because of them, witches have been brought near to extinction."

Claudia casually looks toward Lucia, who then becomes silent.

Turning back to me, Claudia says, "I've told you before that I have no love for the wolves. That hasn't changed, but those ill feelings don't extend to you. Nor to the humans who choose to aid us."

Claudia motions to Longo and Julia.

"I stand by my previous invitation," Claudia continues. "I ask you again, join us."

The last of Claudia's coven then teleports back to Claudia's side. I can see increased satisfaction in her face.

Then, on either side of me, Tobias and Mika appear. I know their individual familiars are hidden inside of them, out of view from the predatory witches before us. I take their hands and magically affirm our union.

"Quaint," Claudia says, "but those two will be of no use to you. They are skilled but ultimately lack what is needed. I had hoped you'd come willingly but now I see that we're going to have to do this the hard way."

Claudia's coven familiars begin to hiss. The air sparks electric around her coven. Storm clouds begin to close in overhead. The sound of thunder rumbles around us. This isn't our doing. What's Claudia up to?

Speaking louder so as not to be drowned out by the sound of thunder, I say to her, "Like you, I just want my people safe. Whatever you have planned, it would be better if we worked together. I still stand with my people, but we don't have to be enemies. Whether you admit it or not, wolves have just as much chance of surviving the onslaught as witches, but not alone."

Divina steps forward and says, "Your people? You are not just a wolf, Devin. You and your coven are witches, too. In my visions, I see a great potential for you. You, not them. Your kin, those wolves, can't be trusted. They've turned on us before. They are destined to do so again."

The clouds become darker as the thunder increases its pitch. I now notice the witch and cat familiar's eyes glowing. The energy emanating from them and their masters feels potent.

Tobias shouts out to Claudia, "What are you doing?"

Claudia yells above the cacophony, "Taking this fight to a more neutral setting and ensuring our survival!"

I close my eyes and focus on my internal magics, letting them amplify my thoughts. I focus on Nicholas. When I sense his awareness, I mentally tell him, "Now!"

Behind me, I immediately sense the arrival of a troop of persons. Just as they appear, the sky strobes with a series of brilliant lightning strikes. My vision goes white from the glaring light for a moment. I feel the same displacement motions that overcome me when I teleport. I try my best to regain my vision. In moments, the world comes into view again. The dock and everyone from before is just as they were, with just one glaring exception. As I look to where the boat previously stood, I see that it is now gone. So has the water it sat in and the city skyline off in the distance. In its place is a large open meadow. It's as if someone has taken a portion of the pier we previously stood on and transported it to another place entirely. Even the evening storm clouds have been replaced with sunny bright blue skies.

To my far left, I see the army of clan wolves who were previously fighting among themselves now stopped in place. They look around perplexed by what they see.

I look on at Claudia, who I expect to still have the same smirk of self-satisfaction. Instead, she carries one of sudden alarm. Her eyes are locked onto the group of persons behind me.

"How did you…," Claudia stammers.

Looking behind me, I see not only Nicholas and the team of Enopo Archons, but also the rest of my family, my squadron of Enopo Emissaries and a large number of Lykaion wolves as well. Idaios and Danae nod to me, signaling their support. I then turn back to Claudia, matching her stare defiantly.

"This could go either way, Claudia," I tell her. "The choice is yours. Side with us and strengthen your chances, or fight against us and potentially doom us all."

Claudia turns to Divina and asks in Italian, "What do you see?"

Divina's eyes gloss over, becoming stark white. After a few moments, they return to their normal pitch. She then says to Claudia, "I see nothing." She then points to the Lykaion wolves and says, "They are the ones. They are the ones who have been blocking my visions."

Idaios speaks up from behind me and says, "Your visions have led your coven down this path of destruction. Now is time for you to stop making judgments based on magic. Now is time for you to make judgments with the sanity of your own heart and minds."

Lucia angrily screams, "They go against us again! They prove their disloyalty! We should kill the wolves now!"

Claudia's coven murmurs its agreement. Claudia turns to Lucia and slaps her across the face. I can see that her hand sizzles from the after effects of touching Lucia, but Claudia doesn't show any weakness. In Italian she says, "I am the head of this coven. You will learn your place!"

Lucia holds her cheek and stares at Claudia coldly. She remains silent, and then takes one step back. Turning back to us, Claudia shouts, "I don't have time for this nonsense! We are taking what we need. The rest of you I leave up to fate." She then turns to her coven and says, "Take him!"

Several witches materialize around me. My coven and several of the Lykaion wolves send hexes at them, hitting deflection fields for some and singeing several others magically. For the people with magical shields, Tobias, Mika, and I kick through them easily, striking the casters square in the face. I thank the goddess for werewolves' natural resistance to outside magics. The witches fall by each of our attacks, thanks to our enhanced wolf strength.

Around me, a new battle takes place, this time between Claudia's coven and my own team of allies.

Before I know it, Nicholas is at my side swinging one of his swords at several newly arrived witches attacking me. His body takes a few hits to the Benandanti's magic, but he shrugs off any effects. An additional hit to his hand does manage to knock his sword away, though. I see Nicholas disappear then reappear behind his witch attacker. He pulls a rod from his thigh pocket and flicks it in the air a couple times. A series of spikes erupt from it. It's then that I realize it's the same weapon Brian gave him a few days ago. Nicholas swings it at the witch's head, and I hear a loud thunk. Claudia's witch falls to the ground dead.

For each new attacker that appears, an additional ally of mine challenges him, keeping me at a safe distance from harm. I look on at Claudia to see that the only people left on the platform with her are her generals Lucia and Divina, along with Longo and his son and Julia. I'm surprised to notice that the Dendronto sisters are nowhere to be found.

"The wall!" Mika shouts to me.

I look over at the group of rival wolves and see that the clear, magical barrier that previously separated them from us is beginning to ripple. With Claudia's coven now focused elsewhere, the dividing wall has no one to support its existence. It soon fades and vanishes altogether. The now freed wolves still stand in place though, unsure of what action to take.

Jason steps out of the group, eyeing what is happening. He then turns to the crowd and says, "These witches confirm what I told you earlier. Stop this infighting and focus on our true enemy!" He then points to Claudia and says, "Kill the witch and her minions!"

A few seconds go by before half of the rival wolves roar themselves into a frenzy, charging into battle alongside of us. The remaining wolves stand their ground, watching the carnage from afar.

Realizing the odds are now in my favor, Claudia gathers a massive amount of energy around herself. She opens her mouth and a siren call escapes her lips. A few moments later, a dark vortex appears behind her. The black swirling clouds grow. Out of the darkness, many child-sized figures emerge. I immediately recognize the hunched monstrous forms. Goblins.

Between deflecting several hexes from Claudia's witches and sending out hexes of my own, I see Tobias and Mika's bodies stiffen in response to the goblin's arrival. I look on at them concerned. A moment later, their familiars shoot out of their bodies. The two familiars race toward the dark vortex and cast a powerful bolt of their own at it. In seconds, the doorway starts to shrink, sending the goblins who have yet to walk through it screaming into oblivion. Their screams remind me of the same screams their demonic brethren gave last year when I cast them back to their hellish realm. Once the dark teleportation tunnel disappears, Claudia turns to look at us in fury. The goblins that made it through shriek their anger into the air above.

Claudia points to Hadrian and Fydan, saying, "Goblins! Capture those two! I need them alive!"

The various goblins' eyes glow with anger. From their heads, the goblins pulse green energy at Hadrian and Fydan. The familiars manage to dodge each attack and return to the side of their witch companions. Claudia eyes Tobias and Mika with the same hunger she showed earlier. I can tell her point of interest just grew to include them as well.

"Get them!" Claudia barks.

The goblins screech and run toward where the three of us are standing. Several Lykaion wolves materialize in front of us, forming a wall. They hold their palms out, sending a wave of mystic energy at the goblins. The goblins fall backward in its wake.

I notice Danae is one of the wolves now in front of me. She turns back and says, "Do not let the goblins touch you. They are energy vampires."

"I know," I tell her. "They managed to steal my familiar from me during our last battle. They are also allergic to silver, like us wolves. You might be able to use that against them."

Danae nods her head. Then, to her companions in her clan's language, she says, "Brothers and sisters, those swords, there!"

She then points to the wolves standing idly by watching the fight, too proud to fight beside my clan. The Lykaions look at the stubborn wolves and suddenly their eyes begin to glow a pale yellow. They then turn back to the goblins. Several Emissary swords appear in mid-air and begin swinging at the goblins. The goblins flee in various directions in terror away from the silver crafted weapons.

I turn to Tobias and give him a hug.

"Be safe," I tell him into his ear.

"I love you," he tells me back.

I give him a quick kiss, then feel someone squeeze my hand. I look to see it is Mika. She smiles and says, "Good luck."

I squeeze her hand back and will myself to appear in front of Claudia. A moment later, I'm standing before her. Lucia and Divina immediately block my access to her with their bodies.

"Stop this fight!" I tell them. "We're both losing members of our own teams. You said we need as much power as we can get." Pointing behind me, I say, "Sending our people to slaughter one another won't accomplish that."

I hear a gun cock off to the side of me. I look to see that it's Longo, ready to aim his pistol squarely at my head. Claudia pushes through her generals and sends Longo's gun flying out of his hands.

To me, she then says, "You know what I want."

"You can have me," I tell her, "but leave them out of it."

With a cold look on her face, she says, "Your coven. I saw their familiars. The three of you surrender, and we'll leave your dogs be."

"No deal," I adamantly tell her.

Angered, Claudia says, "Then, I'll use your familiar's power when needed and kill you both in the process."

"My familiar isn't in your necklace anymore, Claudia," I say. "You saw that yourself earlier. Your coven will die here, along with everyone else. You will be known as a dictator who sent her people to their deaths, not the savior you claim to be. *That* will be your final legacy."

Grabbing her necklace, Claudia pulls it out from under her clothing. I notice that there isn't just one gem on the chain but two.

Now holding them above her head, she says, "Do you think I'm stupid? I sense your magic still in here. That familiar from earlier was a trick. I won't let this go. One way or another, I'll have all your coven's familiars as my own!"

I hear a loud roaring sound from somewhere behind Claudia, and everyone turns to see. Before I know it, Claudia, Lucia and Divina are being knocked forward and onto the ground. Standing over them is a large black and white cat creature. It is double the size of a fully transformed werewolf and bulging with muscles. It's large sabre teeth look as if they could tear through metal, as do the oversized claws protruding from its large paws. Its huge green eyes stare wildly around, looking for its next victim. Sitting on top of the beast is a laughing Brian Gardener, holding a sword in one hand and a shield in the other.

Through his protective helmet, Brian yells, "Eat your heart out, He-Man!"

They both then leap onto a nearby grouping of Claudia's witches who look on in terror as the now transformed Ms. Whiskers makes short work of them.

A series of pinging sounds cause me to look downward. It's then that I see the necklace Claudia was previously holding, now tumbling along the ground toward me.

"No!" Claudia screams.

I quickly snatch it up, barely missing a hex bolt, and teleport back to Tobias and Mika.

When I get there, I notice Mika looking at Ms. Whiskers and Brian. She mutters, "How did you know that…"

Ignoring her questions, I focus on the two gems now in hand. Both are identical so I can't quite make out which is the one holding Fenrus. I use my internal magics to try to break both casings, but to no avail.

"I can't break through!" I say.

Seeing what I have, Fydan mentally says, "Let us help you."

Using my magics again, I feel the added strength of Tobias, Mika, Hadrian, and Fydan assisting me. I hear magical attacks hitting our general vicinity but can only assume the Lykaion wolves are shielding us from harm. A few moments go by, and I hear a cracking sound.

"It's working!" I exclaim. "Keep it up!"

I hear another cracking sound, only this time louder, then again. A bright burst of energy appears. In its wake, I see two figures standing before us. I wrap my arms around Fenrus' neck. Upon our touch, we re-establish our magical connection. I can feel my energies being rejuvenated. Looking down at his newly arrived companion, I'm shocked to also see Anna's familiar, the orange feline Sekhmet.

Surprised as well, Mika says, "Sekhmet! What are you doing here?"

In our heads, we hear Sekhmet say, "It's a long story, and one we don't have time for. Quickly, you must…"

I'm suddenly hit with a powerful bolt. The potency of the spell knocks me back somewhat. I look up to see three Lykaion wolves face down on the ground. Standing over them are Claudia, Lucia, and Divina. Fury completely consumes Claudia's expression.

In Italian, I hear Claudia say, "You just messed with the wrong witch."

As in our previous battle, a green haze begins to envelop the three Benandanti witches. Seeing their master in need, the still remaining Benandanti coven members leave their battle opponents and join Claudia. Now exceedingly more powerful than before, the energy dragon that manifests is colossal. As the dragon throws its head back, the roar that escapes its jaws pierces my ears, chilling my blood.

Frightened by the gargantuan beast, the idol wolves who previously had no part of the battle run for their lives in an attempt at safety. Seeing this, the beast lunges for a few still within striking distance, killing them instantly with its powerful jaws.

"Fall back!" I yell.

Confirming my order, Jason tells the wolves still under his command, "Do as he says! Everyone fall back!"

I notice that even the wolves that previously fought against Jason are now following his orders, too fearful of the prospect of becoming the large reptile's next victims. Even the enlarged Ms. Whiskers now stands behind us, with Brian still mounted upon her. She eyes the dragon defensively.

Next to me, my father asks, "What are we going to do?"

Looking in his direction, I see that he's staring up at the beast with his swords drawn. I know his physical swords won't be of any help against the magical construct.

In my head, I hear Fenrus say, "We need a shield, fast."

I hold my palm out, concentrating on as big a shield as I can manage. When it manifests, I notice it's only big enough to protect two, maybe three, persons. Tobias and Mika hold their palms out as well, joining my cause. With their strength added to mine, the shield triples in size. The dragon sees what we're doing and lunges toward us. The shield manages to stop the monster from reaching us, but shatters as the potent combined energies of the Benandanti coven is too much for the three of us to withstand. Tobias, Mika, and I are knocked to the ground easily as the fragments of our shield dissipate.

My brother Damon steps forward and raises his palm into the air. Just as before, as small shield forms in an attempt to stop the beast. Several Lykaion wolves do the same, further strengthening Damon's limited magic. The three of us quickly get up and rebuild our own shields, feeling our familiars enhancing our strengths in the process. Soon, we create an entire wall of mystical energy. I see that thankfully it's large enough to keep the beast at bay.

The energy dragon lashes at the wall, trying it's best to break through. Our wall holds, though barely. Looking across from us, the faces on the unified coven standing against us are full of pure rage. It's as if they take on the animal persona of the energy beast they create. Despite their ferocity, though, we are at a stalemate, neither set of magics able to counteract the other.

The remaining goblins shriek their disapproval and begin charging at our protected encampment. When they reach the wall, they place their hands upon it. I begin to feel our united magics wane.

Idaios shouts, "The goblins are draining our energies! They're going to break through! They need to be stopped!"

Jason barks at his wolves, saying, "Emissaries! Destroy those creatures!"

Members of each wolf clan raise their swords synchronously and begin charging at the goblins. With their resistance to magic, the wolves struggle through our mystic wall but eventually break free. They then confront the goblins face to face with their silver swords drawn. Several wolves slice through their misshapen opponents easily. Others are attacked by the earth bound demons. Whereas the wolves attacks are graceful yet forceful, the goblins actions are savage as they rake their claws at anything near them. The few that are able to overcome their wolf opponents rip into the lupine assassins' flesh as if it were paper.

"Wolves!" Jason shouts. "Transform! Let these demons know why we are to be feared above all else! Tear them apart!"

On cue, the various wolves place their swords onto their back held scabbards. They then quickly shift their various other weapons and the transformation begins. They bypass their usual hybrid human/wolf guises and let their full inner beasts emerge. Their stretch fabric uniforms easily accommodate their wearer's new larger forms. Soon the troop of military clothed fighters is replaced with a rather large pack of creatures that are the stuff of nightmares.

Behind me, I can hear Brian shakily mutter under his breath, "Oh my God…"

The energy dragon sees their full transformation as well and tries to attack the various werewolves. This, fortunately for us, proves rather hard to do. In their newly formed hair suit guise, the werewolves are now much too agile and fast for the magical energy beast to capture or harm. They manage to scatter to safety before each dragon strike.

When the opportunity arises, the werewolves try to take out as many goblins as possible. Now larger in size, the team of wolves are able to easily scoop up the various dwarf sized demons, shaking them in their jaws before clinching their teeth, making short work of them. The goblin's green colored blood soon litters across the meadow, causing the once green vegetation to shrivel and darken in color.

In my head, I hear Sekhmet say, "Now, while the witches are distracted, reshape your shield and pierce the dragon's hide!"

From the expression on every magical wielding member of my team's faces, I can see that they heard the same sage mental advice as well. I close my eyes and envision our protective wall. I imagine it changing shape. Slowly, I feel our projection elongate. When I open my eyes, I see the wall now isn't a wall at all. The construct is now above us and looks like some sort of long spear. I look at the end closest to the dragon who is now flailing at the various werewolves surrounding it. I imagine the spear's point to sharpen and project my will outward. Sure enough, the spear's end becomes arrow-like and jagged. Looking at my team, I check to see if they are all ready. Head nods abound.

Looking back at the energy dragon, I shout, "Now!"

The spear immediately lunges forward, stabbing the beast in the area where it's heart would have been. The Benandanti coven screams in unison, the result of the psychic backlash of their weapon's death. Several of them fall to the ground, knocked unconscious while the remaining coven members stagger, trying to gain their balance. Slowly, the energy dragon dissipates until there is nothing left.

Seeing their foes are at a disadvantage, the fully transformed wolves on the field begin charging at the witches, ready to sink their teeth and claws into them while at their weakest.

"No!" Tobias yells.

Immediately, earth pillars begin to surround the defenseless witches, blocking the werewolves from finishing their kill.

Turning to Tobias, Jason shouts, "What in the hell are you doing? We have them! Let the wolves kill them and be done with it!"

To Jason, I say, "That is not our way."

Surprisingly, my father then says, "Devin, in this case, Jason is right. We might not get another chance like this again. We need to stop the threat now."

"No," I adamantly say. "If we kill these witches, then we prove they were right. Wolves will only be bringing witches to further extinction. If we do that, it will mean we're no better than they are. I won't let that happen. We do this the witch way."

Fury goes across Jason's face.

"To hell with your bleeding heart!" Jason says. "Wolves! Kill the witches!"

"No!" I yell.

With my connection to Fenrus now re-established, the verbal order is mixed with a sense of magical command. It sends a ripple of strict authority across the field. Every wolf stops in place.

I then turn to Jason and say, "We had an agreement. You agreed to let my coven and me do whatever is necessary to guarantee our safety. Those witches could help us. We need their strength!"

Jason eyes me harshly. His silence tells me that he knows I have him backed into a corner. To go against his word in front of so many wolves under his command would make him look exceedingly bad and may cost him some of his clout as a leader.

Angered, he crosses his arms and says in dead tone, "What do you plan then?"

Looking back at the pillars surrounding the Benandanti witches, I say, "Make an example where it's due."

I will myself to appear beside the earth pillars. My world shifts, and as asked, I see the mounds of earth now standing in front of me. I sense my coven's presence manifest behind me in support. Looking down, I notice Fenrus is still at my side, at the ready to spring into action if needed.

I magically cause Tobias' pillars to explode, leaving only dust and rubble in their wake. Willing the air to clear, I see that the majority of the witches are still incapacitated. The only Benandanti at full attention are the two witches who are masters to familiars of their own. They look on at us, then down at the various familiars of my coven, and stand their ground even in defeat. They know there is no way they could win in a two-against-four familiar battle, especially as weak as they are in their present state. They pet their familiars in hand close to them, unsure of what is about to happen.

"I won't hurt you," I tell them in Italian.

The look on their faces tells me that they aren't all too sure I'm speaking the truth, but they keep still, allowing us to walk among them with no retaliation.

When I see Claudia, she is lying on top of two of her coven members. Beside them, I see the unconscious forms of Longo, Julia, and their son Stephen.

From a nearby location, I hear someone try to say, "Don't you touch her."

Looking toward where the voice originated, I see Lucia. She is on the ground, her face covered with streaks of dirt and blood.

With my magics, I take hold of Claudia and lift her off the ground. I will for her to stay stationary so that everyone can see her. I then tap into Fenrus' magical pool, allowing it to overtake me with added strength. Using that strength, I nudge the many unconscious forms scattered about to awaken. Slowly, the many remaining witches' eyes open, taking in their surroundings. When they see Claudia in my grasp, they look surprised. A few look as if they are about to retaliate, but Tobias and Mika magically restrain them before they can do something they'll regret. Fortunately for us, in their weakened state, the restraint is relatively easy to manage.

Magnifying my voice, I then say through my universal translating necklace, "See this witch. She thought she could steal what she deemed hers and kill whoever stood in her way. She is a disgrace to our legacy. The Wiccan Rede is a simple one. 'That it harms none, do as you will'. Claudia cast aside this simple precept and look where it's gotten her."

One of the Benandanti familiar masters then says, "What she did was for the protection of us all."

Looking at the witch, I say, "No, what she did was needlessly put everyone's lives in jeopardy. Had she come to us openly and asked for our help and told us why it was needed, we would've given it to her without question. Instead, she took it upon herself to try to steal our familiars without our consent for her own selfish purposes. Look where those kinds of actions leave us."

I point to the various dead bodies scattered across the field.

"No one wins when one group takes it upon itself to dictate what others should do," I continue. I then turn to look at Jason. "These dead wolves, witches, and goblins prove that point."

I can tell Jason is chomping at the bit, but some part of me knows that he understands what I'm saying is true.

"Then, what is it you want?"

I look toward who asked the question and see Stephen Carver. His parents stand at either side of him, dirty and disheveled.

I lift my head high and say, "I plan to give each of you the choice Claudia and the other European wolves never gave their people. I give you the choice either to stand by us, or to leave to choose your own way."

Lucia screams, "He lies! Choose against him, and he'll kill you where you stand!"

Mika says, "If you believe that, then you're just as blind as Claudia. I've stood by Devin and am proud to be part of his coven. Devin is no Initiator. None of us are. That said, we need each other if we plan to live through this needless war our gods are destined to fight in, but we won't force anyone's hand."

Tobias continues saying, "Stand with us and you can see for yourself what my sister says is true. Those that wish to leave are free to do so at any time. It's as simple as that."

Struggling to her feet, Lucia says, "They are dogs! They can't be trusted! They will kill us the first chance they get!"

She throws a hex toward me which I am able to easily block. She throws another, then another. Each weak attack, I quickly disperse with magics of my own. I look on at Lucia and see that she is not moved by anything I have to say.

"Fight back!" Lucia screams.

She tries to manifest more hexes but is too physically spent. She collapses on the ground instead, still consumed by anger.

Divina then says, "Stop it, Lucia. We've heard enough from you."

Hurt and in shock, Lucia says, "What? Divina..."

"I said stop!" Divina repeats. Then turning to me, she says, "Your white haired coven members have been blocking my visions. If you are telling the truth, have them lift their binding. Let me see for myself if there's any value in what you say."

In a croaked voice, Claudia says, "No, Divina, you can't trust them. Follow me, stay..."

I can sense Claudia trying to reach out to Divina magically. I block her weakened attempt and Claudia goes slack again.

Turning to Idaios and Danae, I tell them, "Do it. Lift your binding."

Their eyes glow yellow for a moment, then revert to their normal pitch.

"There," I tell Divina. "You're free to use your gifts again. Use your vision, and tell us what you see."

Divina's eyes turn white.

"I see," she says, "I see a coven, large. I see both wolves and witches fighting beside each other. I see a few Benandanti, your coven, some white hairs, and a few others I've never seen before. And Familiars. So many familiars with so much power behind them. The being the coven battles ... it's dark. Even darker than the goblins under Claudia's control. It drains everything in its reach. I..."

A massive energy blast hits Divina. It disintegrates her, leaving nothing but ash and smoke where she once stood.

"No!" Lucia cries.

All eyes turn toward the source of the blast. Standing there is Anna, dressed in her high priestess clothing. She emanates great strength, but the dark circles around her eyes tell me she is near exhaustion.

In an ethereal voice she says, "Ah-ah, can't have you giving away all my secrets."

Several of the fully transformed werewolves gain a defensive position and are about to charge the newly arrived goddess. I yell for each of them to stay where they are. Anna laughs.

"Smart move," she tells me.

I slowly lower Claudia to the ground, but keep a tight magical reign on her. Then to Anna I say, "What do you want, war god?"

Anna chuckles louder.

"I'm here," she says, "to end this little rebellion before it gets out of hand."

Anna looks down and sees the familiar Sekhmet. Her eyes widen, and she roars like a lion. Sekhmet hisses back defiantly at his former master. Obviously Anna, or rather the war god inside of her, didn't expect to see the familiar here. I hope this is something that will work in our favor.

In her new Egyptian voice, Anna says to the limp body of Claudia, "You promised to keep that thing imprisoned! You went back on your word!"

In faint tones, Claudia says, "No mistress, I kept my word. I...I..."

Anna's eyes become a deep crimson color. Beside me, I hear Claudia scream out in pain. A few snaps can be heard and then I can't sense any life emanate from her anymore. I bend down and check her closely. She is no longer breathing.

Another scream erupts, this time from Lucia who angrily begins charging at Anna. Weak though she is, the fury within her takes over at the sight of her Coven Master being killed. Longo takes out his guns and begins firing them at Anna as well.

"No! Stop!" I yell, but its too late.

Lucia falls to the ground and begins to spasm violently. Longo grabs at his neck in a flailing motion, as if he is being choked. Julia and Stephen try to help Longo but are knocked backwards by an invisible force instead. More snapping sounds can be heard and shortly thereafter Longo falls to the ground motionless. Lucia stops moving, too. I know they both are now dead.

Julia screams and is about to charge toward Anna when Stephen stops her, grabbing her by the arm and forcing her down.

"Stop this!" Mika cries out. "If my grandmomma is anywhere in there, fight it! Don't let this monster use you like this!"

Mika grabs at her neck, trying to remove new invisible hands holding her. Anna's familiar Sekhmet sends a bolt at Anna. Surprisingly, it knocks her down, allowing Mika to breathe again. Tobias, Damon, and I go to Mika to make sure she is all right.

Getting back to her feet, Anna roars again. She sends a destructive bolt toward us. I can sense it's just as potent as the one that destroyed Divina. The four of us hold out our palms and create an energy shield. I can feel our familiars enhancing our magical strength. The shield proves to be strong enough to hold off Anna's onslaught, but just barely.

Anna sends another bolt. This time, I'm surprised to see the two Benandanti witches with familiars of their own materialize beside us. They add their magics to ours, causing the shield to become stronger. Once the new bolt strikes, it easily dissipates. Anna's face shows pure fury.

"You think you're strong enough to defeat *Me*? I'll destroy you *all*."

Anna gathers a massive amount of energy around her. I can tell by the determination on her face that she means every word.

"Everyone! Fall back!" I yell.

Just as she's about to let go her energies, Anna is hit with a powerful blast instead. As she topples to the ground, my heart lightens by what I see. Standing there are my gods Gaea, Hecate, Virbius, Artemis, and Apollo. Next to them are the goddess Bastet and another goddess I've never seen before. Upon closer inspection, I notice that this new goddess is wearing a trademark symbol I've seen Anna use in ritual several times before, before her possession.

"Isis," Mika confirms.

I have a feeling that things are about to get interesting.

Chapter Ten
THE GOD WAR BEGINS

Isis speaks first, her voice filled with the same Egyptian dialect as Bastet.

"You have something of mine, insect. Return it to us, or die under my heel."

The power emanating from Isis is almost a match to that of Gaea. Anna slowly gets up, wiping a trickle of blood from the corner of her mouth with the back of her wrist.

I silently motion for everyone on the field to drop back, away from what could potentially be a very destructive battleground. The fully transformed wolves quietly run back to the rest of the wolves gathered behind me. The Benandanti witches are all now at full attention. They quickly move closer to my wolves, too, but not so close as to mingle in with the others.

Anna eyes our regrouping, but does nothing for fear of retaliation. I notice that her body begins to shimmer slightly.

Isis laughs. "Silly godling. You're not running away from this fight."

Desperation goes across Anna's face. She knows she's in trouble. She looks around for anything that can help her.

Bastet says, "You are still too weak to take on all of us on your own, but you *are* now strong enough to live without the aid of the host body you occupy. Leave the shell and face us in your true form."

Anna glowers. "You'd like that, wouldn't you? Me give up your most prized devotee. Sorry mother, but that is not going to happen. I will hold on to this body until it becomes a rotting, withering corpse with no life of its own. One way or another, you will suffer for what you did to me."

Isis says, "You murdered close to half of Egypt with your blood-thirst and made no qualms about killing more. You had to be stopped. I supported your mother's judgment to desecrate you and scatter your remains to the winds. It was a kinder route than what I had in store for you."

Anna becomes livid as she says, "You were all jealous! With all the wars I lorded over I became more powerful. You began to fear me. You were all afraid my power would soon overcome your own!"

Bastet answers, "You fool. Had you continued your course, we wouldn't have had any more subjects to worship us at all! You were becoming the death bringer to all gods of Egypt. No, daughter, we did not do you a disservice by ending your life. By destroying you, we were protecting all life as we knew it!"

Hecate says, "Give up, Sekhmet. You can't win."

Anna stares at Hecate and says, "You are nothing to me, Greek god. Stand with my enemies, and you will soon become one as well."

Artemis manifests her bow and aims it at Anna. An energy arrow appears within it. The crackling energy causes the hairs on the back of my neck to rise. Even from our safe distance, I can feel the potency of the power she wields.

"Stand down," Artemis commands.

The air turns dark and a cold chill sweeps across the field. A strange sickening feeling grows in the pit of my stomach. A black cloud takes shape next to Anna, and then quickly pulls away. In its wake is a dog headed man dressed in black robes. I can tell this is no werewolf, but some sort of dark god.

Isis and Bastet immediately gather their energies about them. My magical awareness goes into overload at the level of magics being manifested. Isis addresses the newly arrived being, saying, "Am-heh. You are forbidden to leave the underworld. Return there at once before I strike you were you stand."

Am-heh raises his head to calmly look at the two Egyptian gods and says, "The underworld isn't as you remember it anymore. You don't scare me, magic god. Atum is no more. I travel where I wish, no longer held to your rules. I stand with Sekhmet now. Soon, we and the others in our union will take over this world, leaving you and yours only memories."

The earth then begins to rumble. On the other side of Anna, the ground begins to rise and open. An enormous spider emerges from the mound of earth, several times bigger than even the largest werewolf I've ever had to face. Like the other newly arrived god, its presence fills me with dread. My gods across from me go noticeably on guard.

Anna smiles, saying, "This is another companion of mine. His name is Anansi, the African trickster god."

Anansi opens and closes his pincers, creating a strange sucking sound.

"Pleased to make your acquaintance," he says in a thickly sarcastic manner.

Gaea says, "Your newly collected pantheon of gods is still no match for ours. Our domain is vast and not as nearly forgotten. The number of mortals who can name even half of you is few and far between."

"Not for long," Anna says. "When they see the destruction we bring, they will fear us. They will know our names again. We will reign as sovereigns once more."

Artemis says, "That's not going to happen."

She then lets go of her arrow, sending it straight for Anna. I hear Mika gasp. Just as the arrow is about to strike, Am-heh catches it, absorbing the energy into himself. Anansi's sickening mouth noises increase, amused by the turn of events.

"As I said," Anna says, "this body is mine. You can't have it."

Anansi shoots webbing at Artemis at lightning speed. It strikes her, encasing her in a thick cocoon. Apollo releases his sword in response. It engulfs in flames once it reaches open air. I hold up my hand to block the brightness and heat it generates. He then slices through the webbing surrounding Artemis, releasing his sister from her hold. Apollo's flames reduce Anansi's webs to cinders.

Tobias then whispers to me, "Do you sense that? Earth magic."

On cue, Virbius' body glows green as heavy vines erupt from the Earth. They ensnare Anansi, holding him firmly in place. Gaea then raises her hands and tree roots also grab the spider, reinforcing Virbius' spell. Anansi's vocal sucking noises increase in agitation.

Am-heh is about to aid his fellow dark god when Isis hits him squarely in the chest with a potent bolt of her magics. The shards of her incredible power spark once he is hit. Am-heh falls to his knees in pain then rolls over to his side in a fetal position. Anna savagely roars her displeasure.

Both groups of werewolves and witches can sense the enormous amount of energy the gods generate. It almost overloads all of our senses. We all fall farther back, finally uniting as a group. I mentally form a protective shield around the people closest to me, afraid of any fallout from the battle taking place. Compared to the collected magics of the gods before me, I possess the magical might of a flea. I can sense other magics being added to mine though, protecting the entire group of us. Looking back, I can see my coven, the Lykaion wolves and the Benandanti coven joining forces to strengthen the protection spell. I whisper a prayer of thanks to Gaea, and then become surprised when I see her look away from her battle for a moment to give me a slight nod.

Anna strikes the ground, causing the earth to ripple around her. The entire group of us non-gods falls to our feet, but we quickly get up and re-establish our magical wall. The resulting earth ripple also manages to displace Virbius' vines, giving Anansi enough leverage to break through the rest of his bindings. The spider immediately jumps into the air, landing on Virbius with great vigor. Their fall to the ground rattles our surroundings again, but this time we hold our footing. The forest god grabs onto the spider's pincers, stopping it from sinking its venomous teeth into his flesh.

Hecate grabs a tuft of fur on Anansi's back, using it to toss the trickster off Virbius. She throws him several yards away, breaking one of his legs in the process. Tobias manifests several earth pillars within our circle to hold on to as the earth again shakes at the spider's impact. Hecate then gathers a large amount of magic in one hand and sends it at Anansi. He shrieks in pain at a high decibel. Every wolf near me immediately covers their ears with their hands, attempting to stop the piercing wailing sound.

I feel a slight movement at my feet. I look down and see Anna's former familiar Sekhmet running by me and out of the protective field. I mentally send thoughts of warning to the orange cat shaped familiar, hoping he will return to the safety of our dome. He ignores my pleas, dashing at an incredible speed toward Anna.

Bastet lunges toward Anna, providing a roar of her own. As Anna prepares for Bastet's attack, Sekhmet leaps onto Anna's back and sinks his teeth into her neck. Anna screams in pain, flailing her arms. Taking advantage of the distraction, Bastet knocks Anna to the ground, pinning her in place. A small crater forms where Anna lands.

Anna screams louder as Sekhmet's body begins to shimmer.

"Let go of her!" Bastet yells.

At first, I'm unsure of who Bastet is talking to. I can sense Mika's agitation through our magical connection. Thinking on Fenrus, I mentally ask him what is happening.

I hear Fenrus respond, "Anna's familiar Sekhmet is calling for his mistress, trying to separate her from the war god, but the war goddess Sekhmet is holding on to Anna tight. Bastet is using her magics to augment Anna's psychic connection to her familiar."

Aloud, I ask him, "Can you help him, too?"

Fenrus looks at me, then to the other familiars near him. They huddle together, and I feel a powerful surge of energy come from them. I then look over at Anna and see Sekhmet grow several times larger.

"No!" Anna's scream seems to linger.

Her body begins to shake violently until all that can be seen of Anna is a blur. A spark of light then appears. It temporarily blinds me. I try to shake off the spotting in my vision. When it fades, I see there are now two bodies lying on the ground. One is Anna and the other, still pinned by Bastet, is the war goddess Sekhmet. Sekhmet's large lioness head looks dazed and confused.

Bastet quickly waves her hand, and both Anna and her familiar appear beside Mika. I notice that Sekhmet has returned to his normal familiar size. Mika whimpers as she bends down to inspect the unconscious Anna. Both she and Tobias lay their hands on her as they whisper a healing spell. Fenrus, Fydan, and Hadrian similarly begin to nudge her exhausted familiar, providing him with needed strength. I'm surprised to see Ms. Whiskers has reverted to her normal size too. She also provides Sekhmet support, through non-magical licks to his face.

I look back at the field and see that all three dark gods are now restrained magically. The terrain around them has noticeably transformed during the battle. The once green field is now filled with hills, rubble, impact craters and scorch marks. Gaea, I can't believe the destruction the gods caused with only a skirmish. My mind can't fathom what could happen during a larger scale battle.

The hairs on the back of my neck begin to rise again. Something is coming. I can sense it. Looking at the gods, I know they sense it, too. I put more strength into my protection spell, unsure of what is to happen next.

Suddenly five more figures appear. One is a tall woman with dark hair and eyes. She wears a thin shift dress, allowing the curves of her fleshy body to protrude out of it seductively. I hear one of the Benandanti witches near me say, "Lilith!"

A shadowy figure stands beside her. It has no human features outside of two red eyes. Its overly long fingers end in points. Next to it is a tall powerful male god dressed in Roman armor. His battle axe looks razor sharp, as does the sword he carries in his other hand.

Before I can get a good look at the other two gods, Lilith swings her arm in mid-air. My gods tumble backwards in a group onto the ground in response. Lilith's energy wave also manages to hit our protective shield, destroying it. Like our gods, we too are knocked to the ground. In my mind, I know that if the protection spell hadn't taken the full brunt of her blast, the lot of us would be dead.

As I thud downward, I hear Bastet give a roar then shriek. I try to regain my composure as fast as possible so that I can see what caused the goddess to cry out. When I do, I see that the newly arrived gods have gathered around their companions and are disappearing with them into thin air. They leave behind Bastet, now lying silently on the ground.

"No!" I yell as I race toward the Egyptian goddess.

I inspect her closely. She is alive, but barely. I then look up to see that the rest of my gods have fortunately fared better than she has.

"Goddess!" I yell to Gaea. "Bastet! She's hurt!"

My gods quickly get to their feet and rush over to us. I stand out of the way so that the others can better access her condition.

"Her life force is low," Isis states.

She places her hands on the cat god and closes her eyes. The air becomes electric around them. I can feel a great transfer of power. Gaea bends down and places her hands on Bastet as well. Then Hecate, Artemis, Apollo, and Virbius follow suit. The potency of their magics begins to bleach the area around them of color.

My father places his hand on my shoulder and asks, "Is there anything we can do?"

A weak voice nearby says, "Pray."

Trailing the voice to its source, I see Anna on the ground. She's raised her head and is attempting to get up.

In a tender voice, Mika says, "Grandmomma, stay where you are. You're still too weak."

Holding tightly to her granddaughter's hand, Anna says, "All of us, we must give Bastet our strength. Gods gain power with the devotion of followers. Pray for her and she will improve."

Using my necklace to translate my words, I say to everyone present, "The goddess Bastet put her life on the line for our safety. She needs our help now. Please, all of you, I need for you to pray to her."

I see looks of confusion on the faces of some of the wolves, but the witches, I can see, have a clear understanding of what I'm asking. The Lykaion wolves similarly gain knowing expressions. The majority of both groups turn to face Bastet, then lower themselves to their knees. They hold out their hands outward, palms side up. They then bow their heads and begin to chant in various languages. The rest of the werewolves look on perplexed.

"Please," I beg of them.

The Enopo Archons mimic the Lykaion wolves and Benandanti coven's actions. The Enopo emissaries follow closely behind. When I notice several non-Enopo wolves begin to gingerly get to their knees as well, I turn to face Bastet and kneel myself. I hold out my hands, palm side up and begin my chanting of devotion. I picture the cat goddess rejuvenated in my mind as I speak my godly wishes. I see her surrounded by a multitude of cats and incense decanters. I see her as she might have been thousands of years ago: young, strong, and powerful. I pray for that same strength to fill the goddess again.

My words fill my head, and I am overcome with euphoria. I can sense a wave of energy emerge from the witches and wolves around me. I feel that energy shift toward Bastet's body, adding to the energies the godly pantheon around her is already generating. Once I feel the pinnacle of the euphoria reach its crescendo, I hear a large gasp from nearby. My head begins to spin upon opening my eyes. I see Bastet now sitting up. One hand is on her chest, and the other is on her forehead.

She looks over at us with a strange expression on her face. She then looks at the gods around her. To us both she says, "I did not expect for you to…" She stops herself to take a few breaths then says sincerely, "Thank you."

It's then that I see Ms. Whiskers race across the field and into Bastet's arms. Bastet holds her devotee affectionately as they both purr their happiness to one another.

I then notice Virbius disappear from his position next to Bastet and reappear beside me.

"Are you all right?" he asks me and the others. I can see he is somewhat weakened by the ordeal.

"We're fine," I tell him. "You're able to leave your domain."

Virbius smiles. "Yes."

"What was that?" I ask him.

"Lilith," he answers with bitterness in his voice. "Evidently, she's still as powerful as she ever was. Come, it's not safe here for anyone. We need to regroup elsewhere."

"Just a moment, please," I ask of the forest god. He nods in response.

Turning to the wolves and witches, I see them all now staring back at me. I focus on my necklace again, asking it to properly translate my words for everyone to understand.

"We have to go," I tell them. "Sekhmet and her other dark gods could return at any moment. Those of you who wish sanctuary, I promise you that whatever actions happened in the past will be put aside. There is a god-protected area where you can find refuge. You all saw the destruction the gods created with only a few of them present. There're more coming still and we have to prepare for what's ahead.

"Those of you who wish to return to the lives you had before, my coven and I will provide you safe transportation back to your homes but know this, the world you know isn't going to last. You've seen what these dark gods can do. We are stronger together. Our invitation remains open."

Tobias leaves Anna's side and stands by me. He asks aloud to the crowd gathered, "Who of you will join us?"

As expected, my parents, Nicholas, Brian, and the rest of the Enopo clan walk over and stand behind me. The Lykaion wolves then do the same. We all look on at the remaining werewolves and Benandanti coven who stay apart.

One of the Benandanti points to Anna still on the ground and

266

says, "She killed our mistress. We no longer have a proper home to go to."

Mika, still at Anna's side, looks at the witch forcefully and says, "My grandmomma is innocent. She didn't kill your coven master. The dark god Sekhmet did that. If you have a vendetta for anyone, it should be against her."

The witch looks at Mika with a scowl. She then turns to discuss the situation with her coven in hushed tones.

Looking at Jason, I can see the conflict in his face. The wolves around him stand silently, unsure of what to do next. Jason then walks over to me, staring directly into my face. I can see he is not happy, but eventually joins my father, showing his allegiance. Several of his wolves look on in confusion. Finally, many of them walk over and join him as part of my pack. Only a few wolf stragglers stay behind.

To those few I say, "I'll honor your decision and will send you home shortly. I do hope you know you'll always have an opportunity to reconsider."

The distant wolves instead transform into their full werewolf forms and race away on their own. I would be lying if I said I wasn't a little disappointed.

Turning to the Benandanti, I ask, "And what of you? Will you stand beside us or will you go too?"

The witch possessing the snake familiar says, "Our coven is divided. Some of us see truth in what you're saying and have hope that you'll protect us like Claudia did before you. The others, though, they refuse to be part of your coven. They will find a way on their own."

The group then splits, half of them walking over to join my pack. I'm surprised to see that Stephen and Julia are among them. Julia eyes me then my mother with hate. My mother matches her enemy's ire with a disdain of her own. I tell myself that I can't pick and choose. I'll have to extend my promise of sanctuary to both Stephen and Julia,

267

too. Unfortunately, I have a sneaking suspicion I'll have to keep a close eye on them in the process.

To the remaining witches who stand apart, I say a silent prayer that they see the light and are protected from what's to come. One witch in that group then raises her hand into the air. The various objects Claudia previously had her coven scatter around the dock back in Boston then fly back toward them. The objects circle the group a bit then land silently onto the ground around the unsympathetic Benandanti. The witches close their eyes and raise their hands upward into the air together. As before, dark storm clouds begin to gather in the sky above. The sound of thunder fills the air and crackling lightning fills the sky. The objects surrounding the witches then take on an eerie glow. A bolt of lightning strikes the objects and the witches disappear completely.

I'm about to turn my attention back to Virbius when I notice something peculiar. Above us, a section of the dark storm clouds opens up, allowing a strange red glowing orb to descend from it. As the orb begins pulsing, I get a strange sense of foreboding.

I hear Gaea cry out, "Virbius! Get the devotees out of here! Now!"

Virbius immediately swings his arms, causing a white field of magic to envelop the lot of us. I begin to feel the traditional sensation of being teleported but then suddenly am violently hit by a series of huge explosive waves. The force of the blasts overcomes me. I have no sense of anything as I fall into the black void of unconsciousness.

When I come to, it's to the sensation of having my face being licked. I slowly open my eyes and see Fenrus standing over me, landing his slobbery tongue kisses to my cheek. Noticing his efforts have worked, he stops. In my head, I hear him say, "You're all right!"

I fold my arms around his neck and say, "Thanks to you."

Looking around, I notice that we're back in Virbius' domain. I'm lying beside the forest god's altar. Around me, I see the rest of the wolves and witches. Virbius is nearby, too, on the ground with the rest of us. He's sitting up and holding his head. I can see he's just as shaken as I am. Realization comes across his face. He quickly looks around him, noticing the other unconscious bodies, some of whom are only beginning to come to. When he sees me looking back at him, he disappears and reappears beside me.

"Are you all right?" he asks.

There's a low throbbing in my head, but I can feel my wolf metabolism beginning to subdue it.

"I'm okay," I tell him "but the others…"

Virbius closes his eyes a moment. I can feel his godly energy spreading out over the bodies on the ground. He then opens his eyes.

"They're all accounted for and alive," he says. "Not all of them are in good shape though."

Upon hearing his words, a feeling of relief washes over me. We all made it through.

I hear a bird screech and look over in the noise's direction. It's then that I see Tobias beginning to stir. Hadrian is gently nudging his side. I immediately go over to the both of them. I cradle Tobias' head in the crook of my arm and wipe away the hair from his face.

"Tobias, are you okay?" I ask him.

He stays silent but gingerly looks into my eyes and smiles. I immediately take the rest of him against my chest and hold him tightly. Thank you, Gaea, thank you.

"Mika…" I hear him say faintly.

I let go of Tobias so that we both can visually scan the rest of the forest clearing together. Across from us, I see Damon already is seeing to her. Fydan looks over her, too, with concern. Beside them, my mother and father are just coming to. Tobias and I both get up and run over to them. Tobias joins Damon to see to Mika while I go over to my parents to inspect them for wounds. When I see they have none, I hold them tightly, relieved that they're okay, too.

Behind me I hear Virbius say, "I must see to the other gods. You all should be fine in my forest. I've mentally summoned the others. They will attend to your injured comrades."

When I look over to see Virbius, I notice his image fade into nothingness. It's then that I hear my father gasp.

"What is it?" I ask him.

I look in the direction my father is staring and notice Nicholas lying still on the ground unconscious. He has blood flowing out of his nose and mouth.

"No!" I yell out.

I race over to Nicholas and check his vitals. They're weak. My mind races as I try a healing spell on him. It's no use as his wolf essence repels the spell outright. I feel a hand on my shoulder and see that it's the Benandanti witch with the black feline familiar.

"Don't squander your magics," she says. "Your friend needs herbs and rest. I was our coven's chief herbalist. Provide me with what I need, and I'll see what I can do."

From across the way, I hear someone say, "I might have what you need in my cabin."

Looking up, I see Fallon has arrived with a band of Halflings and rescued wolves behind him. Several of the Benandanti witches gasp at their appearance.

I turn to the witch beside me and say loudly, "This is Fallon. He and the others are with us. Fallon, can you and the others take Nicholas and…"

I look at the witch, unsure of what to call her.

"Gailen," she says.

"Gailen," I repeat. "Can you take Nicholas and Gailen to your cabin?"

Fallon moves swiftly into action. Then to the remaining rescue wolves I say, "The rest of you, please check the others who've arrived with me. Make sure they're all right. Anyone injured is to be immediately taken to Fallon's cabin."

"Ama!" I hear Damon cry out.

Damon has moved on from Mika and is now beside his mother Gabriella. She, too, is still unconscious. The paleness in her cheeks doesn't look good. Damon gently picks up his mother and quickly follows Fallon and Gailen. Mika and Tobias watch him leave, worried. Gaea, please watch over them.

I'm thankful when I see Anna standing beside Brian, with Ms. Whiskers in hand. Near them, I see Stephen helping his mother Julia get to her feet. My grandfather Jason is also on his feet, moving from wolf to wolf to make sure they are okay.

Vincent then walks over to me with the other Enopo Archons and says, "There are only a few others injured, but the majority of them are wolves. Fortunately, their wounds are mostly superficial and have already begun healing."

I'm about to reply to Vincent when a strong, cold wind sweeps across the forest clearing. I get an immediate chill and notice visible air escape from my mouth. Everyone else begins holding onto his or her arms in a shivering motion. Beside me, I hear Fenrus begin to growl. Feelings of protection and alarm emanate from him.

"What's going on?" I ask aloud.

Tobias, Mika, and Anna stare back at me with confusion of their own. Their familiars, however, gain poses of defense, ready to protect their masters if need be.

The snake familiar witch walks over to me with familiar in hand and says, "Your god, Virbius... I thought his domain was protected."

"It is," I tell her. "No man or god can break through the barriers he and the other of our gods put in place."

In my head, I hear her snake familiar say, "Ssssssomething issssss coming through. Sssssssomething dark."

At that, thick billowing clouds of black smoke appear at the edge of the clearing. The wolves and witches near it quickly recede to a safe distance away. The other wolf Archons and I move toward it, blocking access to our people with our own bodies. Something is taking shape within the darkness. I can sense strong magics within as well. I raise my magical guard, feeling the rest of my coven joining me at my side.

When the darkness disperses, standing there are two gods both dressed in dark robes. They have coal black hair and eyes with marble white skin. I can hear gasps behind me once their full manifestation is complete.

"Who are these gods?" I mentally ask Fenrus.

In a low growl, I hear him reply, "They are Erebus and Nyx, the Greek gods of darkness and night. They are dangerous and unpredictable."

I mentally tell Fenrus, "They are also the gods Luke followed before his death. What are they doing here?"

"I don't know," Fenrus answers. "Be on guard."

The two gods stare blankly at us, then only to me. Nyx eventually opens her mouth and says, "We sensed that the war has begun. My husband and I are here for you, Devin Toxotis."

Fenrus growls louder. Hadrian screeches his disapproval as well. I hear the sound of swords being released from their scabbards. Looking over, I see that it is my father now with his swords at the ready. My mother has also shifted into her wolf human hybrid form, claws at the ready.

Erebus calmly says, "You have no need to fear us, mortals. You misunderstand my wife's meaning. We come, not in wrath, but to provide you with a gift."

I hear Anna say, "You will forgive us if we are suspicious of your timing, Dark Ones. Our gods are currently unaccounted for. We have no knowledge of which group you choose to side with."

Nyx looks at Anna and says, "We choose neither side. Our domain is eternal. No matter which group defeats the other, even when all things eventually come to an end, ultimately, darkness remains forever unaffected."

Erebus continues, saying, "Your gods' protective wards are formidable to any being who may wish you or your people harm. As that is not our goal, we were able to bend the enchantments, allowing us access to you. As we said, you have nothing to fear from us."

Remaining on guard, I eye the two gods carefully. I can't quite gauge their intent, so I ask them outright, "You said you have a gift. What is it, and why do you offer it to us?"

The dark gods look at me intently. Erebus says, "We rarely feel any pull to the mortal realm anymore. Our time with your kind has long since past. When we felt the pull again, it was to a special individual, the mortal you called Luke Barlow. You and he were once comrades, yes? You helped him escape the dangers of your former leader, Malik. Though he has ultimately joined us on the other side, your devotion to keep our follower safe has touched the both of us. For this, you are granted a gift to aid you in your battle ahead."

Nyx continues saying, "Our ties to the underworld have shown us what the Egyptian god Am-heh has plans to do. At the opportune time, he will break the natural order of things and release the spirits of warriors long dead to aid him in battle." Nyx then holds out her hand. On her palm appear Tobias' witch sword and the battle mace Brian had previously given to Nicholas. "These weapons," the goddess says, "have strong ties to the dark realms. They have much magical blood stained on them from over the centuries. With our dark touch, we will release the magic the blood still holds within. With these weapons, you will be provided a gateway to dead warriors of your own. Warriors reanimated with a loyalty to their resurrectors only."

Nyx passes the witch sword to Erebus who takes it from her slowly. They then take each weapon in hand, closing their eyes serenely before placing them gently on the ground at our feet.

"Two weapons, two warriors," Erebus says. "That is our one gift. Choose wisely for we will not aid you further."

Nyx says, "This is also where we leave you, Wolf King. May the next time our paths cross be under better circumstances."

Cold black clouds begin to materialize from the underworld god's feet. The smoke rises, slowly consuming their entire bodies.

"Wait!" I shout. "My gods, they could use your help. Please, help them in their fight!"

The two gods' expressions remain stoic as the smoke covers their faces as well. When the smoke finally clears, the gods are nowhere to be seen. All that is left from their short visit are the magically tinged weapons still lying on the ground before us. I look at them unsure of what to do next. Even from this distance, I can sense the dark magic lingering from the blade and mace.

"I don't trust them," Jason finally says, breaking the silence. "Magic should never be trusted, especially magic from beings like them."

I look at Jason and say, "I reluctantly agree with you on this one. My familiar says that the underworld gods are unpredictable. Maybe they were telling the truth. Maybe these really are well meaning gifts, but I'm not about to take that chance until our gods verify that there are no strings attached."

Tobias walks over and places his hand in the open air above the weapons. The ground below begins to shift and encase the god-touched objects. In moments, a small dome made of earth appears and rises off the ground and into his hands.

Tobias says, "They should be safe in here for the time being. Once Virbius and the others return, we'll let them make heads or tails of this. Until then, I'll place this in our cabin where it can't do any damage."

"Thanks," I tell him.

My father then asks, "Devin, what is this place?"

I tell him, "This is Virbius' forest. We'll be safe here. Come on. I'll introduce you all to the others."

I lead the wolves and Benandanti out of the clearing and toward the main encampment. Along the way, we see several magical creatures frolicking in the forest. Each one completely engrosses the new troop of rescues with me. I could swear I see wonder on even Jason's face. When we finally reach the camp, I am surprised by what I find. The camp is larger than what I remember. Could it really have grown so much in just a few days? Then I remember. It's probably the work of the Lykaion wolves who took over the rescue missions after my coven and I were needed elsewhere. I look back at Idaios and Danae. They nod, confirming my suspicions.

Everywhere I look, there is a buzz of activity. Some repair buildings here, there, others collect water, and elsewhere, others teach small children. The hubbub brings a joy to my heart.

From the corner of my eye I see someone stop and look my way. I realize that it's Lia. She smiles once she recognizes me. She starts to run in my direction then stops, terrified, once she sees the group of persons arriving immediately behind me. I turn to see what she's looking at and notice that she is staring at several of the European emissary wolves that have joined our cause. It's then that I notice several other rescued wolves similarly looking at the new arrivals with panic and fear.

When I see Lia about to run for safety, I shout loudly, "Lia, it's okay! These wolves aren't going to hurt you." Then to the others I say, "They're not going to hurt any of you. They're here seeking sanctuary, just like all of you are. I won't let any of them harm you, I promise."

Looks of uncertainty fill the encampment. My coven and several of the Lykaion wolves push forward so that the rescued wolves and Halflings can see them properly. Once they do, the frightened villagers recognize several of their rescuers among them. Expressions of relief soon replace the fear they had only moments before.

Turning to the crowd behind me, I say, "Trust is a two way street. Please, meet my people halfway."

The newcomers' faces show understanding.

Turning back to the village I say, "We're having a town meeting in thirty minutes. Please let everyone know. I need to fill everyone in on what's happened so far. In the meanwhile, these people I've brought with me need to find available housing if there is any. Please, show them around. My coven and Archons are going to see to our wounded. We'll be back shortly."

Slowly, members of the rescued group come over to the new arrivals. They take them in small groups and disperse throughout the village. When I see everyone is situated, my team and I walk over to Fallon's cabin as a group. Once there, I see two cots resting in the center of the large open living room. On one is Nicholas, and on the other is Gabriella. Damon is sitting beside Gabriella holding her hand. The air bears the pungent scent of earthy medicines. The witch Gailen has placed moist cloths covered with herbs on the two patient's foreheads. I can see that some color has returned to both of their cheeks.

Anna and her familiar walk past me saying, "She may need my help."

Anna then joins Gailen in administering their herbal concoctions. Watching both of them in action, it's almost as if the two had trained together for years.

Mika walks over to Damon and holds his shoulders. I hear Damon ask, "Do you think they'll be okay?"

Mika tells him, "If the new witch is anywhere near as good a healer as my grandmomma is, they should be fine."

At that moment, I notice my father and Jason both walk over to either side of Nicholas. They inspect him for any signs of distress. It's then that I realize that no matter how angry Jason previously was with Nicholas, the tenderness he is displaying to him shows just how much Jason sincerely cares for his nephew. Even the way he's reconnected with my father speaks volumes to me. Despite everything that's happened, Jason's family ties are still strong.

Fallon joins me and motions to Gailen, saying, "She's seemed to have eased their pain somewhat. Now we just have to let them rest and allow their bodies to heal. What happened to them?"

"The god war," I answer. "It's begun. This is a result of the fallout."

Tobias says, "We lost contact with the rest of our gods. Virbius went back to find them."

Looking at the others, I say, "Forgive me. Fallon, these are the leaders of my clan of wolves. This is Vincent, Brice, Ryan, and Shaun."

The Archons nod to the satyr. I can tell they are still amazed at his appearance.

I then pull my mother into an embrace. "And this is my mother, Victoria Marshall."

My mother rests the side of her head against my forehead for a moment before breaking our embrace to shake Fallon's hand. If she is as shocked at Fallon's appearance, she doesn't show it.

I then point toward the two figures standing beside Nicholas. "That over there is my father, Adam Toxotis. Standing next to him is my grandfather Jason Toxotis. Until recently, my grandfather and I haven't seen eye to eye. We're putting aside our differences until this war ends. Archons, this is Fallon. He's Virbius' second in command here."

That's when I notice a figure still standing in the doorway to Fallon's cabin. Looking around the group of Archons, I can see that it's the witch with the snake familiar. She has uncertainty on her face. I motion her to come into the room. She takes a few ginger steps inward, taking in her surroundings before finally joining our party.

I ask her, "I'm sorry. I don't think I caught your name."

The witch gently pets the snake that peaks through her hair and says, "My name is Hellena, and this is Aldo. Claudia's advisor Divina was my sister."

I'm dumbfounded. Before I know what I'm doing, I realize that I've reached out to her and have taken her in my arms.

"I'm so sorry for your loss," I tell her.

Her ridged stance tells me that she, too, is surprised at my reaction. I can feel her familiar's tongue darting the air near my ear. I feel empathic waves of thanks from the familiar. I let go of Hellena, not wanting the awkwardness of my embrace to embarrass her further. I lock eyes with her. I try to convey that I am completely sincere in my condolence. She holds onto her surprise for a few moments, then relaxes her body, showing me her eventual acceptance.

"Thank you," she finally says. "I wasn't very close with my sister, but her death is still pretty raw."

I notice Hellena then look at Anna. There is confliction in her face. I can tell she understands that it wasn't Anna who killed her sister, but there is still pain there nonetheless.

I motion to the others. "These are my allies," I tell her. "The group here have overseen the wolves formerly under my care."

"I know," Hellena says. "Claudia has been watching your group closely."

Mika walks over and says, "I hope you'll give our people a chance to prove that we're not the dangerous lot she's told you we are."

Hellena looks at me then takes in Mika's full measure. "I've learned for myself over the years to never take someone else's opinion as my own. I've already seen that your coven isn't quite what I expected."

Mika nods her head a bit, showing understanding.

"And congratulations," Hellena adds. "Many blessings to you and your children. Your first, correct?"

Her statement takes everyone by surprise.

"My what?" Mika asks her.

"Your children," Hellena restates. "You're carrying a boy and a girl. Didn't you know?"

Damon quickly gets up off his seat and stands behind Mika. Mika, sensing him behind her, falls back somewhat into Damon's arms.

Tobias asks Hellena, "Are you sure?"

She looks at him matter-of-factly and says, "Yes. I've always been sensitive to this sort of thing. See for yourself."

Anna, now at full attention moves over to Mika and places her hands on her stomach. She closes her eyes. I feel Anna's internal magics permeate through Mika's womb. Once the magic recedes back into Anna, she opens her eyes and holds Mika's chin in her hand. I can see tears beginning to form in Anna's eyes as she takes her granddaughter into her arms. Tobias and I go over to the both of them to embrace them as well.

Looking up, I see Damon standing there with a sheepish grin on his face. I let go of Mika and move over to my brother, placing my hand on his shoulder. My father and mother soon join me.

Vincent says, "This is the first birth in our new pack. It's an historic moment for our people."

Anna lets go of Mika and says, "But it's also a dangerous one. There's a god war taking place. It's not safe for any of us, let alone helpless infants. I'm surprised I made it out alive myself."

Damon takes Mika in his arms and says, "I won't let anything happen to Mika, or our children. I'll protect them no matter what happens."

A weak voice then says, "As will I, *mon petite*."

Gabriella looks weakly at the gathered family. The slight smile on her face holds back the exhaustion I know her still recovering body has. Damon and Mika go over to her, each taking one of her hands into theirs.

In the back of my head, I hear a calling. Visions of our gods play through my mind. I know its Virbius. Looking around the room, I can tell the others hear the call, too.

"Come," I tell them. "We've got to go. Gailen and Anna, you two stay here and watch over Nicholas and Gabriella. The rest of you, Virbius needs us in the central encampment."

I can see a slight sign of annoyance in Jason's face at being given orders, but he stays silent and follows everyone else out of the cabin. When we finally get to the camp, I see that the rest of the forest inhabitants are already gathered and waiting for Virbius and the others to appear. They don't have to wait long.

The area becomes a buzz of energy as the various gods manifest in the central square. I'm grateful to see that all of them are accounted for.

Hecate speaks first saying, "As some of you may know, the god war has begun. The war goddess Sekhmet and her allies made their first strike in Italy, and we barely made it out alive. They used their combined strengths to create destructive bombs, not only there, but across the globe."

Hecate waves her hand into the air, causing the skies above us to shift. Images of the same red energy ball descending from the skies appear like before. Unlike our previous scenario, though, the areas the orbs descend onto vary from image to image. In one scene, the orb lowers onto London. In another, it's San Francisco. In yet another scene, it's Tokyo. We see several more cityscapes, each with an orb of their own. All of them, however, end the same. A huge explosion occurs, destroying the cities. Gasps come from our collected group. Some people break down crying. Shock sweeps over me as I think of the millions of people who fell victim to Sekhmet's surprise attacks.

Bastet says, "My daughter no longer hides in the shadows. She and the gods she's convinced to join her walk among their destroyed cities openly. As I speak, surviving mortals are filming their audacity and sending their visages around the globe. Governments are gathering their weapons. Mortals are seeking shelter from the storm. Sekhmet was right. The age of gods has returned, but at a great loss. As these dark gods become more visible, they gain in strength. We have to stay vigilant now more than ever."

Ever the strategist, Artemis adds, "She may have more strength, but Sekhmet's attacks not only help her but harm her. Now that she's more visible, she's also open to more gods wanting to join her cause. Likewise, her actions have also angered many others. She is now the subject of wrath for many deities. In essence, she's become a target for more gods that just this pantheon. That is where our hopes lie."

Julia cries out, "What about Boston?"

Gaea looks kindly at the former mob wife and says, "Boston was attacked as well, but the protective wards we put in place held true. Devin's home and the residents still there, as well as the majority of the rest of the city, remains untouched."

"Over the next few days we will be reaching out to whatever allies will side with us," Apollo says. "You're not to worry. Our protection shields will hold should any god try to come after any one of you. That said, you must promise not to leave the forest. Any of you. We can't guarantee your protection out in the open right now."

Tobias magically raises his earth dome. The gods notice the orb with suspicion. This doesn't surprise me as I know the two god touched weapons are trapped inside.

"My gods," Tobias says humbly. "While you were gone, we were visited by two of your kinsmen, the gods Erebus and Nyx."

"Yes," Isis says. "We can see what transpired in your mind's eye."

Hecate extends her hand, willing the small earth dome to travel toward her. As it does, the earth sphere crumbles away leaving only the sword and mace behind. The various gods examine the levitating weapons closely.

Virbius says, "We will hold on to these items. They could be extremely dangerous in the wrong hands. Thank you, Tobias, for bringing them to our attention. For the rest of you, rest up. You're going to need it. We will be in contact again before you know it."

I ask the green god, "Could you use our help?"

Gaea smiles and says, "Your heart is a precious gift to me, Devin. In time, I'm sure we will call upon your aid. Until then, look over your people and prepare them for what's to come. You and your family have done so much already. It breaks my heart to admit it, but there is still a long road ahead. You will need to be ready for more obstacles coming your way."

Isis says, "I've seen glimpses of you, Devin Toxotis, through the actions of my devotee Anna Geist. I can see from my comrade's honor of you, you are a mortal brave beyond your years. You have my respect and attention."

I'm completely humbled at the accolades I'm receiving from the gods before me. Pride was never something I've particularly focused on in my life. Where my focus does fall, though, is making sure I live up to their ideals of me. It's in this regard I can't allow myself to fail.

"Thank you," I tell them. "Your love means so much to me and everyone else here. We'll wait for your next communication. Please be safe until then."

As the gods fade from our sight, the series of events that lead me to this point play out in my head. I was once a common street hustler looking for a home of my own. Now I'm a werewolf leader helping to protect a pack of varied supernatural beings in what could possibly be the end of the world as we know it. Life continues to surprise me. How this all happened, I couldn't even begin to tell you. Now, for the safety of my people, I'm going to have to come up with a few new surprises of my own.

About the Author

Peter Saenz spent the majority of his growing years in both Southern California and parts of South Texas. He's always held a fascination with various aspects of the fantasy genre. A diverse writer, Peter has contributed original short stories to the anthology books QUEER TALES and NEW YEARS TO CHRISTMAS. Developing one of his previous short stories into a full-fledged novel, he then released the first book of the original supernatural series COVEN OF WOLVES in 2012. Peter is a vocal advocate for several causes including: gay rights issues, animal care and protection, and environmental conservation. Peter currently lives in Los Angeles with his husband Joseph.

Website: www.peterjsaenz.com
Twitter: @PeterJSaenz
Facebook: www.facebook.com/covenofwolves

Other DoorQ/Digital Fabulists Books of Interest

THE PASSION OF SERGIUS AND BACCHUS
by David Reddish
DEMONIC AND OTHER TALES by Garon Cockrell
THE DARK NUMBERS by Luc Descamps
ECHELON'S END by E. Robert Dunn
INVISIBLE SOFT RETURN by Roberta Degnore
KITH AND KILN: SHORT STORIES by Sean McGrath

Printed in Great Britain
by Amazon

All the Gold
in the World

Robert Leeson

Illustrated by Anna Leplar

A & C Black · London

FLASHBACKS

A Candle in the Dark · Adèle Geras
The Saga of Aslak · Susan Price
A Ghost-Light in the Attic · Pat Thomson

Published 1995 by A & C Black (Publishers) Ltd
35 Bedford Row, London WC1R 4JH

Text copyright © 1995 Robert Leeson
Illustrations copyright © 1995 Anna Leplar

The right of Robert Leeson to be identified as author
of this work has been asserted by him in accordance
with the Copyright, Designs and Patents Act 1988.

ISBN 0-7136-4059-6

A CIP catalogue record for this book
is available from the British Library.

Photoset in Linotron Palatino by
Rowland Phototypesetting Ltd,
Bury St Edmunds, Suffolk

Printed in Great Britain by
St Edmundsbury Press Ltd,
Bury St Edmunds, Suffolk

Contents

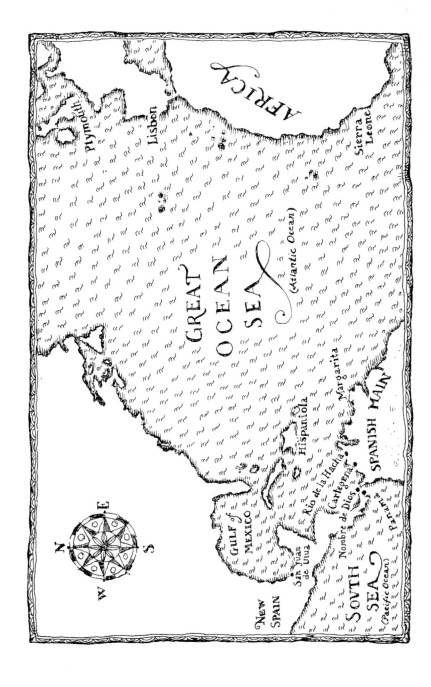

Foreword

Shrove Tuesday, 1573

I sit in the topmost branches of this great tree upon a high mountain ridge. I look north over thick green forest, lakes and swamps, and see the gleam of distant water.

That is the Great Ocean Sea, which they call the Atlantic. Our ship is hidden in a secret bay near Nombre de Dios. If I could step on board her now and sail for fifty days and nights I would reach home.

I am John Marsh, seaman of Plymouth town and I am far from the place where I was born.

Now I turn and look south, over forests and plains where the grass grows taller than your head. Beyond shines another ocean, the great South Sea. Our captain says that if we took ship and sailed on that sea for, who knows, maybe two hundred days and nights, we should sail right round the world.

He says that we would find riches beyond our

dreams and come home again to Plymouth like lords.

I know this is true. The worn little book in my pocket tells of a foreign captain who once sailed round the globe, where no man had gone before. Where he went, our captain can go.

Most of our crew do not believe him. They take no account of dreams. They want gold you can put your hands on. But our captain has promised them gold and they will follow wherever he leads.

Down there by the South Sea shore, lies the city of Panama. Its halls bulge with treasure.

In a few days from now, when the cool of the night comes down, the Spaniards will send that treasure down the forest tracks to Nombre de Dios. Three hundred mules will bear two hundredweight of gold and silver each. From Nombre de Dios, a great fleet will waft it across the sea to their King Philip in Madrid.

But not this time. When the mule bells clang in the dark, we shall be waiting in ambush, sword in hand, to leap down from the trees. King Philip can whistle for his treasure.

In ten days' time, that wealth will be ours.

Now we must wait. And I do not think of

riches. This is Shrove Tuesday. Today my mother would make pancakes. In my memory I smell them, taste them.

I think about my life and how I came to this place.

PLIMMOVTH

Plimmouth mill

the way from Plimmouth

Sut-ten poole

Catte water

Fishers nose

St Nicholas Iland

The Sounde

10

· 1 ·

Brothers and Sisters Have I None . . .

I was born in the house of Master Thomas Poynton above the harbour in Plymouth. My mother, Prudence Marsh, was maidservant to Mistress Poynton.

By chance it happened that on the day I was born Mistress Poynton also had a son, called Harry. She was too ill to nurse him. So my mother took care of him as well as me.

Harry and I were carried at her breast and played around her feet. He was fair-haired and bright-eyed and slender. I was dark and broad and strong. When we fought together I won. But we did not fight often. We loved one another and for years I believed he truly was my brother.

We ran and played around the courtyard, in and out of the kitchen with its cauldrons and turning spits, its smells of roasting and baking.

We ran in and out of the warehouse with its high roof and racks and shelves and stranger smells of Newland fish, French wine, Guinea pepper, Barbary dates and Brazilian wood.

We ran among the legs of men in woollen breeches and leather jerkins, men with sunburnt faces and gold earrings. They would toss us in the air and tickle us in the ribs.

But there was one man who played no games. He was short and broad with a great belly, thick beard and sharp eyes. That was Thomas Poynton, who ruled our world.

For long enough, I thought he was my father. I was small and there were many things I did not understand.

When Harry and I were three, his mother died as she gave birth to a daughter, Alison, small and slender like her brother, with red hair and grey eyes.

Master Poynton would not marry again, he loved his wife too much. So my mother became his housekeeper to look after his children.

Now there were three playmates. Every morning I would come out of the room near the kitchen where mother and I lived and wait at the foot of the stairs. A door in the gallery would open and out would come, first Harry, then small Alison.

They would race one another down the stairs to
the courtyard.

Harry was always in front, but Alison always
won. Three steps from the foot of the stairway she
would leap in the air and I would catch her – she
was so light.

We played a game. She would say: 'Have you a present for me, John Marsh?' and I would answer 'No.' So she would frown fiercely and say: 'Then I must bite you.'

I would cry out in mock fear, 'Oh, Oh!' and pull from my pocket a flower, or a couple of almonds or a piece of ribbon filched from the warehouse. Then she would kiss my cheek.

For her it was a child's game. For me it was more. There were many things I did not understand.

I could not understand why at the end of our play they climbed back up the stairs and left me in the courtyard.

Till one day, after they had gone, I followed in their tracks, up the stairs, along the gallery and in through a great doorway.

I found myself in a tall, empty chamber with high windows. I ran to them, climbed on the window seat and looked out.

I saw down Vauxhall Street, to Sutton Pool, crowded with the masts of vessels loading and unloading at the wharf, and beyond them to Cattewater.

The evening sun shone across the sea as a ship

sailed in. As the light struck the masts they seemed to be made of gold. I stared as in a trance.

But not for long. I was seized by my breeches, hauled up and would have been whipped by one of the manservants. He shouted: 'The little rogue's in the Broad Chamber.' I howled with fright.

Then I heard my mother calling. 'Don't dare touch him,' she said, and I was rescued.

She took me downstairs, dried my tears and told me why I did not belong up there. Harry and Alison were not brother and sister to me, nor was Master Poynton my father.

My father was far away. But that I did not understand, yet.

· 2 ·

Heroes of the Flames

I did go into that Broad Chamber again. I went with my mother on Sunday evenings when the sun shone through those high windows, making golden patterns on the walls.

The room was crowded with folk, some I knew well from the household, some I did not, from the town and beyond. One and all were dressed in sober brown or black, with white collars and frills.

Before us sat Master Poynton in dark velvet and by his side, Harry and Alison in their finery. I could not make up my mind, should I look at Alison, or gaze through the window in hopes of seeing a ship with the sun on its sails?

Then a stranger with a thin, dark face read from the great Bible with brass bindings.

'Men of high degree are a vanity, men of low degree are a lie,' he said, while Master Poynton nodded and others said 'Amen.'

So I said 'Amen' in a high voice. My mother

nudged me. People stared and Alison smirked at me.

Everyone rose and sang. This I loved to hear. 'All people that on earth do dwell.' I thought that all the people on the earth lived in Plymouth and sat in Master Poynton's Broad Chamber.

Yet my father was not here. Where on earth was he, then? Was he in heaven? Would he come back?

And we would pray. For the Broad Chamber was like a church, not grand and gilded like churches I have seen in other lands, but simple and severe. So Master Poynton and his people liked it.

We prayed for the martyrs. The man who stood in front read out their names. There was such hush in the room I could hear the sea birds call over the harbour. Then he said:

'Did not the people of this town pay honour to Queen Mary when she married Philip of Spain?'

'Aye,' said the congregation. But I said nothing. For I had learned my lesson.

'And does not our Catholic Queen torture the Protestant children of God? Has she not sent men and women to be burnt alive?'

'Aye.'

My heart grew cold. I saw, I smelt the smoke. I felt the flames around those doomed people.

'All because they seek to worship God in their own way.'

People round me sighed as he went on: 'And let us not forget one of our own, Ned Marsh.'

As I heard my father's name, the hairs on my neck crawled.

'He had to flee his own land. He carried in his ship copies of the true word of God in our English tongue. And now in the service of truth, he lies in a Spanish prison. No one knows if he will perish in the flames or no.'

In my mind I saw a picture of a man on fire so clear that I screamed aloud and my mother rushed me from the Broad Chamber.

From this time on I would go down to Sutton Pool every day and dodge among the bales and spars and coils of rope and hurrying seamen on the quay. And I would ask them:

'Have you news of Ned Marsh my father?' They shook their heads and said:

'Ned Marsh? Are you his son? Well, lad, he was a good helmsman. He steered a true course. He was a good shipmate. But God alone knows what's become of him.'

· 3 ·

The Monk's Tale

Change came again to my life. An old, limping man called at Master Poynton's house. He was Brother Ambrose, who had once been a monk, but now had nowhere to go for his monastery was closed down.

Master Poynton gave him work, though he despised monks as Catholics and servants of the Pope. But Ambrose offered to teach Harry and Alison to read and charged very little, which pleased Master Poynton very much.

He took a fancy to have Harry taught the Spanish language. One day, Harry too would be a merchant and do trade with Spain, the richest land in the world.

So every day Brother Ambrose struggled up the stairs and I waited, impatient, till lessons were over and my playmates came down again.

But when it was hot in summer, Ambrose taught his pupils in the courtyard. I crept close and listened. While they learned, I learned too.

There were three books. One contained three of Aesop's fables: *The Lion and the Mouse*, *The Fox and the Grapes* and *The Sun and the Wind*. Soon we knew them by heart. Or I did, for Harry and Alison did not pay much heed. Ambrose would ask me to spell the words and say: 'See how well John learns.'

But one day, he snatched the book away and told me to go. I was offended. But I saw the reason. Master Poynton stood behind us.

Yet he only nodded and said: 'Let John learn. He'll be useful in my counting house one day.'

So first I learned to read. Then I learned something of the Spanish language. Harry was quicker than me in this. He picked up what suited him. But I strove to master the strange tongue, because in Brother Ambrose's second book were tales of voyages to far-off lands, to India and America.

Then, when we tired of learning, Brother Ambrose brought out his third book, *The Famous History of Sir Bevis*, a hero who fought giants.

When I heard how Bevis lay in prison seven years amid rats and mice, I shivered for I thought of my father. But still I longed for those tales, most especially the one where Bevis broke the prison walls.

This book was Brother Ambrose's undoing. For Master Poynton discovered what we were devouring. He flew into a rage. 'Trash, fantastic nonsense!' he bellowed and sent the poor old man packing.

After a while, a new teacher, a good Puritan scholar, came to take his place. He told Master Poynton straight: 'I'm paid for two pupils. I shall not teach three.'

Master Poynton nodded. My lessons ended, but I could remember all three books by heart and Harry and Alison came secretly to hear me recite Sir Bevis's adventures.

One winter day I saw Brother Ambrose near the harbour. He was drunk and boys pelted him with filth. I ran and kicked them, then led him back to his lodgings. He stared at me, then smiled.

''Tis you, John. Listen, boy. Beware all those who say they know what God thinks. Only He knows. And He decides who He shall tell.'

He felt in his coat, gave me the Spanish book, blessed me and went indoors. I never saw the old man again.

· 4 ·

Alison's Promise

Soon I was put to work. I swept the warehouse floor, made things shipshape, staggered to and fro with bags and bundles. Or went running with messages to captains down by Sutton Pool.

There I dallied, feasting my eyes on the ships: the *Lion*, the *Primrose*, the *Paul*, the *Jonas*, the *William and John*. Some lay low in the water like the tiny *Swallow*. Some towered over the crowded quay like the *Minion* with her mighty stern and forecastle, her rows of gaping gun ports.

I wished aloud that I could sail in her. But an old sailor said: 'That's an ill-omened ship.' In time I found out why.

I learned the cargoes: wines and salt from Rochelle, sugar, salt and pepper from Lisbon, oil and soap from Seville, sugar and molasses from Santa Cruz.

I learned the names of merchants and captains, Lodge and Castlyn, Hickman,

Towerson, Wyndham, and always the Hawkins brothers, William and John. Poynton grumbled when he heard men speak of Hawkins, but I think he envied them as they grew great and paid their trips to the Queen's court in London.

Hiding in corners, pretending to work, I heard men talk of many things. It seemed they played a double game. In peace they traded, in war they were privateers. They seized other nations' ships and ransomed their cargoes.

But when their own ships were seized, their faces turned dark with fury. They talked of 'pirates' and went to the law to get their cargoes returned.

I was amazed by all this. Greatly daring I asked Master Poynton's clerk, how could one know the difference between pirate and privateer?

He smiled a grim smile. ''Tis simple. A privateer has papers to say he may capture other nations' ships. A pirate has not but does so anyway. Take my word, John, stick by the letter of the law, have the right papers and you may do what you will.'

But whether by trade or privateering, Master Poynton grew richer. He had a great chest in his counting house with three iron locks and once I saw inside. It was full of gold coins that glittered and chattered. I was transfixed by the sight.

Next day, I was in the courtyard, as Harry and Alison were done with lessons. They rushed down the stairs and Alison flung herself right into my arms.

'What will you give me, John Marsh?' she cried. 'A flower, an orange?'

I answered without thought: 'All the gold in the world – when I'm a man.'

She crowed with delight and kissed me on the cheek.

'Then I will wed you, John.'

It was a childish jest. But I took it for the truth.

· 5 ·

A Stranger from the Sea

Time passed. Queen Mary died, so did the fires that burned the faithful. Her sister Elizabeth took the throne. Under her rule Protestants now had charge of the church and Catholics in their turn must worship quietly at home.

And Master Poynton had a swagger in his walk. The world turned his way. 'Mark my words. France may be mighty. Spain may be laden with treasure. But little England will show them all!' he said and banged his fist on the counting house table.

The merchants said 'Aye.' They put their heads and their purses together and sent out more ships across the seas.

One morning a fishing smack came into Sutton Pool. A man was helped up on to the quay. I stared at him. He was tall, but his hair was grey, his cheeks were pale and sunken in. Seamen crowded round and slapped his back.

Of a sudden they all looked at me. The man stepped forward, grasped my shoulders and kissed me. 'You do not know me John, lad, do you?' But I did. It was my father.

What a welcome he had, in town and church. How happy my mother was, though how little she said. How proud I was to walk by his side.

Yet some things were strange. He would not talk of where he had been, nor what he had done in all those years.

Room was found for him in the house. But Master Poynton was wary of him. They had little to say to one another.

There was worse. Often by night my father stayed from the house, or came home unsteady on his feet. My mother wept. They whispered. She smiled again.

But all was not well. I did my work in counting house and warehouse, but my heart was heavy.

At last, one holiday, my father rowed with me out to Cawsand Bay. We sat on the rocks while the tide went out from the level sand. Then my father spoke:

'They take me for a hero.' He pointed to the town. 'I brought forbidden books from Holland. But, John, it was not for religion. I do not give a fig how men worship God, be they Protestant, Catholic, Jew or Hindu. Do you understand?'

I thought I did. 'Brother Ambrose told me no man knows the mind of God.'

'Wise man. All that I care for is to be free, to go where I will and think what I may. When one man says to another, "Thou shalt not read this book or say this prayer," I am angry.'

He scratched in the sand with his toe.

'They all say God is theirs. Can all be right? When Catholic Mary was Queen, she burned Protestant folk. She drove me from England. I sailed in French privateering ships with Protestant captains. We plundered all, Spanish or Portuguese. They sailed in dread of us.'

He drew on the sand two ships, one small, one huge. 'See, that thirty tonner, swift and armed, will overtake the big, slow merchant man. So it was. We took, we sank, we killed. We seized a Spanish ship with forty Catholic priests on board. Our captain said: "Make water spaniels of those papists!" So they drowned. Why did the hand of God not save them?'

When he was silent, I asked him: 'Will you never go to sea again?'

He laughed. 'My pockets are empty. I must sail. Master Poynton will send out his ships and I must go where he commands. But, who knows, I may come back rich, and we shall live like fighting cocks.'

He ruffled my hair: 'What's on your mind, John?'

'Will you take me with you, Father?'

He shook his head: 'No, stay home and count the money when the ships come in.'

· 6 ·

We'll Live like Kings

So the ships sailed out, each time a longer voyage. First to the Barbary Coast, coming home laden with sugar, molasses, dates and almonds. Then further south to the Guinea Coast, for grain and pepper.

Yet further south, risking storms, contrary winds, currents and rocks on uncharted coasts, trading with Negro kings. They took out hatchets, combs and iron rings and brought home gold and ivory tusks.

Master Poynton rubbed his hands. 'My cargo out cost twenty-three pounds. My cargo home earned six hundred.'

The chest with three locks was piled high with gold. Now he did not deal in coins alone but in scrolled papers, each one of which was worth a hundred guineas. 'Lighter in the purse, and safer,' he crowed.

With the help of Poynton's ships, my father

prospered, too, for a while. He rented a house in Stillman Street where my mother could live when he came into port. Master Poynton was not pleased but could not come between man and wife.

But when Father spent his evenings in the taverns on the quay, my mother complained and he said: 'Forgive me Prudence. I miss my shipmates. I'll go less often.'

She answered: 'I do not complain if you drink with your shipmates. It is the money you give away I grudge.'

Father frowned: 'I give to those with nothing. Each time we sail home, we leave men behind, dead, drowned. I can't let their children starve.'

Then he embraced her. 'I'll make my fortune yet. I'll build a house and we'll live like kings.'

When the money ran out, he went back to sea and she went back to Master Poynton's house. Each voyage was longer and each return he was more gaunt and grey.

As my father diminished, Master Poynton grew grander. Great men at court, even the Queen herself, put money into his ships. As his fortune grew, work in the counting house went on till dusk and then by candlelight.

I saw no more of my old playmates. Alison was in Exeter being schooled by a lady. Harry was now apprenticed to the Hawkins brothers, learning the merchants' trade from the most famous men in Plymouth.

One evening as I worked, someone entered and stood in the shadow. A voice said: 'John, is my father here?'

'Alison,' I said amazed.

She came closer. She was taller, her red hair falling becomingly over a green gown.

'You did not know me,' she teased. I could not answer and she laughed:

'You work so hard. Soon all the gold in the world will be in father's chest. You'll have none for me.'

The words rushed from my mouth: 'There's more gold in the wide world than you dream of. One day, I'll take ship and bring it home.'

Harry Poynton's Secret

Next summer a great freight of gold and ivory came home for Master Poynton. But it was borne in one ship. It staggered into harbour with a handful of men on board out of the ninety-two who sailed away last autumn.

One ship foundered in a storm. Another was sunk by a Portuguese galley. Rotten food, bad water, scurvy and yellow fever took the rest.

Father and his shipmates who lived out the voyage were taken to the plague house outside the town lest they spread infection among the folk.

There we went, Mother and I, with food and fresh clothes. An old woman met us at the door. 'Mistress Marsh, bless you, you're the lucky one. Your man will live.'

We turned back home, mother to wait and I to work. In the counting house I found Harry talking to the clerk. I looked him over, velvet jacket, silver buttons.

'So fine, Harry?' I teased him.

He bowed. 'Master Hawkins will not let his folk go round in rags.' He laughed. 'Come John, walk down to Sutton Pool with me. I must talk with the Master of the *Salomon*. She's to sail with the *Swallow* and the *Jonas*, this October.'

'Where away?' I asked.

He took my arm and led me out into Vauxhall Street then spoke low in my ear.

'The public word is that we shall get gold and

ivory on the African coast. But only one vessel will sail home to Plymouth.'

'And the other ships?' I asked.

'They'll sail west to the shores of America – to Margarita and Cartagena, Hispaniola and Rio de la Hacha, and sell their cargoes there.'

I stared at him: 'But the Spaniards rule there. English ships are not allowed.'

'True. That's why no word must get back to Spain. Whatever King Philip may say, there are many Spanish folk in the Americas who want to trade with us. What right has he to forbid it?'

'And King Philip would answer – "Might is right,"' I said.

'Ha! John Hawkins has a way with him that makes folk do his bidding. Meantime, what is not known can't grieve. What we have to sell to merchants on the Spanish Main they'll give their right arms for.'

'What is that?'

He did not answer, but instead, gripped my arm and pointed:

'Talk of the devil,' he said.

· 8 ·

Black Cargo

At the corner of an alley near the quay a man lay on the ground. His rucked-up clothing left belly, legs, arms bare. At first I thought he was drunk. Then I knew by his stiffness he was dead. His skin was dark, near purple.

'A Negro,' said Harry. 'Well made, good muscles. If he were alive, he'd fetch fifty gold pesos on the Spanish Main.'

'Then he may thank his Maker he's dead,' said a voice nearby. Harry and I turned about. There stood my father, scarecrow thin, pale, his hair now white as snow.

'Father!'

He stepped forward. He carried a sack. He pointed to the bare black body on the earth. 'See, made in the image of God, like all His children. His name was Samuel, he was my shipmate.'

With that he threw the sack over the body, hiding its nakedness. Then he spoke to Harry.

'So Master Hawkins is not content with gold and ivory. Now he's selling flesh, alive, eh?'

Harry shrugged: 'In Hispaniola they are mad for slaves. There's a fortune to be made.'

My father said nothing. Harry grew bolder. He pointed to the dead man. 'In their own lands, they kill and eat their own kind.'

'Aye,' answered my father. 'And in this land, the rich eat up the poor.'

Harry was not put out. 'Good Master Marsh. I will not have cross words with you. I'll only say, if Englishmen do not sell slaves, some other nation will.'

My father's face grew dark.

'The French do not. They say a free people shall not enslave others.' He drew in his breath.

'What's more, they say the Englishman will sell his own mother if the price is good enough.'

Harry stared at him, astonished.

'Then Master Marsh, you'd not sail on a slaving voyage?'

'Not sail!' my father shouted. 'Not sail? I must sail or starve like any other poor scrub.'

He turned his back on us and strode away along Vauxhall Street.

Harry and I strolled back to his father's house, he with a smile on his lips. I knew he was pleased with himself – he'd answered my father's furious words coolly, without yielding an inch.

I was unhappy, to see my father so angry – like a stranger. Who was in the right and who in the wrong?

My future lay with the Poyntons. But there was a shadow creeping over my life.

· 9 ·

Spain Will Fight

At first it seemed Harry was right. Next year Hawkins' ships sailed home from the Americas, laden with gold, silver, pearls and hides, in exchange for the slaves they sold. Master Hawkins was now the richest man in Plymouth.

Harry told me, full of pride: 'Here is how it works, John. Spain has power over the West Indian Islands and the mainland, what seamen call the Spanish Main. Spain grows fat on the wealth of these lands and King Philip of Spain will not allow the Spaniards who live on the Main to trade with any other country – English and French ships are not welcome there.

'Yet you cannot stop other countries from trading with the Spanish Main, any more than you can stop the rain from falling. The Spaniards that live on the Spanish Main want slaves to do their work for them. So with a nod and a wink, Hawkins sells slaves to the Spanish merchants there. He pretends to use force to make them buy and the Spaniards pretend to be frightened into buying. Then they tell King Philip that they only traded with England out of fear. Everyone is satisfied . . .'

'But not King Philip,' I said.

Harry nodded in glee. 'Already his envoy is complaining to Queen Elizabeth.'

'So Master Hawkins is in hot water?'

'Not so. He's gone to London to see the Spanish envoy himself. He offers to keep all other nations' ships out of the Spanish Main if he can be free to trade there.'

'So. Play one against another?'

'That's his way.' Now Harry put a finger to his lips. 'Next voyage, my father puts his money in

Hawkins' ships. And, what do you think? I shall sail with him.'

He looked at my long face. 'You'd go too, eh?'

'I'd give my right arm to sail.'

'Then, come, let's speak to my father.'

Master Poynton shook his head. 'No John. I need you here.'

'Father,' protested Harry. 'You can find a clerk to do John's work.' He gave a cunning smile. 'On board John can look after your share in the venture.'

But still his father shook his head. His tone was milder. 'No John. There's another matter. I promised your mother you'd not sail.'

At supper that evening I pleaded with my mother. She said nothing but began to weep. Then my father spoke, slowly:

'Your mother does not want you to go. But no more do I. It was I who said you should not sail.'

'But why then?'

'John. This trade is rich, gold, ivory, or Negroes. Hawkins is clever, talks sweetly to everyone. Is he Catholic or Protestant? No one knows. Does he wish to serve the King of

Spain or trick him? Who can say?'

'Aye John,' my father went on. 'Hawkins is a good navigator. His men are well cared for. He loses only one in eight, where others lose half their crew.'

'Then why not sail with him?' I asked.

'For this reason. This trade is rich. Spain will not let anyone, Master Hawkins included, have a share in it. One day the tricks and the talking will not be enough. Spain will fight. There will be war.'

'Hawkins will not be afraid. Nor will I,' I said boastfully.

'I wager not,' said my father. 'But two can play a cunning game. Philip's admirals will wait their chance. One day, no sweet words will save John Hawkins.'

'Hear me John. The merchants venture their wealth, we venture our lives. They are all we have. The gold piles up in Master Poynton's strongbox and Plymouth bones whiten on far-away shores.'

'Stay home and grow rich.' He smiled. 'Then who knows, maybe you'll wed Alison Poynton.'

Yet Harry was right again. He came home to Plymouth nine months later, his face bronzed, pearls in his pocket. Master Poynton rubbed his hands. His profit on the voyage was sixty per cent.

'Hawkins,' said Harry, 'is now the richest man in England. He dines with the Spanish envoy and tells him tales. The Queen promises to make Master Hawkins stay home. But next year she'll let him slip away. She sends her warships in his fleet and takes her share of the profits when he comes home.'

Now I was on fire to go. I said nothing to my mother but she knew what was in my mind. Father had sailed again to Africa.

I had to work for Master Poynton, counting his wealth while others went abroad and made their fortunes.

The summer wore on. Another Hawkins expedition gathered in the Cattewater, the *William and John*, the *Swallow*, the tiny *Judith*, the *Minion*, that had seen so many of my father's shipmates to their death.

But, dwarfing them all was the *Jesus of Lubeck*, sent by the Queen, a floating castle, bristling with cannon.

I watched them loading hogsheads of beef, stock fish, barrels of biscuit, sides of bacon, tuns of wine and ale. It was to be a mighty venture – four hundred men on board.

As I came back to Vauxhall Street and entered the courtyard I heard footsteps. Alison, tall and stately in a new gown, was on the stairs. I had not

seen her for a year and now she was so fair I could not speak.

She laughed, ran down to the third step and threw herself at me. I caught and held her.

'When shall I see that gold, Master Marsh?' she mocked.

'When your father, and mine, let me sail,' I answered.

I set her down, then saw Master Poynton in the gallery looking down. Next day he said to me. 'John Marsh. Get leave of your father. For you shall sail with Master Harry on the *Jesus* this autumn.'

That October I sailed with Hawkins, but without my father's consent. His ship sailed back into Padstow with only half a crew. Ned Marsh was not among them. He slept his last sleep beneath the waves off Santa Cruz.

My father was gone. He could not make me stay home. I'd never hear his stern, kind voice again. I was free to make my fortune.

· 10 ·

I Sail with Hawkins

Our fleet cleared Plymouth Harbour on the second day of October 1567. My mother stood on the quay at Sutton Pool and watched us out. Her grey hair blew in the wind. Her eyes were dry. She had done with crying. She had lost her husband and now her son was taking the sea road.

I looked out in hope of seeing Alison. But Harry told me she had gone back to Exeter. She wished us both a safe and prosperous voyage.

My hopes were high. There was triple pay and I'd be a fool if I came home with less than twenty pounds, never mind what else I'd pick up on the way. Enough to buy a share in a venture and start on the way to riches.

But, where we bound? Rumours flew about the ship. We were to trade on the Guinea Coast. We were to build a fort on the Gold Coast and drive out the Portuguese. We were to ambush the Spanish treasure fleet.

Harry laughed at all these tales. 'Wait and see,' he told me. 'Trust Master Hawkins.'

And I began to do so. I admired him as he paced the sunlit quarterdeck in his scarlet leather jacket with its silver braid. But was he a man to face foul weather?

I had my answer. In the dread Bay of Biscay a great storm blew up and howled for seven days, scattering our six ships. The *Jesus of Lubeck* was a floating coffin. Her rotten timbers sprang as the waves beat on them. Water rushed in and fish swam in the hold.

Hawkins was all about, shouting orders, hauling on ropes. When all seemed lost he told us to prepare to meet our God like men. We prayed – what else could we do? On the fourth day the storm went down and in the Canary Islands we found our companion ships still afloat.

Hawkins was wise. When we anchored off Santa Cruz he saw that the Spanish ships lying in front of the castle had moved off, leaving a clear field for the cannons to point at us. When night fell, we upped anchor and slipped away.

Hawkins was bold. When we reached the African shore by Cacheo River, the Portuguese

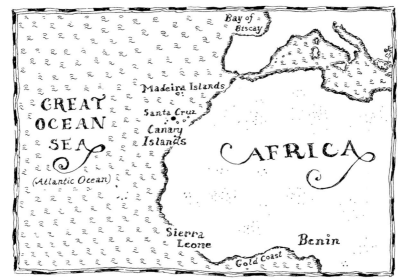

would not play the trading game. So he landed men and guns and took Negro towns by storm.

The Negroes fought back bravely. We lost men. Some died from poison arrows, jaw clenched, eyes staring.

But he led us with a dash. We broke down mud walls, set huts ablaze and led men, women and children captive to the shore.

At night in dreams I heard my father's voice as he covered that black dead body in Vauxhall Street. But I was hardened with blood and war and put these thoughts from my mind. Ninety of my shipmates had died, but we had five hundred slaves in the hold. The voyage was made.

Now we sailed, fifty days and nights until we reached the Spanish Main.

I saw little enough of Harry. He was busy in Hawkins' great cabin. His companions were gentlemen adventurers who sailed with us for glory and the art of war.

My friends were seamen of Plymouth, Tavistock and Padstow, all bent, like me, on making a fortune. And there was a young man, somewhat older than myself, a cousin of Master Hawkins, Francis Drake. He preferred the company of mariners to gentlemen.

He was good to me. His father, a preacher, had been driven from Plymouth, as mine had. He was stocky, red-haired, fierce and merry, and would rather fight Spaniards than trade with them.

Young though Drake was, Hawkins gave him command of the little *Judith*. When he left us to go on board, he bid me come with him. But I felt bound to stay close to Hawkins and said 'No'. That was my error and soon I had time to regret it.

Our ships sailed on to Margarita, Borburata, Rio de la Hacha and Cartagena. At each port Master Hawkins sent a polite letter asking the Governor permission to trade. If he refused we landed with drums beating, fully armed, and merchants flocked to buy.

By summer's end the slaves were sold. A fortune in gold, silver and pearls was packed in the hold. It was nigh a year since we first sailed and we began to long for Plymouth Hoe.

We set sail for the Florida Straits, there to catch the westerlies to waft us home to England. Said Harry: 'What did I tell you? Trust Hawkins.'

But John Hawkins' luck had run out. Mine too.

· 11 ·

Defeat at San Juan

That September, in the Gulf of Mexico, a huge storm seized us. Every plank in the *Jesus* let in water. If we did not repair her we were food for the fishes.

We found shelter in the only harbour, a miserable spot called San Juan de Ulua. Harbour? No more than a space of water, two bowshots wide, between the shore and a sandbank only three foot above high water.

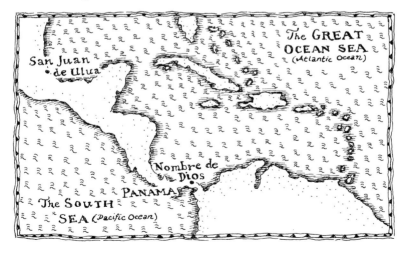

As we sailed in, Spanish boats came out to meet us. Bronze cannon on the sandbank fired a salute. The weather had so faded the colours at our mast-head, they did not know us for English but thought we were ships from Spain come to load Mexican silver.

Before they saw their mistake, we were in and moored to the sandbank. They agreed to let us take on water and food and repair our vessels. They had no choice. We were stronger than they.

But not for long. After two days we saw ships on the horizon, thirteen sail in all. The great Spanish treasure fleet sailed in. We might have prevented them. But Master Hawkins would not. The ship we stood on was the Queen's and that would mean an act of war.

So messages went to and fro. Men were exchanged as hostages. The Spanish fleet entered and we were moored cheek by jowl with them. There was danger in the air.

By night they brought more soldiers from the land, and moved their guns to bear on us. A child would have known what was afoot. Master Hawkins sent Robert Barrett to protest, but they made him prisoner.

Slowly passed the day. We knew it would end in bloodshed and at supper time, it came.

With a trumpet blast the Spanish soldiers sprang aboard the *Minion*. We from the *Jesus*, led by Hawkins, leapt down and drove them off. Then we clambered back to our own ship as the *Jesus* in her turn was boarded. All was dark, noise and confusion.

I took two wounds, in head and shoulder, but in the heat of battle never felt the hurt.

Now the ropes holding us to the shore were cut and the ships swung out to sea. We let the Spaniards have it with our cannons. Soon enough we'd sunk one, blown another apart. But the old *Jesus* was riddled with shot, the *Angel* sunk and the *Swallow* abandoned.

The *Judith*, loaded to the gunwales with men, pulled away out of the range of Spanish cannons. Now the *Minion* came close up to the *Jesus* taking off crew and treasure. Our ship was sinking and we jumped for our lives as Spanish fire ships, set ablaze, bore down on us.

In the water I struck out for where I trusted *Minion* lay. But I was wrong. A Spanish pinnace cut across and I was dragged on board.

As I lay beneath the oars I heard one sailor say: 'Why do we save these dogs?'

Another laughed and answered: 'Those not born to drown, shall hang.'

· 12 ·

Prisoner in Mexico

We did not hang. The Governor of Mexico wanted to execute all prisoners after the battle of San Juan de Ulua. He was quite sure Hawkins did not come driven by the storm, but on purpose to ambush the treasure fleet. We were pirates and should dance the rope-jig.

But in Mexico City, thank God, there were ladies and gentlemen who did not wish us to die, yet. They told the Governor he must wait for commands from King Philip of Spain.

Meantime they had other uses for the Englishmen and one day our guards gathered us in the prison courtyard. We were a sorry band in our torn shirts and breeches, dirty faces, blood crusted on our wounds.

In came a dozen senoras and caballeros. Without a word they paced about and looked us up and down. A handsome lady with grey hair and soft brown eyes paused in front of me and raised her hand. My guard shoved me forward and I followed her.

She was Donna Isabella, widow of a grandee. And I bless her memory. I was her servant for a year and never have I known greater ease.

My work was light. None with white skins laboured hard in that city. Negroes made all the toil. Without them, life on the Spanish Main could not go on.

Donna Isabella had a fancy to learn English. She learned a little of our tongue. I learned much more of hers. She liked to hear me talk for I reminded her of a son who died aged fifteen.

She took me with her to the cathedral. The high ceiling, red, blue, and gold colours of picture and image, the smoke of a hundred candles and the sweet smell of incense made my head spin. She gave me a coin to light a candle for my father. I saw no harm in that and do not think he would, either.

She teased me: 'Have you a sweetheart?'

I blushed.

'Do you have a favour, a ribbon or a lock of hair?'

I shook my head.

'Shame on her. She does not deserve you.'

Donna Isabella was so kind I longed to do her a service. I was a fool to do so. But one day I looked through the ledgers of her estate. I saw at a glance her steward was cheating her. She thanked me and dismissed him.

But a week later she told me: 'Juan my child, you must go away. Someone has whispered to the Governor that you are a heretic and have done awful things. I do not want to lose you, but for your safety you must go.'

· 13 ·

Slaves and Rebels

I was sent to the silver mines, many miles from the city, where an old friend of Donna Isabella found me work, keeping the accounts. My earlier life now became like a dream.

The silver mines were like the gates of hell, the burning sun, the barren yellow rocks, the dust. Instead of church bells and hum of insects in the garden, there was the devil's sound of shouts, screams and endless cracking of the whip.

I saw the Negroes climb with their burdens from the bowels of the earth, like damned souls. I saw them flogged at the stake, flogged till they fell dying. Yet sometimes one would raise his head and yell a word like a curse which made the overseer turn pale.

'Would it not be well to beat them less?' I asked him. 'Beat a man senseless and he cannot work. Why pay fifty gold pesos for a labourer, then destroy him?'

He looked at me with pity and contempt. 'Ingles, you are a fool. Did you hear what he shouted?'

'What word was that?'

'Yanga.'

'Yanga?'

'That is their king.' The overseer pointed to the hills around. 'Yanga lives up there in a hidden cave. When slaves escape, they run to Yanga. For every three slaves brought here, one runs away. Up there are hundreds of them, so hateful, our soldiers dare not venture near. Up there they are no longer slaves, but Cimarrones.'

'Cimarrones?'

'Yes. Wild ones of the mountains. I tell you, Ingles, if you meet one, say your prayers.'

But my danger came from another quarter and come it did. My enemy's spite found me out. When I had been in the mines no more than two months, soldiers came riding from the city.

'Juan – Marsh?'

'That is me.'

'You are to come back to the city. The Inquisition wishes to – question you.'

· 14 ·

In the Inquisition's Hands

Once more I lay in prison. The fine clothes Donna Isabella put on my back were torn and filthy. Rats shared my food, running over my body and poking in my pockets at night. I remembered Sir Bevis in his dungeon but knew I could not burst out of mine.

I was not alone. Other English sailors were there. Word had come from Madrid that the monks of the Inquisition might interrogate us: were we of the true religion, or were we not?

Days, nights passed. I do not know how many, for the sun never shone where we lay. At last my chains were struck off and I was dragged up steps, along passages and finally into a sunlit room where two men sat at a table beneath a great gilded crucifix.

One who spoke most was thin and dark. The other was plump with mild eyes. The questions began and I answered as best I might. Some were on purpose to trick me. But since I barely knew what they meant with 'the body of Christ' and 'the Lord's grace', they got little out of me.

Once, confused by their nagging I answered: 'Who knows the mind of God?' The fat one smiled. The thin one spoke fiercely: 'Who told you that?'

'My old teacher, Brother Ambrose,' I answered, which was true and maybe it saved me. Maybe they thought me a Catholic, ignorant and confused.

Then the thin one picked up a document. 'Are you kin to Ned Marsh?' My eyes showed him the answer. He said: 'Ned Marsh, pirate, blasphemer, ravisher and murderer.'

I threw myself at him, gripping his throat. 'Liar and pig!' I yelled. The plump monk came between us and said with a mild voice, 'No man can endure an insult to father or mother. Leave be.'

With that I was returned to the dungeon.

The next treasure fleet for Spain bore me and thirty shipmates over the sea. In Seville we lay in prison and waited for the Inquisition to decide our fate.

But we did not starve. We were brought food by servants of an English lady, married to a Spanish Duke who was a favourite of King Philip. So we lived in hope.

Others with no more crimes on their conscience than we were not so fortunate. Two hundred lashes, ten years in the galleys for one. Two hundred lashes, eight years in the galleys for another. And poor Robert Barrett was taken out and burned in front of the cathedral steps.

Thank God, we were released. In August 1571, nigh four years after sailing away, I came home to Plymouth town again.

· 15 ·

Sad Homecoming

I knew all was not well, when I landed at Sutton Pool. So I went around the welcoming crowd on the quay and hurried to the tall house in Vauxhall Street.

Opening the door, the old servant gaped at me, then said, 'John, lad, welcome home. I hardly knew you.' But I had no patience and pushed past him, through the courtyard and to my mother's room.

By the light from the window I saw her lying pale as a ghost. Someone was wiping her face with a cloth, then turned round as I came in.

'John!'

'Alison!'

Her face was strange and sad: 'Your mother. I fear . . . we've cared for her, I swear.'

'I know, Alison,' I said, stepping towards her. 'But . . .'

'John, I may not stay,' she answered and ran

from the room, leaving me perplexed.

On the third day, my mother opened her eyes and knew me. 'Thank God, John. I prayed each day I'd see you just once more.'

'Mother you'll see me many times. I'll not leave you.'

'Not so John. 'Tis I who'll leave you. I'm going where I'll find your father.' She smiled. 'Sweet Ned. I missed him so. But now no more.'

Then she grasped my arm and said: 'Look beneath my pillow. Your father gave me that. But I kept it lest you should have need one day. Now God protect you, lad.'

She kissed me and said no more.

· 16 ·

Poynton a Traitor?

There were many mourners at my mother's burial for she was well loved. Master Poynton, Alison and Harry all were there and comforted me, though I do not remember what they said to me or I to them.

For days I wandered up and down the streets of Plymouth, talking to no one, even when they stopped to speak to me. In my mind the thoughts went round, what would I do with this empty life?

Only thoughts of Alison had shape. It seemed to me that in her company my trials might find their reward.

In my pocket was a little leather purse taken from under my mother's pillow – my father's gift to her. Inside were a dozen precious stones that flashed when I opened it. Thanks to my parents I was no longer penniless. I might sell these and buy a share in a venture, one gambler's throw to make my fortune.

I went to a merchant in the city and showed him the jewels. He scratched his chin and pursed his lips. 'There's not much here – maybe fifty pounds. But I tell you what, for your mother's sake I've an offer for you.'

He placed a finger to his long nose.

'Francis Drake of Tavistock.'

'I know him, sailed with him, four years back. Is he still alive?'

'. . . and kicking. Since he came home from San Juan de Ulua he's been twice to the Spanish Main. Next year he'll go there again.' Now he bent his mouth close to my ear. 'They say he'll go openly to seize the Spanish treasure ships.'

He weighed my purse in his hand.

'Let me keep these baubles. I'll lend you, say, seventy pounds. You buy with it a share in Drake's voyage and sail with it. And we both share the profits.'

My father's face sprang into my mind. I spoke in fury. 'You cormorant. You venture your precious seventy pounds, I venture my precious life. I die and you keep my jewels.' With that I marched from his counting house.

Next day I took passage to Exeter. There in a

narrow street I found a Jewish moneylender. He heard my story, took my jewels and said, slowly:

'Sir, I will give you what they are worth. One hundred pounds in gold.' Then he rested his fingers on my arm and said: 'If I were you I'd venture your gold, not yourself. Let others sail. Grow rich at home.'

I thanked him for his money and his counsel and left his shop to go back to the harbour. Now I must find a way to speak to Alison.

But fate had other things in store. I stopped in a tavern for a tankard of ale. Behind in a dark corner, two men talked, low-voiced, and in the Spanish tongue. My ears are sharp. I heard each word. It was beyond belief.

No less than this. In return for forty thousand pounds John Hawkins would lead the English fleet over into the hands of King Philip of Spain. Queen Elizabeth would be overthrown. Mary Queen of Scots would reign and England be Catholic once more.

With care I looked at them from the corner of my eye. One of them was moustached, eyes veiled by a broad-rimmed hat. I did not know him.

But the other I did. It was Harry Poynton.

· 17 ·

Alison Gives her Answer

I waited in the lane outside the tavern. Soon enough the other man, hat down, cloak tight around him, hastened away. In a little while, Harry, finely dressed, hand on sword, whistling, followed him. I stepped out into his path.

'Well met – brother,' said I.

He was thunderstruck and said: 'You were there?'

I nodded.

'You heard. You understood too. How much?'

I said: 'Enough to damn you for a traitor to the Queen.'

His face was pale. His eye was steady: 'You would not give me away, brother?'

'I'm no tell-tale Harry. But I must know what you are about.'

He beckoned me to follow and went back into the tavern. There we sat down in that same dark corner. No one was near. He called for more wine.

I said mockingly, 'Talk Spanish if you will.'

'I will. No one else must know this, John. Master Hawkins plays for high stakes.'

'Forty thousand pounds, eh?'

'Pah. That's just a story. The Spanish believe an Englishman will do anything for gold. But Hawkins is rich beyond greed, John. And has enough fame. He has charge of the Queen's ships.'

'And means to hand them over to Philip of Spain. After the blood we shed fighting the Spaniards at San Juan de Ulua?'

Harry answered in anger. 'I fought there, too. And so did Hawkins.'

But I said, full of hate: 'So did three hundred others. Only eighty came home. Some of us lay in prison. Poor Robert Barrett perished in the flames.'

Harry took my arm. 'John, how did you escape from prison? I'll tell you. Hawkins bought your freedom with his promises to King Philip.'

'He set us free by promising to betray England?'

'If you wish, that's so. But now we play for higher rewards – the safety of the realm.'

'Master Hawkins will save England by betraying it?'

'Hear me John. There are powerful men in England, Catholics like the Duke of Norfolk, who want Elizabeth off the throne and Mary Queen of Scots in her place. They are plotting and Hawkins is pretending to go along with them, to find out what they are planning, and in the end, to trap them. All he does is by agreement with Queen Elizabeth's ministers.'

Harry gripped my arm. 'Believe me, brother. There's no treachery. It is a game of bluff, like chess, for England's sake.'

'And poor scrubs like me are pawns.'

Harry drank from his tankard. 'Your life has been hard. You've lost all. I have been fortunate. But trust me, keep my secret. I'll do all I can to repay you.'

Now a reckless thought came into my head.

'Then repay me, Harry.' Now I gripped his arm. 'You know I love your sister Alison, but dare not tell her. I cannot think of marriage since I'm penniless. But now Harry, I've a hundred pounds – do not smile. I'll venture with Drake, and come home rich.'

'Aye,' he murmured. 'All the gold in the world.'

'So, Harry,' I pleaded. 'Speak for me to Master Poynton. He thinks my father was a heretic rogue, and I no better. But if you speak for me . . .'

He looked sad. 'John, it may not be. Alison is promised in marriage to Sir Richard Dauncy.'

'Marrying up, not down, eh?' I said bitterly. 'Those little promises to John were empty words.'

'John, do not speak so of Alison, if you care for her. She cares for you, as a friend of her childhood days, no one is more dear. But only as a friend. She'll not marry you, John.' His voice grew softer. 'Not for all the gold in the world.'

At first I could not speak. Then I got the words out by force. 'Do me one service Harry. Take a letter for me to Alison. I'll make my plea, with this little silver ring my father gave my mother.'

''Twill do no good John, but I'll do it,' he said. And with that we parted. I journeyed back to Plymouth, took lodgings by Sutton Pool and waited for her answer.

After seven slow days, it came. With her letter was the little ring. She wrote but seven words:

'Forgive me John. God go with you.'

· 18 ·

Drake Raids Nombre de Dios

Alison's letter acted like a powerful medicine, stilling at last my greed for gold. But another hunger remained, companionship. I looked for old shipmates, spent my nights drinking with them. And since the gold I got from the Jew did not go quickly enough I gave it away. There were plenty in the port who needed it more than I.

Now, penniless, I could not stay on land. So winter passed and when spring came, Francis Drake sailed with two ships and seventy-three men and boys, bound for the Spanish Main. And I joined his crew.

He welcomed me as one of San Juan de Ulua, and for my skill with the Spanish tongue. To tell truth though I do not think he planned to talk to the Spaniards. War clouds were on the horizon. Drake was free to sail, and he was not going to trade.

We had fair winds. In nine days we were off

the Madeiras and after that we pushed westward, neither striking sail nor coming to anchor till we reached the Spanish Main.

By July we came to rest in Port Pheasant, Drake's hide-out on the Spanish Main, a deep secret harbour to the east of Nombre de Dios. There, with food a-plenty in the air and the water and no Spaniard for three score miles around, we were snug.

Unknown to us, though, we were being watched.

We made ready. We opened the arms casks, got out pikes and muskets. We bolted together the small boats we'd brought in pieces from England and loaded them with food and gear.

Before July was out, we landed on the beach below Nombre de Dios, by night.

Some of our crew stole round behind the town. The rest of us, led by Drake, marched boldly up the main street, trumpet and drum sounding.

What a panic they were in, bells ringing, muskets firing. For a moment they resisted, then when our lads struck from the rear they broke and fled. The Governor's treasure house stood open before us.

Yet it might have been bolted and barred for all the good it did us. Inside, the chamber was piled high with huge bars of silver, all too heavy to carry away.

We'd had many wounded, our captain too, his blood running down into his boots. So there was nothing for it, but to retreat to our boats, empty-handed.

But this was not the end of the story. And for me it was but a beginning.

· 19 ·

Forest Gold

For two months we cruised the Spanish Main, seizing ships, though never harming their crews. But these were small craft, carrying only wine, grain and meat, welcome enough.

I was content, in a way. The sun shone, the blue sky, the sea, the white shore and green forest were as fine as any I saw. My memories of Plymouth grew dim.

But my shipmates were restless. Their hunger and thirst needed more than meat and beer. Gold and silver was in their talk by day and their dreams by night. But how to get them?

The answer came soon. A slave, by name Diego, came to one of our small boats lurking near Nombre de Dios. He was a rogue for sure, but what he had to tell was worth hearing. He spoke the Spanish tongue and I told our captain what he said.

'I can tell you how to find the Cimaroons.'

'And what are they?' asked Drake.

'Slaves who have run away and live in the forest. They have two kinds, one to the east, one to the west. They hate the Spaniards and they will help you find gold.'

'Brave men, hiding in the forest?' asked Drake.

Diego nodded: 'Before you came, they attacked Nombre de Dios itself. The Governor had to send for more soldiers to defend the town.'

'Captain,' said I, 'I've heard of these folk, the Cimaroons, in Mexico. The Spaniards live in fear of them. If they were on our side, nothing could hold us back.'

Now Drake wasted no time. Guided by Diego, we rowed to a certain river to the eastward. There

at dawn came a troop of Negroes, dressed in the
Spanish style, but armed with bow and spear.
Their leader was a tall man, named Pedro.

'We know of you,' he told our captain. 'The
Spaniards call you the dragon. If you fight them,
we'll help you.'

Drake spoke plainly. 'Can you help us get to
the Spanish gold?'

Pedro answered, smiling: 'If all you want is
gold we could have given you that. Each spring
the Spaniards bring treasure from Peru to Panama
City. Then they take it by mule train through the
forest to Nombre de Dios, where the fleet waits to
bear it to Spain. We ambush them and steal their
gold.'

'Show me, let me see,' demanded Drake.

Pedro shrugged. 'It's buried in the river bed. What use do we have for gold? But now the rivers are in flood. In spring, when the waters run low again, I can show you.'

'Why, spring's five months away,' said Drake.

'Then you must wait, Captain. Let your men come to our town. Be our guests. In the spring, when the mule bells ring, we'll go to battle together.'

Drake was too restless. 'Our thanks for your kindness. We can't stay idle. We'll go raiding. But to prove our goodwill, take two of our men with you and leave two of yours with me.'

He looked at me. 'John Marsh, will you go with Pedro?'

'Gladly,' I answered.

· 20 ·

Pedro's People

So I set out with Pedro and the Cimaroons, first through the swamps, then through the forests and up into rising country. When Tom, my shipmate, fell lame, they made a stretcher of branches and carried him.

After three days' march we were challenged by sentries and Pedro gave our password. Three miles along the track on the side of a hill, we came upon their town.

It had a moat around it, eight foot wide and a wall ten foot high. Inside was a broad, pleasant main street – far cleaner than any in Plymouth. On either side were houses some fifty in all, thatched with palm leaves, each large enough to hold a family of some size.

Cooking fires burned. Down by the river, women washed their clothes. Everywhere children played, ran up, stared at us, laughed and ran away.

They gave Tom and me a house to ourselves and for those winter months we lived like fighting cocks, on all manner of meat, fish and birds of the air, maize and fruit.

But Tom longed to be with the ships. He feared they'd sail away and leave him. And he grumbled when he saw folk with crosses hanging round their necks.

'John mate, we've fallen in a nest of papists,' he said.

I laughed at him. 'Have you seen a priest here, or heard a church bell?'

He had not, but he was not content. He longed for spring. With me it was different. I had been at ease with these folk ever since I'd heard Pedro say they'd buried the Spanish gold, rather than keep it.

Pedro made me his friend. I went hunting with him, using the spear or bow and arrow. They had all manner of arrowheads – burnt wood, fishbone and iron. Iron to them was more precious than gold. 'You cannot shoot a meal with gold,' said Pedro.

He took me along the trail to Panama. And on a great mountain ridge, showed me their look-out

tree. Once they had been taken by surprise. Spanish raiders had killed women and children. Now they kept their guard.

'We steal their gold to make them weak. Then they will leave us in peace.'

From the treetop he pointed north and south and I saw the two great oceans. And I knew I must tell our captain. 'He'll be afire to sail on that South Sea,' I told Pedro.

He replied: 'Juan, your people and the Spaniards are mad to sail on seas. I only sailed but once on the sea and it was not by choice – the ship carried human cargo, out of Africa.'

At that, I fell silent. But he said, 'Come, what's done is done.'

We went secretly into Panama, I, posing as a Spaniard and Pedro as my slave. We learned that treasure would be landed there in four weeks' time.

'Hey, Juan,' Pedro told me, 'soon you'll be back with your friends and back at your trade again.'

I told Tom. At first he smiled at the news. Then he was sad. 'Four weeks you say, John? I wish it were four days.'

I was sad too, for I wished it were four years and more. I had good reason. Pedro had a sister, Conseula, also called N'kansa. She was tall, straight-backed and walked with swaying hips. She smiled much and laughed often. When we talked, her eyes were friendly. They looked full into mine.

A new life beckoned me, in the forest. Yet the old life on the sea, my loyalty to captain and shipmates, held me fast.

Soon the mule bells would clang along the track. We would make an ambush, seize the Spanish gold and silver, load our ships and sail away.

· 21 ·

John Marsh's Choice

When Tom and I rejoined our shipmates, bad news was waiting. Of our seventy-three, now twenty-eight were dead and buried, killed in fighting or struck down by fever and in that number were Drake's brothers, John and Joseph.

But Drake had done his mourning. When he heard about the treasure train his spirits rose. And when I told him of the look-out tree he said: 'That sight I must see, and in good time, I'll sail that South Sea. But meantime, let's to our work.'

We formed our raiding party, eighteen sailors, thirty Cimaroons and marched into the forest for our rendezvous with the Spaniards.

At first, though, things went badly. We set our ambush, outside Panama City. But in the dark, one of our men got drunk with spirits and rushed out of hiding. The Spaniards were warned and ran back to safety.

Our captain was undaunted. We made another sally. That failed. Then we made a third and caught our enemies where they could not escape. Fierce was their defence, yet our attack was fiercer.

Pedro's men wanted their hands on Spanish throats. Drake's crew wanted their hands on Spanish gold. In the end, revenge or riches, all got what they sought.

On ship and shore the feasting and the singing made the air ring. Only one man was silent amid the rejoicing. And that was John Marsh, deep in his own thoughts.

Three days later, Drake gave the order to load the ships and weigh anchor. Our old Devon craft were long gone – battered, holed and sunk. But in their place were fine Spanish ships seized off the coast near Nombre de Dios.

Drake's little fleet was going home famously,

though many of those who left Plymouth a year ago would never see their home town again, for they were dead of wounds or foul disease. I knew what pain lay in wait for their families, for I had been down that road.

In these days of work and thought, I made up my mind and when my chance came, I seized it.

The day for farewells came at last. Sailors and Cimaroon comrades gathered together on the shore. Drake saluted Pedro for the last time and made him a present of a fine French sword. Then he said 'John, shipmate. Be so good and ask our friend, what other gift I may offer him.'

I did so and Pedro smiled. Turning to the small boats we had brought out with us from England, now worn-out and broken up for burning, he told Drake: 'We'll have the ironwork from those pinnaces, from that we'll make a thousand arrowheads.'

To each man, thought I, some thing is precious. Now was my moment.

'Captain,' I said, 'I have a wish.'

Drake looked at me. I knew he guessed what was in my mind. 'Speak, John.'

'I have no more life to live in Plymouth, no

family, no one . . .' I fell silent. 'Go on, lad,' he bid me.

'Release me from your service. Let me stay here.'

Drake nodded, then he smiled and turned to Pedro.

'What do you say, sir? Have you a place among your folk for John Marsh? I give you my word he's a good true seaman, faithful to death.'

Pedro smiled in his turn. 'Captain, we know John Marsh. He already has his place among us.'

So I had my wish. The ships sailed and I went back into the forest with my people.

That, then, is the story of John Marsh, of Plymouth town.

Further Reading

Now that you have read **All the Gold in the World**, you might like to read some other books about life in Tudor times. You might like to read other novels or general information books. Here is a selection of the books available.

Fiction

Leon Garfield   **Shakespeare Stories**,
Gollancz Children's Books (1995)

Avril Rowlands   **The Shakespeare Connection**,
Oxford University Press (1994)

Rosemary Sutcliff   **The Armourer's House**,
Red Fox, Random Century Children's Books (1994)

Geoffrey Trease   **Cue for Treason**,
Puffin Books (1994)

Non-fiction

Richard Balkwill   **Food and Feasts in Tudor Times**,
Wayland Books (1995)

Roger Coote   **Tudor Sailors**,
Wayland Books (1995)

Elizabeth Newbery   **Tudor Farmhouse**,
A & C Black (1994)

Elizabeth Newbery   **Tudor Warship**,
A & C Black (1996)

Rachel Wright   **Tudors** *(in the* **Craft Topics** *series)*,
Watts Books (1993)